LITTLE RED HOUSE

Also available by Liv Andersson (writing as Wendy Tyson)

Allison Campbell Mysteries
Fatal Façade
Dying Brand
Deadly Assets
Killer Image

Greenhouse Mysteries
Sowing Malice
Ripe for Vengeance
Rooted in Deceit
Seeds of Revenge
Bitter Harvest
A Muddied Murder

Delilah Percy Powers Series
A Dark Homage

LITTLE RED HOUSE

A NOVEL

LIV ANDERSSON

CROOKED
LANE

NEW YORK

Published in the United States by Crooked Lane Books, an imprint of The Quick Brown Fox & Company LLC.

Crooked Lane Books and its logo are trademarks of The Quick Brown Fox & Company LLC.

Library of Congress Catalog-in-Publication data available upon request.

ISBN (hardcover): 978-1-63910-203-7
ISBN (ebook): 978-1-63910-204-4

Cover design by Nicole Lecht

Printed in the United States.

www.crookedlanebooks.com

Crooked Lane Books
34 West 27th St., 10th Floor
New York, NY 10001

First Edition: December 2022

10 9 8 7 6 5 4 3 2 1

To Jonathan. Keep reading. Keep writing.
Keep questioning.

CHAPTER

1

Kelsey Foster
Somewhere in New Mexico—1997

NIGHTS SEEM ENDLESS, days are worse. He's going to die, I tell myself over and over. It's the only thing getting me through. The floorboards squeak overhead. My shoulders tense, my muscles constrict. It's the asshole, home from wherever he goes from morning to sundown. I've been following his movements, up, down, around this godforsaken hellhole for the last hour. He likes to taunt me.

I'm waiting. Always waiting.

I wiggle my arms, trying to get blood to flow to my hands. The board beneath me splinters into my back, a thousand tiny pinpricks. The pillow smells of mildew and rot. A thick animal pelt covers me. It's hot down here in the basement, hot and dry and overrun with things that scurry at night, and the pelt stinks of mothballs and body odor. Every morning he swabs my body with a cool, wet cloth, wiping away the sweat, looking, he says, for spider bites. It's a fake show of humanity—one I'll use against him.

I hear the bolt slide open, and I hold my breath. It'll take him thirteen footsteps to reach the cellar, and I count along with the plodding slap of his loafers. At footstep thirteen, he'll stop again to pick out his supplies. I can picture the table, picture the tools. An inquisitor's arsenal.

Seven more footsteps and I'll feel his hands on my feet, unbinding me—only my feet, never my hands, the palms of which dig into rough board. I'll feel his tongue on my neck, and his fingers groping, grasping, probing . . . worse than the scuttling things moving along the bare length of my skin under the pelt at night. Worse than the splinters in my hands.

I'll make no attempt to hide my repulsion. It won't matter. I've played the submissive victim, the scornful conquest, the nagging mother . . . the result is always the same. He wants only one thing, getting his fucking rocks off using whatever instruments turn him on that day. Grunting. Moaning. Sweating his acrid slimy disgusting sweat. I will lie still, watching him. Watching the flow of light that trickles into the bare, dingy room, oozing around the cardboard that blocks the narrow window above my prison. Meeting stone-cold eyes with stone-cold eyes. In my head, it's another item to record. The day, the brightness of the moon, the level of cruelty measured one through four. Keeping my internal log, biding my time.

Always waiting.

It's a challenge, I tell myself. One I will win if I can just outsmart my opponent. The endgame is clear. Only one of us will leave this house alive.

And it won't be him.

2

Constance Foster
New York City, New York—Present Day

I COULD TELL BY the way the shadows fell across his bare midriff—ribboned, dancing—that it was nearly noon. The sheet under me scratched like sandpaper, the sheet over us felt crisp with sweat and something cruder. I rolled over, head throbbing. Twenty-two nights in and I was already nearly out of cash, crashing on some guy's floor in an apartment near Chelsea. Brian. Bruce. Brent. Who the fuck knew. The point was, I'd done exactly what Eve said I'd do—squandered the little money I'd had and ended up on the streets.

Not for long. I'd figure something out.

Last night's meal ticket lumbered out of bed, pulled the shades up so that sunlight poured in from the dusty window above the mattress on the floor, scattering roaches. He tossed me a towel redolent with sweat and cum.

"You can shower first." Eyes strayed to the clock over the studio kitchen table. "You need to get out of here soon, Connie." His tone was apologetic, but his eyes polkaed in panic.

I dug around in my duffel bag. "No longer single?"

"I said I'm not married, and I'm not."

"But you have a girlfriend."

"I have a girl who is a friend." He turned away. "She wouldn't understand. Having you here and all."

"No, I'm sure she wouldn't."

Based on the dingy blandness of the apartment, I guessed a girl who was a friend was just that—a friend. Otherwise she would have made some impact on his dump of an apartment, or at least she would have inspired him to clean up. But I'd scouted for signs of another woman two nights ago, when we'd first arrived. No second toothbrush, no tampons, no lavender-scented body wash. He wasn't married, and if he was, he and his significant weren't together. This apartment wasn't even nice enough to be a love nest.

He'd said he was a lawyer. Based on the address and the quality of his clothes and electronics, I could believe he was some sort of bottom feeder attorney—and not too good at his job. Or maybe a pro bono lawyer. Or a paralegal. Or maybe he was a liar and cleaned toilets at Penn Station. Whatever his occupation, he stood there now with a pathetic shadow of a beard sprouting across his ruddy face, covering his chest with his arms—making no effort to hide his shriveled penis.

I stretched and rose from the bed, hugging the dirty towel as a cover-up.

"Do you have somewhere to go?" He looked genuinely concerned. I would have been touched had it not been for a rising erection and the claw marks down his chest. Last night's fifth of bourbon and tussle on the floor came back to me in a cloud of regret. My mouth tasted like gunmetal, my eyelids ached to close. Score another for Eve.

"Sure," I said, suddenly wanting more than anything to get out of his place. I pulled on cargo pants, a black turtleneck sweater that felt constricting around my neck.

"Do you need cash?" He was watching me while he pulled clothes from a hamper on the floor.

"I'm not a pro."

"I know." He blushed. He'd put on boxers, but his cock still strained against the tartan plaid, hopeful. "It was fun, Connie. And the girl . . . she *is* just a friend. Will I see you again?"

"Doubtful." I turned, saw the confusion in his eyes, and heard Eve's voice in my head. *Once a whore, always a whore.* I thought about kissing his cheek. Decided against it. "Thanks for the bed—and the good time."

He grabbed my hand, pulled it to his crotch.

I jammed a fist against his stomach, growled "asshole," and pushed my way out the door.

*   *   *

I had nowhere to go. Twenty-two days of rationing my money, and I was down to $68, plus the $10 I took from Brian/Bruce/Brent's kitchen counter—money rescued, I reasoned, from the cockroaches—plus a Metro card. Jobs were hard to come by when you had no address, and the first room I'd rented turned out to be in a crack house. I stayed for five nights. On night six, the smell of the live corpses in the room next door drove me out. I needed a way to make money. Eve would send it to me if I called . . . but I would die before I called. Her price was too high.

Clouds pressed in overhead, coloring the space between the skyscrapers an irritable gray. I wandered down East 42nd Street, deciding what to do next. The first drops hit when I reached Fifth Avenue and I bolted inside Grand Central, just ahead of the early May downpour. Inside, I bought a baguette and a small bag of almonds. I traded the Metro card for a seat on the subway. Once on, I didn't need to get off. A person could ride the subway for a very long time.

*   *   *

I must have fallen asleep. My eyes opened with a start, that unbearable feeling of disorientation gradually waning. The light in the subway car seemed unnaturally bright. An apocalypse worth of blank-eyed travelers sat steadfastly ignoring one another. A woman, crumpled face awash in dirt and wrinkles, was staring at me, her hand outstretched. An open sore festered on the skin of her right forearm, and her fingers bore the telltale knots of too many nights spent outside. She could have been sixty, she could have been forty.

I glanced away, toward the window, and rubbed my face. The reflection staring back at me was gaunt and thin and angular—not a trace of the old beachy Constance. I supposed that was the reason for Eve's little games. When other measures hadn't worked, she pulled out the big guns. Sink or swim. Live or die. Blur the lines between crazy and sane. A game my sister Lisa wouldn't have to play.

The homeless woman grunted. She stood, holding the rail in front of me, her head tilted in supplication. Bruises dotted her neck, she stunk of sweat and rotting dumpster. I reminded myself that she was somebody's daughter.

"Dammit." I reached for my duffel, figuring a five-dollar bill would do her more good than it would do me. Only my bag was gone. I'd tied it to my leg in case I dozed, and someone must have cut it loose in the dead zone between stations.

"Did you see who took my bag?" I asked the woman.

She held her hand out again and moaned.

"Anyone see who stole my bag?" I didn't like the hysteria in my voice, and apparently neither did the homeless woman. She backed away into the shadows. The half dozen others in the car locked gazes on the walls and floor. The unspoken code of New York's destitute: don't see, don't hear, don't tell.

"*Fuck.*" I stood, thankful my phone and small backpack were still there. I kept my money separated—some in my bag, some in a little pouch I'd sewn into my bra, and the rest in my backpack. I'd learned that the hard way in my first test city—Chicago. But the duffel had held my clothes and my iPad—things I couldn't repurchase with the little money I had left.

A scream gurgled and died in my throat. Closing my eyes, I sat back down. Like it or not, I had nowhere else to go. I still had my phone—Eve had left me that, at least. I'd find a shelter for the night, then head to SoHo tomorrow. I'd try again to find some kind of job. Sign holder, ticket taker, floor cleaner—what did it matter? I would make this work. The hell with college, the hell with my inheritance. The hell with Lisa. The games were getting old. Maybe I could actually be rid of Eve.

The homeless woman was back, her eyes burrowing into mine. "Scram," I said, feeling a wellspring of rancor toward everyone, and waved her away. She flinched, cowering back into her corner. I pushed away the shame.

The car pulled into the last stop on the line. It would head back to Grand Central, then quit for the night. I'd had enough of my fellow passengers' zoned-out stares. I tucked two dollars into the homeless woman's hand and hopped off the subway. I'd take my chances here. What more could I lose?

*   *   *

He said his name was Irving. He had long arms and white teeth and hair the color of dirty snow. I hated him on sight. His mouth brushed against my neck. The scent of Italian hoagie and stale tobacco permeated his pores. My traitor of a stomach growled—the baguette and nuts had been in my duffel, too. He heard it, smiled.

I pulled back, eyes darting about, searching for an exit.

"How much?" he whispered. "For anal?"

The bar was nearly empty. I'd used the john to wash up, then nursed a glass of water as long as I could, looking for a friendly face and free peanuts. I'd found neither—just Irving. I refused his offer of a drink, but he must have sensed my desperation. A predator like him could smell it on me, sweet perfume to his perverted senses.

His tongue swiped my ear. "Come on, how much?"

I could leave and take a cab—except I didn't have enough for the fare. The subway was just a block away. I could make a run for it if he followed me. Keep riding the cars until dawn. I stood.

He grabbed my arm. I shook it free, slapped a buck on the bar for my water, and headed toward the door. The place smelled of loneliness and regret. I watched a Black man in a business suit watching us from across the square bar. Irving followed me through the double glass door out onto the deserted street. The cold air felt like a slap across the face, waking me up.

"Hey," Irving yelled. "Come back here."

I kept walking, picking up my pace. He was fast for an older guy. I felt his grip on my neck, an impossibly long arm around my waist.

"I said get back here." Irving pulled me against him. He had a knife against my ribs. With one hand he tugged my backpack off my shoulders. "You want this, you come with me."

I took a deep breath, then let it out, calming my nerves. My heart was pounding into my throat. I willed it to slow. I'd known men like Irving. Fear was his drug.

He kissed my ear, clawed at a breast. "Just a few hours. I tried to be nice about it."

"Okay."

"Good girl."

I relaxed my muscles, leaned into him, away from that knife. The streetlights were pulsating, a trick of my narrowing vision. I heard something rustle behind us, saw the glow of more streetlights down the block. He was still holding me.

"Fifty bucks," I whispered.

"Twenty." He dangled the backpack in front of my face, beyond my reach. "And I do what I want."

"Fine."

He started to let go. With a sudden push, I grabbed his wrist, twisted his arm backward. Something snapped. The knife clattered to the ground. We both locked eyes on it, but I pulled on his bent arm harder, shoved my knee in the small of his back, aiming for his kidneys. He moaned, a mean sound that started low and curled around itself until it was a rumble.

"Run," a voice said behind me. It was Business Suit from the bar. He picked up the knife. "I'll make sure he doesn't follow you."

I kicked Irving in the back again for good measure, then did my best to shove him toward Business Suit and the outstretched knife. Business Suit had six inches and twenty fit pounds on Irving.

"Thanks," I said.

Business Suit nodded.

I bolted, hit the subway entrance, and didn't look back.

*　*　*

Dawn came slowly. From the corner of a subway car, I watched a parade of human cockroaches come in and out. Some sober, some stoned. Some honest, some not. I didn't care. I had no valid ID, no money, and nowhere to go—certainly not back to Vermont and Eve. I knew what she wanted: for me to fail. For me to come running back, telling her she was right, and I needed to stay with her forever. I wouldn't do it. I'd rot here first, a victim of my own stubbornness.

At seven fifteen, I climbed into the sunlight, back near Grand Central. The day was bright and hopeful, the city wide awake. My ribs throbbed where Irving had jabbed me, my saliva felt gummy in my mouth. I clutched at the money I had left and weighed whether to visit a soup kitchen.

At 7:24, my cell phone rang. With the charger gone, I was lucky it still had juice. I glanced at the ID. Lisa. What did my sister want?

She wasted no time telling me. "She's dead."

"Who?"

"Aunt Eve." Flat tone. I wondered whether she was telling me the truth.

"What? How?" My mind spun with the implications.

"An accident. In the lake."

"What kind of accident?"

A pause. "She drowned during her morning swim."

"That doesn't sound like Eve."

My blonde-haired, blue-eyed, rich-as-fuck mother had succumbed to something as mundane as an accident? Impossible. Her demise would be of the grand variety. A push from a tower, a fiery plane crash. The Joan of Arc of the Ladies Who Lunch. Only Eve Foster had no ladies with whom to lunch. No friends, no attachments, no warm feelings. She was the ice queen.

"You need to come home," Lisa said.

Home. I had no home.

"I'm sending a car for you," Lisa said. "Your fight is over." She paused. "It's time for you to be *here*."

"I'm not coming." But even as the syllables escaped my mouth, I knew how feeble they sounded. Of course I would come back to Vermont. Where else would I go?

Lisa didn't wait for me to change my mind aloud. She knew I would, just as she had always known how to appease Eve.

"I'll send Dave with the Town Car," she said. "Hurry, Connie. I'll be at the estate, waiting for you." She paused, and when she spoke again, I heard the crack in her façade. "I need you."

3

Eve Foster
Nihla, New Mexico—1997

KELSEY WOULD BE the death of her. Eve Foster cursed her daughter under her breath, saving her strongest words for their reunion. Her daughter may have looked like her, but she was headstrong and manipulative like her father. Headstrong, manipulative, and too smart for her own damn good.

Officer Timothy Mayor tipped his cap in an old-fashioned gesture of respect. He was older, balding, with a broad chest and arms that seemed too short for his towering, lanky frame. "We believe she's gone from Nihla, Mrs. Foster. You're poking around the wrong gopher hole."

The sun was an orange disc in the sky. Eve looked up, frowned, and adjusted her sunglasses against the glare. She pulled her pashmina tighter around her shoulders and stared into the eyes of this stranger. Gray-green eyes, the color of a fast-running river. They were standing outside by the police station, on the outer edge of a town that sat on the outer edge of civilization, and Mayor's eyes matched the muddy color of the desert around them.

The officer leaned forward. "Ma'am, did you hear what I just said?"

Eve tugged a cigarette from the case in her purse. "I hate this godforsaken state," she said, lighting it. "The dryness, the searing heat, the damn cacti." She shook her head, sucked on the cigarette, and let the smoke out in concentric circles. Watching the rings dissipate into dry air, she shook her head again. "I can *feel* my daughter here. Keep looking."

"No one's seen her in days."

"That doesn't mean she's not here. My detective says he tracked her here. No one has seen her leave, have they?"

"Kids hitchhike. They meet strange . . . well, let's call them new friends. They leave with those new friends."

Strange men, he was about to say, Eve thought. And he wouldn't be wrong. Strange men were Kelsey's weakness. Kelsey enjoyed taunting them. God knows how many strange men she had slept with during her little adventure across the country. Eve took another puff, letting the smoke fill her chest and push out the angst. No use dwelling. Eve had no illusions when it came to her daughter. With her cigarette pressed between red lips, Eve removed her sunglasses, taking her time to put them back in their case. Slowly, deliberately, flaunting the brand, flaunting her jewelry, flaunting the power she was used to having—the power that came with Swiss bank accounts and multiple companies. But if this man was fazed by her show of wealth, he hid it well. She turned her focus on his face, let her cool blues drill into his mud-colored eyes.

"My detective told me there have been other disappearances in and around Nihla. Were they caused by *new friends* as well?" When Mayor didn't respond, Eve said, "Find my daughter. It's your *job*."

Mayor didn't move, just kept his obstinate gaze on her face, his hands on his hips. She looked away first, detesting herself for the failing. He would be of no more help. Everywhere she turned in this town she felt stonewalled. A runaway. Drugs. Sex. Parties. *Strange men*. She knew what was going through his mind. What was going through all of their minds. Kelsey. Young, nubile, rich. At best a naïve young girl. At worst, a criminal. Picked up by some creep— maybe for money. Probably in Mexico by now, fooling around with some brown boy in the back of a pickup truck. Or stoned out of her mind on a pile of pillows in an old VW van.

The cop's condescending stare said it all: an overbearing mother with more money than sense. A teen runaway with too much time and too little discipline.

Only he was wrong. So very wrong.

Eve threw her cigarette on the ground so it landed right in front of the officer. She turned to go with a toss of her blonde hair. If he wasn't going to do anything, it would be up to her.

* * *

The bar was a half mile from the station. It was a dusty dive in a row of derelict houses, with a smeared window front and the name "Jack's Place" written in scrawling brown scribble across a wooden plank. Eve took a seat at the end of a long, wooden bar, in the shadows, her back to an empty makeshift stage and a door that said "*Hermosas*" in black-markered square letters. An ornate mermaid stared at her from over the bar.

"What can I get you?" The bartender's eyes were black orbs feathered with dark lashes.

"Gin and tonic. Martin Millers, if you have it." She lifted her chin toward the mermaid. "No ocean for many, many miles."

Ignoring her, he swiped the bar top with a gray cloth, then grabbed a glass from a mirrored shelf. "We've got Seagram's."

"Seagram's then."

The bartender held her gaze for a pulse too long. "Where you from?"

"Philadelphia."

"You came a long way for a gin and tonic."

Eve's smile widened. "I wanted to see beautiful Nihla, New Mexico."

He tossed the cloth into a sink behind the counter and finished fixing her drink. "Now I know you're a liar. No one comes to Nihla on purpose."

"Funny name for a town so close to Mexico." Eve tilted her head. "Sounds Middle Eastern."

"Does it? We may seem out of the way, but all roads lead to Nihla. You'll see." He placed the drink in front of Eve and studied her, his mouth turned up in a half smile. With a glance at his other two customers—an old white man nursing a Dos Equis and a young guy whose shaved, tattooed head was currently resting on the bar—he said, "Really, why are you here?"

Eve took a sip of her drink. Despite the cheap gin, it went down easy. "Looking for someone." She pulled a picture of Kelsey from inside her purse and slid it across the bar. "Perhaps you've seen her."

The bartender picked up the picture and walked toward the front of the bar, where murky sunshine washed over the drunk's shaved scalp. The bartender was medium height and lean, with muscular, tan arms, and a scarlet slash of a burn that crisscrossed a bare bicep. A tattoo of a mermaid, similar to the one on the wall, encircled a thick wrist. His face was all hard planes bisected by a surprisingly soft mouth. He stared at the picture, then held it up to the sun.

He returned to the darker side of the bar and handed Eve the picture. "Nope. Never seen her." Black orbs slid sideways, toward the *Hermanos* bathroom door. "Pretty kid. Your sister?"

"Daughter." Eve tugged a cigarette from its metal case. "She's sixteen."

The bartender shrugged. "Probably why I've never seen her. Underage."

"Yeah, right." Eve finished her drink and pulled cash out of her wallet. "What's your name, cowboy?"

"Jack Cozbi." He nodded toward the sign outside the glass window front. "This is my bar."

Eve slid a ten, and then two hundred dollar bills across the counter. "If you remember something, Jack, anything whatsoever, call me." She scribbled her name and the number for her hotel on a piece of embossed ivory note paper. *"Anything."*

Jack's eyes danced from the bills on the counter to Eve's face to her cleavage. He nodded.

"Sixteen," Eve repeated.

"That's not that young around here."

Eve slid off the stool. "That's what I'm afraid of."

* * *

The pillowcase was an ivory polyester blend. Eve ran her hand over the outside, clutched the corners, and pulled it forward so that it cradled her head. She watched Jack's eyes get wide, then go dull, his mouth pull back into a grimace, then slacken until his face was buried against the silk of her blouse. She wrapped her thighs around his back, but let her gaze fall to the doorway, silently counting the seconds until he would be finished. She hated men's orgasms. They were not just messy, they were downright *ugly*.

"You next," he murmured.

Eve pushed him off her. "I'm fine."

"You didn't come."

"I don't need to."

"Suit yourself."

He sat up and grabbed his pants. Jeans buttoned, he turned back around and looked her over. Eve stared right back at him, admiring the view. He wasn't her usual type, but there was an unmistakable masculinity to him that both amused and attracted her. He was a fun diversion.

She rolled over, smoothing out the cheap sheets. She could forgive the room's heavy-handed floral air freshener, but the décor—a Tex-Mex version of a high-end motel, if there was such a thing—was too much.

Eve forced a smile. "I enjoyed this."

"I can tell."

Eve rose. She pulled on her panties, then her skirt, taking her time with the zipper. Jack had been a decent lover, making up for a lack of technique with unbridled enthusiasm. But now she was ready for him to leave. She chose a cigarette from the case by the bedside table and watched as the bartender tied his work boots with calloused fingers. His hand was shaking.

"Do I make you nervous?" she asked, smiling.

He scowled. "I need to go."

Eve made her way to the other side of the room, her movements languid, exhaling smoke as she walked. When she reached Jack, she stood in front of him, waiting.

Boots tied, he stood straight. Eve felt the heat coming off him in waves. She pulled him close, pressing her breasts against his still-bare chest, and kissed him. She waited until his body relaxed, giving in to the kiss, then she pushed him away, locking her eyes onto his.

She said, "My daughter."

"Is that what this was about?"

"I only fuck men I want to fuck. But I still need to find Kelsey."

"I told you, she's never been in the bar."

"But you've seen her."

Jack looked down, then back at Eve, who'd stood so she was haloed in the dying light seeping in between the blinds. She knew the impact she had on men, and she stretched tall, aware of the sun's worship on her slender body. Her nipples were hard, the skirt hugged shapely thighs. Despite beginning her third decade, she was toned and taut, her skin all milky shades of cream.

Jack said, "Yeah, I've seen her."

"Where?"

"Not at the bar."

Eve tapped ashes into the glass on the bedside table. Calmly, icily, she held Jack's gaze. "Forget the bar, Jack. Where did you see my daughter?" She waited. "*Tell me.*"

"Damn it, Eve. Outside the bar, okay? She was there with a guy. I noticed her through the window because," he looked away, "well, I just noticed her. She seemed to be having a good time."

Just like Kelsey to taunt fate. "When was this?"

"Few weeks ago."

"Who was the man?"

"I have no idea."

"*Bullshit.*"

Jack rubbed his eyes. "Damn it, Eve. It's not a crime to go out with a pretty girl."

"A girl who's now missing. A girl who's sixteen."

He shook his head. "She looked older. Twenty-one. Twenty-five even."

"Did you fuck her?" Jack shook his head. She waited a beat. "*Who was it?*"

"Antonio Leroux."

Eve recognized the last name from the hours spent at the police station and driving around Nihla. "The judge's son?"

Jack nodded. Sweat had collected across his brow. "Same."

Eve snubbed the cigarette out. "You need to leave now."

"What are you going to do? You can't mention me. Judge Leroux won't appreciate his son's name being brought into this, and he might take it out on the bar—"

Eve's cold stare stopped him short. "Get. Out."

Jack grabbed his shirt and left without another word.

4

Constance Foster
Shelburne, Vermont—Present

N OT A DAMN thing had changed.

Dave Dagger, Eve's driver, wound the car down the long drive that led to the gate that led to Eve's house on Lake Champlain. I asked him to stop along the driveway so I could get my bearings and have a smoke. Eve never let me smoke on the property. I figured a cigarette along her precious entranceway was as good a "fuck you" as any.

And I didn't even smoke anymore.

I lit up, took a drag, and stared off into the distance. The house loomed from the top of the hill, its white Victorian façade glaring down on Lake Champlain. A strong breeze blew the cigarette smoke toward the house, and I watched it dissipate into the cool air. Even though it was early May, I pulled my fleece tightly around me, suddenly chilled. From here, I could see the lake through the trees. It would have been a perfect vista—the choppy blue waters, the majestic Adirondack Mountains in the distance, their peaks still snow-covered, but I could feel Eve's presence like a malignancy that couldn't be excised.

Dave coughed, and I glanced in his direction. He'd been a fixture in the household for the last few years, a quiet shadow in a home of shadows, identifiable by the smells of pipe tobacco and menthol cough drops. Never a verbose man, today he seemed especially somber.

I slid back into the car.

"How are you holding up, Dave?"

Through the mirror, I watched gray bushy brows arch. "Okay."

"Missing Eve?"

"Indeed."

He was lying. Eve had been almost as cruel to her staff as she'd been to me. No one lasted in our household—not the cook, not the private tutors, not the gardener, not the housekeepers. Ours was a revolving door of unhappy people when it came to help. Then again, it dawned on me that Dave had been with her for more than five years. She had to have been doing something right. I took a fresh look at the driver. Saw the thick gold watchband, the Italian wool pants, pressed to perfection, the Brooks Brothers shirt. Eve was paying him well—maybe that was why he'd stayed.

Dave drove through the gate and up toward the house. I rolled down the window. There were few things I missed about Eve's house, but I loved the smells and sounds of the lake. Nature was waking up, and I could already hear the frogs and birds whose calls would get louder as the day melted into night.

Dave held the door for me as I climbed out of the car. I walked slowly across the sprawling porch to the house's French-door entrance. From there, I could see the soft peaks of the Green Mountains and the rugged White Mountains of New Hampshire beyond. I understood why Eve stayed here. I didn't understand why she chose never to leave.

A seagull called out from the shoreline, and I watched it fly overhead. The breeze had kicked up the waves, and the lake's surface was angry and white-capped. As a kid, I'd waited for Champ, the mystical creature that was said to live in the lake much like the Loch Ness Monster haunted the waters of Scotland. Champ never showed.

The only monster I'd known was my mother.

*　*　*

I had expected Lisa to greet me at the door, but I found myself alone in the great hall. I'd been gone for three consecutive game periods, almost three months, but the house hadn't changed. The hall floors gleamed, and my shoes click-clacked their way across the marble. The sound echoed, bouncing off pristine white walls and the high ceiling.

I hated this house. Hated the way it made me feel—small and insignificant and always, always unsafe. Maybe that was why I hadn't minded the games so much. They weren't here.

"You made it."

I turned to find my sister standing in the entry to what Eve had always called the parlor. Her face remained in its shadows.

"I just got here."

"Your room's ready."

"*My* room? No thanks."

I couldn't see if my sister had the decency to blush. "A room," she said. "The Paris Room."

My mother had named her six guest rooms after places she'd visited. The Paris Room, the Athens Room, the Avignon Room, the Versailles Room, the San Francisco Room, and the London Room. Growing up, I'd thought it was pretentious, but listening to Eve talk about her travel was as close to bedtime stories as we got, so the guest rooms mostly held benign memories. Not that we ever had guests. In fact, I couldn't remember Eve entertaining even one person at the house. Instead, these rooms offered a place to play and imagine when we were kids. And a place to hide.

Lisa explained when dinner would be, what time we were meeting with the attorney, how I should dress. I paused, waiting for more, and we stood there, me alone in the great hall, Lisa in the shadows, until I couldn't take the tension any longer. I turned to head up the stairs, to Paris.

"Wait," Lisa said. She stepped into the light, and I took a moment to study the sister I hadn't seen in months. Unlike me, Lisa had golden curls and ivory skin. Where I was darker-skinned and angular, Lisa was soft and round, almost voluptuous. People never believed we were sisters, much less twins. Today she looked especially pale. Dark shadows like bruises lined the delicate skin under her eyes. Her hair framed her face in lifeless waves. It looked like she'd been crying.

"How are you?" she asked finally.

"I'm here."

Lisa glanced away, turning her body in dismissal. Over her shoulder, she said, "I'll see you at six."

*   *   *

Dinner consisted of beef consommé (good for the digestion, according to now-dead Eve), a wedge salad, broiled salmon, and small talk so painfully boring you'd never know Lisa and I were twins.

*   *   *

The lawyer was someone I'd never seen before. Ancient, with bored gray eyes and a mass of thick white hair, he sat at Aunt Eve's desk as though he might catch a disease if he touched any of her belongings. His fingers—long and elegant except for deeply ridged, yellow nails—paged through a manila folder while he stared resolutely at his phone.

Lisa and I sat across from him, in the two damask-encased Queen Anne chairs that faced the ornate mahogany desk. This posturing was Lisa's idea. I would have been just as happy in the dining room or out on the balcony. My sister was a stickler for tradition. Getting called to Eve's office—never a harbinger of good things as a child—held no power over me now. I could sit in this chair and no longer feel the bite of our tutor's ruler on my ass. Or the cold damp of the basement floor on my bare thighs. Or the hot sting of vomit and tears.

I owed a lot to Eve Foster. Not the least of which was an incredible ability to tolerate pain.

"Uh-hum." The lawyer cleared his throat. He shifted gray eyes toward the ten-foot ceiling, then the fireplace mantel. He seemed to be watching the mantel clock, oblivious to me and Lisa sitting patiently on the chairs in front of him. It was as though we didn't exist.

"Hey, Grandpa," I said.

"Please stop," Lisa hissed.

At exactly eight he began talking.

"Your mother left very explicit instructions, down to the time of day I was to provide the details of the will." He cleared his throat. "As detailed as her unorthodox instructions for how I am to present this seem to be—in the study at exactly eight o'clock in the evening and shortly after her death—the will itself is quite simple. I will read her words to you now." He cut through an old-fashioned wax seal with Aunt Eve's letter opener and pulled a single sheet of paper from the envelope.

He scanned the document before glancing first at me, then Lisa. His eyes softened for the briefest of moments. In the instant he let his guard down, my own stomach clenched. Eve was reaching up from the grave, and whatever she'd planned would not be pleasant. Her choice of timing, the litany of rules, said enough.

Eight o'clock had been the witching hour in this house. If you were to be punished, she called you at eight, right before bedtime. Infractions could be major—a failing grade, yelling at the staff—or minor. I'd once had to sleep naked in the basement for two nights because I took a slice of cake to my bedroom without asking.

"Girls," the lawyer said in his gravelly voice, "if you're hearing this it's because I'm gone. Cliché, perhaps, but true. I'm not sentimental enough to believe in an afterlife. Or perhaps I'm simply not a masochist, for although I would stand by all of my worldly actions, I don't know that God would have approved of my methods. But then, He didn't go through what I have gone through." The lawyer paused, and I watched as he scanned the page, reading ahead.

He continued. "That's perhaps not a fair statement. Lisa, you have always been a good daughter. You've had the sense to listen and the grace to obey. For that, you will be rewarded. Constance, I fear that whatever I say to you now won't matter. The distance between us remained cavernous, and I am, and will always be, an easy target for your feelings of failure and inadequacy. The real failure is mine, of course, because a parent's role is to teach humility and instill wisdom, and with you I've managed neither. Selfishness should not be rewarded, nor should ungratefulness or stupidity."

The lawyer shifted in his seat. His discomfort as he read Eve's words bothered me more than my aunt's backhanded self-deprecation. She wasn't saying anything I hadn't heard a million times. He apparently had the unfortunate luck of hearing it for the first time.

"So," he continued, his voice wavering, "I'd like you, Lisa, to continue my role in our corporate holdings and maintain the Foster estate. I'm leaving the properties, the houses, my business interests, and all other assets to you in trust, except"—the lawyer looked directly at me—"for the property in Nihla, New Mexico, which

I leave to Constance. There are other matters, small and inconse-
quential for now, that will be shared later. Craig Burr, my trusts
and estates attorney, who is no doubt reading this to you now, will
provide you both with all the necessary details and see that assets
are transferred in accordance with my directives. You must do as
Mr. Burr says. And one more thing," Craig's gaze traveled from me
to Lisa and back again. "Under absolutely no circumstances are you
to question my decisions. I want a quiet cremation with no public
announcements or inquiries."

The lawyer stopped reading.

Pale-faced and bright-eyed, Lisa said, "I want to split everything fifty-fifty."

Craig pursed his mouth and continued reading. "Lisa, being
the decent person you are, you will no doubt balk at the terms of
my will. Please know that I have given much thought to this. If you
attempt to alter the terms in any way, you will forfeit everything.
And Constance may not simply live here with you, a ward of my
estate. You may give her exactly $5,000 for airfare and food and
initial expenses, and thereafter $5,000 per twelve-month period,
but that is all. In fact, she has seventy-two hours after the reading
of this will to gather her belongings and leave the premises."

Lisa stood. "No—"

"Please sit," Craig said. Once Lisa returned to her seat, face
ashen, he said, "Constance may return for one week each year, if
scheduled ahead of time and approved by Craig in accordance with
my instructions to his firm. She may not rent out or sell the New
Mexico property for three years after the date this will is read. If she
attempts to do either, the estate will be sold and the proceeds given
to charity." Craig looked up at me and blinked. "And if you think
you're going to challenge this in a court of law, Constance, think
again. I have already received affidavits from two well-respected
psychiatrists attesting to my sanity. I assure you, everything is legal
and in order."

Craig put the paper down. "Your mother's wishes will have to
be followed, or I'm afraid you could both lose everything."

Tears trekked down Lisa's pretty face. I grasped her hand. She
moaned.

"I'll be fine," I said. "It's more money than I've ever had. And a
place of my own."

"You know nothing about the property in New Mexico," Lisa said, round brown eyes swimming in tears. "And I don't want to be here alone. You're supposed to be here, with me."

"You'll have Dave," I said, "And Cook," trying to lighten the mood.

Lisa shook her head. "Please," she said to Craig, who was already packing papers back into a leather briefcase. "She's dead, what does it matter? There has to be some way to change this."

"I'm sorry. I truly am. But unless you want to tie everything up in court, this is the way it must be." He finished fastening the clasps on his bag before addressing me directly. "I'll make your flight arrangements, Constance. The property in New Mexico is . . . well, you'll need the money if Lisa is willing to give it to you. Five thousand dollars. Lisa?"

Lisa sniffled, then nodded.

Craig said, "Very good. Then I'll see about the arrangements and get more information to both of you on your respective assets and the terms of transfer." He moved toward the door, body movements screaming with relief that this was over. "Seventy-two hours, Constance. And one week a year, which will be monitored. So please, don't put your sister's inheritance in jeopardy." He peered at me over his briefcase. "Eve wanted it this way, and it was, after all, her money."

I didn't argue. There was no use. *Eve wanted it this way.* Eve Foster saw the world as cut and dried, good and bad. In her world, there was no in between. And for one sister to be rewarded, the other had to be punished.

5

Eve Foster
Nihla, New Mexico—1997

JUDGE ANDREW LEROUX lived in an oversized, ornate adobe home six miles outside of town. The house, a series of flat boxes built around a central courtyard with an oversized pool, sat on a scrubby patch of property so brown that it was hard to tell where the house started and the land ended. A five-foot wood and wire fence surrounded the acreage, but Eve followed the dirt road that encircled the property and finally found the entrance to a concrete-slab driveway. She parked the rental in front of a short stone wall, behind a white Chevy with a The Clash sticker on the bumper and climbed out of the car.

Three knocks later a small, slim woman opened the door. She frowned when she saw Eve.

"Mrs. Leroux?" When the woman nodded, Eve poked one pointy-toed pump in the doorway and said, "I need to speak to your son, Antonio."

"And you are?"

Eve detected a hint of a southern accent, but the accent couldn't mask the woman's annoyance. Slightly slumped shoulders, linen cardigan hanging too large off her small frame, dark circles under her eyes. This was a troubled woman—troubled, or ill.

Eve pushed on the door, letting herself into a dark entryway.

"My name is Eve Foster."

"I'm afraid I don't know you."

"Is there somewhere we can talk?"

"It's a bad time."

By now, Eve had pushed her way completely inside. From this angle she saw the reason for the woman's exhaustion. A skeleton of a person, sex unidentifiable were it not for the pink hat sitting precariously atop tufts of white hair, dozed in a wheelchair in the living room. Eve raised her voice. "I'd like to talk to Antonio about my daughter, Kelsey Foster. Perhaps you've met her?"

Mrs. Leroux's eyes widened. "Could you keep your voice down?"

"Mrs. Leroux?" Eve's voice was a near scream now. The old woman jumped. Eve took some satisfaction from the look of panic on her host's face. "My daughter?"

"Brenda," the woman said finally. "I'm Brenda Leroux. Come into the kitchen. My mother-in-law is trying to nap."

Eve followed Brenda through a narrow hallway and into a cheerful kitchen. The cabinets were oak, the floors white tile, and the walls the same smooth brown adobe as the entryway. A carton of Ensure sat on the counter; dirty dishes littered the sink. A skinny black cat perched on a wooden stool and stared reproachfully at Eve. She stared back.

"Antonio isn't here," Brenda said. "He's at work."

"I saw his car outside."

"That's not his car. It belongs to my mother-in-law."

"That woman listens to The Clash?"

Brenda frowned. "What do you want?"

"Is he always a prankster, Brenda?" Eve's eyes locked on a book wedged under a copy of *Modern Italian* cookbook. It was a title she recognized, by the author Ayn Rand. Slowly and deliberately, Eve took out the photo of Kelsey and slid it across the tile countertop. "Maybe he was playing a prank on my daughter and it got out of hand?"

Brenda turned her attention to the photo. Eve watched as Brenda studied Kelsey's image, wondering if this other woman saw what she saw. Unsmiling green eyes. A face that would have been beautiful had it not been for the meanness that lurked under the surface. Skin so pale it seemed translucent.

A Ferris wheel sat in the background of the photo, a symbol of gaiety caught forever in Eve's nightmare. Two other girls stood a few feet away, their backs turned. Friends? Kelsey had said so, but Eve hadn't been so sure. A snapshot taken at a convenient time, when the strangers nearby seemed to be her daughter's age? Or mere acquaintances, girls met in gym class or Spanish who agreed to meet up at the local fairgrounds if Kelsey paid their way?

Eve might never know. Kelsey liked to keep her guessing.

"She's . . . lovely." Brenda slid the picture back to her. "I'm sorry, though. I can't help you. We've never met your daughter."

Eve snapped the photo off the counter and tucked it back into her bag. "I don't think that's true, Brenda."

"You should probably leave."

"Where's my daughter?"

"I don't know."

Eve closed her eyes. "*We the Living.* There on the shelf. It's her book. Her father gave it to her."

Silence. Eve heard the whir of the ice maker, the light snore of the skeleton in the other room, the low drone of a news program in another part of the house.

Brenda turned back around. Somehow her dark circles had deepened until her eyes were two holes sunken into her bird-like face. "That's my son's book."

"He reads Ayn Rand?"

"He's a college student. Or at least he was."

Eve walked over to where the book sat. She took it out from under its Italian companion and flipped to the dog-eared title page, her gaze all the while on Brenda.

"Shall I read this to you, Brenda?"

Brenda shook her head.

"To my daughter, Kelsey—one whose life is surely worth a million. Fondly, your father." Eve looked up. "Your son's name is Kelsey?"

"I wasn't lying. I've never met your daughter."

"Clearly your son has."

"It was a short fling. Nothing. A passing fancy for both of them."

"Where is she?"

"I have no idea."

Eve made it across the room in the instant it took Brenda Leroux to back up against the wall. Eve stood over the smaller woman, nudged her leg with a beige stiletto. "Where can I find your son?"

Brenda closed her eyes. "Mike's Knives. On Main. But he doesn't know anything." She swallowed. Her eyes were watering. "He's a good boy. We told him"—she swallowed again—"we told him they weren't compatible."

Eve placed two fingers on the older woman's neck. Her face close to Brenda's, she pressed a sharply manicured nail into the soft flesh above Brenda's collarbone, leaving two red half-moons in fragile skin, and smiled. "Is that so?"

Eve backed away.

Brenda placed a hand on her chest. She panted.

Still carrying *We the Living*, Eve turned to leave. She paused in the living room on her way back to the front door and bent down in front of the elderly woman in the wheelchair. She peered into the shriveled old face.

"Boo!" she said loudly.

The woman jumped.

"Pathetic," Eve muttered. She didn't bother closing the front door behind her.

CHAPTER

6

Constance Foster
Shelburne, Vermont—Present

"WILL YOU BE alright?" I asked. Lisa sat on a king-sized bed in the Paris Room. She'd pulled her hair into a tight chignon, and with her tailored black pantsuit and a thick strand of diamonds and pearls, she already looked the part of mistress of the Shelburne estate. "You seemed particularly distraught tonight."

She said, "I'm just really sorry."

"What do you have to be sorry for?" I put the last of my jeans in my backpack and secured the zipper. "You didn't write the will or create the terms of the trust."

"No, I didn't."

"And you didn't know what she planned to do."

"True."

I placed the backpack on the floor next to the door, beside my computer case and hiking poles. Then I settled in on the bed next to Lisa. My sister was in many respects my polar opposite. Where I'd always been stubborn, she was accommodating. Where I struggled to sit still in our homeschool classroom, Lisa flew through her assignments, earning the praise of whatever tutor we had at the time. Even our physical appearances were different. My sister's gentle features and soft curves elicited warmth from women and appreciative stares from men. Eve said I looked like a biblical harlot—dark, hungry, and ready for anything. And despite my best attempts to prove her wrong, I found myself in bad situations again and again.

Poor judgment. It had been her excuse for every mean thing she'd done to me.

"She was a cruel woman, Connie. You can't internalize what she did."

It was rare to hear Lisa bad-mouth our adopted mother. Me, yes—all the time. But Lisa saw the good in everyone. I nodded. "Sure."

"We'll contest it. Figure out a way to give you half."

"Don't bother. We both know she used belts and suspenders. No court will overturn her decision, and even if her conditions can be challenged, do you really want to go through the time and expense?" My gaze strayed to the window and Lake Champlain beyond. "What happened to her? You said she drowned?" Unlike Lisa, Aunt Eve had been a strong swimmer. She did open water swims the same time every morning, never missing a non-winter day. We'd see her orange flotation marker bobbing behind her as she made her way back and forth in front of the house, rain or sun. It seemed unlikely she'd drown.

Lisa clenched her hands in her lap, knuckles mottled red and white. My sister was terrified of getting into the water. Eve had insisted she learn to handle herself in a kayak and a canoe, but Lisa never willingly went near the lake.

"The wind came on, sudden and gusty. The police think she got overwhelmed by the swells, tried to use her flotation marker as a life preserver. She was wearing a thick wetsuit, which may have hampered her mobility. The tether . . . the tether wrapped around her chest and neck. She must have struggled in the deep water, but it only made things worse."

Lake Champlain was a massive natural body of water known for its deep swells. I'd kayaked on the lake before a storm and knew how dangerous the waters could be. But Eve had been careful. Although if she'd been out far enough when the winds came on, getting back would have been tough. The lake, like my adoptive mother, was unpredictable.

"What a way to go," I said.

Lisa's eyes watered. We stayed quiet for a few minutes. Finally, she said, "You should have half of everything."

I threw another pair of socks in my bag before climbing onto the mattress. "I don't want half. I have a house. That's all I need."

"Take her jewelry collection. It alone is worth at least a million."

My mother had been a recluse, but She'd loved jewelry and had it flown in from around the world. Tempting as the offer was, I couldn't risk Lisa's security. "I have a house. I'm fine."

"I'm sure it's beautiful." Lisa's voice sounded anything but sure.

We sat again in silence. My gaze wandered to the Parisian prints, the wrought iron bed frame, the antique French country dressers. For all her faults, Eve had had good taste. She'd owned the Vermont estate, and before that, a beautiful house in Corfu. Surely the New Mexico place would be similar.

"Why haven't we been to New Mexico?" Lisa said, echoing my thoughts. "Why didn't she ever mention that she owned property in the Southwest?"

I shrugged. "I have a feeling we'll learn more about Eve now that she's dead than we ever did when she was alive."

Lisa wiggled down on the bed and placed her head on my lap, like she used to as a kid. She looked up at me, eyes round and pleading. We'd grown distant lately. Lisa saw my refusal to disobey Eve's cruel demands as an annoying character defect. Florida, Alabama, New York. She had no idea what compelled me to play Eve's sick games—and it was better that way. And so with each town I had to conquer, our relationship grew more strained. But now she sat beside me, the closeness filling an ache I hadn't known I had.

"Promise me you'll visit that one week a year," Lisa whispered. "Promise, promise, pinky swear."

Pinky swear. A memory swam before me, just out of reach. I saw a red circle, red nails, blonde hair under blue water. My heart raced. Just the echo of a memory from long, long ago. Or a child's imagination.

"Come on, pinky swear," Lisa said again.

Pinky swear. Despair marred my sister's pretty features. I would have said anything to take away the pain.

"Pinky swear. You won't be able to get rid of me."

Lisa closed her eyes, smiled. I knew it was a lie—I'd never come back—but Lisa would accept it. She was good at lying to herself. It was a strength I'd never had.

* * *

Later that night, I slipped past Lisa's suite of rooms and down into the great hall. From there, I made my way across the marble floor, to the door that led into the basement rooms. The door was locked. Hardly a deterrent because I knew just where to find the key. Lisa, God bless her, was as unimaginative as she was well behaved.

Sure enough, I found the large iron key hanging in the utility room on the other side of the kitchen. I pulled it from the hook and padded my way back across the downstairs until I reached the door. I wasn't sure why I was taking such pains to be quiet. It wasn't like Eve was going to catch me and send me to the basement.

The key slid in easily. I turned it, listening for the familiar creak as the door opened into the black abyss beyond. I flipped the switch by the doorframe, flooding the cavity with light. The staircase itself—walls painted a deep gray, arctic white trim—looked the same. I followed the steps as they wound their way down, deep beneath the house. My breath caught in my throat, my heart thumped wildly, but still I made it the three small flights to the bottom.

Pinky swear.

The basement had long ago been divided into three sections. One housed the building's vast utilities—furnaces and water heaters and extra deep freezers filled with meat that Eve would never eat. The second area was for entertainment. It contained a wine cellar and a game room we were rarely permitted to use. The third section, the part of the basement that was darkest and dankest and creepiest, contained two rooms.

The punishment room. And another.

Door one—the punishment room door—was closed. I knew the key I held in my hand would open that door. I knew also what I'd find: a bare cot, a single bare light bulb dangling from the ceiling, a toilet, a concrete floor, a light switch with a metal cage over it—a cage that also opened with this key. A vent that led into *her* old room. Or so Eve said.

I held out my hand, ready to open that door, ready to vanquish my ghosts once and for all. But something stopped me.

The door to the other room was closed, just as it always had been. But now a thick metal padlock hung from a second lock, high above the ground. Why a padlock? Why now?

Something in the depths of the basement click-clicked across concrete. I jumped, my hand shaking so badly I dropped the key.

My eyes were once again drawn to the padlock.

"Don't go in there," Eve used to warn us.

That door had always been kept closed. A test of our obedience. We never knew Kelsey, but the staff spoke of her, an insane daughter kept in a twenty-by-twenty concrete box. It was a warning to us—obey, or else. At least that's what I believed growing up.

I heard many things in my nights in that basement. Crying. Moaning. Screams.

But lying in the dark, under that big house, alone and terrified, I had never been quite sure whether I was hearing another girl's terror. Or my own.

I snatched the key from the ground and raced up the stairs. My ghosts would have to wait.

*   *   *

I left the following morning while Lisa was still asleep. It was easier that way.

7

Eve Foster
Nihla, New Mexico—1997

M IKE'S KNIVES EXISTED in a faded blue box of a building at the end of a dusty street. Eve pulled slowly up to the curb and parked directly in front of the store. The day was drawing to a close, and with it the fairer weather. Storm clouds gathered overhead, blocking out the relentless sun. From the safety of her car, Eve watched as the sky opened up, raining down judgment on this dusty town. When the worst of the downpour had ended, she climbed out of her rental and popped open her umbrella. She walked unhurriedly to the front door, aware of a man's gaze following her progress from behind a barred window.

She was the only customer. Two men—one older and mustachioed, the other much younger, with wavy black hair and a quarterback's body—stood behind the counter. Both stared; the older man acknowledged her with a wary nod. Eve glanced around her surroundings. Leather goods—belts and riding crops and knife sheaths and purses—hung on racks and hooks. Knives, some ornate Native American designs, others basic hunting tools, sat in cases near the register and around the shop. The floor was worn linoleum, the walls apartment white. All color came from the feathers that adorned the leather goods and the intricate designs on knife handles. The smell of animal hide left a foul taste in Eve's mouth.

Eve plastered on a smile and headed for the register. The younger man attacked a folding knife with a polishing cloth, downcast eyes refusing to meet hers.

"How can we help you?" the older man asked.

"I assume you're Mike?" Eve smiled when he nodded and held out a hand. "Eve Foster."

Out of the corner of her eye, Eve watched the younger man's face as she said her name. If she was expecting him to act surprised, she was disappointed. He didn't react at all.

Eve engaged in a moment of small talk with the store owner before turning her attention to the younger man. "You must be Antonio."

Hands still moving over the sharp metal edge of the knife, focused on his work, he said, "Who wants to know?"

"I do."

The younger man swallowed. Mike stood by, watching.

"What do you want?" Antonio asked.

"You know my daughter, Kelsey."

A flash of recognition before eyes darkened to slits. "Yeah, so?"

"Where is she?"

"How should I know?"

"You were the person last seen with her."

Antonio glanced at Mike before putting the knife back in the case. He took his time folding the polishing cloth, only to leave it sitting on the counter. "The cops already talked to me. I have no idea where Kelsey ran off to."

"But you admit meeting her."

"Yeah, sure." He glanced at Mike, shrugged. "So what?"

Eve turned her attention to Mike. "Is there an office or somewhere I can talk to Antonio for a few minutes?" She pulled a hundred-dollar bill out of her bag and slid it across the counter. It was gone before she could say more.

"Back that way." Mike pointed to a cube-size office at the rear of the store. "Ten minutes."

Antonio glared at him, but Mike was busy pulling boxes out from beneath the counter. Eve didn't wait. She strode past a rack of leather caps and entered the cramped office. Antonio followed.

"Close the door and sit." When Antonio was seated, Eve perched on the edge of the desk so he had to look up into her face. "You knew I was coming."

"My mother called me."

"Of course she did. I bet she still makes your lunch." She leaned down, slammed a hand on the desk, startling him. "What did you do to my daughter, Antonio?"

"Nothing."

"You were together, now she's gone."

"I told the cops. We went out four, maybe five times. She got restless, we split. That's it."

"Did you sleep with her?"

Antonio flinched sharply. "I don't need to answer that."

"How old are you?"

"Twenty-two."

Eve tapped a pointed shoe against Linoleum. "Sleeping with a minor is a felony offense."

"Kelsey wasn't a minor."

"*Wasn't?*" Eve raised her eyebrows. "She's only sixteen."

"Shit." Sweat beads popped out along Antonio's forehead. His left knee started to pump up and down. "She told me she was twenty-one. She looked—looks—older." He swallowed. "Sixteen's probably legal in New Mexico."

"Legal? Maybe, maybe not. Young, either way." Eve stood. She walked to a metal shelf on the back side of the office and picked up a framed photo of Mike and two little boys. "Tsk, tsk," she said. "You could get in a great deal of trouble, Antonio."

"I don't believe Kelsey's sixteen." Voice stronger now, convincing himself. "She knew too much."

Eve spun around. Antonio had the decency to blush, but nevertheless, she shot him a withering stare. "Help me find Kelsey, and I won't report you."

"You can't prove anything."

Eve smiled. "Do you really want to go down that path?" She watched the young man squirm, sympathetic to his plight. She knew her daughter as well as anyone. Antonio was a handsome boy. Athletic, a little naïve, maybe even gullible. Cool, sophisticated Kelsey would appeal to a small-town boy like him—especially one bent on defying his judge of a father. And as for Kelsey, she loved nothing more than a big, dumb plaything. Eve could understand what her daughter saw in the boy—despite his utter lack of balls. He was cute and clueless. "Your father is a judge. I don't think he would appreciate it if his son was accused of having sex with a sixteen-year-old."

Antonio's leg was still working up and down.

Eve placed two fingers under his chin and pulled upward, so he was looking into her eyes. She made sure he could feel her breath on his cheek, her breasts pressed against his arm. He tried to shift his gaze away, squirmed against her body.

"I really don't know where she is."

"Where did you last see her?"

His breathing was rapid, shallow. His pupils darted, looking at anything but her. Finally, he said, "We'd gone out into the desert with a few friends. Drinking." Another eye shift. "Getting high."

Eve let go of his face. She saw the owner, Mike, looking at her from behind the glass, and she held up a hand for a little more time. "Go on."

"There's not much to tell. Kelsey got drunk. She decided she'd rather be with someone else. I think she expected me to be jealous." He shrugged. "Anyway, she went with him. I'm figuring she left town after that."

"Who was the other man?"

He shrugged again.

"Were you and Kelsey fighting?"

"Is that what the police said?"

"I'm asking you. Were you fighting?"

Antonio sighed. "She was angry at me, yes."

"About what?"

"I was flirting with someone else, and she got mad, okay?"

"Flirting, or—"

"It's not like we were boyfriend and girlfriend." His expression turned sullen. "Look, when we head out to the desert like that, everyone knows there are no rules. Kelsey saw me with someone and got pissed. She stormed off. Next thing I knew, she threatened to leave with someone else. Go for it, I told her. What did I care? It's not like we were dating. I told the police this. All of it."

"She'd been staying with you before that?"

"She crashed on my floor a few times."

"How generous of you."

"Look, she left town. Like I told you, she was restless. If it hadn't been that night, it would have been another, soon after. She was getting tired of Nihla." His eyes focused on something beyond her, out into the store. "Can't say I blame her."

Eve tapped a shoe against the desk. "Did you hurt my daughter, Antonio?"

"No." Eyes wide. "You have to believe me. I would never hurt anyone."

Reluctantly, Eve nodded. This boy-man was no match for Kelsey. "Who did my daughter leave with?"

Antonio shrugged.

"*Antonio.*"

"Like I told the cops, some drifter. I didn't know him."

Eve studied his face. "You're lying."

"Mike's waiting on me. I need this job. I have to go."

Eve walked in front of the office door, blocking his exit. "Who did she leave with?" Voice lower. "Tell me his name."

"Oh, man," Antonio ran a hand through his hair. "She left town. She was a runner, looking for adventure, escape. Maybe she caught a bus. Who knows? Something wasn't quite right about that girl." Eve's arched eyebrows stopped him cold. He backed up, arms fluttering by his side. "I'm sorry. I know she was—is—your daughter."

"*Tell me his name.*"

"Motherfucker." Antonio wiped his forehead with the back of his hand. "Dude, my father will fucking kill me."

"His name, Antonio, and you get to leave. Kelsey had just turned sixteen. You fucked her, made her sleep on your floor like a dog, left her to her own devices in the desert. *Sixteen.* You're twenty-two. Think your father will like that?"

Eve waited. She could wait all day if she had to, but she suspected that wouldn't be necessary. The office phone rang. The sound seemed to jolt Antonio into awareness.

"Fuck, fuck, fuck. I'm so fucked." He pulled a hand through his hair. "Kyle Summers, okay?" Antonio wiped at his eyes. "Kyle fucking Summers. Happy now?"

"Kyle Summers? Should that name mean anything to me?"

Antonio backed up, away from her. He slumped down in a chair. "Maybe not to you. He's my uncle. My mother's brother."

"My daughter left with your uncle? That must have been a blow to your ego, Antonio."

The boy shrugged. "He's older, has money. Girls like that shit. Anyway, we're not that close."

"Where does Kyle live?"

Antonio mumbled something unintelligible.

Eve stepped on his foot. She pressed the toe of her stiletto into his ankle bone. He winced.

"Where does he live?"

"Mayberry Street, in the nice section of town."

"I didn't know there was such a thing."

Antonio bit his lip, looking close to tears. "Don't tell him I told you." His eyes pleaded. "The cops already knew."

"Why are you protecting him?"

"You haven't met my father."

Eve crouched so her face was close to Antonio's. "No, I haven't."

Antonio closed his eyes, a gesture that echoed the one his mother had made earlier. For some reason, the show of cowardice enraged Eve. She kicked the desk. "You don't know who you're dealing with."

Antonio's eyes remained closed. "Please," he said.

Eve grabbed her bag and left the office, leaving Antonio cowering in his seat.

CHAPTER

8

Constance Foster
Somewhere in New Mexico—Present

I LANDED IN ALBUQUERQUE midafternoon and took a taxi to a
dusty used car sales lot, where I spent a portion of my dwindling
funds on an old white Acura Integra. No rust, and it had a manual
transmission. The sales guy was a jowly man in his forties wearing
checked brown polyester and a Braves baseball cap. He handed over
the keys with a bored yawn and watched as I climbed into my new
wheels, pausing only to stomp on a centipede that scurried from
beneath a signpost.

Centipedes and desert. I wasn't so sure I'd like this place.

As I drove out of Albuquerque, I marveled at the Sandia Mountains that sprang up around the city. Imposing, beautiful. But so
much barren brown. I found myself longing for the ubiquitous
green of Vermont and wondered what Lisa was doing now.

Lisa. My twin. We'd been so close growing up—yet so distant.
It was as though Eve had monitored our relationship, stepping in
whenever we grew too intimate. Purposeful or not, her punishments
caused rifts between me and my sister, and served to highlight the
differences between us. Differences that meant little to me—but
the world to Eve.

As I headed northwest on Route 25, I watched the scenery
change. Brown gradually gave way to green, flat earth to hills.

By the time I reached Santa Fe, the landscape had softened, and I was starving and tired. Three fish tacos and a Diet Pepsi later I was back on the road. But night had fallen and any optimism I was feeling had given way to despair. Little in the way of funds, a house I'd never seen, and all but forbidden from returning home. I couldn't face the new house in the dark. None of Eve's stupid games matched this.

Neon flashed in the distance. I pulled over at the one-story Motortown Motel, captivated by the "vacancy" sign and the promise of a bed. A sour-looking white woman with rotting front teeth held out my key, and I handed her $47 in cash. She opened her mouth, about to request a credit card, I was sure, and I slid another ten across the counter.

"No male visitors."

I smiled. "Wouldn't think of it."

"No entertaining."

"It's just me."

She relinquished the key with a curt nod and an appraising glance at my midriff. "No soliciting."

I got the feeling she'd exhausted her vocabulary for prostitution. "Got it. I'm actually with the health department." Blank stare, so I left.

Room 16 was a mess of orange floral polyester and pressboard furniture, but the sheets looked clean and the water ran clear, so after pulling the drapes tight, I stripped down and showered. I was toweling off in the bathroom when I heard a thump at the door and the click of a key entering the lock. I scrambled for my T-shirt, slid it over my head, and, otherwise naked and wet, stood next to the door, my heart thumping. I'd been careless—the cheap chain lock dangled like a limp dick. It would have offered some protection, at least.

"Who's there?" I called.

The door slammed open, and a baby-faced man stood in the doorway. He held a wrench in one hand and a clipboard in another. His eyes soaked me in, embarrassment and interest fighting it out.

Loud traffic noise through the open door. "Go away," I said.

With a pronounced stutter, he told me the front desk clerk had sent him to fix my pipes. I bet she had. Checking up on me, more likely. I told him my pipes were fine and locked the door behind

him. I propped a chair beneath the door handle, slipped on a pair
of jeans, and lay down on the bed. I listened to the cars go by for
hours and thought about Eve until sleep finally came.

*   *   *

Eve had been my adopted mother. She was young when she took
us from an orphanage in Greece. She changed my name from Kon-
stantina to Constance and my sister's from Líza to Lisa, and eventually she had us call her "Aunt Eve" rather than Mother. My first
recollection of Eve remains hazy and distorted, as though I was
seeing her through a film of water or a veil of smoke. I remember
blonde hair and green eyes and the color red.

To this day, I hate the color red.

*   *   *

I crossed into Nihla at 9:12 the next morning. My eyes were red
and swollen from lack of sleep and dust allergies, and my head was
pounding despite three ibuprofens and a large cup of coffee. I don't
know what I expected to find. New buildings, paved roads, some
kind of hip Southwestern Santa Fe vibe. Naïve, I know.

Nihla was a dust bowl.

I drove down the main thoroughfare, taking in my new surroundings. A wide strip of faded asphalt ran about half a mile
through the center of what passed for a town. On either side, squat
concrete and faux-adobe buildings advertised breakfast, check
cashing, drugs, *comestibles*. Every fourth store was boarded up,
abandoned. Dirt roads intersected Main Street like the legs of a
silverfish. An old woman stood on a cracked sidewalk, her walker
decorated with three plastic bags and a paper copy of the Mexican
flag.

I pulled over in front of an empty diner and checked my directions. I was looking for 13 Mad Dog Road. My new home. The
name sounded appropriate.

*   *   *

It took me another twenty minutes of driving to find Mad Dog
Road. It was less of a residential street and more of an afterthought.
Only three houses sat along the dusty stretch. The first two huddled
close together, bright blue doors, rectangular adobe twins fighting

off the encroaching desert. Farther down the road, a handful of short, twisted trees were interspersed with low shrubs and cacti. Mountains rose up majestically in the far distance, but the land here was flat, flat, flat. A chain-link fence marked property lines.

It wasn't hard to spot the home Eve had bequeathed to me. It stood alone at the end of the road, a good mile from the blue-doored twins. A low-pitched roof capped a tiny red rectangle; the only bits of folly were the white picket design below the roofline and the black framing around the door. Two ancient metal chairs sat on a concrete slab out front, next to a wheelbarrow filled with crushed Coke cans.

I killed the engine and looked around. Behind the house sat another building, this one smaller, flat-roofed, and also red. An empty chicken coop perched next to a small raised-bed garden. The ground for miles was dirt, brown and barren, but directly around the house I saw green. Green shrubs, green potted plants, green trees. Interspersed within the green were beautiful pieces of furniture: a small round bistro table fashioned from tiger maple, a backless bench, what looked like a low chair carved from wood and padded with a red cushion. It was as though someone was fighting nature and winning one small victory at a time. Yet there was something distinctly off-putting about the property. I couldn't put my finger on what it was.

I stared at that plot for a long time, confused. *Home* rang in my head. Would this finally be home?

How could I live here? It felt foreign, unfriendly. *Wrong.* And yet there was an odd, familiar pull. But my feelings about the compound didn't matter. It was clear someone already lived here.

An aging Ford truck sat alongside the house. Its owner stood in the window of the smaller house, his bearded face glaring out at me, a gun extending from beneath the glass.

9

Eve Foster
Nihla, New Mexico—1997

KYLE SUMMERS.

She had a name. Somewhere to begin.

Eve left the knife shop and headed west down the main street. A fine coating of dust already covered the windshield of her rental, and she turned on the wipers, mulling over her next move. She made a sharp left into the police station.

Officer Mayor was out on a call. Eve told a husky receptionist she'd wait. She perched on a chair in the lobby, tapping her shoe against the floor and enjoying the receptionist's angry glares. Mayor showed up an hour later.

"I told you all I know," he said as he passed her. She hated the way he avoided looking at her. She walked briskly by his side, refusing to be ignored.

"I have more information," she said. "I need to talk with you. Now." When he kept walking, clicking worn heels down the avocado-tiled hallway, she said, "Judge Leroux."

Mayor stopped mid-stride, the eyes that met hers suddenly wary. "You have five minutes."

* * *

"You weren't honest with me."

They were sitting in Mayor's cube-size office, she on a brown folding chair, he on a patched swivel seat. A clunky metal desk squatted between them.

"I don't have time for games, Mrs. Foster. Exactly what are you insinuating?"

"Kyle Summers."

Mayor rubbed his bald head. He was trying to maintain an exasperated expression, but Eve could see through it. He was buying time, thinking about what to say. He landed on, "What about him?"

"You let me believe Kelsey simply left town without a trace. You implied that she'd run off with a stranger."

"That's exactly what we believe she did."

"You suggested she was . . . wanton."

"I never said she was wanton."

"That's what *suggested* means, Officer Mayor. You didn't have to say it. Don't underestimate my daughter. *Never* underestimate my daughter." *My daughter will do anything,* Eve wanted to say. *She will play you—all of us—like the fools we are.* Instead, Eve stretched her hands out before her, letting him see the three-carat rock on her finger. She tugged a cigarette out of its case and took her time lighting it. "And now I find out that she was last seen with the brother-in-law of the local judge, a small fact you failed to disclose."

Mayor's gaze was on the cigarette as it traveled to Eve's mouth. "It was, frankly, none of your concern. We'd spoken with Kyle. He had nothing to contribute."

Eve studied the man in front of her. He was sitting there calmly, but she saw the beads of sweat on his forehead, the way his fingers grasped the ratty edge of his seat.

She leaned forward. "Tell me about Judge Leroux."

"What do you want to know?"

"Why everyone seems to be protecting the Leroux family."

"No one is protecting anyone."

"Antonio slept with my daughter. He brought her to a party, and she left with a man. A *grown* man." Eve kept her voice low and growly. "Need I remind you that Kelsey is barely sixteen?"

"You need not."

"Kyle Summers is an adult."

"There is no arguing that point."

Eve raised her eyebrows. "And he was the last person to have seen my daughter."

"You have no proof of that."

Eve stood. She walked to the window and looked outside at the dusty street beyond. A woman walked down the sidewalk, one hand clutching a dark-haired toddler, the other pulling a wagon loaded with garbage bags full of something bulky and large.

"So what *did* Kyle Summers have to say about my daughter, Officer?" Eve spun around. "If he didn't take her home that night, what did he do?"

Mayor stood. He walked to the door and opened it. "Your five minutes are up."

"I'm not leaving until you tell me what he said about my daughter."

Mayor let out a sigh. "Nothing. He said nothing. He gave her a ride into town, and she must have hitchhiked from there."

"With whom? Someone local?"

"I have no idea. Maybe a trucker. Maybe she walked off into the sunset. Kyle just dropped her in town. He didn't know what she did from there."

"Again, so he says." Eve frowned. "A grown man left a sixteen-year-old in the middle of town at night and that doesn't concern you?"

"She hitchhiked her way here, didn't she?" He pushed the already open door. "Goodbye, Mrs. Foster. If we get any new leads, we'll be sure to contact you. Leave your home information with the receptionist before you go."

"Oh, I'm not leaving just yet." Eve lingered by the window. She glanced around the small office, taking in the hopelessness in the air, the stale scents of mediocrity and laziness. Her gaze fell on a framed high school diploma. "You're a graduate of Nihla High School, Officer Mayor."

Mayor's square jaw set, his eyes narrowed.

"You've invested a lot of your life in this small town. Grew up here. Graduated high school here. Probably married your high school sweetheart." When he didn't react, Eve continued. "I don't imagine there are a lot of opportunities in a dusty little forgotten town like Nihla. You probably had to fight and scratch your way up the ladder." She smiled. "Or maybe you just had to know—and please—the right people." Mayor still didn't respond, but Eve was sure he understood where she was headed. "I imagine it wouldn't look too good if you crossed a town icon."

"I'm a police officer, Mrs. Foster. It's my job to protect."

"Ah," Eve said. She stubbed her cigarette out on an ashtray on Mayor's desk. "But whom exactly are you protecting?"

10

Constance Foster
Nihla, New Mexico—Present

"WHAT DO YOU want?" The voice calling from the open window was deep, wary, with a slight Texas twang. I watched the gun; it stayed trained on my chest.

"My name is Constance. Connie Foster." A little louder: "This is my property."

The gun lowered—slightly. I saw two laser-sharp blue eyes above it. "What's your mother's name?"

"Eve Foster. She's dead."

The gun slithered back from the sill. A few moments later, the door of the smaller building opened. A tall, broad man in his late thirties walked out. A closely trimmed beard couldn't hide a steely jaw or distrustful stare. He wore a plaid button-down shirt rolled up to the elbows, and huge, deeply scarred hands still clutched the gun from beneath those sleeves. Before he could close the door, a skinny black Lab-looking dog darted out. She rushed at me, barking madly.

"Micah, down," the man said. The dog sat behind him, her watchful gaze on me. "ID," he said brusquely to me.

"ID? I should be asking who the hell you are. This is *my* house."

"ID."

"Fine." I opened the Acura's trunk, keeping my gaze on the stranger. I poked around in my purse until I found my wallet. From this I pulled my driver's license. I waved it in front of him. He tried to snatch it, and I pulled it away. "No way. Look only."

He frowned, leaned in, glancing from the photo to me and back again. "You look younger."

"I was younger."

He grunted. "Okay, so you're Constance. There's your house." He shrugged in the direction of the red house and started to walk away.

I said, "Hey, who are you? And how do I get in?"

He stopped walking. "You don't know?"

"I don't know anything. I was only told a few days ago that I owned this place. The lawyer gave me no other details."

He turned slowly. His body was lean, but muscles rippled beneath the fitted shirt. I noticed patches on the elbows, intelligent eyes, the intense way he was staring at me. I glanced around for something I could use as a weapon.

"Relax," he said. "I'm the caretaker, Jet."

"Caretaker? The lawyer never mentioned a caretaker. Where do you live?"

"In the shed."

"The shed?" I pointed to behind the house. "You mean back there?"

"Yep. Shed." He shrugged toward the smaller structure. "House." He pointed to the house. "Did my job, now it's all yours."

"I'd call you a smart-ass but you're carrying a gun." When he didn't even smile, I said, "Wait here. I need to make sure you're who you say you are." Quickly and from my car, I called Eve's lawyer, Craig. He was unavailable. His admin confirmed that a caretaker came with the property, but that's all she could tell me.

Back in the yard, I said, "Since apparently I'm paying you, can you put that thing away and show me around?"

"Eve's paying me."

"Same thing now, isn't it?"

"Not really." He sized me up for a long moment, his gaze snaking from my worn sneakers to my face and lingering on my eyes. Without another word, he jogged back to his shed. Micah stayed in her spot, staring at me.

"Good girl." I put my hand out. She growled.

I was about to give up on Jet's return when the door slammed open and Jet-with-no-last-name came back outside. He walked to the red house and opened the door.

I followed, apprehension like a vise grip on my temples.

It took a moment for my eyes to adjust to the darkness. Dust. Cobwebs. Broken floorboards and peeling walls. A gaping hole of a house. *Thanks, Eve.* I closed my eyes again, willing this all to go away.

*   *   *

Eve had a sick sense of humor.

When I was twelve, she promised to throw me a birthday party—not Lisa, my twin, just for me. We were living in a stately marble house on the island of Corfu, in Greece. The house sat on the shoreline of the Ionian Sea, overlooking a narrow beach. A hauntingly beautiful place, with marble floors that echoed Eve's comings and goings, and a view from the roof all the way to Albania. I had one friend in town, Nicholas, a frail, pale boy with a thick shock of black hair and a languid smile. After school, I was excited to spend time with Nicholas during the party, excited to have something just for me.

Only when I arrived at the house for the party, it was filled with kids from the area—Lisa's acquaintances, not mine.

"Where's Nicholas?" I asked Eve, a sense of dread rising in me like a fallow tide.

Eve smiled, a smile so beatific that even God could have been fooled. She glanced out the floor-to-ceiling windows that gazed out upon the sea.

I saw him, my small friend, floating on a red raft. His face was a dot in the distance. Nicholas couldn't swim. Neither could I, despite Eve's insistence that I learn.

"Happy birthday," Eve said.

Lisa sat hunched in the corner, her head in her hands. Kids sat around her, perplexed preadolescents unused to Eve's machinations.

"I don't understand," I said.

"My gift to you—swimming lessons." When I continued to stare helplessly at my friend, floating farther and farther out from the shore, Eve said, "Nothing motivates like fear, Constance."

I saved Nicholas that day. We celebrated with a feast. Nicholas never spoke to me again.

* * *

I said, "This has to be some kind of joke."

Jet stood in the doorway, waiting, his face impassive. I, on the other hand, felt queasy. When it became clear explanations would not be forthcoming, I searched the wall for a light switch.

"The power's off. Been off for years."

"Years? What about you? Do you have power?"

A grunt that I took as a yes. "No use powering an empty house."

"Why has it been empty? Why not rent it out?" I searched his rugged face. "Why would Eve even keep this place?"

Jet didn't answer, and so I ventured into what could only be called the living room. Raw, torn floorboards covered plywood. The walls and ceiling were overlaid by horizontal plank siding. Curls of peeling blue paint hung from the walls, and a third of the ceiling looked damaged and in need of fresh paint. Two dirty windows—one on each side—let in a milky haze of light. A single rocking chair stood in the corner, its curved rails covered by dust and cobwebs. A doorway, its frame once white, led into another room. Standing here I could see three rooms total—their doorways stacked, one behind the other.

"It's called a shotgun house," Jet said. Rusty voice, as though he was unused to speaking. "Each room leads into the next."

I stepped farther inside, and only five strides later I was in the next room. An iron bed frame had been propped against one wall, next to a stained nightstand. On the other side of the room sat a rusty cast iron tub that didn't appear to be connected to plumbing. Like the living room, this room had the same peeling blue paint, the same rutted flooring.

Bewildered, thinking of Eve, I said, "There're no doors. What do you do for privacy?"

Jet shrugged. "Put in doors."

The final room served as the kitchen. A single row of rough-sawn pine cabinets was topped by a scarred vinyl countertop. Other than the dust and cobwebs, the cabinets appeared to be in decent shape. A large old refrigerator stood against a wall, and a small stainless sink sat at one end of the counter. No stove.

"That refrigerator must smell lovely," I said. I opened a cabinet door and heard something scatter inside. Reminding myself that at least these rats weren't human, I forced a smile. "Running water?"

"You have a well."

Sounding hopeful: "Bathroom?"

Jet nodded toward a peeling white door right off the kitchen. I pushed it open. A low, metal toilet sat next to a small stainless sink and a child-size shower stall. A single dusty window let in a trickle of light. The room was barely the size of a closet, but at least it was something. Assuming the plumbing still worked.

Jet examined a spot on the wall next to the bathroom. "Move the bathtub into the kitchen. Then you can hook it up to water." He pointed to a patched area on the floor. "Looks like that's where it was at some point."

"Nice." I jumped up and down, testing the floors. "At least the place feels solid. This is it? This is the entire house?"

Jet shrugged noncommittally. "Plus the basement."

"There's a basement?"

"Kind of. You enter from outside. It's low-ceilinged, more of a crawl space—for me, anyway."

I noticed the door at the rear of the kitchen; like the other doorways, it lined up with the front door. Its white paint had peeled in places, revealing the rough wooden frame underneath.

"Can we go out this way?"

"Suit yourself. It's your house."

I followed Jet onto a lopsided wooden stoop and down into a small courtyard. The greenery I'd seen from the front brightened the landscape. Raised garden beds, green shrubs, potted flowers, and that furniture. It was then I saw another shed, this one smaller. Its door was opened onto the courtyard and I could just make out the glint of machinery.

"You make this stuff?"

Jet nodded.

"It's beautiful."

Jet didn't respond. I found his reserve unnerving, but I refused to show my unease. I spun around until I saw the Bilco doors. "Basement?"

"Go for it."

"Aren't you coming?"

"You seem like a big girl, and I have work to do. Hold on." He walked slowly into his shop and returned with a flashlight. "You'll need this."

I accepted the offering. "How long's this house been empty? It looks like the last tenants didn't treat it so well."

"There were no last tenants."

"Since when?"

"Since I came."

"Which was?"

Jet pulled a hand through thick hair. "Years ago."

"And before that?"

Another shrug. "Mrs. Foster didn't tell me much."

Go figure. I studied him. He was a handsome man in a hungry, brutal sort of way. I wondered why Aunt Eve had chosen him. Did he come cheap, quiet—or both? And why had she needed a caretaker for this dilapidated place?

Thinking of the trust and all its conditions, I said, "Did she tell you anything about the home's history, about why she never visited?"

"She paid me to watch this place. I wasn't allowed to live in it or change the main house. Some other stipulations. She paid a fair wage and left me alone."

"Did you know I was coming?"

"I was contacted."

"By a lawyer?" No answer. "Yep, I figured. So now that I'm here, Mr. Jet, when do you leave?"

"Sorry." He started walking toward his shop.

"What the hell does 'sorry' mean?"

"I'm here for now. That's all I can tell you."

"For how long?" Silence. "This is bullshit."

His back to me, he said, "I didn't set the rules of engagement."

Rules. *Game* rules. Fuck Eve, always with the games. Even now, playing her stupid games from beyond the grave.

Jet turned. His face was a mask of forced patience, as though he were working with a difficult child. He studied me for a moment, and without a word, he disappeared into his shop, returning a moment later.

While we walked back toward the main house, he asked, "You sure you want to go down there?"

I sighed. "Why not? I might as well get the full picture." I kicked at the dirt. "This place isn't even livable."

He handed me a set of keys. "Don't reach under anything. Recluse spiders are common here."

"I thought you didn't believe in keys."

"The basement is different."

"Why?"

"Watch out for the snakes. Rattlesnakes, especially. They get in through the holes in the foundation. Have a gun?"

So he was going to ignore my questions. "No, Jet, I don't have a fucking gun."

"Then grab a shovel." He pointed toward the gardening tools lined neatly up against the house exterior wall. "See a rattlesnake, kill it. Before it gets you."

11

Constance Foster
Nihla, New Mexico—Present

THE LOCK WAS old and rusty, but after a few stabs, it gave way. I pulled the device off the door and pocketed it, then wrestled with the entrance, Jet behind me. After a few tugs, the Bilco door fell into place and the basement opened up below, a black abyss. The stink was strong. Years' worth of disuse and dust and something nauseatingly sweet wafted from below. I turned my head, took a deep breath, and descended, gripping the shovel in one hand and the flashlight in the other.

I said, "You sure you don't want to come with me?"

"Don't much like cramped spaces."

Who did? The beam swept over the tight space. Low ceiling. Cobweb streamers. I walked slowly along a path in the center of the room, taking stock. The space was cluttered. Four broken chairs, an old recliner, an end table, and a small wooden dresser, painted robin's-egg blue and decorated with tiny crimson flowers and sprays of green leaves, took up most of the right side of the room. The left side contained a dusty plaid couch, stacks of unmarked cardboard boxes, and a small pile of old children's toys.

Something scurried. I flashed the beam toward the back of the room, holding my breath. A mouse, most likely. My breath came out slowly, quietly. I felt hypersensitive to everything: the musty air, the silence, even the rhythm of my own mad heart. I thought of the man outside this room. Could I trust him not to lock me in down here? Could I trust him to be on the same property? And where the hell was I supposed to sleep?

Fuck Eve.

Another rustle, this one closer. I saw something long and brown, and I jumped backward. The largest centipede I'd ever seen shimmied into the light and scurried for cover under the couch. *It's just a bug,* I told myself. *Just a bug.* Still, echoes of another basement room. Scratching. Moaning. Crying. Nighttime noises. I closed my eyes. This was New Mexico—far away in time and place from *that* basement.

She'd know that. Of course she would've. This was all some twisted attempt to mess with my head, to invade my psyche from the godforsaken grave.

"Constance?" came a voice from above.

"I'm fine."

Steadying my hand, I forced my eyes open and surveyed the room anew. There didn't appear to be anything valuable. Maybe in the boxes—but I didn't have the strength or courage to go through them now. The small table could probably be salvaged. And maybe that painted dresser.

Another rustling sound. My eyes surveyed the room, looking for movement. Something brushed against my ankle. I swung the flashlight wildly downward, but whatever it was had disappeared into the darkness.

I backed up until my heel hit the steps. Using the shovel as a crutch, I made my way up the steps, pausing at the top until my pulse slowed and my breathing sounded normal. I was grateful for daylight.

"You have cobwebs in your hair." Jet stood a few feet away, on the cusp of the courtyard. He was using a piece of fine sandpaper on a small bench. He paused, his hand over the smooth, light wood, before snatching the keys from my hand. "Any rattlers?"

I closed the Bilco door and reattached the lock, swiping at my hair as I did so. "Just a centipede. And maybe a mouse." Or twenty.

Jet nodded. "Probably a few dead ones, too." He took a few more swipes at the bench before sitting back on his heels and studying his work. "You'll need power. I called the electric company to have it reconnected. Will take a day or two. You can stay there anyway."

"Part of the agreement with Eve?"

"Mrs. Foster was very specific."

I wiped my hands on my jeans. "She's dead, you know. No longer the boss." The words sounded hollow, even to me. Wasn't she still pulling strings from the Great Wherever? At the very least, she had arranged for his pay; that would be strings enough.

While Jet put his tools back in the shed, I wandered back to the house. By now it was after noon, and the sun beat down relentlessly from overhead. The mountains in the distance glowed pink and red, grand, barren landscapes that might as well have been Mars— so different from the lush greens and blues of Vermont. I climbed the stoop to the kitchen and swung open the door.

I turned the faucet. After a number of sputters and spurts, brown, rusty-looking water squirted into the basin. I let it run, hoping the color would clear. Meanwhile, conned by the relatively benign look of the refrigerator, I pulled open the door and quickly closed it. I'd eat only canned food before getting that piece of filth workable. It had to go.

The water was still brownish.

What the hell was I going to do with this place? Questionable water. No furniture and little money to buy any. And a strange man on the property. I wanted to get Jet kicked out, but not before I learned what I could about this place.

For starters, why had Eve even owned it? And why had she left it to me?

*　*　*

An hour later, I looked around for Jet. He wasn't in the wood shop or the terrace. The door to the smaller building was ajar, and the whir of machinery could be heard in the still air.

"Jet?" I was about to poke my head into Jet's house when the door slammed shut. I pounded on the door. "Hey, I need the keys to the house." No answer. I pounded harder, competing with the noise in the house. "Jet!"

The noise stopped, and the door slammed open. "What?"

"My keys, please."

Jet stared at me, eyes narrowed to slits. He was wearing a T-shirt soaked with sweat. I smelled cigarette smoke and wood dust and musky male body odor. I held out my hand. "The keys. All of them."

"Where are you going?"

"Out. Does it matter? You may not think locking the place is important, but it is to me."

He disappeared inside and returned with one key. He plopped it in my hand. Before he could leave again, I said, "You must have more than one key."

"Nope. Just that one."

"The basement key?"

"No."

"What do you mean 'no'?"

"Mrs. Foster wanted me to have sole access to the basement."

"Mrs. Foster is dead." The words came out more loudly than I intended, and I saw a flash of amusement cross Jet's face. "Mrs. Foster's wishes don't matter anymore."

"To the contrary." He wiped his forehead with the back of his hand before reaching for the hem of his T-shirt. He pulled it up and over his head. I tried not to glance at his broad, well-muscled chest. He caught me looking anyway. "Mrs. Foster's wishes mean everything. You and I both know that—or you wouldn't be here."

True. "Whatever."

"You're leaving the house, huh?" His eyes scanned the horizon before he tossed me the basement key. "Night is absolute here. If I were you, I'd get back before dark. And watch out for the coyotes. They're attracted to Oliver's chickens. They can be ornery. Mountain lions, too." He said everything with that same condescending, amused tone, and it was pissing me off.

I turned to leave.

"One more thing. Eve wanted me to give you this." He handed me a small business-size envelope.

In my car, I contemplated the paper in my hand, torn whether to open it or throw it away. I opened it. Some information—however twisted—was better than none.

Inside was a slip of white paper with a single line, typed in bold, all caps, in her favorite Garamond font.

DON'T SLEEP WITH THE HELP, CONSTANCE.

My eyes squeezed shut. Fuck you, Aunt Eve. *Fuck you.* I crumpled the paper and threw it on the floor.

* * *

Lisa called while I was on my way into Nihla.

"I wish you were here. Are you okay?" she asked.

Her voice sounded so forlorn that I could only say, "I'm great."

"Did you see the house yet?"

"I did." I swallowed. "It's nice."

"Really?" A half octave higher and worth the lie. "Oh, thank goodness. I was so worried."

"No need to worry about me."

A few beats passed. "It's lonely here. Too much house for one person."

"You'll be fine." I passed the two houses at the base of Mad Dog Road. A chicken ran out in front of me, and I swerved to miss it. "Just stay out of the basement."

Lisa's laugh was tinged with nerves. "Connie?"

"Yes?"

"Do you hate Aunt Eve?"

It seemed an odd question. "Yes," I said, thinking of the slip of paper, of her cold and nasty will. "But that should be no surprise."

"No, I guess not." She paused and I heard Vivaldi in the background—Eve's favorite. I pictured Lisa sitting in the enclosed porch that overlooked Lake Champlain, sipping French burgundy and eating quiche and fresh fruit while she watched the sailboats.

No, I corrected myself. Lisa didn't drink. Make that Evian or some other bottled water, chilled to just the right temperature. Maybe a twist of lemon or a slice of fresh cucumber. Always Eve's pet, well fed and pampered.

"Do you think she somehow meant well with all of this? I mean, do you think she somehow knew that this was what each of us needed?" Lisa asked.

Did I think Lisa needed thirty million dollars and a large estate, and I needed a shack of a house in bum-fuck New Mexico? Sometimes Lisa's naïveté bordered on cruelty. I followed the highs and lows of Vivaldi's "Four Seasons" before answering. "No," I said truthfully, knowing this would hurt my sister. "I think she meant to mind-fuck us one last time."

12

Eve Foster
Nihla, New Mexico—1997

AFTER THE UNFRUITFUL visit to the police station, Eve headed back to Jack's saloon. Outside, the air was uncomfortably hot and dry, and bugs were frying on the pavement. She needed a cool room and a spot to think. She took a seat at the end of the bar and waited while Jack steadfastly ignored her. The place was empty.

Eve tapped long nails against the bar's blemished wood. "Hey."

"What do you want?" His voice was gruff. He wore a tight gray shirt that hugged sculpted biceps. The biceps flexed as he wiped the glass beer mug in his hand.

"A glass of French burgundy to start."

He brought the drink to her along with the bill and walked away.

"Not so fast," Eve said. "I wasn't finished."

"That's too bad, Eve. I'm finished."

"Always so testy with women you've slept with?"

Jack stood, rigid. The afternoon sun flooded through the windows, and Jack squinted against the glare. The front door opened, and a pair of denim-clad Mexican cowboys claimed two stools at the other end of the bar.

"The usual," one called.

"What do you want?" Jack grabbed two shot glasses and began pouring an amber liquid. "I'm busy, and I told you what I know."

"Kyle Summers."

"What about him?"

"So you do know him?"

"Of course. Everyone knows Kyle. Why? What's Kyle to you?" Jack looked genuinely curious. He disappeared down the aisle to deliver the drinks. When he came back, he said, "You don't think Kyle has something to do with your daughter's disappearance, do you?"

"I don't know."

Jack looked thoughtful. "You're grasping at straws."

Eve sipped her drink, thinking. "He left a party with Kelsey."

Jack shrugged. "So what?"

"I think he brought her home."

"Kyle's older than your daughter. Significantly older."

Eve smiled at his feigned innocence. "Kelsey likes anything that's a challenge—or a middle finger to me. She prefers older men, so it fits that she'd be with him. And if he's married? Even better."

"Kyle isn't married."

The tone of his voice gave her pause. "No?" She sat back. "I heard there've been other disappearances. Murders, too. It seems Nihla has its very own serial killer. Maybe this Kyle has something to do with that."

Jack looked suddenly uncomfortable. He glanced down toward the men at the end of the bar. When he turned back, he was chewing on his bottom lip, which was red and swollen. "He has a mistress. An illegal. It's the worst kept secret in town."

"An illegal as in illegal alien?"

Jack nodded. He looked about to say more but closed his mouth. Two more men entered the bar and sat at one of the high-top tables, and Jack walked away to wait on them.

Eve lit a cigarette and stared at the mermaid painted over the bar. Watching the smoke waft upward, she thought about what Jack had said. A mistress. No wife. That meant he lived alone. That also meant he could do what he wanted, including with a sixteen-year-old girl. She needed to visit this Kyle Summers. When Jack was back behind the bar, Eve took a final sip of her wine and threw a twenty on the counter.

Jack picked up the twenty and started to make change. Eve waved him off.

"Leaving town?" Jack asked, pocketing the tip.

"Why does everyone seem so anxious to be rid of me?"

"Not exactly a place used to strangers."

"Maybe." Eve tapped her cigarette case into her hand and pulled out another smoke. "Or maybe I'm getting close to something like the truth."

Jack shook his head. "I'm sorry about your daughter, but I don't think your quest ends in Nihla."

"I need to be sure." She took a small pad of paper and a silver pen from her purse. "Do you know where I can find Kyle Summers?"

"He owns businesses all over town. Most of the apartments as well."

"And he has a house on Mayberry Street?" Eve smiled at the look of surprise on Jack's face. "Where on Mayberry? I checked it out—it's a long street with lots of houses."

"I have no idea. Kyle and I aren't exactly chummy."

"How about this mistress?"

Jack shrugged.

"How about where she works?"

The two men at the end of the bar slammed their glasses down at the same time. "Jack!" one called. "Stop flirting with the lady and get us another round."

Jack said, "I have customers, Eve."

"The mistress, Jack? Tell me her name, and I'm out of here for the night."

"You're the most determined woman I've ever met." He studied Eve for a second, his gaze gradually hardening. "And if I help you?"

"I'm still in the same room at the motel. We can talk."

Jack's nod was curt. He left to attend to the two men at the other end of the bar. When he came back, he said, "The Cat's Meow, a rooming house off Main Street. She works in housekeeping. Her name is Flora." He cocked his head. "Watch it, though. You might catch something there. Locals call it the Pussy Palace."

"I'll be sure to take precautions."

Jack shook his head. "I have a feeling it's them who should be afraid."

CHAPTER

13

Constance Foster
Nihla, New Mexico—Present

"I'M GOING TELL you a ghost story." The woman leaned over the bar and squinted, her eyes red-rimmed and unfocused. "It's about Nihla and her love affair with darkness."

The bartender pushed a shot of tequila to me from across the bar. "Amy filling your head with nonsense?" He wiped a puddle of beer in front of her and shook his head in mock annoyance. "She'll have you up all night with her horror stories." He made a loco motion with his hand.

I put a ten on the counter. "She's fine."

Amy stuck her tongue out at the bartender. "Finally, someone who'll listen."

The bartender sighed and retreated to the other side of the counter. The room was wood-lined and stuffy—the only art to speak of a painting of a mermaid painted in primary colors over the bar. Van Halen blared from hidden speakers. Only three people remained in Jack's Place other than me and Amy, and the bartender turned his attention to the soundless television on the wall, watching the shitshow that was the news.

The woman said, "Six girls over five years. Kidnapped, then raped, tortured, mutilated, and dumped. Some were held for days, some for weeks. Imagine being one of those poor girls. Out there alone, at his mercy?" She shook her head. "And now it's started again."

"Six girls, huh?" I gulped my drink. "Unbelievable."

She slid an arm down on the bar, into a fresh puddle of beer, and grimaced. "You're not from here."

"How can you tell?"

"Six girls in the nineties," Amy said. "And here we go again." She was a sloppy drunk. Her blonde hair, ends dyed Easter-egg blue, hung in her face, covering one eye. Her mascara was smeared, and her linen top was a mess of wrinkles and one Italy-shaped beer stain. The booze didn't slow her down, though. She pulled her stool closer to mine and whispered loudly in my ear. "Two girls in the past four months alone."

Amy slapped the bar top. She swayed backward and her blouse hiked up, revealing an angel tattoo across her midsection. She could have been nineteen and she could have been thirty, damn if I could tell. However old she was, they'd been hard years.

"Two dead women. Raped, tortured, hidden away." She pointed to the television. "Why aren't we hearing about it on the news?"

"You'd think we would. That's eight dead girls."

Drunken nod. "No witnesses, no one caught. Why is that, do you think? I'll tell you why. Because no one gives a damn about these women. One day they're lurking around Nihla, the next day they've disappeared. They show up days or weeks later in plastic bags, quartered like chickens." She put a hand over her mouth, eyes wide. "Poor things. How am I supposed to feel safe here?"

I felt an involuntary shudder run through me. Old murders were one thing; fresh ones were quite another. "All of this happened in Nihla?"

"Yep. In fucking Nihla." Amy took a long gulp of beer. "Another shot!" She glanced around, and in a conspiratorial tone, said, "And the police aren't doing shit. Maybe I wasn't born here, but ask me and I—"

The bartender spun around. Smooth as whipped cream, he pulled Amy's beer and replaced it with water. "Time to sober up, Amy. You're bothering this poor lady, and I think your boyfriend is calling."

The pair exchanged a look. "Low blow, Ron." She moved back, away from me. "My boyfriend is an ass. Ron knows I left him. Ron thinks it's funny. Don't you, asshole?"

The bartender poured another shot of tequila and placed it in front of me. "On the house. For suffering through Amy's stories."

"I don't mind."

Amy beamed at me. "See." She took a sip of water and grimaced as though she were drinking gasoline. "Ronnie here is looking after me. Always does. He knows—"

The bartender leaned over and whispered something in Amy's ear. Her face paled, and she nodded and stood. With a final nod at me, she left the bar without paying.

Ron watched her leave, shaking his head. "Sorry about that." He wiped a damp towel across the bar where Amy had been sitting, leaving half-moon marks on the polished wood. "She's a little mental when she drinks. Makes up stories to get attention."

"Is she right? Two girls in four months?"

The bartender seemed to be weighing his words. "We get a lot of transients through here. People on their way to Albuquerque or Mexico or parts west."

"That doesn't really answer the question."

"You going to drink that?" He pointed to the free tequila.

"Maybe." I picked up the glass, swirled it around. "Two girls?"

"The drug trade brings a lot of undesirables."

"Hmm." I threw the tequila down my throat, relishing the burn. The first one had barely made a dent in my nerves. With this one, I could feel a veil of calm settling over me. I'd come into Nihla proper in search of food and cleaning supplies, and I'd settled for booze and company. "You don't say."

The bartender chewed at his bottom lip. He was short and squat, with a thick black mustache that reminded me of a hairy caterpillar. "Where you staying?"

"Why do you want to know?"

"Wondering if I need to drive you there."

I pushed the shot glass back, away from me. "I'm fine."

"Still. You at the boarding house?"

"Nope. Mad Dog Road."

"You Oliver's granddaughter?"

I smiled at the idea of being anyone's granddaughter. "No. I have the little house at the end of the street."

"Ah," he studied me. "The red house. Jet's girlfriend? Never knew Jet to have any girlfriends." He tilted his head. "Or any boyfriends, for that matter."

"Nothing to do with Jet. I own the house. Own Jet's house, too."

Ron frowned. His gaze strayed to the other people at the bar, and when he looked back at me, his demeanor had changed. His spine straightened, and he tossed the cleaning rag into the sink.

"Last call," he yelled, dismissing me.

Overhead, the newswoman droned on and on about a crash in Santa Fe. I watched television and drank water until I felt like I was sober enough to drive. Ron remained coolly professional. It wasn't until I was making my way back up Mad Dog Road that I realized Ron had never really answered my question. Had two girls died in Nihla recently? Murder wasn't uncommon, but if they'd been killed in this town, why the secrecy?

* * *

I slept in my car that first night and woke up at dawn to a rooster's crowing. I had a skull-gripping headache and a kink in my neck. My stomach rumbled. I stretched my way to wakefulness and thought about coffee before trading my jeans for running tights and pulling on a light sweatshirt—no easy feat in the cramped space. The morning air felt dry and chilly. I popped two Excedrin and chased them down with yesterday's flat soda, debating what to do next.

Might as well get started on the house. The sooner I had the place livable, the sooner I could sleep on something other than a back seat. And the sooner I could make my own damn coffee.

Jet's place was dark, and his truck was gone.

I threw my duffel bag on the living room floor. The place was quiet—too quiet. Not even the sound of Oliver's chickens penetrated the building's thick walls. I wandered through the three rooms, making plans in my head. A fresh coat of paint, some secondhand furniture, maybe new appliances, a new color on the exterior. I'd need cleaning supplies and tools.

I'd also need a job. And a bank account.

But first I needed electricity. When was that supposed to be turned on?

I wandered out the back door, hoping Jet was back from wherever he'd been so early in the morning, but his truck was still gone.

Somewhere in the distance, a coyote howled. I rubbed my arms with cold hands, wondering what to do. Nothing would be open this early. Maybe Jet had cleaning supplies in his shop. I could start there.

The shed that housed his workshop was closed up tight but unlocked. I pulled open the door and cringed when it creaked. The interior was dark. I squinted, looking for a light switch. Something brushed my face, and I jumped before realizing it was a string. I pulled it and voilà—light.

The inside of the shop was immaculately clean. Woodworking tools, a simple wooden workbench, a half-formed chair sitting upside down on a wooden platform on the far end. I spotted a cabinet near the chair and made my way across the concrete floor. The doors were fastened with a padlock. I felt along the top of the metal structure, hoping for a key. Nothing but dust bunnies.

No other cabinets or cubbies graced the small space. Disappointed, I turned around and bumped into the chair. It started to fall off its platform, but I was able to catch it before it hit the ground. *Damn*, I muttered to myself. As I righted the chair and the platform, I saw that the platform's wooden base was sitting on a door in the floor—or at least the outline of what appeared to be an opening to *something*.

I pushed the platform aside, one hand steadying the chair. The door in the floor was about two by two, just large enough for a person to get through. I felt along the edge for a button or trigger of some sort, but the edge was smooth all around. The wood was a discolored reddish brown in spots, a lacy pattern that bled across the door's edge and onto the adjacent floor before meandering under a worktable. I traced the stains with my finger, feeling a strange sense of foreboding.

I couldn't help but think about the woman from the bar, Amy. Two girls killed in four months. A locked cabinet. A hidden space under the floor. A man with no last name.

I knelt down and studied the door. I jammed a fingernail under the edge, and a splinter stabbed my nail bed. Blood trickled along my knuckle. I hissed under my breath and stuck the nail in my mouth, sucking away the blood.

The lacy patterns seemed to dance along the wood, taunting me. There was something familiar about the pattern. I reached for my phone to take a picture and realized it was in my backpack in the house.

I started to stand when I saw it: a shadow falling across the wooden floor, long and distorted and very distinctly human. I started to turn, but it was too late. A whooshing noise, then pain seared my skull. The last thing I remembered was the starburst shape of my own blood as it landed on the floor, mingling with the lacy patterns and creating something new.

CHAPTER

14

Constance Foster
Nihla, New Mexico—Present

I CAME TO IN a darkened room. A single bulb illuminated the
space overhead, leaving the edges in shadows. My head hurt, and
the blow exacerbated my hangover. I flexed my muscles, doing a
physical inventory. Other than my pounding head, my ribs ached,
and my finger felt stiff. I made a fist. There was a bandage on the
finger where the splinter had been. What thug takes the time to
bandage the victim's finger?

The room was tiny—not much larger than a walk-in closet.
Wood-paneled walls, a single bed. Spartan but clean.

"I don't trust her and neither should you," I heard a voice say.

A man grunted in response.

"What are you going to do with her? You can't let her stay here.
She should have never come."

"Like I have a choice in the matter."

"We always have a choice."

The first voice was unfamiliar, but I recognized the second
voice as Jet's. I tried to sit up and was rewarded with a wave of
nausea. I clenched my jaw against the onslaught and pushed myself
onto my elbows. I groaned.

"I think she's awake," Jet said. "Stay here."

Footsteps, then a door opened wider, spilling in more light. I closed my eyes. I heard Jet cross the room. He touched my shoulder and handed me a glass of water. "You're lucky he didn't kill you."

I rubbed the back of my head. It felt sticky. My scalp was tender to the touch. "I don't feel so lucky."

"Yeah, well." Jet put out a hand, and I took it. He helped me stand. "Oliver's not used to strangers. He didn't know who you were—just that you were where you shouldn't have been."

"Oliver as in chicken Oliver."

"Don't call him that. He's a sensitive guy."

Jet led me out into another room. This one was small, too, but not as claustrophobic. A pair of plaid armchairs sat on a rug, across from a two-person rectangular wooden table. I recognized Jet's handiwork in the table's sleek lines. Along one edge of the room was a bank of kitchen cabinets, a small refrigerator, a microwave, and a sink. An induction burner perched on a butcher block–topped rolling island that had been pushed up against a wall. On the other end of the room, next to the table, stood a computer desk. A tiny television hung on a wall behind the desk. Two windows looked out on the red house and the driveway beyond.

My eyes were drawn to the man sitting at the table. He blended into the shadows, but as he leaned forward, into the light, I saw tufts of red-gray hair and an elfin face. He was older—sixty, maybe seventy. His hunched back and impossibly long arms gave him an ape-like appearance. Micah lay at his feet.

"You must be Oliver," I said. "You have a hell of a way of welcoming new people to the neighborhood."

Oliver scowled, then stood. "Good luck with her," he said to Jet.

I watched him disappear through the front door. "Not much for social skills, I guess."

Jet gave another of his maddening grunts. "He doesn't take well to strangers poking around my place."

"It's my place. All of it."

"The shotgun is your house. I still have rights to the outbuildings."

"Eve's lawyer never mentioned that."

Jet shrugged. Somehow he made even that simple gesture seem arrogant. "Call him. It's in my agreement with Eve. It survives her death." Jet regarded me as he made his way to the kitchen area. He opened the freezer and pulled out an icepack, which he tossed my way. "Put that on your head."

I placed the pack against my skull. "Damn." It hurt, and the ice only made it worse.

"What were you doing in the shed, anyway? Oliver said you were nosing around on the floor."

"I was looking for cleaning supplies."

"On the floor?" He stared at me, his expression unreadable.

Jet had the kind of masculinity I normally loathed in men. Strong, quiet—above the need to explain himself. Impatient with feelings and convinced that only his brand of logic mattered. Used to getting his way with most women because of a handsome face. Only I wasn't most women. As much as I hated Eve, I'd learned a few things from her, and I viewed men—nearly all men—with the same wary pragmatism I reserved for large dogs and black bears. Unless they served a purpose, I admired them from a distance.

I wanted Jet gone from the property. He was a complicating factor I had neither bargained for nor agreed to. I said as much.

"Call your lawyer, then. Ask him. I'm afraid you're stuck with me. For now, at least." He took the ice pack from my hand and repositioned it against my head. "I'll ask again, Constance. What were you looking for in my workshop?"

"Nothing."

"Oliver said you were nosing around."

"I saw a trapdoor on the floor. I was curious about it."

"It's just a cabinet. I use it to store chemicals."

My foggy mind flashed back to the lacy stains. "The wood flooring—is it old?"

"Old as the house, I guess."

Another wave of nausea hit, and I put my head between my legs, riding it out. With my eyes closed, I pictured the shed floor, the reddish-brown stains interspersed across the wooden planks. Like fans. Like pinwheels.

"Constance, are you okay? You probably have a concussion. Constance?"

Not fans. Not pinwheels. Small red . . .

"Constance?"

Like . . . hands. With dawning horror, I realized what I'd been looking at. Handprints. Like a macabre finger painting captured for posterity across the floor of Eve's shed.

* * *

Jet hooked me up with a bucket, a scrub brush, and some cleaning solution. I thanked him, although after realizing what the pattern on the workshop floor was, I had trouble looking him in the eyes. But if those were handprints, they were old—or so I told myself. Jet had nothing to do with whatever had happened in that shed.

Jet, the man who had constant access to my property. The man whom I knew nothing about.

Maybe you're imagining things, I said to myself. *Maybe they weren't handprints. Or blood for that matter. That could have been paint or wood stain. Stay calm. You're safe.*

But was I?

As I scrubbed floors and washed walls and windows, I thought about Jack's Place and the woman, Amy, I'd met the night before. Two dead women in four months. Had Amy been right? It seemed unlikely that two gruesome murders would go unnoticed by local media. Had this little town of Nihla really been haunted by the deaths of eight women? Or had the bartender been telling the truth—and Amy was an attention-seeking liar?

I forced myself to stop thinking about Jet and Amy and unsolved murders. I had more pressing issues to address, after all. Like a place to sleep.

That afternoon, I took a ride into Nihla. First stop would be the store for some plumbing supplies, paint, and two door locks for front and back. I knew they wouldn't do much if Jet was determined to get in, but short of buying a gun, I wasn't sure what to do. And guns cost money—money I didn't have.

As I drove back down Mad Dog Road, I called Lisa.

"I'm so happy to hear your voice," she said. "How is the decorating coming along? Do you need ideas?"

I didn't waste time with niceties. "Lisa, I need you to contact that lawyer. The one who read us Eve's will."

"Craig Burr. Sure . . . why?"

"Ask him about a man named Jet. He's the caretaker of the property Eve left me. I want to know the terms of his employment."

Silence. Then, "You can call him, Connie. I'll give you his number."

"Do this one thing, Lisa. Please? I'm trying to get this place ready and livable, and I don't have the money for attorney's fees. It feels like his time should come out of the estate."

"You said the place was nice."

I had, hadn't I? "It's fine, but it needs work."

"What if Craig thinks we're disobeying the terms of Aunt Eve's will? What if he asks me questions I can't answer?"

"You'll figure it out."

"It really would be better if you called him."

Something in me snapped. I took a deep breath and accelerated the car. "You're there by the lake, watching your reality and talk shows, and meanwhile my house has no furniture or electricity or clean water. I don't even have a stove. Can you do this *one* thing for me?" I regretted the words the second they escaped my mouth, but it was too late to retreat. "One thing."

She said, "I didn't know your house wasn't livable. You didn't tell me that, Connie. How would I know if you didn't tell me?"

There was reproach in the tremble of Lisa's voice. Of course she didn't know—how could she? I'd told her the house was nice. I'd told her everything was fine. She had been eager to believe it, but I had been eager for her to believe it. Why? Because I didn't want her to worry? Or because I didn't want to deal with her neediness?

I sighed. "I'm sorry. You're right. I'll do it."

"Don't bother. I'll call." No more tremble, just indignant anger.

"I said I've got it."

But Lisa had already hung up.

*　　*　　*

The Handyman's Hideout was a cluttered mishmash of tools, household items, building supplies, fishing and hunting equipment, and animal feed. I pulled together a cart's worth of stuff and waited patiently while an elderly woman with a pink baseball cap checked me out, my argument with Lisa still heavy on my mind.

"Doing some home improvements?" the cashier asked.

"Yep."

She nodded. Her white hair was thin and wispy, a contrast to her mocha-colored, weathered skin, and it stuck out from beneath her cap like a snowy Medusa. "You new here in Nihla?" She peered into my face. "I haven't seen you before, and I would remember you."

"I'm new."

"Whereabouts you living?"

"On the outskirts of town."

The woman put down the paint can she'd been scanning, and a broad smile creased her face. "Now, sweetheart, that could be anywhere."

Her smile—the first one I'd seen in days—made me smile. I told her where I was living, and like that, her smile disappeared.

"Ah, near Oliver."

"Right down the road."

"You be careful, living among all those men. Oliver's brother, Raymond, he's no peach. Jet mostly keeps to himself." She tilted her head, gave me a forced smile. "Renting from Jet?"

"It's my place."

The woman's eyebrows shot up. "That little red house? Figured Jet owned it. Had been vacant for years—abandoned. Until he showed up."

"My mother owned it. She recently passed."

"Your mother?"

"Eve Foster."

The woman pressed her lips into a stingy frown and returned to scanning my items, completing the job in silence. I wasn't sure what I'd said to shut her down that way, but I was getting used to the people in Nihla turning on a dime.

When she told me the total, I peeled off four twenties and handed them over reluctantly. "You need any help here?" I asked. She seemed friendly enough—my bar was low these days—and I needed the money.

The woman looked around at the empty store. "We're not hiring, sweetheart. No one in Nihla will hire you."

At least she was saying it aloud. "Because I'm new in town, or because I'm a woman?"

She smiled again, but this time her expression was tinged with sadness. "Because Nihla is dying. And dying towns don't hire."

CHAPTER

15

Eve Foster
Nihla, New Mexico—1997

THE CAT'S MEOW was a dump of a building sandwiched between a discount liquor store and a taco shack. The front door welcomed visitors with a set of chipped and scarred front steps and a sign that read "No Loitering/No Dogs/No Drunks." Eve used the hem of her blouse to turn the knob. A steep set of steps led to a dirty foyer painted institutional green. A small, battered desk sat in the corner, a phone tethered to the surface with a metal chain. Hallways led from either side of the foyer, each dank and dim. Under the overpowering scent of Lysol lingered the pungent smells of urine and vomit.

There was a bell on the desk, and Eve hit it three times in quick succession. When no one arrived, she shouted, "Hello?"

A few moments later, a man emerged from the first door down the hall on the left. He was short and fit, with a collage of tattoos running down the length of both arms. The name tag on his pressed white shirt read Raul. He eyed Eve up and down, his eyes full of questions.

"You want a room?" he asked in a thickly accented voice.

"I'm looking for someone."

He held up a thick hand. "No way, lady. You have trouble with your *viejo*, that's not my problem."

"This isn't about my husband. My husband is dead."

He huffed out, "What then?"

"I'm looking for Flora Fuentes." When his eyes morphed into distrustful slits, Eve added, "I found something I think belongs to her."

"Flora is not here."

"Maybe you can tell me where she lives."

Outside, a car horn blared. The man followed the sound with his gaze, his expression hard. "You have something for Flora, you leave it with me. I'll see that she gets it."

"I'm afraid I can't do that."

"Then I am afraid I can't help you." He turned to go back to his apartment.

"Wait!" Eve closed the space between them with long strides. She held out a fifty dollar bill. "Please. I need to see Flora."

The man studied Eve's hand, regarding the money like it was a rattlesnake. Eventually he shook his head. "I don't get mixed up in people's business. You got issues with Flora, you find her yourself."

"When does she work? Maybe I can stop by again when she's available."

The man shook his head. He reached for the door to his apartment and opened it before turning back to look at Eve. He mumbled something under his breath in Spanish. Eve didn't understand all of it, but she heard *perra blanca rica*. Rich white bitch.

She'd show him what a bitch she could be.

*　*　*

"He wouldn't help you, huh?" Jack ran his finger lightly over Eve's nipple. They were lying in Eve's bed at the hotel. Evening had long since passed into night, and Eve sucked on a cigarette and watched Jack's finger, feeling oddly at peace. "Short guy? Lots of tattoos?" When Eve nodded, he said, "That's Raul. He manages the Pussy Palace. Sorry, The Cat's Meow." He flicked a tongue along her collarbone. "He's not a bad guy."

"Never said he was."

Jack took Eve's hand and rubbed it along his groin. He was hard. Eve pulled her hand back and shook her head.

"Come on—"

Eve sat up, tugging the sheet with her so it covered her breasts. "Help me find Flora. I want to know where she lives. I want to talk with her."

"Are you just sleeping with me so I'll help you?"

Eve smiled. "I'm sleeping with you because it's pleasant enough. I'm being nice so you'll help me."

"You really are a cold bitch."

Eve put the cigarette out in a tray next to the bed. "I've been called worse."

Jack smiled down at her, his eyes a misty mix of longing and confusion. She wondered if she hadn't made a grave mistake in bedding Jack. He was cute and he was fit, but emotional attachment meant ego, and ego meant trouble. She needed to nip this in the bud immediately. She needed to keep it transactional.

She slid down slightly so that she was pressed against him and ran a hand down his side until she found what she was looking for. She rubbed the length of him, using her nails to trace waves along tender skin. He shivered. She stroked him lightly.

"I need to find my daughter. You understand that."

"Are you so sure she's in Nihla?"

"I know she is. This is where the trail went cold." She moved her mouth next to his ear. "Will you help me find Flora?"

Jack closed his eyes. Eve tightened her grip. His breathing quickened. Eve stopped, and his eyes fluttered open. "What?"

"Will you help me, Jack?"

He lifted his hips. Eve touched him lightly again. Teasing—no promises.

"Jack?"

"Yes." He rolled over, on top of her. "*Yes*. Fine, yes."

When they were finished, Eve found her eyes closing. Sleep was seducing her, promising her relief from this relentless drive to find her daughter, to show Kelsey that she couldn't win, ultimately, and that Eve was always the stronger one, the smarter one.

And if someone had hurt her daughter? There would be hell to pay.

"You must really love her," came Jack's voice, an unwelcome intruder in this pressing, sweet oblivion.

"Love who?"

"Your daughter."

Eve frowned into her pillow, turned over so she was staring at the ceiling. "The truth is, loving Kelsey is like loving a cactus. She's hard to love and even harder to hold."

"She ran away from home?"

"It was a game. Her version of hide and seek. I forbid her from going, but she went anyway." Eve sighed. "Typical Kelsey. I had her followed, of course. Then in Nihla she simply *poof*, disappeared."

"What will you do when you find her?"

"I don't know." *What can I do?* Eve wondered.

Jack said, "Kids need consequences."

"Is that so?"

"They need to know who's boss."

Eve's smile was faint. "When she told me she was leaving, I took her out of the will. She stood to inherit quite a bit."

"But did she know you did that?"

"Of course. It wouldn't have been a deterrent otherwise."

"She must think you're one of those soft parents. The kind who caves."

Eve laughed. "I'm not the caving type."

Jack moved closer, his front pressing against Eve's side. He pushed the hair back from her face. "You come from some kind of rich family? Rolling in here with a fancy car and throwing around bribe money."

"It's not bribe money. It's incentive."

"Whatever you call it. Did you grow up with a trust fund, Eve?"

Eve tensed. "Hardly."

Jack pressed his lips against her forehead. "The Ice Queen has feelings after all." It was a statement, said with neither judgment nor pity, and at that moment, Eve both hated and adored him. They lay in silence for a few minutes, silence broken only by the occasional sound of a car on the road below.

Jack broke the silence first. "You're angry at me."

Eve said, "I was only fifteen when Kelsey was born. Fourteen when I got pregnant."

"Who is her father?"

"My late husband, Liam Foster the Third. He was twenty-seven years my senior. A doctor at the hospital where I volunteered." Eve nodded at the surprise in Jack's eyes. "Can't see me as a hospital volunteer, bringing cheer and hope to sick people?"

"Not really."

"Clearly I was meant for other things. Liam was power personified. Surgeon, inventor, businessman. He had more patents than patients. Held ownership shares in two companies." She closed her eyes, exhaled. "He screwed me in the broom closet with the hospital president right outside. Knocked me up." Eve reached for her cigarettes. Took her time lighting one, then took deep breaths and let them out in concentric circles, watching the smoke rings as they disappeared into the darkness.

"You married him?"

"Three months before Kelsey was born. He was single, and my father, who had some power in his own right as a local preacher, forced his hand. Liam resented me, and I resented my father. Perfect all around." Eve traced the length of Jack's bicep with a fingernail, digging in harder than necessary until she felt him flinch. "Kelsey is her daddy's daughter. Spoiled. Headstrong. Determined. And always, always playing mind games."

Jack took the cigarette, inhaled, and handed it back to Eve. She felt his muscular, hairy calves against her own.

"Like mother, like daughter," Jack said. "Liam's dead?"

"Yeah, he's dead. Killed in a car accident when Kelsey was only ten. Left us well off." Eve's smile was melancholy. "Kelsey never really recovered. Or maybe she did." Another half smile, this one bitter. "It's hard to tell with Kelsey. Was she already fucked up because of Liam, or did Liam's death fuck her up?"

"Chicken and egg?"

"Something like that."

"Your daughter sounds like a handful."

Eve slipped out of bed, still nude. She walked to the window and opened the curtains wide, aware of Jack's stare, aware of the cold air flowing from the air conditioner onto her body. Hairs stood up on her arms. That feeling of lazy, hazy sleepiness left her.

"You should leave," she said.

"I'd be happy to stay."

Eve tossed him his pants. "Call me when you've arranged a meeting with Flora."

"Eve, listen—"

But Eve was past listening. Her mind was on Liam and Kelsey and all that had transpired in the years since her husband died. She'd become a recluse, a shadow of the woman she could have been. And her daughter—well, the six years since had twisted Kelsey into a fun house mirror version of a teenage girl—both smaller and larger than life.

She waited while Jack dressed and showed him to the door, making no attempt at covering her naked body.

"Lock the door behind me," Jack said.

Eve nodded. He didn't know about the gun. "Good night."

He kissed her before she could turn away. "I'll call you tomorrow."

"Flora," she said. "Don't forget, Jack."

"You are single-minded." He glanced at her body and swallowed. "Flora."

With Jack gone, Eve returned to bed. Pleasuring herself, she closed her eyes and thought about Liam. What it felt like to fuck him. What it felt like to watch him sleep. What it felt like to wish someone dead so badly that you cried for joy when the wish finally came true.

16

Constance Foster
Nihla, New Mexico—Present

THE WOMAN AT the store had been right. No one would hire me. I visited six establishments, including, reluctantly, the boarding house off Main Street, with no luck. I had a finite amount of cash, the house needed repairs, and I had no job prospects. Eve's final hand had been well played. If her goal had been to punish me, she'd succeeded.

I was scrubbing the bathroom in the little house for the third time, trying like mad to remove the rust stains from the sink, when my sister finally called back about Jet. I'd bought a sun shower off the sale rack at the hardware store and used that to wash my hair, but I had to do that in my bathing suit, and even then, I felt Jet's cold stare on my naked back—imagined or not. I was desperate for a hot bath. And some privacy. The tub sat in the bedroom, unconnected to plumbing. That was a future job. I could leave it in the bedroom—with the doors locked and the shades pulled, I would have some privacy—or maybe I'd expand the bathroom to enclose the tub.

The electricity was turned on, hallelujah, and I'd also bought a compact refrigerator from Habitat for Humanity, so I had food—or at least something to eat, if you considered yogurt, carrots, and beef jerky food. When I heard Lisa's voice, I was feeling melancholy, as though every baby step forward was met with a giant step back.

"Warning," Lisa said without preamble. "You're not going to like what I have to say."

I stood, pulled off my rubber gloves, and went outside to my car, where reception was better, and I was assured no listening ears. "Nothing can surprise me," I said once I was settled in the Acura. "Go."

"You can't get rid of Jet."

So Jet had been telling the truth. "Because?"

"He comes with the property, locked in for three years after you take possession."

"Why?"

"Why did Aunt Eve do anything?"

Because she could. Because she was cruel. Because deep down, she hated us. Who knew?

"Is there anything else about him you can tell me?"

"Full name is Bernard Jetson Montgomery. Originally from Texas. Lived in New York City, Asheville, North Carolina, and LA. Earns five thousand a month as caretaker of the property on Mad Dog Road, plus a free place to live."

I whistled. "Five thousand a month? For what?"

"Craig the lawyer wouldn't say. Just called him the caretaker."

I slammed my head backward against the seat. The bastard received as much in a month as Eve had given me for a year. And for what? It wasn't like he actually took care of the house. It was a mess. I said as much.

Lisa hesitated. "Craig said Jet's not allowed to help with the main house. It's all on you."

"Seriously?" Her lack of response was all the response I needed. "I can't fire him?"

"No. Not for three years."

"What's so magic about three years?"

Again, Lisa didn't answer. She didn't need to. She didn't know either.

"Any background info on him? College, jobs, police record?"

"No."

"Any history on the house? Why Eve owned it, for example?"

"I'm sorry, Connie. Nothing."

I sighed. "Thanks for checking."

"Sure. Connie . . . ?"

"Yes, Lisa?"

"I'm sorry. For flipping out on you. I'm just so . . . lonely. It's so quiet here now."

"You have Cook. And Dave."

"We both know I have no one." She sighed. "Listen to me, always feeling sorry for myself. Will *you* be okay?"

No. "Yes, of course."

"I could give up what Eve left to me. We could move in together somewhere. Start over without her money."

My breath caught in my chest. I had a sudden vision of the two of us living on the coast of Maine in a small cottage by the sea. Simplicity. Sure, we'd be poor—but so what? We'd be together, and free from Eve.

"Really?" I asked. "Is that what you want?"

"I want you to be safe."

I closed my eyes against the disappointment. No, that wasn't what she wanted. And why should it be? She had everything a person needed—the comfort of money and more. From the driver's side of my car, I watched Jet leave his house and lock it behind him. I watched as he and Micah climbed behind the wheel of his truck, his focus on the little house. He wouldn't see me in the car, which was just as well. I could watch him unnoticed for once.

I said, "Goodbye, Lisa." Hearing the bitterness in my voice, I added, "I love you."

Her response practically dripped with relief. "I love you, too, Connie. I always will. We're sisters."

* * *

A trip back to the Habitat for Humanity store proved fruitful. I purchased an armchair and a side table for fifty dollars, a small bistro table for ten, two kitchen chairs for fifteen, plus a bed frame and dresser for another seventy-five. They were ugly, but beggars couldn't complain, and I wanted to sleep in a bed almost as badly as I wanted a bath.

Everything would be delivered the next day for another twenty-five dollars.

Now all I needed was a mattress. I was heading to the only discount mattress store in town when I saw a flash of blonde hair, ends dyed blue, out of the corner of my eye. It was Amy-from-the-bar, and she was walking toward the taqueria next to the boarding house.

I slid the Acura into a parking space and jumped out just as Amy disappeared inside the restaurant. Opening the taqueria door, I was assaulted by the scents of frying meat and onions. Grease hung in the air, competing with heat and noise. My stomach grumbled, and I realized I hadn't eaten since yesterday. I glanced around, looking across a dozen occupied booths and tables, until I spotted Amy at the counter. I stood by the entrance and waited.

Five minutes later, she walked toward me carrying a bag of food in one hand and a drink in the other. Her gaze brushed over me dismissively before she turned to take a second look. She flashed a smile of recognition—a pretty, youthful smile—before her expression turned wary. I realized she was young—maybe early twenties. Even younger than me.

"Amy, right?"

She nodded. "I'm sorry, I don't remember your name."

"Connie. We met at Jack's Place."

"That, I remember." She gave me a chagrined smile. "I'm afraid I wasn't . . . at my best."

I waved away her apology. "We all have those nights."

"Yeah, well, I've had a lot of them."

On impulse, I said, "You want to join me for lunch?"

She stood open-mouthed for a moment, clearly torn on how to respond. "Sure. Why not?"

I ordered a trio of chicken tacos and joined Amy at a table toward the back of the restaurant, near the window overlooking Main Street. She'd waited for me to eat, and her tacos were spread across their wrappers in a neat row, bits of stray lettuce in a tidy pile occupying one corner of the wrapper.

"What do you think of Nihla?" she asked as I sat. She was gazing out the window. I saw a fresh scratch across her jawline and the yellowish remnants of a black eye on the edges of her brow bone.

I said, "It's . . . quiet. Kind of pretty."

She turned back toward me. Arched eyebrows, a wide sneer. "You don't know Nihla well."

"No?"

"No."

We made small talk for a few minutes. She asked how I came to live in Nihla, I gave her the skinniest version of the truth, avoiding any mention of Eve, Jet, or the inheritance. I asked her why she'd moved here, and she briefly described a turbulent relationship that ended with her living in the rooming house next door.

"It's a hole, but I have a bed, and for now I can afford it." Amy took a bite of a taco, frowned. "Truth is, it used to be called the Pussy Palace. Popular spot for truckers who wanted a bed and a warm body in it. New owner kicked out the hookers, but it's still gross."

I considered inviting her to stay with me on some kind of help-for-rent deal. I could use the extra hands, and she could obviously use a nicer place to stay. But I didn't know her at all, my place was not very nice, and, remembering the drunk girl at the bar, I figured the last thing I needed was drama. So instead I asked her about the murders she'd mentioned.

Eyes suddenly downcast. "Just drunk talk."

I'd survived Eve's tests by learning to read people. She was lying, and she knew I could tell. She wiped her mouth with the corners of a paper napkin, keeping her gaze on her food. She cleared her throat, fidgeted in her seat.

"Where'd the murders happen?" I asked.

She shrugged. "Honestly, I may have heard some vague rumors, but that's it. When I get drunk . . . you know how it is. I tend to say things I regret later."

I was pretty sure the only time she was truthful was with alcohol running through her veins. "You mentioned at the bar that this had happened years ago."

"Did I?" She scrunched her face. "I don't remember mentioning old murders." I waited, and she said, "But yeah, I heard they happened. It was a long time ago. Like the nineties."

"Six girls?" I asked, trying to nudge her memory.

"So I heard. Runaways and druggies . . . you know, girls no one cared about. Throwaways." She glanced out the window, her expression troubled. "But the person who told me that was probably just trying to scare me." She started to fidget in her seat, glancing nervously toward the door. "My ex-boyfriend. He liked to control me with anything he could. I'm sure they were just rumors."

We sat in silence for a few minutes. I finished my tacos—they were decent—and Amy sucked on her drink. Finally, she stretched and stood.

Amy said, "I need to go. I have a job interview in an hour. Wish me luck."

"Who's looking for help?"

"Local gas station needs an attendant." Her eyes narrowed. "You're not going to apply now that I told you, are you? I really need this job."

Tempted as I was, I promised her I wouldn't.

She started to walk away from the table, stopped, and turned around. "Take care of yourself."

"You, too." When she continued to stand there looking unsure of what to say next, I added, "We should do this again some time."

Amy looked uncomfortable, as though a thousand reasons why she wouldn't want that were running through her mind, but after a pregnant pause, she nodded. "Sure."

When she left, I realized how much I'd like a friend. Bad drunk or not, Amy was someone I could maybe talk to. I was lonelier than I wanted to admit—lonely and, for the first time in a long while, a little afraid.

Something about Nihla, about this whole setup, spooked me. It may have been the town, which had a ghost-town-meets-backwater-shithole flavor to it, and it may have been the rumored murders or the locals' reactions to them. It may have just been Eve's ever-present shadow. She rarely did anything for the hell of it. Everything from the food on our plates to the games she made me play were orchestrated to prove a point.

But what was the point of *this*? Why would she leave me an unfinished house in a small town in a state I'd never visited? As I watched Amy walk back to the boarding house framed through the restaurant window, I thought about what she'd said. Throwaways—what a horrible term for real people with real feelings and real problems. I rested my head on the table. I wanted a drink. I wanted the sweet sting of alcohol to wash away Nihla.

To wash away Eve.

17

Constance Foster
Nihla, New Mexico—Present

I COULDN'T GET AMY off my mind. If drunk Amy had been telling the truth, and there *had* been two women murdered in Nihla in the past four months, then someone in or near town was likely to blame. I sat in my driveway and stared at the house I'd inherited. I saw the peeling paint along the roof line, the rusting roof, the small, dark windows. Why had Eve left it to me? Who lived here before she bought it? Why had it been deserted? And why the hell had Eve hired a caretaker, told him to do nothing, and let the house sit here, fallow and deteriorating further, only to bequeath it to me? What was here—in this house, in Nihla—that made it the final destination in Eve's latest game?

It was nearing dusk, and the coyotes were howling in the distance. The hairs on my arms stood up, a shiver ran through me. I couldn't take my eyes off the house, though. The place still seemed deserted, even with the small touches I'd made today—shiny glass on the windows, a fresh coat of paint on the door, even a planter on the porch. Deserted and somehow . . . malignant.

I took a deep breath. I still didn't have a bed, and while the electricity had come on late that afternoon, I didn't relish the idea of sleeping inside that mausoleum. Another night in the car for me. Jet's truck was gone and had been since I'd arrived home. If he stayed out, perhaps it was another chance for me to learn something about my new neighbor. I'd wait until dark, reducing the chance, I hoped, that Oliver would use me for target practice again.

Nightfall in the desert is breathtaking. The stars. The stillness. The absolute abyss-like blackness in every direction. The short walk between the house and Jet's shack had my adrenaline racing. The coyote pack was still howling, their haunting sounds too close for my liking. Something slithered into the brush beyond the workshop. Startled, I realized my own breathing was coming in odd, ragged gasps. This place felt foreign to me, with its endless views and imposing mountains and dry air and scrubby landscape. I missed the gentle mountains and valleys of Vermont, the safety of a landscape with firm boundaries.

Boundaries. The curse of living with Eve was that I longed for structure and boundaries but resented them at the same time. Rules felt confining. Openness felt overwhelming. Eve had dedicated her life, it seemed, to making me feel unsettled. She'd succeeded. Even here, now, when I should be relieved to have her gone and have a place of my own, I felt like unfinished business was waiting around the corner. Waiting to get me.

The coyotes howled and yipped from what sounded like Oliver's yard. They were after the chickens. I turned the knob to Jet's front door, hoping it would be that easy, wanting—needing—to get away from the coyotes' constant wailing. The door was locked. I knocked, listening for Micah. Silence, so I walked around the shack looking for another way in. It took me ten minutes to find a small window with a broken latch in the back. I opened the window, wiggled inside, dropping into the dark. I wedged a piece of wood between the sill and the window to keep the window open and flicked on my flashlight. I'd landed in a utility closet. The only things I saw were a broom, a mop, and a vacuum cleaner.

The closet door was open and led into what passed as Jet's living room. I pulled down the shades and glanced around. I didn't see any cameras, and I'd known from my last stay there was no alarm. I headed for the small computer desk in the main room and starting sorting through the drawers. Bills. Receipts. Woodworking catalogues. An old copy of *Penthouse*. Nothing that could be considered personal, and certainly nothing from Eve.

I moved on to the kitchen. The galley area told the story of a longtime bachelor with decent cooking skills. A few cast iron pots and pans, a freezer full of meat, vegetables in the refrigerator, and a pantry well stocked with spices. The bottom drawer of the small cabinet unit contained a first aid kit, a hunting knife, and flares. I was careful to put everything back as I'd found it.

The rest of the main room was clear of clutter. I opened the bedroom door, ignoring the thump of my heart against my ribcage. Jet was gone for the night. If I did this right, he would have no idea I'd been here. I'd have to hurry, though—in case he returned.

My gaze swept the interior of the space. Jet was a neat man. The bedroom was clean, if austere. The small bed was made, covered with a navy blue wool blanket and two pillows. Beside it sat a beautifully made bedside table, clear of belongings except for a lamp. A quick check of the single drawer revealed three pens, a blank notebook, a few porn magazines—nothing too kinky—a box of condoms, and a tube of lube. His only dresser contained neatly folded clothes and nothing else.

The condoms said he was sexually active—or wanted to be.

The clothes in his dresser—all casual, all worn—said he wasn't a man of fussy tastes.

Discouraged, I opened the door to the small bathroom. Single shower stall, toilet, sink. The medicine cabinet over the sink was nearly empty except for three razors, a bottle of ibuprofen, some antiseptic, and a box of Band-Aids.

Frustrated, I went back into the main living room. I rechecked the computer desk and found nothing else in the drawers. Thinking of the ways I'd hidden things from Eve, I searched on top of the refrigerator, under the chair cushions. My hand was sweeping the underside of the computer desk when my fingers grazed something hard. I squatted down and shined my flashlight beam on the spot. A tiny box had been glued to the underside of the wood.

Gently, carefully, I pulled it out. Inside where two silver keys and a small black key.

I stared at them for a long moment, thinking of the shed. I had a hunch as to what they likely opened. Corralling my nerve, I put the house back in order and climbed back outside through the broken window.

*　*　*

Many things happen under the cover of darkness. Terrible things, things that test the fortitude and will of the human spirit and make me certain that it's the capacity for sheer cruelty that separates us from the other beasts of the world. I've witnessed such things during Eve's survival tests, and it's often the most vulnerable among us who suffer. I'd like to portray myself as some kind of hero, a vigilante whose courage saved lives and souls during the dead of night.

That would be a lie.

The truth is, I crept along the edges of humanity, closing my eyes to the pain whenever I witnessed it. It was the only way to stay sane. I tried not to add to the suffering; that was the best I could do. Live and let live. Believe that things would someday be better.

I had prayed for Eve's death. It was a silent prayer, one my subconscious suppressed. But looking back, it was my mantra, my meditation, my hope. Without Eve, I thought, and her need for absolute control, I could be normal.

Normal.

And yet here I was, once again slinking around the inside of Jet's workshop. Did I even know what normal was? Adopted, home-schooled by a series of stern tutors, made to live in solitude with Eve and Lisa and a handful of staff, and then thrown into the streets again and again by my mother. No, I was not normal. But maybe, just maybe, I could create a new normal for myself. I would start with the house on Mad Dog Road. Make it my own.

Once I knew I could be safe here. I'd try. I'd really try.

This time the workshop was locked, but the black key took care of the thick padlock that fastened the two doors together. One of the other keys fit the metal cabinet toward the back of the building, as I thought it would. What was in there, I wondered, that he kept the keys hidden in a separate building, tucked out of sight?

I started with the top cabinet. Stacks of files sat upon a few books and some expensive-looking carving tools. A quick review of the files revealed sales receipts, presumably for furniture sold, tax documents, order forms, and some expense reports. Nothing earth-shattering, nothing that seemed to require carefully hiding the keys—other than, perhaps, from identity thieves. I tried the third key in the bottom cabinet. No good—the lock didn't budge. I looked around, curious as to what else it could open. I didn't see anything with an obvious lock.

It was after one in the morning, and I was getting tired. My mind wandered to the little box under the computer table. Had he done that here, too—hidden another key in the shed? I felt around the inside of the cabinet. Nothing. I reopened the files, then the books.

Bingo. No box, but one of the books had been carved out and inside was another key. It opened the lower cabinet. I pulled open the doors, expecting bodies or blood or confessions or something heinous. Instead I found two boxes marked "clear polish" and a large metal lockbox. I opened the polish boxes: inside sat a half dozen knives and guns and a set of what looked like nunchucks. Strange assets for a woodworker.

The third key from the house fit the lockbox. I steadied my hand and opened it.

Inside were two more guns.

And stacks and stacks of hundred dollar bills.

* * *

"There had to be a hundred thousand dollars in there," I whispered to Lisa from inside my car. I'd put everything back, including the keys from the house, and took pains to make sure all was as it had been. Still, I couldn't push away the feeling I'd missed something, something that would give me away. Even now, my hands were quivering, my heart twisting in my chest.

"Maybe he's from a rich family."

"Lisa, *think.* If he were from a rich family, he'd have his money in a bank, or tied up in the stock market, not locked in a shed."

"A mobster?"

"That sounds more like it. A mobster or a criminal. Why else would he have all the cash?"

Lisa was quiet for a moment. There was a time difference between Arizona and Vermont, and it was crazy late in Vermont—well past Lisa's bedtime. I'd clearly awakened her. She sounded sedated and tired, but once I told her about the money and guns, she'd livened up. Finally, she said, "Aunt Eve."

"Eve?"

"Yes. Consider this, Connie. What if Eve paid him all that cash? What if that was just his salary for watching the property?"

"We know what she was paying him. Besides, he had tax documents. He's clearly not living completely off the grid or under the table."

"Unless . . . ?"

I knew what my sister was thinking, and I finished the sentence for her. "Unless she was paying him to be more than a property manager—and the cash was the bonus."

"Connie, what if this guy's job is to kill you? What if that's why Aunt Eve sent you there?" There was panic in Lisa's voice, and I rushed to reassure her.

"Nonsense. Even Eve wasn't that evil."

Lisa didn't respond. She didn't have to. We both knew deep down that she *was* that evil. Even Lisa, who'd spent half her childhood defending Eve, knew Eve was capable of horrible acts of cruelty. She was just creative with her methods.

"You need to leave," Lisa said. "Rent an apartment. Or a hotel room. Something. The lawyer didn't say you couldn't do that."

"I don't have the funds."

"Then I'll do it."

"That's supporting me, Lisa. I'm not going to let you risk your inheritance."

"I don't care."

"Yes you do. And if that happens, we'll both be on the street. It's not like we have anyone other than each other." The thought of Lisa on the street was frightening. Lisa with her face creams and sedatives and white noise machine. She wouldn't last a day. "I'll be fine."

"Go to a shelter, or a church. Somewhere." Panic was slurring her words.

I unlocked the car door. "Nope. Staying here." I pushed open the car door and walked toward my house. It was time for me to start sleeping here, even if it was on the floor. I had to stake out my turf, make this place mine. "It feels like I've been running my entire life. I just want to be somewhere, anywhere, that's *mine*. I want a home."

"That's not a home, and you know it. You can't stay there."

"Thanks for talking to me."

"Connie, I'm going to figure something out. I really will. Something so that you'll have money, we will both have money. Connie, *please*—"

Inside the house, something felt amiss. I looked around the room, searching for tossed furniture, movement. Anything.

"Connie?"

My eyes locked onto a crucifix hanging on my living room wall, above a freshly patched section of plaster. It was brightly painted Mexican majolica, colorful, ornate, and beautiful—and not something I'd placed there. A fist formed in my gut.

"Lisa, I have to go."

"Connie, wait! What if—"

I clicked off the phone, my gaze still affixed to that cross. When had someone broken in here? Had it been Jet, sneaking around my house while I was sneaking around his? I thought of two dead girls, then the box of cash in Jet's shed. Another possibility occurred to me, one almost too horrific to contemplate.

What if Jet was the serial killer? Jet was a mystery. Other than knowing his full name and the fact that he made furniture, I knew nothing about his background, his tendency toward violence, or the reasons he was holed up here in Nihla. I didn't even know his age. What if Jet was a murderer? If Eve had somehow known that, then she'd sent me here for the ultimate game of cat and mouse.

18

Eve Foster
Nihla, New Mexico—1997

JACK USED HIS connections to arrange for Flora to meet Eve at his bar at seven fifteen the next evening, after Flora got off work. He'd given the pretense of a job prospect for Flora, who, he said, was always looking for extra cash. It was decided that Eve would wait outside until the other woman showed up so she wouldn't scare her. Eve sat impatiently in her car, watching the bar's comings and goings. At 7:14 she saw an attractive Latina woman enter. Assuming this was Flora, Eve locked her car and went inside.

Unlike during her previous trips to Jack's, the place was crowded. It took Eve a minute to spot Flora across the room. She was standing next to the bar, a brightly colored embroidered floral handbag bag clutched in front of her. Eve studied the other woman. Long, thick black hair. Almond-shaped hazel eyes that shone with intelligence. Her nose was prominent and regal, her mouth full. She was on the tall side, with a full figure packed into tight jeans and an even tighter button-down blouse. Men stared at her; Eve did, too—although for different reasons.

This was Kyle's mistress? She was barely out of teen-hood herself. *Maybe* early twenties, if that. She seemed self-conscious—in fact, everything about her, from her timid glances around the bar to the fidgety way she waited for Jack to speak with her—suggested nervousness. Grudgingly, Eve admitted she was pretty. Beautiful, even. But so were many other women. What was the brother of a judge doing with her?

Maybe she was a fantastic screw.

Eve remained across the room, watching as Jack and Flora chatted, heads bent together over the bar. Flora was frowning, then glanced around, wariness turning to panic. She shook her head firmly side to side, eyes wide, and backed away from the bar. Jack reached out, grasping Flora's arm. She snatched it away and hurried toward the exit. Jack's eyes met Eve's from across the room. He nodded toward Flora, a warning look that Eve heeded. Eve took off, zigzagging through the bar behind Flora.

Flora pushed through the exit. Eve followed.

The night air was cool against Eve's skin. Although Flora was rushing away, hurrying down the sidewalk as fast as her tight jeans would allow, Eve felt no rush. Flora was walking back toward The Cat's Meow, where, presumably, her car was parked—if she had a car—which made her easy to follow. Eve started her own rental car and followed her, trailing the younger woman along the dark road back to the rooming house. Twice Flora turned back and glanced over her shoulder. Eve knew she could see her. She wanted Flora scared—scared enough to talk.

Once at The Cat's Meow, Flora dug into her purse and struggled to open a beat-up silver Datsun. Eve memorized the look of the vehicle, the license plate number. She watched as the other woman glanced back, toward the car Eve was driving. Eve still made no attempt to hide her presence. She hovered a quarter football field behind Flora, lights on. When Flora had managed to turn the lock in her door, Eve pulled her car up next to her and rolled down her window.

"Good evening, Flora" she said.

Flora jumped. She turned, clutching her bag and the key. She tried to open her car door, but Eve had pulled close—so close that Flora couldn't open the door wide enough to slip inside the Datsun.

"I just want a few minutes of your time," Eve said, keeping her voice low and calm.

Flora shimmied around the side of the car, shaking her head the whole time.

"It's not about you, Flora." Eve slipped out of her own car and closed the door. "I don't want anything from you."

"Then what *do* you want?" Soft voice, milky smooth, accent thick but understandable.

"Information."

By now, Flora was at the passenger side of the door, but Eve was quick, and she leaned against the vehicle, blocking Flora's entrance. A car drove by, and both women watched as the driver made his way down the road and turned at the corner. Heavy metal music blared from one of the rooms at The Cat's Meow. Somewhere in the distance, a truck horn blared.

"Please leave me alone."

"You give me five minutes, I walk out of your life."

Flora threw her head back, her face twisted in aggravation. "Why do I not believe that?"

Eve waited. Someone in The Cat's Meow shouted, and the music stopped playing. The sudden silence felt jarring. Eve pulled Kelsey's picture from her pocket and handed it to Flora.

"Have you seen this girl?"

Flora took the photo. The light along the street was dim, and she bent closer, studying it. "No. I have never seen her before."

"You're sure?"

Flora nodded. She handed the photo back to Eve. "I am sure."

"That's my daughter. She's missing."

"I do not understand what that has to do with me."

"Kyle Summers."

Recognition, a frisson of panic. Flora's full mouth set in a grim line. "You know him?"

"No."

"You're lying." Flora reached for the car door, but Eve slid over and blocked her way. "Why are you lying?"

"I do not know him, okay? Please go. I told you what you wanted to know. I do not know that girl."

Eve was taller than Flora by at least two inches, and she was wearing heels. She squatted slightly so she was at eye level with the other woman. When she spoke, her voice was a low growl. "I've come to understand that not only do you *know* Kyle Summers, but you're his girlfriend. And as his girlfriend, you know where he lives and what he does." Eve gave her a cold smile. "So, Flora, where does Kyle live?"

Flora spat at Eve's face. A spray of spittle landed on her ear. *Ah*, Eve thought, *there's the fire*. She grabbed Flora's wrist.

"Where does he live?" Eve hissed. "Is he keeping my daughter there? Tell me."

"You're hurting me."

"Tell me."

Out of the corner of her eye, Eve saw a police cruiser coming down the road. She let go of Flora's wrist, annoyed at herself for losing her temper. The cruiser slowed next to the two women. Eve didn't recognize the cop sitting behind the wheel, but she calmly met his appraising gaze with one of her own. She felt Flora tense beside her.

"Everything okay here?" He was looking at Eve, but he addressed Flora.

Flora nodded. "Yes, sir."

After a long moment, the cop drove off.

Flora took advantage of the break to open the passenger door. She slid over to the wheel and jammed her key in the ignition. Eve walked around the back of Flora's car, thinking. She knew she'd missed this opportunity, but she'd get another. She could follow Flora now, see where she went. But Flora would be expecting that. No matter. Eve would find out where Flora lived. She knew where she worked, so it was just a matter of biding her time. She'd do what she needed to do, pay whom she needed to pay. All that mattered was finding Kelsey, and Eve knew in her gut that Flora could lead her to Kyle Summers. Whether or not he had hurt her daughter, he had been the last one to see her. That meant something.

Eve felt a wellspring of exhaustion followed by a wave of rage. Why was everyone protecting Kyle Summers? Or were they? Maybe she was losing her mind. Nihla could do that to a person, it seemed.

She forced her breathing to slow, her mind to focus. She had one goal.

Calmly, Eve watched as Flora locked her car doors with shaking hands. Flora stared straight ahead, ignoring Eve, her beautiful face shadowed, unreadable. The night was still, and Eve stood by Flora's car, silent and unmoving. Finally, Flora drove off, her hands gripping the steering wheel.

The artificial lighting caught Flora as she pulled away, shattering the wetness on her cheeks into a million luminescent sparkles. Tears of terror. The question was whether she was afraid of the police, of Eve—or of Kyle Summers.

CHAPTER

19

Constance Foster
Nihla, New Mexico—Present

"HAND OVER ANY additional keys to my house." I placed my palm up, willing it to stay steady.

Jet's smile was smug. "No."

"The crucifix. You broke into my house and hung in on the wall."

"It's not breaking in if I have a key."

I stared at him, exasperated. "Just give me the keys."

Jet was hand-sanding what looked like a table top. He took his time, pushing sandpaper across the already smooth surface over and over, ignoring me. His hands were large and callused, his nails neatly trimmed.

"Do you admit you hung the crucifix?"

After a moment, he said, "The crucifix is yours. A gift from Eve."

Of course. "And she wanted you to sneak in and hang it to rattle me." When Jet didn't answer, I snatched the sandpaper from his hand. He glared at me, and I backed up, momentarily frightened. Watching his face was like watching time-lapse photography: his expression went from rage to serene in seconds out of what I could only assume was sheer will. "Bloody hell, Jet. You did this—why?"

He wiped his hands on his pants. "I have no idea what Eve's motives were. She just told me that if you should move in, I was to place that very crucifix on your wall when you weren't home."

I closed my eyes. More of Eve's antics, this time from beyond the grave. When I opened my eyes, Jet was studying me with something close to empathy—or pity.

Jet sighed. "I can't give you the key. And don't try to have the locks changed, or technically I'll have to break in and change them again. Eve's stipulations are many, and I'm afraid she had everything checked out by an attorney and notarized. I'm effectively the landlord for the duration of my contract."

I wasn't so sure that would hold up in court, but I didn't have the money to fight it. "What other stipulations?" I asked.

Jet pursed his lips, sighed. "I have to watch for influxes of cash. You aren't allowed to have any of your sister's income, and I'm to report any suspicions to the same lawyer."

"Craig Burr?"

He nodded.

Not a surprise. "What else?"

Jet's face turned the color of beets beneath the beard. He shook his head and held a hand out for the sandpaper. I gave it to him in a sort of truce.

"What else?" I asked again. "I know there's more. Does she want you to drive me mad? Get me to leave?" I edged closer, hating the hysteria in my voice. "*Kill me?*"

He returned to sanding. I wasn't going to get more out of him, but I suspected Lisa had been right. That cash may have been from Eve—a bribe for whatever crazy shit she wanted him to do. She had Jet by the balls—or at least the wallet.

Only I had an advantage.

Whatever game she was playing now, she couldn't change her moves to fit the situation. Figure out the game, and I could win. *My move*, I thought. *What next?*

* * *

The rains came unexpectedly that afternoon, flooding our yard and turning dusty desert into raging rivers. The sound of it pelting the metal roof was comforting, or would have been had it not solidified my sense of isolation. I couldn't hear Jet in his workshop, but I knew he was there. I worked in the kitchen, scrubbing and painting the old walls above the cabinets while simultaneously keeping an eye on the door to his shop through the window. Melancholy rippled over me. I found I missed my sister and the semblance of family she represented.

By two in the afternoon, my wrist hurt and my back ached and the paint fumes were making me feel high. I rinsed out my tools and changed into a linen blouse and pants. I'd make another attempt to look for work in town. If nothing else, I could use the internet at the local library—there had to be one nearby and they had to have Wi-Fi—and pick up a few more things at the hardware store.

I glanced around my house before locking the door. *Why bother*, I wondered. But I did it anyway.

*　*　*

I threw my raincoat in the car and slid behind the wheel. I was plugging my phone in the charger when I felt someone staring at me. I glanced up. A tall figure was standing between Oliver's house and its blue twin. The man had a long, gunmetal beard and wore a gray T-shirt over his swollen belly. But I wasn't looking at his beard or belly. I was looking at the knife he was wielding in front of him, rubbing it back and forth along the smooth silver edge with short, deft, reverent strokes.

He watched me as I pulled out of the driveway, as I passed his house. I slowed down to tell him off, and as my car slowed, he stepped back into the shadows. I could no longer see him, but I could still see the glint of the knife, moving up and down in rhythm with his hands.

*　*　*

The Handyman's Hideout was practically empty. The same woman waited on me, eyeing my motion-triggered door and window alarms with thinly veiled curiosity.

"These won't do anything," she said finally. "You'll hear a little beep if you're not a sound sleeper, then before you know it, some bastard will be on top of you." She sounded as though she spoke from experience.

"It's the best I've got."

She frowned, chewed her bottom lip. Her white hair was tamed into a slicked-back cap today, but she still had the wild look of a forest goddess or a witch. I felt an odd pull.

"Booby trap your house. Explosive trip wires. Or sound grenades."

I laughed. "Do you think I need those?"

She shrugged. "I used to have a trip wire attached to a gun. Had to give it up when I shot my now ex-husband. Law didn't much favor my 'aggressive means.'" She put air quotes around aggressive means. I smiled, and she said, "Woman alone has to watch out for herself. Especially around here."

"So I've heard."

"Don't believe everything you hear." She lowered her voice. "Things are worse than they're letting on."

"What things? I heard there have been several murders."

The woman—her name tag identified her as Stella—placed my purchases in a paper bag and slid the bag across to me. She glanced around the empty store.

"Don't ask a lot of questions. The wrong people may hear you. This is a small town, but people have long memories." Her hand shot out and she ran a finger along the outline of my cheekbone. "You're a beautiful girl, like my daughter. Such high cheekbones."

I stepped back, the feel of her finger like the burn of a cigarette— unexpected and unwelcome. I grabbed my bag and turned to go, too taken aback to speak.

"I'm sorry," Stella said. "It's just . . . You still looking for a job?"

I spun around, nodded.

Her smile seemed apologetic. "Try Manuela's. It's a few miles down the road, near the gas station. Food is surprisingly good for a diner. Tips won't be great, but I think you'll like Manuela."

I nodded. "Thanks."

A man walked in, glanced at us, and nodded curtly. Stella nodded back.

So many questions swam in my mind, but Stella's focus was on the new customer, so I took my bag and left.

On the way out, I heard someone yelling for me to wait. Stella ran outside and stuffed something in my hand. "You forgot your receipt." I hadn't—I'd seen her slip it into the bag, but I took the paper anyway. Before I could ask any questions, she disappeared back into the store.

I slid into my car and drove away without looking at the paper.

20

Constance Foster
Near Nihla, New Mexico—Present

NIHLA, I FOUND out, had no public library. I drove eighteen miles down a rutted road until I connected with the biggest nearby town with a library. Wells was another one-avenue affair, more has-been than up-and-coming, but its library had exactly what I was looking for: a decently fast Wi-Fi connection and microfiches of old newspapers. I found a pitted pine table, pulled out my laptop and notebook, and set to work.

The crumpled paper Stella-with-no-last-name had handed me contained only a name: Josiah Smith. No address, no phone number, no other identifying information. I assumed Josiah Smith had been—or was now—a resident of Nihla. Another job prospect? Or something else?

Like someone who knew about the murders in Nihla.

I started with Josiah. Not surprisingly, his name turned up no definitive hits. There were six Smiths in Nihla, according to the internet—none named Josiah. When I used the White Pages to see who lived in the house with the other Smiths, I did get a "J. Smith" who lived with Rebecca Smith on Lowry Lane. A search engine's maps feature suggested that Lowry Lane was across town from me, close to the interstate. This J. Smith seemed to have no social media presence, no recent internet presence at all. I jotted the address in my notebook and moved on.

The name "Bernard Jetson Montgomery" didn't net me much, so I tried "Jet Montgomery," "Bernard Montgomery," and a host of other name and location combinations. Nothing new or helpful came up in my online search other than Jet's current address, which I already knew. Frustrated, I decided to widen my search to the murders.

Things became more interesting.

While the national online news hadn't covered the recent murders, I found multiple fleeting references to them in local online papers, and one longer article in a Taos-based site. Amy had been right. Two girls, one named Heather Agnew and the other as yet unidentified, had been found in or near Nihla. Heather's mutilated body had been dumped in a garbage bag by the interstate. No details on what constituted "mutilated," but clearly there had been enough of her body left to confirm identification.

The other body was that of a Latina woman in her late teens. She'd been found in a dumpster two months ago, behind the hardware store. Handyman's Hideout. Tortured, raped. I wondered why Stella hadn't mentioned that.

The condition of both bodies suggested a long imprisonment. The women had been starved, beaten. I put down the paper, closed my eyes.

The Taos article was the only one that mentioned the past killings in Nihla. Amy had said there were six, but this article said nine. Nine people dead or missing from Nihla over a period in the late eighties and nineties. Most of the past killings had been similar: girls ranging from thirteen to thirty found dead in dumpsters, garbage bags, or, in one case, the trunk of an abandoned car. Mutilated bodies. Rape. The usual psycho-bastard shit that sick men did to women.

And now more murders. Related? The author didn't connect the dots, although he did everything but. The article asked for anyone with knowledge of who the Jane Doe behind the hardware store might be to come forward.

I skimmed the piece a second time, looking for the author's name. His byline was buried at the end: Alberto Rodriguez. No photo or additional details. I saved the article and made a note of

Alberto's name before searching for more by Mr. Rodriguez. I was rewarded with over three dozen articles, all appearing to cover crime in and around Taos—everything from car theft to murder. Six of the articles related to the deaths and disappearances in Nihla. The earliest one had been written in 2000. I wondered if more existed in the microfiches, because the early murders occurred before the internet was much of a thing.

I rubbed my eyes and looked around the library. I was the only one in the common room, which consisted of four large tables surrounded by shelves of books. Light filtered in through pristine windows, bathing the lone computer in a haloed golden glow. Despite what was likely a lack of funds, someone took pains to care for this lonely place. Someone who valued books or knowledge or history—or all three.

I decided to go look for that person. I found her in the back room, where the old magazines and microfiches were kept. She was jotting notes on a yellow legal pad, her hand curled around a fountain pen. She was short and thin and in her fifties, with facial features that suggested a Native American heritage. Dark brown eyes studied me when I entered, then softened when I smiled a hello. I chatted with her about the library for a few minutes—she seemed to appreciate my appreciation for the condition of the library—but she stiffened when I asked about the murders.

"Oh, those," she said, looking down at her notebook. "That was a long time ago."

"The eighties and nineties. You were here then?"

"I grew up near Nihla."

I waited for more. When nothing came, I asked about the recent murders.

"We get a lot of transients through here," she said, echoing the bartender, Ron.

"Do you think the new killings could be connected?"

"Connected to what?"

"To the old ones?"

She frowned. "I have no idea what the police think."

"Not the police . . . you, the townspeople. Do you think the killings could be connected?"

The librarian put her pen down, and in one whirl of movement shoved the notebook in the drawer of a corner desk. She rubbed her temples with both hands. I noticed a thin gold wedding band, but otherwise her hands were unmanicured and unadorned. She stopped rubbing when she realized I was staring at her.

"Could there be a connection?" I asked again, more softly this time.

"Why are you asking? Are you a journalist?"

Something stopped me from telling her anything personal. Instead, I said, "I have a friend who lives in Nihla. She's worried."

"Is she *from* Nihla?"

Thinking of Amy—and myself—I said, "No."

The woman's nod seemed almost one of relief. "I can understand worry, but I don't think it's warranted. These girls were runaways, hitchhikers. Who knows what they got involved with. Drugs. Trafficking." She shrugged, a defeated gesture that brought on a fog of hopelessness. "It's tragic. Tell your friend not to wander at night alone."

With that, the librarian made to leave the small room. I stopped her with an outstretched arm. "Can you help me set up the microfiche?"

Her eyes narrowed. "For what?"

"I'd like to see for myself. About a connection."

"I'm afraid that's not possible. Our records are very old—nineteen fifties and sixties. Nothing from the eighties or nineties."

That seemed odd. "But you could order materials."

"Borrow from another library? I suppose, if you know exactly what you want. I need the name of the periodical and the issue and page numbers. Do you have that?"

I didn't—and I said so.

"Well, come back if you know what you need. Or you might try the library in Taos or Santa Fe. They're more likely to have a broad selection."

Taos. I could go there. And I could try to track down Alberto Rodriguez while I was at it. In fact, if I talked with Rodriguez, maybe I could save myself the pain of studying microfiches for hours. He seemed to be a knowledgeable man, one with his pen aimed at Nihla.

* * *

My last stop was Manuela's Diner. Stella hadn't been kidding—it wasn't much to look at. A ten-seater with a long counter and six stools, it inhabited an old modular home with a shed attachment. The adjacent gas station was a two-pump dump, and you had to drive through the gas station area to get to Manuela's. But the smells coming from that diner . . . my stomach growled.

I opened the door and was met by the stares of half a dozen men. Mostly truckers, I guessed by the three semis parked in the lot. One older couple shared a piece of pie in a rear booth. I slipped my backpack off my shoulders and pushed my hair back from my face. I didn't see wait staff, so I sat down at a stool and waited.

The man next to me, a dark-haired, thick-mustachioed guy, leaned over and whispered, "Manuela's shorthanded, so this could take a while. She cooks *and* serves."

No wonder Stella suggested the place. A few minutes later a woman walked—no, sashayed—out of the kitchen. She was exceedingly tall and busty, with a thick head of blue-black hair. I soon saw that part of the height came from stilettos, and the Adam's apple suggested that the rest of her extreme height was related to a Y chromosome. Manuela placed a plastic-coated menu in front of me, said "no more tamales" in a husky whisper, and cleaned off the counter in front of two of the men. To the mustachioed guy, she said, "Five minutes and your meatloaf will be ready."

I ordered a plate of enchiladas, served with posole and the largest sopapilla I'd ever had. Manuela slid a jar of honey to me with a tired grin. "Try it," she said.

I did, and it was delicious. Everything was delicious. I realized I hadn't had a good meal in weeks. Maybe months. Satiated, I watched Manuela work her way through the diner, serving plates of food and collecting cash. She handled even the most gruff men with diplomacy, letting subtle and not-so-subtle stares roll right off her slender back. When only the older couple, Manuela, and I were left in the diner, I told her why I was there.

"Stella from the hardware store, huh?" she asked. Her lashes would have been the envy of a Paris runway model. "What skills do you have?"

"I'm a hard worker. I learn fast." I nodded toward the kitchen. "And I can cook a little."

"Do you clean toilets?"

"Sure."

Manuela eyed my arms, skinny from too much worry and too little exercise. "You don't have an eating issue, do you? I don't need medical drama. Some girl fainting on my watch."

"I'm just thin."

She swung her hair back behind her. "And how about men? How do you handle the men, because we get a lot of them in here? Truckers. Construction crew. They like a little teasing with their tamales, a little slap with their sausage, if you get what I am saying."

I stood up. I'd scrub toilets, I'd wash floors, and I'd cook onions in the greasy kitchen, but if Manuela was suggesting a quickie in the bathroom, no way. I said as much.

Manuela clapped. "Good! I like a woman with boundaries. You're hired. Can you start now?"

Sure, why not. "Now is good," I said.

"There's an apron in the back room. Slip that on, wash up, and let's get started." She squinted at my face. "And what do I call you?"

"Connie."

She nodded firmly. "Connie from nowhere and everywhere," she said and laughed. "You'll make a good addition to Manuela's. I can feel it."

21

Eve Foster
Nihla, New Mexico—1997

THE PUSSY PALACE was an apt name for the roach motel called
The Cat's Meow. Eve watched man after man leave the place.
They all had the same stupid look on their faces going in: half
expectant, half terrified. Some looked around nervously while
entering the building; others barged straight ahead, focusing on
the entryway as though worried the least distraction would derail a
meeting of the needs, tawdry as they were.

Eve had little patience for men. She knew all about their needs.
She had little patience for those needs, either.

She wondered who the men were visiting because she rarely saw
any *women* enter or leave the boarding house. Only Flora and one
other woman seemed to come and go, and while Eve wouldn't have
been the least surprised to learn that they were the prostitutes, the
timing of their comings and goings and their uniformed attire suggested otherwise.

So were these gay hookups? Or were the women who were ser-
vicing them living there? And if they were living there, was it vol-
untary? Eve didn't necessarily care about the plight of these women,
but if there were captives at the Pussy Palace, one of them could
be Kelsey—and that *did* interest her. She could stop one of the
johns on his way in or out, but she doubted he would talk, even for

cash. The men had too much to lose—wives and jobs that could be threatened if news of their indiscretions got out. She grabbed her purse, clutched her cream cardigan to her chest, and stormed inside.

The superintendent lived in the first apartment on the left, she recalled. She knocked. When no one answered, she knocked again, harder.

"For chrissakes," someone yelled through the door. "Fucking hold on a minute. I'm taking a shit. Can't a guy take a shit?"

A minute later, Raul the super opened the door. He was holding a cordless phone under his chin while buckling his pants. His scowl turned to pure annoyance when he saw Eve standing there.

"I told you, I'm not Flora's fucking keeper. You want to talk to Flora, you figure out a way to talk to Flora."

Taking advantage of his momentary incapacity, Eve pushed her way into his apartment. It was small and outdated but surprisingly tidy. Before he could object, she held out a hundred dollar bill.

"I don't care if you're running a brothel. Frankly, I don't care if you have twenty girls locked in your basement. I just want to know if my daughter is one of them."

The guy looked genuinely confused. "What the hell . . . ?"

"Men. Coming and going. I've been watching the place, and it doesn't take a genius to know why they're here. There's a reason they call this dump the Pussy Palace." She waved the money. "Where's Kelsey?"

He seemed to be grappling with what to do. Finally, he snatched the money from Eve. "She's not fucking here. I tol' you that already."

"Prove it. Let me search the place."

"Are you fucking crazy, lady? People live here. I can't let you in their rooms." He glared at her, his gaze cold and calculating. "You are crazy. *Fuck*. Fine, if I show you, will you leave me the fuck alone?"

Eve nodded.

"Another hundred," he said. "No guest rooms. And you don't come back."

"First the tour, then the money." She pointed at the bill now clutched in his hand. "I've shown you some good will."

Raul murmured something under his breath. He slipped on a pair of slippers and opened the door to the hallway. "Come on," he said. He grabbed a gun from inside a drawer by the door and stuffed it into his pants. "For good measure. You never know what kind of dicks you'll run into around here."

* * *

Eve followed the superintendent through the first floor hallway and down to the bottom floor. "Upstairs are rented rooms. We want to go down," he said. "That's where . . . well, that's where the nickname comes from, if you know what I mean."

The air was damp and dank. They passed four closed doors. At the fifth, all the way at the end of the hallway, Raul stopped to find his keys. He opened the double locks and pushed his way inside an inner chamber of sorts—part waiting room, part storage. Two wooden chairs, a small desk, a bookshelf lined with canned goods and toilet paper took up two walls. Three more doors led off the room. He opened the first one. It led to a small bathroom—sink, toilet, shower stall. Clean, no frills.

"Happy?" he said.

"The other doors."

He nodded. With a sharp bang, he knocked on the first.

"What?" came a woman's voice.

"You decent?"

"That you, Raul? Am I ever decent?" A throaty laugh, an Eastern European accent. "Come in. Use the key."

Raul unlocked the door with another key. The interior of this room was dark and smoke-filled, the only light filtering in through a small window at the far end of the enclosure. Eve tightened her hold on her bag, feeling suddenly unsettled. Across from her, beside a second small window, this one shaded, stood a statuesque blonde. She was wearing a red lacy camisole and red panties, and she held a lit cigarette out in front of her like a weapon. When she saw Eve, she gave another throaty laugh.

"You want I fuck a woman? Extra twenty." She eyed Eve up and down with a haughty confidence Eve found maddening. "She look uptight. Maybe thirty."

She crushed the cigarette out in a crystal container and seemed to float toward them. In the muted light, Eve noticed the lines around her eyes, the beginnings of wrinkles on her neck and in the delicate skin between her breasts. A camisole strap fell to the side, exposing one large breast, a dark nipple. She made no move to cover it. Instead, she pouted her rouged lips and leaned forward, showing off her cleavage and the flat, smooth stomach beneath.

"Come in," she purred. She pointed to a full-size bed behind her. It was draped with a thick ruby comforter. Eve could only imagine the germs that lurked on the bedding.

"Bojana, she's not here for that."

"Oh. Then what the hell does she want?" The woman called Bojana fixed her strap, straightened. Her features hardened. "Immigration? You bring them here, Raul?" To Eve, she said, "I have papers. I am here legally. I can show you."

Raul said, "She's not here for that, either. She thinks I'm locking women in the basement, making them turn tricks for me. She thinks her daughter is here."

Bojana's laugh was shrill and mean. "It's only me. No other girls, no locks." She glanced at the super. "There had better be no one else, Raul."

Eve said, "I want to see."

Raul nodded, and Bojana took a step backward. Eve walked gingerly through the set of rooms: bedroom, kitchenette, small living room. All reeked of smoke and cheap perfume and stale, salty semen. Eve searched for hidden doorways, trap doors, anything. She saw no signs that anyone else lived in the tiny apartment. Bojana was a one-woman show.

"How about the other door? The bathroom, this place, and a third door. Where does that lead?"

Raul and Bojana exchanged a look. Bojana nodded. They walked back into the hallway, and Raul unlocked the third door. He let Eve open it. It led outside, to a small concrete area. A Chevy sedan was parked there.

"It's how Bojana comes and goes," Raul said. "Without raising the suspicions of the police or our tenants. Without men stalking her."

"My private entrance," Bojana said, and laughed at her own little joke.

"It means you could also bring other women—and girls—in here," Eve said. "Without anyone noticing."

"Why would we do that? I have a good thing going. Not that many men coming through Nihla. Give this jackass a cut for my rent, and I make a decent living. I involve other girls, now I bring attention, *and* I have to share my space. I am too old for that shit."

Eve didn't know whether to believe her, but the number of men she'd seen coming and going matched what Bojana was saying. Maybe this was just a small operation. She didn't feel Kelsey here. She didn't feel anything much other than repulsion.

Eve closed the door. As she was doing so, she felt the cold sting of metal against the back of her head. She tried to turn, but the gun pressed harder against her skull.

"Raul says you have monies," Bojana said. The throaty laugh was back. "You share."

"Of course. Let me get it." Eve started to open her purse, but Bojana grabbed the bag before Eve could reach the small handgun concealed at the bottom.

"We will do that for you." Bojana opened the clutch, pulled out the wallet, and sifted through its contents.

Eve was always careful to bring enough money—but not too much. She feigned panic when the other woman took five one hundred dollar bills from the wallet. Enough, hopefully, to appease two low-level crooks.

Bojana took four of the bills and handed the other one to Raul. "For breach of my privacy."

Raul pocketed the money and the gun. He grabbed Eve's arm and tugged her back out to the hallway.

Eve said, "My purse?"

Bojana tossed the bag back to Eve along with the now-empty wallet. Eve followed Raul dutifully from the mini-brothel, her eyes on the ground, her hand on the clasp of her purse.

When they'd emerged back into the dank hallway without Bojana, Eve acted quickly. Her tiny pistol was tucked in a makeup bag in the bottom of her purse. She pulled it out and grabbed the gun from Raul's pants pocket while simultaneously jabbing the tip of her gun between his shoulder blades. Oh, how she loved being underestimated.

"Never do that again," she hissed. With the pistol still pressed to his back, she released the safety. It made a satisfying *click*. She reached her arm around his front and grabbed his balls. She squeezed until she heard him groan. "Where the fuck is my daughter?"

"Not here."

Eve squeezed harder, and Raul let out a low moan. Wary of attention, she let go, but she poked the gun harder into his flesh. "You'd better not be screwing with me," she said.

Raul gasped in an attempt to catch his breath.

"Hands up and walk up the stairs. At the top, go into your apartment and close and lock the door. You can keep the cash, but I'm keeping the gun."

"You're a real bitch," Raul said. "Jack was right."

At the mention of Jack, Eve stiffened. She caught herself and let it go. *Focus.* She drilled the gun tip into Raul's back. "Move. Now."

Only when Raul was safely in his apartment and she was in her car did she let out a long breath. Jack had been talking to Raul? She thought Jack, at least, she could trust—because he was decent or because she liked the sex, it didn't matter. Clearly, she'd let her guard down, and now she would pay for it.

Worse than Jack's disloyalty, though—she'd screwed this little engagement up royally. She let Raul the superintendent see her desperation, and she'd managed to piss him off. He'd want revenge—or, at the very least, he wouldn't give her any more information.

Not all is lost, she reminded herself as she pulled away from the curb. Jack didn't know she knew he'd spoken to Raul. She could use that to her advantage. And then there was Flora. She had to crack Flora. Perhaps using a little sugar would work better this time around. Sugar, or cash.

Eve drove back toward her hotel. She was running out of time. The locals were getting angsty, and now she'd pushed things too far.

She needed to get out of this godforsaken hellhole.

Where was her goddamned daughter?

22

Constance Foster
Nihla, New Mexico—Present

THE GAMES BEGAN when I turned sixteen. Like that, Aunt Eve stopped my homeschooling and declared me incorrigible. I was to have "life lessons," which meant, for starters, spending a week alone in Chicago. She gave me a hundred dollars, a burner mobile phone, and let me pack a backpack of clothes. The rules were simple: stay alive and don't call home.

I found out quickly that a hundred bucks in Chicago isn't enough to eat for a week, much less sleep. I tried panhandling and was robbed at gunpoint. I tried sleeping in a church and was kicked out. I considered going to the police to turn Aunt Eve in, but I knew she'd lie and say I was a runaway. I settled for a homeless shelter where I refused to speak, ignoring the old woman who snuck in my cot every night and spooned my prone body. By the time they contacted Child Services, I was ready to return to Vermont. Eve had me picked up downtown and flew me home first class. I stunk up the cabin.

Eve had one thing right: it was a life lesson. A series of life lessons. I learned that restaurants and grocery stores throw out perfectly good food, which can be found intact in their dumpsters. I learned how to use a knife against an attacker. I learned that cops can't always be trusted, and strange homeless men sometimes can. I learned that three AM is called the "dead of night" for a reason:

nothing is more terrifying than being alone, outside, in a sleeping city. Except maybe not being alone, outside, in a sleeping city. And I learned that the one person I should have been able to trust was, in fact, my biggest tormentor.

When I returned to Vermont after the Chicago trip, Lisa followed me around like a wounded puppy, as though she had been the one turned loose in a strange city. Aunt Eve gave me a private tutor to continue my studies. Nothing was said about my week in Chicago, and when Lisa brought it up, *I* was sent to the basement to sleep for three nights.

Two months later, I was awakened in the middle of the night by an angry Eve. She stripped me naked, made me put on warm clothes, and handed me a backpack, a new burner, and another hundred dollars. This time, our driver drove me two hours north, crossing the border into Canada. With an apologetic smile and a slipped extra twenty dollar bill, he tossed me out at a McDonald's. I stayed in Montreal for ten days.

Next time, I refused to go. Eve threatened to send Lisa instead.

And so went my teenage years. And my innocence.

Why would Eve do that? Why would I put up with it? Questions I've asked myself over and over through the years. Eve clearly got some sort of sick pleasure out of her game. Perhaps, eventually, I did too, relishing the challenge and my ability to survive as a sort of "fuck you" to my adoptive mother. But I had come to realize that a part of it had to do with Lisa. I could handle the come-ons and grime and uncertainties of living on the street. I could debase myself on a street corner or in the bed of a stranger if I knew it was for a higher cause: keeping my sister safe.

Because Lisa could never live this life, and I truly believed that if I had not been Eve's sacrificial lamb, Lisa would have been.

Only survival came at a price. Paranoia. Jadedness about human intentions. A gray approach to morality that some—from the comfort of their living rooms—would view as fundamentally immoral. Eve had taught me that sometimes you had to do the wrong thing to have the right outcome. Means justifying the ends and all that shit. But with mind fucking and suspicion came a sort of mistrust of reality. Paranoia as a by-product. Was what I was seeing real? Were there hidden meanings in people's actions, or motives that belied their behaviors. Could I take things at face value?

Here in Nihla, for example, was I just being paranoid? Were the murders a coincidence and the house a true gift from Eve? A small token for the daughter she hated, the only string being a caretaker to make sure the place ran well for the first three years. Or was there something more sinister afoot? I asked myself again—was this Eve's final performance, the grand denouement of all the twisted games before?

*   *   *

These thoughts plagued me during my fourth day at Manuela's.

"Here, Connie." Manuela tossed me a sponge. "Wipe down the counters and refill the napkin holders."

I did as she asked. So far, Manuela was proving to be a fair boss. She was paying me a fair hourly wage, plus whatever I made in tips. In exchange, I was waitress, line cook, maintenance crew, gardener, receptionist . . . whatever she needed. I worked hard and quietly, just thankful for the money. Soon I'd have enough to buy a decent mattress.

"Pity you're living here," Manuela said while she chopped onions and peppers in the kitchen. The diner would open in thirty minutes, and this was my favorite time of day—before the customers, when it was just the two of us. Manuela was chatty, but in a friendly, benign way that made me momentarily forget all I had going on. "Nihla's no place for young people. And you can't be more than what, twenty?"

"Twenty-six."

"You look younger and act older." She studied me for a moment, her garnet-red lips pursed in a disapproving frown. "Shouldn't you be working as a barista in an overpriced coffee shop in some sexy West Coast city?"

I smiled. "I inherited a house."

Manuela cocked her head. "Here, in Nihla? Who left it to you?"

"My mother." I gave her the highly edited version of my reasons for being in town. "So that's what I have—that house and a car."

Manuela tossed the chopped onions and peppers into a stainless steel bin. She began shredding potatoes for hash browns, uncharacteristically silent.

"Have you lived here your whole life?" I asked her.

"Nah. Came here for love about ten years ago. Love left me, but by then I'd scraped together enough cash to buy this diner." She glanced up at me. "Lemon wedges, please. Then you can get the cheese ready for omelets."

I knew the routine by now, but it seemed like Manuela was looking for a new topic, so while I sliced fresh lemons into neat wedges, I decided to give her one. "I heard about the murders in and around Nihla," I said casually. "The recent murders of the two girls—and the older murders."

Manuela placed more peeled potatoes into the shredder attachment on her industrial food processor. "We'll need extra cheese today. Fridays are big with truckers. They all want omelets, for some reason. Extra cheese." She shouted over the shredder. "Heart attack on a plate."

"Not you, too."

Manuela flicked a switch, stopping the industrial shredder. Despite shapely nails, her hands were large and thick-knuckled. She didn't seem self-conscious about them; rather, everything about Manuela exuded a kind confidence. Stella-from-the-hardware-store had been right. I was at ease here. But that ease didn't stop me from feeling frustrated that even Manuela was reluctant to discuss the murders.

She placed those hands down on the stainless steel counter. "Me too, what?"

"Everyone in this town seems hellbent on ignoring the recent murders. From the bartender at Jack's Place to Stella at the hardware store, to the neighboring town's librarian, and now you. It's a taboo subject."

"Not taboo, just nothing to tell." Manuela did that shift of her eyes that told me she didn't want to deal with something. "Cheese done?"

"Working on it." I pleaded with my eyes. "Come on. What's up around here?"

Manuela sighed. She leaned against the counter and tapped two nails against its surface over and over. "There really is nothing to tell. Three girls have been found—"

"Three?"

Manuela nodded. "It's a tragedy, Connie, so no one wants to talk about it. You can understand that."

"But these women—"

"They're runaways and transients. Drugs, prostitution, trafficking. Has nothing to do with Nihla. It's a sad sign of the times."

My mind was on the number three. "I thought two girls had been killed."

"Heard something on the news this morning. Police found a woman's body in the desert." She squinted, thinking. "Not far from you."

I swallowed, considered the vast expanse of scrubby desert behind my property. Thought about Jet. I forced my voice to sound calmer than I was feeling. "Do you know who she was—the woman who was murdered?"

Manuela was clearly done with the discussion. She pointed to the large bag of onions I'd pulled from the walk-in. "No idea. But I do know that customers will be here soon. You haven't experienced a really heavy day." She smiled, but her eyes looked tired. "Today will be baptism by fire."

I cut open the onion bag and grabbed a chef's knife. Another girl dead. In the desert. Two things to do tonight: find out more about the third murder and resume my search for Josiah Smith. Maybe I would hit up the local police. I'd been reluctant to go there, but if the latest body was found near my house, it felt like it was time.

*   *   *

I didn't have to wait to go to the police. As it happened, they came to Manuela's later that day.

Manuela's former love, the love who had brought her to Nihla, was a commercial pilot. While Manuela had clearly moved on, he had not, something he proved during his layover in Albuquerque by driving across the state to harass Manuela at her place of work. His name calling and belligerence didn't sit well with the locals, who, while not exactly the type to promote transgender rights, knew a good cook when they had one. A fight ensued.

Pilot boy was drunk, and the locals were large men itching for some excitement, so the fight took all of one minute. A subdued and sorry ex sat at one of Manuela's booths with his hands tied and his head on the worn Formica, waiting for the cops to show up. The locals toasted with a free round of coffee.

The Nihla police sent two officers: Officer James Riley, a Black man not much older than me, and an older, red-faced white guy, Officer Little, whose gut matched the size of his ego and mocked his name. Officer Little eyed Manuela with disgust.

"Did he hurt you?" Little asked.

"No," Manuela replied.

"Did he cause damage to your establishment?"

Another no.

Little glanced at his partner, who was studying me. This caused Little to stare at me, too. "She illegal?" he asked Manuela.

Manuela laughed. "Hardly. And if you have questions, ask her yourself. Despite the existence of a vagina, she *can* talk."

Snickers from around the diner. An older man in a corner booth gave Manuela a thumbs-up. Officer Little reddened. Officer Riley put a hand over his face to hide his expression, but I saw the amusement in his eyes.

"Can we talk to you privately, ma'am?" Little said to me. His question was polite, but his tone was condescending. "In the kitchen, perhaps." He threw an angry glance at the customers, most of whom were still watching the spectacle with rapt attention. "Or anywhere with some privacy."

"I have to cook," Manuela said. "Go outside. And she's on the clock, officer, so please be respectful of her time." Manuela pointed at her ex, who still sat with his head on the tabletop. "Besides, he's the one you came here for."

Little glanced at me, then back at the pilot. When one of the customers cleared his throat, Little seemed to make a decision. "You take her outside and question her," he said to Officer Riley. "I'll take care of this mess."

His partner nodded. He motioned for me to step outside before him, and I obeyed. The air was pleasantly warm and dry, the sun a disc overhead. A light breeze blew, and a cellophane wrapper skimmed the blacktop in front of the diner. Officer Riley bent to pick it up, shoving it in his pocket.

"Hate litter," he mumbled when he caught me watching.

I smiled. People rarely surprised me. He surprised me.

From across the pavement, the gas station attendant, an older man with a noticeable limp, one of Manuela's regulars, waved. I waved back before returning my attention to Officer Riley.

He took out a notepad and a pen and looked at me with just the right amount of official gravitas. "Your name?"

I told him.

He paused, nodded. "Tell me what happened."

I recited the events in a monotone voice. Police, I knew from experience, distrusted emotion, especially in women, no matter how justified.

"Did he hit or otherwise attack the alleged victim?"

"No. He harassed her verbally." Again, I repeated the vile things her ex hurled. He took notes, glancing up on occasion. Finally, he thanked me for my time. His eyes—deep brown, thick-lashed, and gentle—regarded me with obvious interest. "What are you doing in Nihla?" He spat out the word "Nihla" as though it were a place to avoid.

I gave him the same edited version of the truth: dead mother, inherited property, nowhere else to go. He nodded, those eyes slightly pitying.

I said, "Are we done here?"

He glanced at his notepad. "I think so."

"Can I ask you about something else? Something unrelated to Manuela and her ex?"

"Sure."

I mentioned the recent murders.

He snapped his notebook shut, glanced toward the diner. "I should get back inside."

A semi pulled into the lot and parallel parked against the curb. We both watched a bowlegged man in flannel amble out and across the pavement. He disappeared inside.

"The last body you found, it was near my house," I said. "I think I have a right to some information." I waited a beat before continuing. "Who was she? How did she die?"

It was a long time before the cop responded. With a deep sigh he said, "Cause of death? Strangulation. Wasn't that simple, though." He frowned. "Her body was in . . . rough shape."

I wasn't surprised, not after what Amy had told me at the bar. "Who was she? A drifter? A local?"

Officer Riley shook his head. "I can't say anything else until we've notified the family. You'll have to wait until the details are released to the media."

"And what should I do in the meantime?"

"Lock your doors." He turned to look at the highway and the horizon beyond. "Or go back to wherever you came from. That would be your smartest move." He returned his attention to me. His look was kind. With a quiet voice, he said, "Leaving is your absolute best bet."

23

Constance Foster
Nihla, New Mexico—Present

I DIDN'T HAVE TO wait long for details to be released. Her name was Amber Whitefeather, and she was an eighteen-year-old girl from a neighboring reservation. Her body was found along the highway. Her murder made the local papers; I noticed the national news didn't even mention Amber Whitefeather—or the string of killings that had occurred near Nihla. Once again, I wondered why.

The news seemed to set Jet on edge. I watched him in the days that followed the announcement of Whitefeather's murder. As the townspeople steadfastly pretended nothing bad had happened, Jet became surlier than usual, remaining in his house or his workshop with barely a nod in my direction. Of course, it could have been something other than the news that had set him off. I wouldn't know because he wasn't talking to me, either.

I didn't trust him.

Monday was my day off, and I'd decided not to sit around watching Jet avoid me. Instead, I loaded the Acura with crap from the basement—which I'd been slowly cleaning out—and headed toward the dump, then Taos. I was going to seek out Alberto Rodriguez. At least that was the plan.

I looked around the basement before I left, pleased with my progress. All that was left were an old crib, a couch I couldn't move by myself, and a few boxes I was too scared to open for fear of scorpions or spiders or worse. I was about to leave when something caught my attention. An object sparkled from the darkest corner. I hadn't brought a flashlight, but there was enough daylight streaming through the open Bilco doors for me to venture toward the back of the space.

I leaned down, curious, and picked up the object. It was a framed photo. Small—three by five inches—and the picture captured the image of a woman. She was beautiful by any standards. A brown-skinned Latina with dark eyes and flowing hair and a wary smile. I stared at that picture for a long moment before tucking it into my bag.

The photo preoccupied my mind during the drive to Taos. Was she the previous owner of the house? Had all the stuff in the basement been hers? Was she somehow related to the mysterious Josiah Smith I'd yet to find? Had Aunt Eve known her, and, if so, had Eve planted that picture?

My God, I was getting paranoid.

I reminded myself to track down Rebecca Smith on Lowry Lane, the woman who lived with a J. Smith. If I didn't keep moving, finding practical things to do, I would go crazy.

I glanced at my bag, thinking of the woman memorialized in the photo, beneath that glass. I thought of Amber Whitefeather, dead in the vast desert behind Mad Dog Road. I thought of Jet and his dark moods, the money he'd hidden in his workshop. I could leave. I could go to a shelter and find a job doing something menial to sustain myself. Maybe eventually I could go to college and get a degree, work some hourly job to pay my way.

But as I drove along the dusty highway that led northwest, toward Taos, I realized I wasn't going anywhere. Not yet, anyway.

Maybe I was already crazy.

* * *

The newspaper office in Taos was housed in a squat, rectangular building meant to look like authentic adobe. Here and there, bits of plaster had chipped away, exposing the ugly cement underbelly. A straggly flower bed adorned the front walkway, which led to a glass front door on which a sign that said "No Loitering" had been posted. The door was unlocked; someone had graffitied the sign.

Inside, three people sat at cheap desks in an institutional-looking room. An air purifier hummed in one corner, and a set of small table speakers played Bach so low I could barely make out the composer. A graying golden retriever greeted me at the door with a half-hearted tail wag before disappearing under a desk.

"That's Dottie, our secretary," said an older woman dressed in head-to-toe white linen. She was tapping away at a keyboard and just kept typing without so much as a glance in my direction. "What Dottie lacks in energy she makes up for in loyalty." The woman finally looked up at me. "What can we do for you, honey?"

The room's other two occupants included a balding man in his thirties and a bearded man who was somewhere north of sixty. The younger man was watching me, his long, shadowed face telegraphing mild curiosity. The other man ignored my presence completely.

"I'm looking for Alberto Rodriguez," I said.

"You came to the right place. What do you want with Al?"

I hesitated. "It's about a story he wrote."

"That hardly narrows it down," said the older man. He'd pushed himself away from his keyboard and was contemplating me with what could only be described as contempt. "You here to ride me about my portrayal of the so-called transfer station? Or maybe Rudy sent you over to bitch about my article on his so-called gentleman's club?" He snorted. "That's it, isn't it? You're one of his so-called dancers."

I smiled at this. "I'm neither a so-called dancer nor a dump advocate."

The younger man laughed.

"Enough already," Rodriguez snapped. "Then what do you want?"

"To talk to you." I glanced around the office, looking for a private room. There was none—other than the door marked "toilet." "Can I take you for coffee?"

He returned his attention to his computer screen. "I'm busy."

This seemed to be the signal the others were waiting for. They all turned back to their computers, shutting me down. Even the dog lost interest and tucked her head under her tail.

"Please," I said. No response. Then, "Amber Whitefeather. Carla Deerling. Maria Sanchez." He looked up, so I continued. "Nancy

Cane. Roseanna Scarletti. Simone Moore. Stephanie McFarlane. Two Jane Does."

Rodriquez chewed on his pen, regarding me with cool interest. "Thirty minutes," he said finally. "There's a pizza place down the road. Pizza sucks, but it's quiet. You can buy me lunch."

*   *   *

The pizza did suck, which probably explained the quiet, but that didn't keep Rodriguez from wolfing down four slices and a Coke.

"Nine girls over a twenty-year period. And there are probably more." He waved his last slice at me, took a swallow of Coke, and bit into the pizza crust. "Nine girls," he said between bites, "In or near Nihla, but the cops won't acknowledge that it's the pattern of one perp."

"They think it's random?"

"Before I answer that, what's in it for you? Why are you asking?"

Alberto Rodriquez squinted at me. He had dark eyes, almost black, and a bitter slash of a mouth. But his cheekbones under his peppery beard were high, and his eyes shone with intelligence, giving him an undeniable, if not handsome, presence. I was at once drawn to him *and* repulsed.

"I live in Nihla. Recent transplant. I heard about the murders from another transplant, but when I ask around, no one will tell me anything." I realized I'd wrapped my arms around my torso, as though to protect myself from the words, and I forced my hands on the table. "It's as though everyone thinks if they don't talk about it, it's not happening. Like there's some tacit agreement in Nihla to pretend women aren't being murdered."

That seemed to be the right answer. Rodriquez nodded. "The police insist these latest ones are random, and the national rags aren't interested because the women are nobodies."

"Nobodies?"

"Throwaways and runaways." He met my gaze, his expression softening. "Whitefeather was a drunk from the reservation up in Touring. Cops knew about her because she was always loitering at the rest stations. Even the victims from the nineties fit the bill. Deerling was a druggie and a prostitute. Sanchez, a drug addict and runaway, here illegally from Mexico. Cane was homeless. Scarletti was a stripper—the kind who turns tricks in her car afterwards.

Couldn't find anything about Moore, which also speaks volumes. McFarlane came from a wealthy family, but she'd run away from home at fourteen. One of those oppositional types, always lying and getting in trouble, so her parents said they could never control her. They weren't surprised when she turned up dead."

"Were any of them from Nihla?"

"No." Rodriquez paused to take a drink. "Not really."

"Not really?" When he didn't respond, I said, "How about the Jane Does?"

Rodriquez picked up his last piece of crust, looked at it, and threw it back on the plate. "The first one? Her body was burned beyond recognition. Cops tried to use her teeth to identify her. No hits. The other? No one knows. She had been tortured and raped and mutilated, but her identity remains a mystery." He pushed at the crust on his plate. "As alone after her death as she was before."

I sat back in my chair. Nine girls, one small town. "Were all of them tortured and raped?"

"Those nine? As far as I could find, yes. Not sure about the latest round." He glanced out the window. "There are others, girls who were coming through Nihla because of the interstate and disappeared. Missing persons reports, rumors. Who knows whether there are nine or twenty." He shook his head, returned his attention to me. "That's part of the tragedy. How many are simply lost?"

I chose my next words carefully. Rodriguez struck me as a journalist who was more invested in these murders than met the eye. I sensed an emotional connection, and I didn't want to say the wrong thing.

"Do you think the recent string—the ones over the past months—are related to what happened in the eighties and nineties?"

He let out a derisive snort. "Well, I think something is wrong in Nihla. Something is putrid and rotting and stinks to hell." His voice was low, his tone like steel. "Are all of the deaths connected? It seems far-fetched, doesn't it? The last round and this round were separated by two decades. Related? Something a crazy bastard would say, especially because the local police have declared the deaths to be random, caused by the unfortunate choices and circumstances of the victims. As though they should ever be blamed. The cops point to the proximity to the highway, a highway that brings traffic through the area." He shifted his focus to me, and his eyes were like lasers, pointed and full of rage. "But yes, I sure as hell think they're connected. Only I seem to be the only one."

"What if I said you're not the only one?"

"Are you referring to yourself? No offense, but so what? What clout do you have?"

"None whatsoever."

Rodriguez sat there, silent, his eyes continuing to deride me.

I said, "What are you trying to accomplish with your articles?"

"Justice."

"For these girls?"

He paused. "For my mother. And my sister."

I let his statement hang there until he was ready to explain.

"In 1995, a young Latina named Gloria went missing. Her family lived twenty miles from Nihla, in a little town called Springs. They searched for Gloria for months, to no avail. She was a good kid, a straight-A student, had a big heart. The New Mexico authorities labeled her a runaway, but she wasn't. Her body was never found, but I'm convinced it's out there somewhere, in the desert." He pushed away his paper plate. "Gloria was my baby sister."

"I'm sorry."

He nodded. "Gloria was one of many Latina girls who went missing across the Southwest that year. Two others turned up in or near Nihla, including a young woman named Esmerelda. She was only fifteen. She had been my sister's friend."

"Her name never came up in my searches." And neither had his sister's.

"Does that really surprise you?"

No. "And they never caught anyone?"

Rodriquez's smile was twisted and bitter. "Oh, they arrested people. Two men in late 1997. Cops claimed they were responsible for the deaths of several of the girls. But I know that's bullshit." He glanced at his watch. "Look, I have to go. This story is old, and frankly nobody cares."

"I care."

He seemed to remember that he was actually talking to a person. His eyes softened with sympathy. "You're afraid, and I understand that. Don't wander around by yourself. Or better yet, get out of town."

"I can't."

"Bullshit."

"The house is all I have."

He stood. "Well, be careful. And if you hear or see anything . . . call me."

"And the police?"

"Don't bother."

With a sigh, I scribbled my number on a piece of napkin. "Will you do the same?"

He glanced at the number. "Eight-oh-two? That's not a local extension."

"Vermont. The house on Mad Dog is my inheritance. The only thing I own, other than my car."

Rodriguez's face froze.

"What is it? Surely you've met people from Vermont before." My attempt at humor fell flat. "Mad Dog?" he asked.

"Mad Dog Road. Strange name, I know."

"Mad Dog Road in Nihla. Small red house?"

"You know it?"

The color drained from his face. "In 1996, they found Esmerelda's body a quarter mile from that house. She'd been raped and held captive somewhere. By the time they found her strangled, mutilated body, she weighed only eighty-eight pounds."

How awful. I couldn't even contemplate what it would have been like for her, for her family. "Was there a connection between my house and Esmerelda's death?"

Rodriguez shrugged. "Not that I know of. The only person living there at the time was a young Mexican woman named Flora Fuentes. She claimed she heard nothing, saw nothing."

"Did she find the body?"

Rodriguez shook his head. "Man named Oliver Bard. Mean motherfucker."

I rubbed the spot where Oliver had hit me. It was still tender. "Yeah, I know Oliver. He's my neighbor." I paused, thinking. "Do you know a man named Jet?" When Rodriquez gave me a blank stare, I said, "Bernard Jetson Montgomery. Ring a bell?"

"No. Should it?"

"He's the caretaker of my property. My mother hired him."

Rodriguez stood up and grabbed his plate and cup. "Sorry—not familiar. I really do have to go."

"Please, call me if you learn something."

I watched him walk out the door and down the road and wondered whether Flora was the name of the woman whose photo I had found.

CHAPTER

24

Eve Foster
Nihla, New Mexico—1997

Back at the motel, Eve used her cell phone to contact her lawyer. He was no help. Jim Kelly had been with her since Eve's husband died, when Kelsey was still a kid, and he'd generally humored her demands with stoic grace and not a hint of the condescension she was sure he felt. Today, though, he seemed out of ideas—and patience.

"You've threatened to disown her if she leaves, you've actually disowned her, you've hired a private detective to no avail, and now you're spending time in New Mexico looking for your daughter. Have you ever considered that Kelsey simply doesn't want to be found?"

Eve put her head against the cool glass of the motel window. Of course she'd considered it. "I can't exactly leave without knowing what's happened to her."

"She's her father's daughter, Eve."

He didn't realize how true that was. Eve had only been fifteen when she'd had Kelsey. Sure, she'd been drawn to her late husband's charisma and confidence, but what had she known? She'd only been a child herself. For the next ten years, until his untimely death, Liam Foster had tortured his child bride. Not in ways that left visible scars, he was too cunning for that, but in smaller, more insidious, ways. With mind games. And sex games.

And, sometimes, with pain. He knew she had nowhere to turn. Shunned by her religious parents, hers was an opulent prison, and Liam had been both prison guard and rescuer. Torturer and healer. God-figure and Satan himself.

Eve rubbed her arm absentmindedly. His death had freed her, but it hadn't freed Kelsey. She'd only gotten worse. Her youth was littered with warning signs, a veritable field of psychological land mines. Friends who came over once and never returned. Small animals that disappeared. Lies told with so little guile that it would terrify even the most accomplished politician. Kelsey made her mother the target of her games, with this little disappearing act her grand finale.

Eve stared at the phone in her hand. Kelsey could be dead in a ditch somewhere. Or held captive by some psychopath. She should be worried sick. But she also knew that Kelsey could be waiting, setting a trap for her mother so she could claim victory. Eve could sense her daughter here, in Nihla. She'd like to call it the result of a strong mother–daughter bond, but it was more like the second sense a deer has when it *feels* the hunter nearby.

She had to know what happened to Kelsey, for her own sanity, if nothing else.

But her lawyer knew none of that. He saw a young mother, a teen who was smart beyond her years, and a fortune.

Eve said, "I understand what you're saying, Jim, but I have to do everything I can."

Liam's longtime lawyer was silent for a moment. When he spoke again, there was resignation in his voice. "I'll wire you the money from your account. But please be careful. I know you want to find your daughter, Eve. I know a parent can't rest until they locate a missing child."

"Right," Eve said into the phone. "If something's happened, I need to know." *And then, God help me, I will truly be free*, said a tiny voice inside her. Eve closed her eyes and shut out the voice. What kind of mother had she become?

Never mind Liam and Kelsey—what kind of monster was *she*?

* * *

Mayberry Street may have passed for the nice section of town in Nihla, but in Eve's view, it was *meh* at best. What it lacked in polish it made up for in length—and distance from the highway. The road, which horseshoed its way around the northeast side of town and skirted the encroaching desert, consisted of five long blocks of single-family homes. One end housed the smaller homes—a mix of adobe-style cottages and Craftsman one-stories. The nicer homes were on the eastern end of the street, so that's where Eve concentrated her efforts. She'd found a phone book at the local library, but Kyle Summers's address was unlisted. She was left watching—and hoping.

She spent a half hour parked on the second to last block of Mayberry, mulling over next steps. At 2:37, a woman in a Volvo pulled up to one of the larger homes, parked in the driveway, and went inside. Well-dressed and silver-haired, she approached the front door with the confidence of someone who lived there. Her presence gave Eve an idea.

Eve turned on the engine and pulled into the woman's driveway, behind the Volvo. She got out and strode up the driveway with assurance, arriving at the front door just as the woman was opening it.

The woman glanced at Eve. "May I help you?"

"Kyle asked me to stop by."

She smiled. "Kyle? Oh, you must mean Kyle Summers. I'm afraid you have the wrong house."

Eve read the numbers off the side of the building. "I'm sure he said four-sixteen Mayberry."

The woman's smile broadened, softening stern features. "Four-forty-eight. Easy mistake to make."

Eve smiled back. "Thank you. Yes, I suppose it was."

*   *   *

Four-forty-eight Mayberry was a nouveau riche version of Greek Revival. Set on a scrubby half acre, with only the briefest nod to landscaping evident in its weedy border beds, it landed points for size, not style. Eve sat in her car, staring at the house. Its ostentation hardly screamed kidnapper. Then again, she reminded herself, she had nothing but gut instinct to tell her Kelsey had been kidnapped. She could be holed up in this place, stoned out of her mind and screwing this Kyle Summers like some tramp turning tricks in a drug den.

Eve wouldn't put it past her daughter to be here voluntarily. She wouldn't put it past Kelsey to be *running* the drug den.

Reluctantly, Eve climbed out of her car. She scoped out the house. Double wide entryway. A small sign near the entrance that warned of an alarm system. She pressed the doorbell button twice in quick succession, waited a few seconds, and then she pressed it again. It was 3:13 in the afternoon. Kyle was probably at work—whatever that meant.

Eve was about to leave when the door opened, only it was Flora who stood on the other side of the threshold. Her beautiful face was marred by a bruise that covered one eye and left her right cheek swollen. She wore a shapeless blue shift. One hand grasped the doorframe, the other held on to the door as though she meant to slam it in Eve's face.

"What do you want with us?"

"I just want to talk."

"I have nothing to say to you. *Nada*. Go away."

"Your face," Eve said. She held a hand out, tentatively, and quickly pushed against the closing door. "Please. Just a few minutes?"

Flora closed her eyes. The damaged one was too engorged to close all the way, and Flora covered it with the back of her hand. She glanced behind her, sighed, and walked out onto the concrete landing, closing the door behind her.

"Follow me." Flora walked around the side of the house and stood in the shade of the lone tree, tucked between the house and a shed, out of the sight of anyone on the road. Eve joined her.

Eve pulled her photo of Kelsey out of her purse. "That's my daughter. She's missing." Eve watched the other woman's expression, looking for some sign of recognition. "She was last seen in Nihla."

"So?"

"So, she was last seen with Kyle Summers." Eve waited a beat. "Your boyfriend."

Flora wrapped her arms around her ample chest, jutted her chin forward. "I don't know where your daughter is."

"But you know where Kyle is."

"He is not here."

"Then where can I find him?"

Eve followed Flora's gaze, which strayed to the big house. She seemed to fixate on the second story windows.

Flora said, "He's traveling."

"Are you sure he's not here?"

"No. He is away, I swear it to you. He is not at home."

Eve took a step closer. She made a show of studying Flora's damaged cheek. "Why are you protecting him?"

"I am not protecting him." Flora turned away. "If that's all you wanted, you should go now. I don't know where your daughter is, and Kyle isn't here."

"What does he have on all of you that everyone seems so scared to cross him?"

Flora answered without turning around. "We are a tight community. When someone threatens one of us, we band together."

"You're not even from Nihla, are you?"

Flora turned her head ever so slightly. Sunlight fell on her swollen face, turning purple bruises blood red under olive skin. When she spoke, her voice was heavy with sadness and resignation. "Leave it be. There's nothing to see in Nihla."

"I think there's a lot to see here, Flora. Girls have disappeared, there are rumors of murder. Things that lurk beneath the surface, things that no one will admit."

Flora gave Eve a defeated smile. "We have a saying in my birth country: '*Donde el diablo puso la mano, queda huella para rato.*'" She shook her head. "Go home, Mrs. Foster."

Eve watched Flora hurry across the yard, back toward the front of the house. She was limping.

Only later, settled in a wooden chair at the local library, did Eve look up the saying. She closed the Spanish-English dictionary, feeling pensive. Roughly translated, it meant, "where the devil put his hand, there is a trace for a while."

In other words, evil always leaves its mark.

CHAPTER

25

Constance Foster
Nihla, New Mexico—Present

Lowry Lane jutted off Main Street like an afterthought. I found Rebecca Smith's house without much fuss. It was a simple Craftsman-style cottage, small but cozy-looking. Wooden façade, blocky porch, expansive windows, and a metal fence that surrounded a dime-size property. A Honda sat in the driveway, its bumper sporting a "Love One Another" sticker—and stickers from a dozen state and national parks. The interior of the vehicle was cluttered with garbage, clothing, books, and blankets. I wasn't sure how anyone was able to drive it.

The third knock on the door brought a woman running from around the back of the house. "Please stop." She waved one gloved hand at me while the other pushed back a chunk of silver-gray hair. "You have no idea how hard it is to get him to sleep."

"I'm sorry." I put my hands in the air in surrender. "I didn't mean to cause issues."

The woman took a moment to catch her breath. She was short and stodgy, her round face accentuated by chin-length hair. She looked down at muddy knees and laughed. "That's what I get for wearing shorts." She pulled a glove off and eyed me sideways. "When I find the time, I like to garden. It keeps my mind off other things."

I gave her as warm a smile as I could muster. She seemed friendly enough, and it was nice to see a friendly face. "Are you Rebecca Smith?"

"Who's asking?"

"I'm Connie Foster." I held out a hand and she shook it half-heartedly. "I'm actually looking for Josiah Smith."

"Becky Smith." A curt nod. "Well, you came to the right house, but I'm not sure it'll do you any good. What do you want with my uncle?"

"The truth is, I'm not sure. I'm new to Nihla, and someone gave me his name. Suggested I speak to him."

"Are you a lawyer?"

I shook my head. "No, ma'am."

"A reporter?"

"Nope." I knew I needed to come up with something, and not knowing what Josiah had to do with me, I didn't want to mention Stella from the hardware store. I settled on, "A friend from home told me to look him up. I guess they went way back, and she thought he could help me." I glanced down at the ground. "Adjusting to a new town's been tough."

"You're new to Nihla?"

I nodded. "Moved here recently. Still trying to acclimate."

The woman sighed. "Well, I wish Uncle Joe—that's what we call him—could help you. Maybe on a good day he'd enjoy the company." She smiled. "He liked the ladies. He was a catch in his time."

"Does he suffer from . . ."

"Dementia? Not really. He had a stroke a year ago, but the docs say it was mild and doesn't explain his symptoms. We moved in together, and I try to take care of him. On good days, he can hold a conversation, feed himself, walk a bit. On bad days," she shrugged, "I pray he'll sleep."

"I guess today was a bad day?" When Becky nodded, I said, "I'm sorry to hear that."

"Yeah, well." She waved a glove. "I need to get back to the garden. I only have so much free time with Uncle Joe's schedule, and I still have half a bed to weed." She must have seen the disappointment on my face, because she added, "Tell you what, why don't you give me your number. If he has a good day, I'll give you a call. I promise."

I wrote my number on a piece of scrap paper from my bag. She stuffed it into her pocket, and I had a brief vision of her losing it in the mess in her car.

Before leaving, I said, "What did your uncle do here in Nihla?"

Becky pulled herself a little straighter. "He was the assistant district attorney for the whole county. In fact, that's why I thought you were here. People contact him now and again about those murders years ago. Journalists, civil rights lawyers, law students." She cocked her head, looked me over from head to foot. "If you come by when he's feeling up to a visitor, Connie-from-away, I'm sure he'll tell you *all* about it."

* * *

So why had Stella from the hardware store given me the name of a prior assistant DA for the county? The question plagued me as I drove back to my house. I decided to give Alberto Rodriguez a ring.

His office patched me through.

"You're getting to be a pain in the ass," Rodriguez said.

"Does the name Josiah Smith mean anything to you?"

Alberto was quiet. Finally, he said, "Why?"

"I just want to know."

"That's not a name you'd just come across, Connie."

"Please."

He huffed out a sigh. "Smith was the assistant DA for the county back in the 1990s and early 2000s. He was involved in the case against the two alleged murderers, Norton Smallwood and Mark LeBron."

"The men you talked about. The girl—Esmerelda," I said. "He put away her purported killers."

"Yeah, well, that's a load of bullshit. Those two were truck drivers, not serial killers. But they were Black and convenient, and it made the force look like heroes. This area belched out a collective sigh of relief. But that's the guy—Josiah fucking Smith. He retired a few years after Smallwood and LeBron were imprisoned. Rewarded for good behavior, I guess." He took a deep breath, let it out. "I told you, now you tell me. Why do you care about Josiah Smith?"

"Someone suggested I speak with him."

"Someone as in?"

"Just someone I met." I closed my eyes, rubbed my temples. "Look, I don't really know why this person gave me this guy's name, but he lives with his niece, and she says he's incoherent most of the time."

"*Connie?*"

"So now I'm at a loss. What's he have to do with anything? Why would she give me his name?"

"Connie!"

I opened my eyes. "Yes?"

"Stop asking questions in Nihla. Please. Just stop."

His tone caught my attention. "Why?"

"Because you have no fucking idea what you're doing."

"What am I doing? Asking questions about something that should be in the news? That normal people would care about?"

"For chrissakes, please stop. Don't ask questions. You want to know something, call me. Look it up. Call the president of the United States. Do anything, but don't ask questions in that god-forsaken town."

"Why? Can you just tell me that?"

He took an audible breath, let it out. "Notice that most of the women who died were strangers to Nihla?"

"Yes."

"I said most. There was a girl murdered in late 1997. She didn't quite fit the bill. Her body was found in a garbage can, but she'd been strangled—not raped or, from the what the authorities could tell, tortured."

"I'm not following you."

"It happened right around the time of the arrest."

I saw where he was headed. "After the alleged murderers were in custody."

"Yes."

"And this girl . . . she'd been asking questions?"

"Not her, but someone close to her."

I slowed the car, pulled over to the side of the road, letting this sink in. He didn't need to spell it out further. "Who was this person? The one who asked questions?"

"Think I'm going to tell you so you can go to them and dig your hole deeper? Or cause trouble for them? No way, Connie."

"If I can't ask questions, and nothing is online, and you won't tell me, what am I supposed to do?"

"Get a job. Fuck a few guys. Learn to knit. How the hell should I know? Just keep your damn mouth shut."

"What if I'm already a target?"

Alberto said quietly, "Do you have a gun?"

"No."

"Get one."

* * *

The gun would have to wait; I had neither the money nor the desire for one. And I wouldn't stop asking questions—although in retrospect, perhaps I should have. I was too close to all of this, too worried these murders and Eve's intentions were tied together in some savage knot. Alberto had pointed to a quid pro quo: ask questions and you're next. But those murders were years ago. Was it possible the same murderer was at work here in Nihla today? Alberto thought so, but I wasn't so certain he was a reliable judge.

I knew my next stop. Anyway, I figured after that bash on my head, Oliver Bard owed me.

His house was larger and more modern than my own, but not by much. A brightly painted blue gate opened to a red-tiled courtyard. I climbed out of my car and locked the doors, stepping over grayish-brown scrub to reach the blue-doored entrance. The place was quiet. A chicken pecked around in a courtyard, pausing only to glance my way before continuing to hunt insects in the dusty earth.

"Oliver?" I called from the courtyard threshold.

The chicken raced in front of me, complained, and darted farther into the tiled courtyard. I followed. Large planters, now empty, sat upon chipped terra-cotta Mexican tiles. Three more chickens eyed me from one corner; another raced across the courtyard, squawking a warning. A lone beach chair, its red, white, and blue webbing worn and dirty, perched next to a metal bucket that overflowed with cigarette butts. I heard the buzz of Jet's machines from down the road and the low hum of a sitcom's canned laughter. The courtyard smelled like fresh cigarette smoke.

I knocked on the entrance to the house. The door swung open, and Oliver glowered at me from the dark interior of his house.

"What?" he said.

"Can I talk to you?"

"No." He slammed the door shut.

So much for hospitality. I knocked again. "Oliver, please. Just for a few minutes."

"I said no."

I pounded this time. "Oliver!" When he didn't respond, I said, "Esmerelda." No answer. The chickens scolded me from across the courtyard, and I backed away from the door, frustrated and angry. "Esmerelda!" I yelled again. "Coward! You're a fucking coward, Oliver. Come out and talk with me."

I had the car in first gear when something made me look up. Reddish gray hair, full beard. Tall and lumbering. No knife this time, but he was watching me from the yard between the blue houses with that same glazed interest.

I rolled down my window and yelled, "Hey!"

He ran like a jackrabbit to the house next door and disappeared inside.

*　　*　　*

Night was beginning to fall. By the time I returned to my house, the horizon was aglow with bands of red and orange, silhouetting the rugged mountains in the distance. Mesmerized, I almost missed Jet's lanky form leaning against my house, his body a shadow melding into the many shadows of the desert beyond. I called out to him, and he moved forward into the weak porch light.

"Leaving me another crucifix?" I asked.

He smiled. "Something different this time."

"Oh, yeah?" I'd changed the locks on the house, so I was anxious to hear how'd he gotten in. "What?"

"Follow me."

Jet disappeared around the back of the house. A coyote howled, and I jumped, unaware until that moment just how tense I was. Instead of following Jet, I let myself into the house and turned on all of the lights. Once convinced that he hadn't left me a new surprise, I tucked a Swiss army knife—the best I had—into my back pocket and waited. Alberto's warnings weighed on my mind.

Jet knocked on the door a few minutes later.

"Where'd you go?" He peered beyond me, into the house, but I blocked his view.

"I'm tired, Jet. Not in the mood for games."

"No games." He held up his hands. "I promise. I just made you something, that's all. Come see."

Reluctantly, I followed Jet outside, into the night. I locked my door behind me. The coyotes had friends now, and a pack had set to wailing in the expanse behind the house. A chill ran over me, and I wrapped my arms around me for warmth.

Jet led the way to the shop. Inside, he flicked on the lights and pointed to the center of the room where a simple desk stood atop a paint-splattered canvas tarp. It had been crafted with curly maple, and the intricacy of the wood defined its beauty.

"For you. A housewarming gift." He gave me a lopsided grin that brought out a deep set of dimples. "And an apology—for the cross, and for Oliver's bump to your head."

I stared at the desk, unsure how to respond. People rarely did nice things out of the blue, and certainly not for me. I wasn't sure if this relieved some of my distrust—or deepened it.

Jet laid a strong hand on one edge. "I need to put a few coats of poly on it, and then it'll be ready."

"It's beautiful."

"I'm happy you like it." Jet took a step back, studying me. His tan and the beard lent him a cowboy allure. I could see how women would find him attractive. I shifted my gaze to avoid his eyes. There was something raw and hungry there, and I didn't want to acknowledge that it reached a hungry part of me.

"I have to go." I turned to leave and felt his hand on my shoulder.

"Oliver called me just now. He says you stopped by. Want to talk about that?"

"Not really."

"He's not a man to mess with, Connie. He and his brother are a little . . . mentally unstable."

How unstable? I wondered. "Yeah, well, he wouldn't talk to me anyway. And his brother—I saw him playing with a knife the other day, watching me."

"Raymond is mostly harmless. Exists on the mental level of a twelve-year-old from what I can tell. Oliver, though." Jet tapped his own head. "Smart but in a shrewd way. Just stay off their properties."

I was about to tell Jet that I'd spoken to Alberto, that I knew Oliver had found Esmerelda's body, but I stopped myself. The less said to Jet the better.

"You need to be careful," Jet said. "Nihla's not a friendly place when it comes to strangers."

"So I keep hearing. Especially strange women?"

Jet's eyes narrowed. "Especially strange women." He glanced toward my house. "Have you eaten?"

"Not yet."

"I made a cassoulet. Want to join me?"

I smirked. "Pretty fancy food for a cowboy."

He shrugged. "Oliver slaughtered a pig, gave me some cuts." Another lopsided grin. "But I am a pretty good cook."

I was tempted by the offer, if only because I was starving and hadn't had anything at home in weeks that hadn't come from a can. But I declined. No use playing into his—or Eve's—hands, whatever those hands were up to.

Jet looked disappointed. "Let me know if you change your mind. I have plenty."

"Thanks, but I won't."

Jet held the door of the shop, letting me go out first. Outside, the furnace of a sky had settled into an ethereal canopy of stars. He looked up. "Beautiful, huh? This never gets old."

"It is something." I started toward the house.

Jet flicked on a flashlight and aimed it past me. "You're a weird girl, you know," he said.

"Others have said that."

"Not what I expected."

I took the bait. "What had you expected, Jet?"

"Eat with me, and I'll tell you."

I started to walk toward my house, avoiding the light from his flashlight. "I'm not that interested in your opinion."

"Okay, fine, since you're so anxious to know, I'll tell you," he called. "I figured you'd be spoiled. Someone unable to tie their own shoes without a butler."

I spun around. "Why in the world would you have assumed that?"

"Eve seemed entitled, almost viciously so. I figured you'd be the same and that this little . . . deal . . . was to teach you a lesson. How to live in a rough world on your own, that sort of thing." He shook his head. "But I can see you already know how to do that. You've fixed up the place, found a job." He ran a hand through his hair, crossed his arms. "Tell me, Constance Foster, if Eve didn't want to teach you how to be self-sufficient, then why these rules? What are you supposed to learn here in Nihla?"

"I have no idea, and that's the truth."

"The house is really just that—an inheritance?"

"Eve hated me."

He turned off the flashlight. "She never said she hated you."

I threw my head back and laughed. I sounded crazy, even to myself. "She would never say it. That wasn't her way. She would find some passive aggressive or downright cruel way to get her point across."

"She sounds like an awful mother."

Was that empathy or mockery in his tone? I wasn't sure. "You know why I can't eat with you, Jet? Because I would never know why you invited me. Were you following Eve's playbook? Was she paying you to be nice to me? Or maybe she told you to poison my food. Or seduce me." I watched his face as I spoke, but I couldn't read his expression in the dark courtyard. "I could never trust anything to be real."

"Even friendship?"

I glanced down at my feet. "Especially friendship."

"That's a sad way to live."

Tell me about it.

26

Constance Foster
Nihla, New Mexico—Present

"THREE EGGS, OVER easy," Manuela barked. "And make them *easy* this time, love. Easy as in Pam Anderson after a Kid Rock concert."

I smiled at the dated reference. Sometimes I forgot that Manuela was almost twice my age. "Got it."

Manuela peeked at me from across the kitchen. She was training me to cook, and she let me handle the griddle when we only had a few customers. This morning, though, I just wasn't feeling it. Burned bacon, undercooked eggs, unmelted cheese. We'd already had two orders returned. Manuela was patient, but I knew even she had her limits.

"What's gotten into you? Normally you'd call me out for some tired comparison like that. Pam Anderson? And here you are saying 'got it'? You got something, love, but I'm not sure what it is." She walked closer, leaned down, and peered into my eyes. "You sick?"

I smiled. "I'm fine." I poured three round portions of pancake batter on the griddle. "Just preoccupied."

"Tell me all about him."

I laughed. "What makes you think there's a him? I live in a house with a bathtub in my bedroom, a refrigerator I can't bring myself to open, and a scary caretaker in my back yard. There is definitely no *him*."

Manuela's skinny brows shot up. "Scary caretaker?"

"He came with the property. I don't trust him, and I can't get rid of him."

"He have a record?"

"Not that I know of."

Someone called Manuela from the dining room. She picked up a fresh order pad and pointed it at me. "Find out. Get a background check done. You don't need that kind of hassle in your own backyard. A little money and a good PI or lawyer, and you can dig up what you need."

She was right, of course. I didn't have money, but someone else did.

After the lunch rush, I called Lisa. She didn't answer, but she called me back five minutes later.

"Do me a favor," I said. "Get a background check run on Jet, my caretaker."

"You know I can't."

"What do you mean you can't? Why? Because of the will?" I was standing outside by the dumpster and had to pause every time a truck drove by.

"Aunt Eve's lawyer won't do it. I already asked. Aunt Eve said Jet had to stay, and they have to comply with the terms of her trust."

I closed my eyes, felt my jaw tighten. "Then hire another lawyer, Lisa. Or a PI. You're a big girl."

"Wouldn't that be supporting you financially? We're not allowed to do that."

"It wouldn't be supporting me if you were the one concerned and did it of your own volition."

"Has this guy hurt you?"

"No. I just don't trust him." *I want to trust him*, I thought. *I want to trust someone.*

It felt like minutes went by before she spoke again. "I'll do it."

"Thank you."

"Connie."

"Yes?" I waited.

"I'm thinking of visiting you. Aunt Eve didn't say that wasn't allowed, and I've been making some plans. For us. I think we should talk about them in person."

I thought about my conversation with Alberto Rodriguez. The last thing I wanted was my sister here in Nihla. It wouldn't be safe. Whatever I was meant to do here, I had to do it alone.

I couldn't say that to her, though.

"Sure, I'd love that. Just wait until the house is ready, okay? Right now I'm still sleeping on the floor."

"Surely there's a nice hotel in town."

I laughed out loud. "Well, there's a rooming house. You can get a room for about twenty-eight dollars a night. You'll have some nice creepy-crawly roommates. It used to be affectionately called the Pussy Palace, if that tells you anything."

Lisa took a sharp inhalation. "Oh."

"Yeah." Manuela was waving at me from the diner's back door. "I have to go, Lisa. Call me when you have that background check."

"What if I find something awful?"

"Then you'll tell me, and I'll deal with it. Look, I really have to go."

"I miss you, Connie."

You miss Eve, I thought. I hadn't really been home in years. But I would never say that. My sister's neatly packaged life was set on a foundation of lies she'd told herself over the years. No use wrecking it now.

*   *   *

"You have a visitor." Manuela pulled me inside. She grabbed a damp cloth and wiped at my forehead before pushing me backward to have a closer inspection. "Some lip gloss would be nice, but this will do."

"What are you talking about? Who's here?"

"That nice cop. James Riley."

Officer Riley. "The guy who came when your ex was harassing you? What's he want with me?"

"He came for a late lunch. Asked for you." Manuela's smile lit up her eyes. "Go, go. I'll take care of the cooking for now. You can wait. We only have one customer." She pushed me toward the dining area.

Officer Riley was sitting in a booth with a paperback thriller in front of him and his phone next to his left arm. He wasn't in uniform.

"Day off?" I asked, climbing into the booth across from him. I slid a menu across the table.

He smiled. "As a matter of fact, yes. How are you, Connie?"

"Fine. Manuela said you asked for me, so here I am."

Another smile, shy this time. He opened the menu. "How's the grilled cheese?"

"Cheesy and grilled."

"Grilled cheese versus burger?"

"Hmm. Grilled cheese."

"I'll have two of them and a Coke. Maybe some fries?"

I took the menu. "Are you always this decisive?"

"Fries. Definitely fries." He tilted his head. He had soulful eyes, and I noticed how quickly they brightened when he was talking. "As a matter of fact, no. I'm usually a man of action."

"I'm glad to hear that, Officer Riley. Life can be tough for the indecisive. Give Manuela a little time, and your lunch will be ready." I stood, and he motioned for me to sit back down.

His voice low, he said, "I actually did come by to see you." Before I could respond, he added, "It's about the girl who was murdered. The one you said was found near your home."

"Amber Whitefeather."

Solemn nod. "She was young."

"I'd read that."

"Then you also read that she was from a local reservation." His gaze pivoted to the front entrance where a retired couple, regulars, were entering. Another man, older, short, and well-dressed, was with them. They all laughed as they entered. James lowered his head, and said, "There's stuff you wouldn't have read."

The couple and their friend were staring at me impatiently. I put a hand on James's hand and said, "Give me a minute."

With their order and James's turned in, I returned to James's booth with his Coke. He accepted it gratefully, refusing the straw. The couple had resumed their chatter, but their friend was watching me and James. I met his gaze, wondering if he wanted something else, but he simply smiled and returned his attention to his friends' discussion.

I said, "Amber?"

"Amber." He leaned across the booth so he was barely audible. "Her body was found in three garbage bags. Preliminary reports suggest she'd been raped and tortured, maybe over weeks."

I had no words. What kind of sick person does that?

"Bastard, I know." Riley's eyes darkened. "Anyway, I didn't stop by to scare you, but I did a little digging, and the other deaths, they follow this same pattern. Dismembered bodies, rape, and torture." He swallowed. "Kidnapping."

"I'm not surprised." It echoed what Amy had told me. "I just don't understand why it's not bigger news."

"I asked the same question and got shut down. My first thought was race and social status. Victims have been mostly kids. All girls, many from broken homes, and most are runaways. Sometimes they're Native American, like Amber, or Black or Latina. But not all."

I thought of my conversation with Alberto Rodriguez. He'd said the same thing—runaways and throwaways. Despicable terms. "There's a 'but' here, right?"

"There is. *But* I think there's more than racism at work." He glanced toward the people at the other table. "Connie, I'm trusting you. Please don't repeat what I'm saying, or I could get canned, and I need this job."

I promised him.

"The *but* is that no one seems to be following up on any leads. I don't understand why."

"What do you mean?"

"We've interviewed witnesses who saw Amber hitchhiking along the highway. She'd been a troubled kid. Drugs, problems with the law, even turning a few tricks at the truck stops. Her parents say she'd left home and was heading east this time, had mentioned something about New York. We have a trucker and another driver who've come forward with information. They saw someone pick her up. Gave a pretty specific description of the car. But after that, nothing. No follow-up by the police that I can tell."

"You've not been assigned to her case?"

"Me?" He laughed. "I'm just a beat cop, not homicide. And I can tell you, my questions weren't welcome."

I considered what he was saying. I shared with him my own experiences of getting shut down every time the topic of the murders came up. "Even the bartender at the local pub and the librarian the next town over had the same reaction."

Manuela rang the bell in the kitchen, and I retrieved James's meal. I placed it in front of him. He stared at it sullenly.

"You going to eat?"

"Yeah." He still looked distracted. "There's something else."

The bell rang again.

I said, "Hold on."

This time the other table's food was up—two enchilada specials and a hamburger. I served their food, got them the extra salsa they requested, and returned to James. By now, he was through both sandwiches and was picking at his french fries.

"Good grilled cheese?"

"Sure. Very grilled and very cheesy." His smile fell flat. "I read the interviews. Someone saw her with a man the day she was murdered."

I felt the tiniest flush of excitement. "And? Description?"

"That's just it." Riley balled his paper napkin and threw it on his plate. "There wasn't one. The cop who interviewed the witness just stated 'a man' was seen with the victim. No description, not even an age."

Disappointed, I said, "Is that normal protocol?"

"No way. Our report on Manuela's ex was far more detailed, and that was a simple harassment case."

"How about the witness? Was there a name? Someone who could be contacted separately?"

James shook his head. "Even if I wanted to get that involved, and I don't, whoever wrote that report didn't even record the witnesses' names. Not the person who saw her with a man, and not the trucker who saw her get into a car."

"A real breach of protocol?"

Riley sat back, arms crossed, nodded. "Even if the witness refused to cooperate and provide a name, that would have been recorded."

Manuela poked her head out of the kitchen, saw me, and ducked back inside. I glanced over at the couple and their friend. They were still eating, drinks half empty.

"None of this makes sense." James stared at his mostly empty plate, then up at me. "I don't like it."

"It sounds like they know who the killer is, and they're protecting him."

"It sure does."

"What are you going to do about it?"

He picked up a french fry, stared at it, and tossed it back on his plate along with a balled-up napkin. "Not a damn thing."

"Then why are you here telling me this?"

"Because you're young and alone and new to Nihla." His eyes pleaded with me. "The questions you asked me . . . be careful. These girls won't get justice, Connie. They'll be data points, unsolved murders that get filed away. Shit, I'll bet you a buck that the files will be lost within the year." He shook his head slowly back and forth. "Within months."

"And you're really not going to do anything?"

"What can I do? The guy who took the interview? Top of the heap."

"I have something you can do. Something that won't get you into trouble. Will you help me?"

James looked up sharply. "What?"

His point about the victims as data points had sparked an idea. "Do you have access to databases?"

"Of course—some."

"Can you get to them without getting noticed?"

He thought about that. "I don't see why not."

"Do you think you could do some searching? Look for similar patterns in the area?"

"Why?"

"Because the murders stopped for two decades and then resumed. I'm wondering whether the same murderer has returned, or whether there's a new killer in town."

"The old murders were solved. The killers were put away."

"That's bullshit, James, and you and I both know it." I realized I was shouting, and I lowered my voice. "Given what you've told me, it seems unlikely that the two guys put away for the nineties murders were the actual killers, wouldn't you say?"

"And you think that if I can track similar patterns, and the dates work, it may show we have the same killer back in Nihla."

"It's a long shot." A very long shot. "But yes, that's what I'm hoping. Maybe we'll see a pattern."

"Worth a try."

James reached for his wallet, and I told him to put it away. "Manuela never charges cops."

He took a twenty out anyway and placed it on the table alongside a business card with a phone number handwritten in blue ink. "A tip then."

"That's a big tip."

James smiled. I liked his smile. "That's how I roll."

* * *

On my way home that evening, I stopped by the rooming house. I wasn't the only young, new woman in town, the only woman who could be a target. Amy-from-the-bar should be warned, too. I could do it without breaking James's confidence. Just let her know to be careful. She was the one who had alerted me first, after all.

The property manager let me into a nondescript lobby. Linoleum floors, white walls, stainless steel fixtures, a few framed pictures of the nearby mountains. Whoever bought this place had at least made an attempt to modernize it, but the result was a cold, institutional atmosphere that still hinted at despair.

I told him I was looking for a tenant named Amy.

"Amy Bombardi?"

"I don't know her last name. About this tall." I motioned with my hands. "Hair with blue ends."

"That's Bombardi. You a friend of hers?"

"Acquaintance."

The manager's eyes disappeared in folds of fat. "A friend would know her last name." He regarded me with unabashed curiosity, chewing the inside of his cheek. "You sure you weren't sent by the ex-boyfriend? I don't want no trouble."

"Nope, just an acquaintance. I met her at a . . . library. Wanted to catch up. Is she here?"

"Room seven. Wasn't here this morning, though." The manager started to walk away.

"Could she be at work?"

"Not my job to keep tabs on the tenants."

I waited until he left the lobby and made my way down a dank, dirty hallway to room seven. A half a dozen knocks got an angry reprimand from the old man in the room next to her, who banged on his door and told me to shut the fuck up.

"Have you seen Amy?" I asked through his door.

"Fucking go away," he answered.

I took that as a no.

27

Eve Foster
Nihla, New Mexico—1997

O FFICER MAYOR AGREED to see Eve the next day. The sun beat down on the cracked and bleached pavement leading to the station, and Eve walked over the crevices wearing new black stilettos. She'd dressed for the occasion in a fitted black suit. She was the owner of Foster Technologies, after all, she reminded herself. Liam Foster had been a terrible husband, but he'd been a genius when it came to business. She had his money at her disposal, money that Jim Kelly had wired just an hour ago.

"What can I do for you today, Mrs. Foster?" Mayor asked. He was sporting a few days' worth of mustache, and the facial hair added a decade.

"Arrest Kyle Summers. He has my daughter."

Mayor looked amused, which only increased her resolve. "On what basis are you alleging such a serious charge?"

"I know he has her."

"We need proof. You know that."

"Get a warrant. Search his house. I'm sure Kelsey's there."

"I don't know how they run things in Philadelphia, but in this town, you need reasonable cause to get a warrant. No judge in his right mind will grant a warrant based on one woman's unsubstantiated allegations."

Eve sneered. "And especially when that judge is the brother-in-law of the perpetrator."

Mayor's amusement turned crypt cold. "I suggest you reconsider your antics, Mrs. Foster. I've had complaints from multiple people that you've been snooping around, asking questions, causing trouble. I've let it go for now, worried mother and all. But when you come in here and make accusations against one of our own, well, you need to stop."

Eve held Mayor's stare with a cool gaze of her own. She broke away first and walked over to the officer's metal desk. She picked up a framed photo of a baby girl dressed in a pink frilly dress with a bow around her bald head.

"Your daughter?" When Mayor didn't answer, she put the picture down and turned to face him. "Being a parent is special, isn't it? You worry all the time. What would you do if something happened to your child? If she disappeared?" Eve shook her head. "It's the biggest burden, that worry."

"Are you threatening me, Mrs. Foster?"

Eve flashed him her most saccharine smile. "Hardly, Officer. I'm merely talking parent to parent. When your child goes missing, there is nothing you won't do. Nothing." Another smile, this one sadder, and she glanced again at the picture in her hand. "You understand, I'm sure."

"You need to leave."

Eve shook her head. "I'm not leaving without a commitment. Will you look into Kyle Summers again?"

"Yes. Fine. I'll send someone over there today."

Eve placed the picture back on the shelf, letting go a moment too soon. The photo fell to the floor, and the glass shattered into a million tiny shards.

"Oh, my!" Eve jumped backward. Her smile was apologetic, her eyes icy orbs. "Look what I did. I'm so sorry."

"I'm sure you are." Mayor picked up the phone to ask for maintenance. With the phone back on its cradle, he looked down at the mess. "Please go, Mrs. Foster." His tone was stern, but Eve caught a flicker of fear in his eyes.

The fear was what she wanted.

* * *

Eve sat in her car, waiting. Armed with several sandwiches, a thermos of coffee, and her gun, she could stay in the car as long as her bladder would hold out. The Pussy Palace was a busy place today. *Bojana must be thrilled*, Eve thought, and watched two men leave the Palace at the same time.

But it wasn't Bojana she was after. Or Raul, the superintendent of this shithole.

Eve glanced down at the notes she'd made after talking with her private investigator. He'd been a disaster when it came to tracking Kelsey, but he was good for background information, at least. She'd asked for the scoop on Kyle Summers, and he'd given it to her.

Divorced, never remarried. Thirty-nine years old. Owner of nine local businesses, including a laundromat, an apartment complex, a gas station, a hardware store, and the lovely Pussy Palace. Brother to Brenda Leroux. No prior arrests, not so much as a DUI. Lived in Nihla his entire life.

Her investigator had found nothing on Flora Fuentes. She was a ghost.

Judge Andrew Leroux was clean other than a parking ticket, one speeding citation when he was eighteen, and some unsubstantiated allegations of a prison pay-to-play operation. He smelled bad, the PI said, but the source of the smell wasn't clear.

A whole fucking town full of goody two-shoes and one questionable judge, but someone had her daughter. Kelsey's trail didn't just stop in Nihla for no reason. The hospitals in the area were a dead end. No cash withdrawals from her bank account, no charges on the one credit card she maintained on her own. No nasty postcards, no citations to the house. Many had seen her arrive in Nihla; no one had seen her leave.

Another ghost.

Eve glanced behind her. She saw the police car a block back and the undercover cop sitting inside. She knew she was being followed, which was why she was here at the Pussy Palace.

She wanted to talk with Kyle, but they'd expect her to go there. Looked like they expected her to track down Flora as well.

Let them follow her, she didn't care.

Eve glanced down at her notes one more time. Kyle's ex-wife was a woman named Bella Minooski. Remarried, she was a salon owner who lived in a nearby town. Eve had Bella's work telephone number and address. Maybe Bella Minooski would have some insights to share.

Eve glanced at her watch. A few more minutes and she'd need to pee. Just then, the front door opened and Flora emerged. She climbed into her junker and drove away, seemingly oblivious to the woman watching her. Eve smiled. Oblivious people were her favorite kind of people.

Eve pulled away from the curb slowly. She watched as the cop did the same. She had a plan to lose him, but for now she'd let him follow.

She trailed Flora through town and down a dusty road with no name. Hovels lined the road on either side—small one-story shacks with lean-to roofs and pin-sized yards and corrugated metal fences. Dogs and chickens roamed freely, snot-nosed kids played tag in a back yard. Flora drove past a cluster of these houses and stopped at the end of the road, at a nicer version of the same shack. This one had flowers planted outside and a fence made of chain link.

Eve watched Flora disappear inside. She watched the cop car hover at the end of the narrow road, waiting. She put her head back and breathed in, silencing her bladder's urgent need. After a half hour, her bladder won and she did a three-point turn to leave the neighborhood. The cop did the same.

They don't even care whether I know they're watching me, she thought. *They want me to know.*

Eve swerved to avoid a rangy brown mutt that had darted into the center of the street. Cursing, she glanced back in her rearview mirror, at the house at the end of the road. Flora's car was still there, the house was still buttoned up.

Later, Eve thought, *I'll follow Flora again*. She raced back to the hotel feeling frustrated, the cop a few cars behind.

CHAPTER

28

Constance Foster
Nihla, New Mexico—Present

THURSDAY WAS MY next full day off. It was a scorchingly sunny morning, with a high of eighty-eighty and a dry, bitter wind that made me homesick for my lush green state of Vermont. I'd decided this was the day I would make some progress on the house and clear out the basement. The bedroom needed paint, and I wanted to check that off my list. I had enough tips from Manuela's diner saved to buy a mattress, but I wanted the bedroom to be finished first, and a can of soothing blue paint was waiting.

I'd already discarded the old bed frame and scrubbed the walls and floors. I'd carefully prepped the room for paint—walls cleaned, spackled, and sanded, windowsills taped off—and I was just opening the can of paint when I heard a sharp knock on the door.

It was Jet, carrying the desk he'd made me. Micah was trailing dutifully behind him. He said, "A hand?"

I opened the door wider and let them both in.

"Where do you want it? The living room?"

"Sure—thank you," I said. "I mean that. It's gorgeous." In truth, I wasn't sure how I felt. The piece *was* gorgeous, and I had almost no furniture—certainly nothing this nice—but it felt like a string, and I wanted no strings attaching me to Jet.

Jet wiped his hands on his jeans. "Truce? I feel like we got off to a bad start." When I didn't answer, he said, "You have another paintbrush?"

"You don't seriously want to paint."

"I have a few hours to kill while some varnish dries. I can give you a hand."

I considered his offer. "Actually, there's something I could use help with even more than the painting."

"What's that?"

"The basement. I need to carry up the remaining boxes and saw apart that awful couch so I can get rid of it."

He shrugged. "Whatever you want. I'm at your service." He held up a hand. "And before you ask, no, this isn't in my contract."

"Even better. Happen to have a chainsaw?"

"As a matter of fact, I do."

It took over an hour to disassemble the couch and drag it up the steps. Painting I could do alone. Had I done this job myself, it was the only thing I would have accomplished all day. With the pieces in a pile near my car, I grabbed two beers from the small apartment refrigerator and tossed one to Jet. I nodded toward Micah, who was hovering shyly behind him.

"Can I give her a treat?"

"You have dog treats?"

"Picked up a box at the hardware store."

"Sure." He opened the beer. "It's only eleven in the morning, you know. A little early for booze."

"Think of it as lunch." I took a long gulp and welcomed the cooling sensation. It was hot and musty in the basement, and I was feeling sweaty and light-headed.

Jet gestured toward the fridge with his beer. "Still haven't cleaned out that thing?"

"Volunteering?"

He glanced over at the old appliance, which I hadn't moved from its spot against the wall. "I'd offer to help, but I think that's past even my pay grade."

I smiled. "One of these days, I'll down enough of this stuff to tackle it."

"Do you always drink when you're stressed?"

I studied him over the edge of my can. I couldn't tell whether he was joking. "Are you always so blunt?"

"Only when I care."

"*Uh-huh.*"

He cocked his head. "It must be hell going through life so full of distrust."

"I get by."

"Maybe I understand better than you think. Ever consider that?"

I squatted down and reached a hand out to Micah. She regarded it anxiously, so I moved away, sorry I'd invaded her space. "So share."

He took a swig of beer and shook his head, grinning. "You do realize that letting go of some of this paranoia would be one way of getting back at Eve? Seems to me she *wanted* you to be on edge. She *wanted* you to be alone in the world. You're basically letting her control you."

"Easy for you to say."

"Not really."

I drained the last of my beer and tossed the can into the sink. The dog biscuits were in the cabinet next to the jar of peanut butter and cans of Campbell's soup, and I pulled one out for the dog. "How about you, Jet? What's your story? No Mommy Dearest in *your* childhood?" I held the bone out for Micah. She inched forward, eventually taking it from my fingers with wary gentleness.

He looked mildly amused by the question. Finishing his own beer, he tossed the can beside mine and said, "Misspent youth. Took me a while to find my way, but I did eventually."

"What does that mean, exactly?"

"Typical shit."

"Stealing? Breaking curfew? Underage drinking?"

Jet glanced at his watch. "It means you have thirty minutes of my time left, then I have to finish the table I promised a woman in Santa Fe. This Jet honors his commitments. So how about those boxes?"

"You're as squirrelly as that dog of yours."

"And about as fond of people. Come on."

I followed Jet outside and down into the cellar. He told Micah to stay at the top of the steps, and she crouched beside the Bilco doors, watching us. The cellar didn't feel any more welcoming without the clutter. If anything, it seemed creepier, the air heavy, the tight space claustrophobic.

"I hate this place," I said. "Can you feel it?" I wrapped my arms around my chest. "Once it's empty, I'll be happy never to come back down."

Jet patted the walls. "You're lucky to even have a basement. Most houses around here don't." He looked up at the rafters overhead. "This one was a retrofit."

I followed his line of sight. "Why would someone do that?"

He patted the cinder block again, then pointed to the dirt floor. "The house is pretty old, probably ninety or so years. I'm thinking some Easterner—a medic or a missionary, maybe—moved here and wanted a basement, so he dug one out under the house."

"How can you tell it wasn't original?"

"For one, the construction is different. Cinder blocks are newer material, postdating the upstairs. Two, I think the footprint of the basement is narrower than the footprint of the house."

I saw what he meant. "It looks like there's a good foot or more difference."

"At least."

I'd been kneeling by the boxes, and I stood and wiped off my pants. "What do you know about this house? Its history?"

"I told you—I don't know anything, really. It was likely built in the early 1920s. Oliver would know more. He's lived on this road for over forty years."

"He won't talk to me. I tried stopping by, and he slammed the door in my face."

Jet had the decency to look embarrassed. "He'll warm up eventually."

"Will he? I don't know about that. What's his story?"

Jet rubbed his face with his hands. "Damn if I know. He and his brother are fixtures here. Don't talk much, but they've been good to me. They keep an eye on the place, give me chickens and eggs and occasionally meat." He shrugged. "Lots of people around here are odd, as I'm sure you've noticed. At least they're neighborly."

I frowned, rubbed the spot where he'd hit me. "Not sure I'd second that. What does he have against me?"

"He distrusts strangers. Something you two have in common."

But I wasn't letting him off that easily. "You were a stranger once. He accepted you."

Jet bent down and picked up a box. "I can't answer for the guy, Connie. His first interaction with you was when you were skulking around my place. Maybe he holds a grudge."

"Or hates women?"

Jet looked toward the open Bilco doors and Micah, who'd started to whine. "Come on. Let's get these boxes out of here."

"You're not going to answer me, are you? Does Oliver hate women?"

Jet had started making his way up the stairs, back to me. "Where do you want the boxes? This one is heavy."

In the garbage, I thought. "Outside by the front door is fine."

* * *

There were three boxes—two large, one small. I started with the largest. It had been sealed tight with duct tape, and I cut my way through slowly, peeling the box back with trepidation. I stayed outside, by the car, so I could bundle the garbage up and take it into town. As curious as I was about the contents of the boxes, I didn't want any poisonous insects or other contaminants inside.

I lifted the contents out gingerly, using gloves. No centipedes. No scorpions. Just two embroidered pillows, a matching tablecloth, and several sets of plain yellow bed linens. The pillows' white cotton was now a dirty gray, but that didn't mar the beauty of the handiwork. Fuchsia, violet, and sunny yellow flowers danced on a wave of green foliage. I pictured these items in the house as it once was, adorning a table and chair. Handmade, loved. Originally festive, now they just looked sad.

The second large box held clothes. Jeans, tops, bras, nightshirts. Cheap stuff, clean but dated. All women's, size 9/10 and medium. Nothing remarkable; a box of items someone had stored and forgotten.

I opened the smallest box, expecting more of the same. I stared at the contents, confused at first, then with dawning horror.

I picked the box up and brought it inside. There, I studied its contents, reluctant to reach inside. Nestled in the box was a crucifix. Ornate, colorful Mexican majolica. Hand-painted, from the look of it.

And an exact replica of the one Jet had hung on my wall.

What the fuck?

I slammed my way outside and around back, to Jet's workshop. Without knocking, I kicked open the half-closed door. He stood there with a paintbrush in his hand and a can of varnish next to his elbow. Micah was sleeping under a workbench.

"Connie, what's wrong?"

"What the fuck! *Let's be friends.* Such bullshit!" I shoved the nearest table with two hands. "You fucking *asshole!*"

Jet dropped the paintbrush. "Calm down."

Behind him, Micah growled.

"Connie, seriously, what's gotten into you?"

I closed my eyes, took several deep breaths. "The crucifix. You *knew.*"

"What are you talking about?"

I felt the rage building. My head began to spin, my breath got caught in my throat. This wasn't me. I was the calm one, the rational one. The survivor.

"Fuck," I said half under my breath. "Come with me."

Jet followed me around to the front of the house and inside. I pointed to the crucifix he'd planted on my wall, which now sat atop a garbage pile on my living room floor. "Look in the box." I nudged the box from the basement toward him with my foot. "Now tell me you didn't plant that down there."

Jet looked inside the box and back at me. "I didn't put that down there."

"But it's the exact same crucifix."

He picked up the one from the box, turned it over, and then did the same with the original. "Same artist, almost the exact same design." He frowned. "And you say this one"—he held up the second crucifix—"was in the basement box."

I nodded.

"I don't know what to tell you, Connie. I didn't put those boxes down there. And I didn't get my crucifix from the basement."

"Eve made you put this crucifix on my wall."

"True, that was her instruction."

"And that crucifix matches the one in the basement." I could hear my voice spiraling again, and I fought to keep it even. "If you didn't put it there, who did? How would Eve have known that the same cross was sealed in a box in this basement."

"It is her house, Connie. She owned it. Maybe she put it there."

"The boxes were covered in dust. They'd been there a long time."

"Eve has owned this house for a long time."

That stopped me cold. We'd never come to New Mexico growing up. Lisa and I didn't even know this house existed, but that didn't mean Eve hadn't been here. But to set me up so far in advance? Pretty calculating, even for her. And to what end?

I sat down on the lone living room chair, head in my hands. Jet put the crosses down and joined me, sliding on the floor beside my legs.

"Hey." He pulled my hands away from my face. His touch was gentle. "Look at me."

Dark eyes expressed concern and confusion, but how could I know that those sentiments were genuine? What did I know about Jet—other than his connection with Eve? Nothing. He could have been a master gaslighter. He could have been a serial killer.

I pulled away and stood. While he sat there, staring at me, I wrapped both crosses in newspaper and put them in the box from the basement. I'd take them to the dump. For now, I wanted them out of my sight.

Jet said, "You know I had nothing to do with this."

"I don't know any such thing." The anger had left me, and I felt only helpless frustration. "I don't know you. I don't know what you promised Eve. For all I know, this is an act, all part of the plan." I didn't need to look at him to know he'd be studying me with disbelief on his face. And why not? I sounded crazy. But better crazy-sounding than dead.

"Connie, I can help you."

"As long as you're beholden to Eve, you can't."

He was silent. I taped up the box and sprayed down the area with cleaner. I was about to head outside with an empty garbage bag to collect the rest of the stuff when Jet said, "Wait."

I turned around slowly. "What?"

"If I show you my contract with Eve, will you believe me then?"

I thought about that. "It would help."

"Wait here."

While I waited, I went outside and bagged the old clothes from the basement box and placed them in my car. Overhead, the sky was an angry bruise, and I could feel a storm coming. I longed for rain, for release.

The drops started to fall, softly at first, then hard like tiny pellets. I looked up, welcoming the sting against my face, my arms. Welcoming the distraction. Only the reprieve didn't last. My thoughts were on Eve; she swam in my brain like a shark with hungry, bloodshot eyes. Eve *had* to have known there were two identical crosses in the house. She must have been the one to pack the boxes, keeping one out for later. *Such hate*, I thought. Only hatred could lead someone to be so cunning, so cruel.

I spun around in the rain, whipping my wet hair against my neck. I closed my eyes, shutting out the red house, its lines blurred and smeared in the downpour, but still all I saw was red. A red sky, a red orb, thin red lines, harsh and demanding.

"Connie?"

Jet startled me, and I stumbled.

"What are you doing? Come on. Get out of the rain."

I followed him into the house. He handed me a towel. In the bathroom, I slipped off my clothes, put on a robe. I felt shaky and worn out despite the early hour. I craved a drink and a nap.

"Here." Jet motioned to a kitchen chair. On the table, in front of the chair, were three sheets of white paper. "Sit. Read." He took the other seat, and Micah lay beside him.

I sank down on the chair with the papers in my hand. Knuckles white, my head still trippy, I read through the catalog of responsibilities Eve had laid out for Jet. Maintain the property. Live on site. Secure the property. Remain on the property for at least three years after the transfer of ownership to her daughter, Constance Foster.

In return, money. A lot of money. My mind returned to the cash in the workshop. If Jet had been living here cheaply, it's possible the money was simply his way of saving. I wanted to ask him, but then he'd know I'd broken into his house, borrowed the key.

Instead, I said, "I don't see the cross mentioned in here."

"She asked me to do that separately." Jet frowned. "Her lawyer sent the crucifix with instructions after she died."

I sat back against the chair, my head against the plaster. Micah's breathing was rhythmic, soothing, and I rooted myself to the sound. "Then you really don't know anything about the boxes downstairs?"

"You saw that basement. You saw the layers of dust, the old furniture. I would have had to have planted all of that years ago."

He took the contract from me, folded it, and stood. "I don't know what game Eve is playing from beyond the grave. I'm only a pawn."

"I only have your word. Surely you understand that. She could have asked you to do other things, things not in this document."

Jet's eyes softened. I saw pity reflected there. *Pity.* He shook his head. "I think she's already won."

29

Constance Foster
Nihla, New Mexico—Present

I HEARD IT BEFORE I saw it. The *hiss* of its tail startled me from a vodka-induced haze. It was curled in a ropey ball by the old refrigerator, its head up, its rattle-tail waving. *"Ohmygod."*

Slowly, carefully, I stood up from the seat I'd been holding down and backed into the bedroom, looking around for a weapon. A broom was wedged against the wall, my large bucket next to it. I grabbed the pail and walked back into the kitchen. The snake was small but agitated. I considered trying to shoo it out the back door with the broom, but I was afraid it would strike. I got as close as I dared and, using the broom as a handle, dropped the pail over the snake.

I let out my breath, quietly and steadily. *Great, now what?* It was dark outside—no one would come to get it until morning. I was on my own. There was no way I was sleeping with a rattlesnake in the house, and while the car was an option, what if it somehow got loose? I needed a hook, something I could use to pick the snake up and place it outside. Quickly.

I slipped on my sneakers and went out the front door. Jet's lights were on. He answered my knocks with a gruff, "What the hell, Oliver? Oh . . . it's you."

"Don't look so excited to see me."

"What do you want, Connie?"

Ignoring his cold tone, I told him about the rattlesnake.

"In your kitchen?"

"Yeah, right by the old refrigerator. It must have gotten in through a crack in the foundation."

Jet didn't look convinced—whether he doubted there was a snake in my kitchen or that it had crawled in through the foundation, I wasn't sure. He receded into the house and came back out with his black workshop key. "Give me a minute. I have something we can use."

As we made our way across the courtyard, toward his workshop, I said, "I don't need you to do it for me—"

Jet took an audible breath, turned around. "Seriously? What do you think I'm going to do? Put the snake in your bed? Toss it at you? I've lived here way longer than you, and I'm used to handling rattlers. Anyway, it's my goddamn job, Connie." He didn't wait for me to respond before opening the shed. A few seconds later, he was back in the courtyard with a long-handled hook. "Show me the snake."

I brought him into the house through the front door. The snake was still under the pail, where I'd left it. Jet walked around it, opened the back door, lifted the bucket, and with one quick movement, hooked the animal. He disappeared outside, returning a few minutes later with an empty hook.

"Thank you," I said.

He nodded. His hair was disheveled, and he was wearing plaid pajama bottoms. I'd been too distracted to notice earlier.

I opened a cupboard and pulled out the vodka. "Drink?"

"No." He was walking around my kitchen, studying the perimeter of the walls.

I poured myself a shot.

"Your back door was unlocked."

"Okay—"

"The snake didn't get in through the foundation, Connie. This place is tight—no cracks, at least up here."

"Maybe it was in one of the boxes from downstairs?" Grasping at straws, but the alternative made ropes of my stomach.

"You opened them outside, and they were sealed up. Plus, the small box was too small—you'd have seen a snake."

"What are you suggesting?" Although I knew exactly what he was suggesting. I just didn't want to acknowledge it. "Who would do that?" I didn't add that the only person I could think of was Jet.

"I don't know." Jet's mouth set in a frown. "We should go through the rest of the place, make sure this was the only one."

I trailed Jet around the small house, looking under the little furniture I had. Other than a dead cockroach and a crispy moth, we didn't find anything.

"Damn, Connie, you don't even have a bed."

"I'm working on it."

Back in the kitchen, Jet said, "Looks like someone opened your back door and placed the snake in here. You have to face that."

"I've been here the whole day. I would have noticed."

Jet stepped closer to me, until he was inches from my body. Beneath the beard, his face was as lean and angular as my own, his eyes as haunted. He leaned over me, his lips near my forehead, so that I could feel his breath on my skin.

I felt my own breath quicken. "Jet—"

He took the glass from my hand and dumped it in the sink. "You were here, but you weren't paying attention. Probably weren't even awake."

"You were home. You would have heard a car."

"I was working. The machines would have drowned out the sounds. Besides, someone could have parked and walked."

"With a snake?"

He shrugged. "A snake in a pillowcase will stay calm."

"Oliver."

"He wouldn't have done this."

"You sound sure."

"Not his thing. He likes to be left alone, not create drama." He locked the back door, put my vodka back in the cabinet. "I need to go. Micah doesn't like to be by herself." When I didn't respond, he asked, "Will you be okay?"

I nodded, my thoughts on the vodka he'd wasted and the fact that my makeshift bed was on the floor. How would I sleep tonight knowing it was possible we'd missed a snake? How could I sleep knowing someone may have done this on purpose?

Jet had his hand on the door. He was watching me with concerned curiosity. "You sure you're okay?"

"Go. I'm fine."

"Micah gets crazy when she's alone."

"So you've said. I understand. I'll be okay."

Jet stood there another moment before leaving through the back door. I locked it behind him, then pressed my back against the wood. Crucifixes, snakes, neighbors who hated me. This place would never feel like home. I wrapped my arms around my chest and sank down onto the floor. I wouldn't cry, I told myself. I would never cry.

*   *   *

This time a sharp knock woke me up. I'd fallen asleep against the back door, and my neck was stiff and sore. I hopped up, my head clearer than it had been earlier. That, at least, was something. The clock read 11:14. I'd only been asleep for twenty minutes. I turned my neck, trying to loosen the muscles. Those twenty minutes had felt like an eternity.

"Who is it?"

"Jet. Let me in."

"What do you want?"

"I saw your lights still on."

"So?"

"Just let me the fuck in, Connie."

I unlocked the door and opened it to find Jet and Micah standing outside. Jet, still in his pajamas, was carrying a large box. The rain had stopped, and the night was clear and cool, the stars a canopy overhead. I glanced from man to dog, ushering them inside.

I eyed the box. "That to bury my body when you're finished with me?"

"You're a regular stand-up comedian. Air mattress. Figured it would get you up off the floor, at least until you have a real bed." Jet walked past me into my bedroom, Micah slinking behind. "If I'd found that snake, I wouldn't want to sleep on the floor."

I doubted that was true. Jet seemed pretty unflappable. Still, I appreciated the mattress and told him so.

It took him a few minutes to set it up. I sat in the kitchen, watching him, thinking about who could have placed the snake in my house. He worked quickly, unpacking the full-size mattress and filling it with air. The noise from the pump scared Micah, and she bolted into the kitchen. She pressed her side against my leg, surprising me. I reached down and rubbed her head.

Jet looked up. "Traitor," he said to the dog.

"Where'd you find her?" She felt warm and real, and I was happy for her presence.

"Hanging around a truck stop. She'd had puppies. Was eating scraps from the dumpster, and she and her pups were living underneath." Finished with the mattress, he stood. "They didn't make it."

"I'm sorry, girl." I rubbed behind her ears. She looked up at me, those dark eyes liquid and sad. "Too young?"

"Too many parasites. I tried, but . . . well, Micah nearly died, too. Heartbreak, I think."

The dog left me, trotting back to Jet. She walked with her head down low, as though apologizing for existing. Her body undulated as he scratched her back. She wagged her tail furiously.

"She loves you."

Jet moved to behind her ears. "I'm just her meal ticket."

I didn't challenge him, but watching the way he looked at her, I knew it was more than a partnership of convenience. On both sides.

"Can I get you anything?" I asked, surprised to find I didn't want them to leave.

"No thanks."

Jet collected the box and walked past me, toward the door. He paused, then turned back to face me. "I can stay, if you'd like. There's nothing wrong with wanting company."

I reached out and stroked the side of his cheek. He leaned forward, and I met his lips with my own. The kiss was long and hard and full of wanting. He pulled back first.

"I didn't come here for that," he whispered.

"I know." I took his hand, used it to trace the curve of my waist.

I led him to my makeshift bed and dropped my robe to the floor. The sex was rough and tender, hurried and languid all at once. Afterward, we slept entwined in each other's arms, Micah on the floor beside us. As I curled my body around him, I felt, for once, like I belonged.

When I woke up, he and the dog were gone.

CHAPTER

30

Eve Foster
Nihla, New Mexico—1997

EVE MADE AN appointment at Bella's Best for ten the next morning. It took her an hour to find an unassuming car service willing to make a short trip, but money talks, and eventually she was successful. That evening she went to the local retail outlet that masqueraded as a mall and bought jeans, a sequined button-down shirt, and cheap cowboy boots. The cop followed her to the mall but stayed in his car, leaving her to shop in peace. Back at the hotel, she made a point of going to the front desk to ask for a two PM wake-up call for the next day.

"I'm not feeling well," she told them. "I plan to sleep in."

The next morning at seven fifteen, a jeans and sequin-shirted Eve waited at the back of the motel, near the pathetic pool, until a car picked her up. The car drove her to a nearby car rental agency, where Eve picked up a plain gray sedan. She drove the sedan to Evansville, twenty-two dusty miles from Nihla, and parked behind Bella's Best.

Bella's Best was a sad disappointment. Four hundred square feet of unimaginative décor and mind-numbing country music, the salon offered a sink, two padded metal folding seats, a small manicure table, one stylist chair, and a checkout counter. Gaudy jewelry was displayed on clear plastic shelves, alongside polyester scarves and rhinestone sunglasses. Eve sat in one of the folding chairs and waited until Bella was finished checking out a blue-haired biddy with an old-fashioned bouffant.

"You must be Edwinna Martinelli," Bella said with a smile. "And you're here for a cut and color?"

Oh God no. She'd only pretended to want that much done to secure the slot. "Just a manicure."

"Oh." Bella sounded deflated. She glanced at the appointment calendar again. "Wonder why I blocked a whole hour-long hair appointment then. Oh well. Come on. Let's take a look at those hands."

Bella sashayed Eve back to a card table covered with a tablecloth and nail equipment. She had a derriere that was twice as wide as her narrow shoulders, and she wiggled it furiously with each step. She was an attractive woman, Eve thought, if a little rough around the edges. A pleasantly round face was accentuated by caramel-colored bangs and long, straight hair. She swung the hair behind her as she sat across from Eve. Taking Eve's fingers in her own, she inspected the nails as she chatted away.

"Why, these are nice nails. Not sure what you need done, Edwinna. They're perfection." She bent closer. "Wow, you must have paid a pretty penny. Whoever did this knows her stuff. Frankly, you don't need a fresh coat, cuticle work, or any repairs."

"I'm tired of the color."

"Hmmm. Well, there's my selection." She pointed to a shelf on the wall on which sat a rainbow of polishes.

"That red." She pointed to the reddest red on the shelf. "I'll take the whole bottle when you're done. For my toenails."

Bella smiled. "Let's get you started."

Bella removed the old polish and then soaked Eve's hands in what looked like dish soap. "What brings you to town? Not exactly the hub of tourism here in New Mexico."

"A divorce," Eve lied. "A nasty one."

"I'm sorry to hear that."

"Yeah, well. I feel lucky to get a fresh start."

"Are you moving to Evansville?"

"I'm visiting a friend in Taos. Thought I'd take a tour through the state while I'm here."

Bella's face lit up. "I do love Taos. I thought about moving there after my marriage ended." She frowned. "You know the saying, 'Man plans, God laughs.'"

"I hear you." Eve frowned. "You're divorced, too?"

"Yeah, but I have a new husband now. He's a love." She glanced up from the massage she was giving Eve's hand. "I lucked out with this one."

"How long have you been married?"

"To this one? A little more than four years."

"How about your ex? Were you married long?"

Bella dug hard into Eve's palm, and Eve flinched. "Two years too many."

"I'm sorry."

Bella nodded. She grabbed the other hand and started working on it, using more pressure than needed on the downward strokes.

"You're hurting me," Eve said. "Maybe thinking about your ex isn't a great thing when you're doing nails."

Bella flashed a wry smile. "It's never a great thing." She put Eve's hand down and patted it with a warm towel. "I'm sorry. It's been over five years, and I still loathe the man."

"Difficult marriage?"

Bella rose to get the nail polish. "I guess you could say that," she said over her shoulder. "He and I weren't compatible, that was apparent pretty quickly. I like tequila, he doesn't drink. I like party boat cruises, he likes lake fishing. I like to dance, he encouraged me to go alone. A woman doesn't get married to do everything by herself." She shrugged, sat back down. "Gets old after a while."

"My ex was gone a lot, too," Eve said.

"Yeah? I feel you, honey. Not really a marriage in my opinion."

"At least your divorce was amicable."

Bella snorted. "Not hardly." She was shaking the polish, hard, and paused. "I didn't fare so well." Bella waved her hand, gesturing toward the folding chairs and the single stylist station. "As you can tell."

"I'm sorry to hear that."

Bella shrugged. "Always was a controlling bastard. I should have known by the way he had to have every little thing just so when we were married. His way or the highway, as the saying goes."

Eve sat up a little straighter. "He was controlling?"

"Oh, yeah." Bella stopped shaking the polish and unscrewed the cap. She placed the bottle on the table, tapping the side with a long, lavender-sparkled nail. "Not like some husbands, who tell you who you can see or where you can go. Nothing like that. He was controlling in other ways, weird ways. Like he had to get his way, even about stupid things. The color of the bathroom towels, the make of the car I drove, how I made the bed." Bella took Eve's hand in her own. "I'm not even sure he actually *cared* about those things, but he sure got mad when I crossed him. Quiet, scary mad, if you know what I mean." Bella shook her head. "I can take a yeller, but the silent treatment for days on end? No thank you."

"That sounds awful."

"Got old real fast."

"He controlled the terms of the divorce, too?" Eve tried to sound casual, but her heart was racing. She was hoping Bella couldn't feel her pulse thumping against her wrist.

"He had the right connections. I didn't."

"Connections?"

"Helps when your brother-in-law is a judge."

"Yikes."

"You're telling me. I had a successful hair salon in Nihla. Good customers, lots of business. My ex owned the building, of course. That's how I met him—he was my landlord. It's a laundromat now." She snorted. "I hear he hooks up with some Mexican woman in *my* house, probably in *my* bed. Bet he was doing her before we even split." She steadied one hand against the table and pulled Eve's fingers across her own with the other. Her hands were warm, her touch firm. "Bastard."

"Maybe that's why he was gone so much."

"Sleeping with other women?" Bella ran the brush against Eve's nail, leaving a streak of blood red next to the pale peach of her skin. "Maybe. Probably. Who knows?" Bella snorted again. "Honey, I say good riddance. Let someone else deal with the man. I'm sure they deserve each other."

*　　*　　*

Eve returned to the hotel a little after noon. She parked in the back lot, pulled a wide-brimmed cowboy hat down to shade her face, and used the rear entrance of the building. Back in her room, she stripped out of the jeans and sequined shirt and traded them for a linen pantsuit. She put the night goggles and wigs she'd purchased outside of town in the drawers of the armoire. When the wake-up call came at two, she asked whether anyone had come looking for her.

"A gentleman was asking about you," said the motel manager. "I told him you were sleeping."

At two thirty, Eve left the hotel. She made a show of getting into her car, all the while aware of the man watching her from across the parking lot. She had some errands to run. She'd let the cop follow her, leading him around in an old-fashioned game of chase.

With a twist.

31

Constance Foster
Nihla, New Mexico—Present

THE CROSS AND the snake continued to plague me. If it wasn't Jet playing these games, then who?

Before work, I headed back to the library. I set up my laptop, connected to the free Wi-Fi, and starting searching. I looked up the old cases in and near Nihla, hunting for some connection to the house on Mad Dog Road. Other than proximity to where Esmerelda's body was found, there didn't seem to be any real nexus. I switched gears, looking for any mention of the two truckers who were imprisoned for the earlier killings.

It took me an hour and two phone calls to confirm that Mark LeBron and Norton Smallwood were both dead. LeBron died from a knife wound. Smallwood had a stroke at sixty-one and died shortly thereafter. Both men passed away in prison, which, of course, meant that even if they were behind the original murders, they weren't behind these.

Two things about Smallwood and LeBron caught my eye. The first was a mention of Smallwood's funeral service. He was survived by his widow, Anita Lynn Smallwood, of Wells, just a few stops down the highway. I couldn't find an obituary for Anita, so she could still be alive, and while I couldn't locate an address, I finally found her name listed as the manager of a store in Santa Fe. I'd go tomorrow. It was worth a shot.

The second thing that caught my attention was a vague reference buried in a 1997 article about the murders. The reporter mentioned a missing girl from Philadelphia, a girl whose body was never found.

Philadelphia. Eve was from Philadelphia.

Outside the library, I called Alberto Rodriguez. He didn't answer, so I left him a message. Thinking about Philadelphia made me think about Eve's family. She had not been close to her parents, at least that I knew of, but she'd had a cousin she'd mentioned from time to time whenever we asked about our family. Sandy Jenkins, her father's niece.

It took me another twenty minutes, but I finally found a phone number for Sandy. She didn't answer either, and I left another message. Maybe she could shed some light on my adoptive mother— who she was, why she married Liam Foster, what happened to her daughter Kelsey, and whether there had ever been a family connection to New Mexico.

I didn't hold out much hope that either lead would pan out, but I was getting desperate for answers, and doing *something* was better than waiting.

Waiting for what, I didn't know.

* * *

"A slice of apple pie and a cup of coffee." I placed the cup and plate in front of the trucker sitting at the end of the counter. He rewarded me with a ten and a "keep the change."

Manuela had been right. The afternoon was slow, which was good because I didn't think I had the energy to juggle a crowd, but it picked up as we neared the dinner hour. Two singles sat at the counter, an empty stool between them, and an older businessman took up a rear booth, nursing an unsweetened iced tea and a special and splitting his time between a crossword puzzle and the *Wall Street Journal*. He'd been in before, but he was too involved in his puzzle to engage in small talk, and that was just fine with me.

At four thirty, Stella from the hardware store walked in and took a seat at a booth. When she saw me, she grinned.

"Thought I'd see how things were going. Looks like you and Manuela hit it off."

I returned her smile, happy for a friendly and familiar face. "Thanks for the tip. Manuela's great."

I placed a menu in front of Stella, but she shook her head. "Just a green tea and a few cookies, if you have them." Her white hair was wild and free today, and she swept it back from her face with an impatient push of her gnarled hand. "Manuela makes good sugar cookies, if she has any. If not, whatever will do."

I cashed out the two truckers and brought Stella her sugar cookies and tea.

She said, "Join me."

"I'm the only one on."

"You can take a five-minute break, right? Blame me, your cranky old customer." She touched the plate, pushed it toward me. "Have a cookie."

"No thanks."

I slid into the booth across from Stella and watched while she ate—gingerly, slowly. The only other customer, the businessman in the back, was preoccupied, so I didn't rush.

After a few minutes, Stella said quietly, "The name I gave you. Did you contact him?"

"I tried." I told her about my trip to Josiah's house, his niece, and her explanation of his illness. "Why did you share his name?"

Stella nibbled on the end of the cookie. Her brown eyes stayed locked on the table. They seemed sunken and tired, her friendly energy suddenly gone. She swallowed with difficulty.

"You should leave Nihla," she said. Her voice was so low I barely heard her.

"Why? You can't say something like that and not give me a reason."

Stella stirred sugar into her tea. Her eyes were pleading, but she didn't respond.

I heard the businessman clear his throat, and I rose to take his plate and reconcile his bill. As I was getting his change, three more men came in, one after the other, including Norman from the gas station and two strangers. Each situated himself along the counter. While I was attending to the three men, Stella slipped away through the front door. She left enough for the food and a small tip on the table, next to her uneaten cookies.

Manuela joined me in the dining area. "Getting busy."

"Seems that way."

The businessman took his jacket and walked out of the building without so much as a nod. A new customer opened a crossword puzzle and pulled a pencil from his shirt pocket. He was in his fifties, fit and pale, with a blondish combover and a pair of sunglasses on a lanyard around his neck. He asked for an enchilada plate with a loud growl from across the room. Manuela sighed.

"Men," she said.

"Men," I agreed.

*   *   *

Sandy from Philadelphia called me back later that day. Her voice was high-pitched and pleasant, but she seemed confused about my inquiry. I snuck outside and took the call from the parking lot.

"I haven't spoken to Eve in ages," she said. "I mean *forever*."

"Were you close as kids?"

Sandy took a moment to respond. "Not really. Eve was . . . let's just say not one to have girlfriends, if you know what I mean."

"I'm afraid I don't."

"She was competitive—about boys, clothes, money. I guess I wasn't surprised when she ended up with that rich guy, although for the record, no one in the family believed she should have been forced to marry him. That was a mistake. After that, most of us stopped talking to Uncle Richard, her father. That caused some issues. You know how it is."

I knew about Liam, about his accident, about the money Eve had inherited. I knew Eve's father had been a fire and brimstone preacher. I wanted to know about New Mexico.

"Eve lost a daughter," I said. "She disappeared?"

Sandy sighed. "Yes, and that seemed to change her. After Kelsey disappeared, so did Eve for a while. She went off to Greece, and no one in the family heard from her for years. When she came back . . . well, you know, of course. She'd adopted you and your sister."

Through the window, I watched a man in a BMW rental park the car and enter the diner, a briefcase and newspaper in his hand. I'd need to wait on him, but I wanted a few more seconds with Eve's cousin. "Did you speak with Eve after that?"

"No, not really." She paused. "Come to think of it, we never connected again. Her mother died three years before Eve returned to the States, her father a few months beforehand. She shut herself off in Maine or wherever after she came back to the U.S."

"Vermont."

"Yes, Vermont. How about you, Constance? Are you okay? I heard that Eve passed."

"I'm holding up." I told her about the house in New Mexico. "Do you recall Eve ever talking about the state? Or a town called Nihla?"

While I waited for Sandy to respond, I made my way back to the diner. The latest customer was reading his paper, waiting for service.

Sandy said, "I think Eve went to New Mexico to look for Kelsey. Yes, I remember that. After that, nothing. She took it hard. It was like she dropped off the face of the earth—at least for most of us." She sighed. "I'm sorry about that, Constance."

"Sorry for what?"

"We're your family. We should have been there to welcome you when Eve brought you home from Greece. I'm sure you and your sister could have benefited from the connection."

"Thank you for that," I said. "It means a lot." As I hung up, I realized just how much I meant it.

* * *

It was after seven when Manuela gave me the okay to leave. I was wiping down the counters one last time when I got to the pile of newspapers at the end.

"You're off tomorrow?" Manuela called from the kitchen.

"Yeah. You need me?"

"I'm thinking of closing. I could use a day to myself."

I didn't blame her. She worked nonstop. "Want me to come in for you?"

I pulled today's newspapers out of the pile. Manuela's rules: if they were clean and current, we kept them for the next day. We recycled the rest. And we threw away crossword puzzles unless they were completely blank.

Manuela joined me in the dining area. She'd changed into a pair of jeans and a white blouse.

"Date?" I asked. "Maybe something fun tomorrow?"

"Nah. Court date over my ex's little show here. Afterwards I may treat myself to a long hike and a massage." She leaned over the counter and threw a cloth into a bin of hot, soapy water. "I deserve it, right?"

"Absolutely. Are you getting a restraining order?"

"Decided not to pursue it. It wasn't worth the effort unless he does something more aggressive."

I wasn't so sure I agreed. "Sorry to hear that."

She flexed a strong hand, raised her eyebrows. "That's life and love."

I bundled the good newspapers and placed them on the counter for the next day. As I was getting ready to throw the crossword puzzles into the garbage, I froze.

"Connie, you okay? I think I lost you for a moment."

I stared at the papers. The crossword on top had been completed, but in every column and row there were only three words, written over and over in red pen in square, neat letters.

LITTLE. RED. HOUSE.

32

Eve Foster
Nihla, New Mexico—1997

RAIN FELL IN large, greedy drops, bringing with it high winds, thunder, and bursts of lightning. Eve watched the storm from the safety of her motel room. She was waiting for a call from her lawyer, who, she knew, was still sore that she'd remained in Nihla and was siphoning money from her accounts.

The call came at 9:48 AM. "You were right. A number of girls have been killed in and around Nihla, Eve. More have been reported missing. Most of them were passing through, some were from the nearby reservation. These were poor girls, runaways." He coughed. "I don't think you have to worry. They weren't savvy or well off like Kelsey."

Jim was merely confirming what she'd heard. "Kelsey likes to take risks, play games. Who knows what she told people? She could have made up some nonsense about her past, she could have courted danger."

"Now why would she do that?"

Eve didn't like the reprimand in his tone. "The flight?"

"You're sure this is what you want?"

"I'm positive, Jim. Book me a flight." Thunder boomed overhead, and she waited until it was over before saying, "I'm not sure when I'm leaving, but they need to believe I'm gone." More quietly, "They're following me."

"That's ridiculous. You're really being paranoid."

"For all I know, this room is bugged."

"If you really believed that, you'd be staying somewhere else."

He was right, of course. Eve stretched out on the bed, her silk-clad legs spread out before her. "I may have made a half-hearted threat against an officer's family, just to make a point." She waited for his judgment. When it didn't come, she said, "It's a small town without a lot of resources, so bugging my room is unlikely. I know I'm being followed, but I've figured out a way around it."

"I'm sure you have, which is why you want me to book the flight."

"Yes."

After a beat, "I'm your lawyer, not your travel agent."

Her voice crisp, Eve said, "Do this for me, keep the remainder of your retainer, and we part ways."

"Eve—"

"I mean it. It's time. You were Liam's lawyer, not mine, and face it, we never really liked each other."

"Eve, you're being childish—"

"Goodbye, Jim." She hung up the phone. She'd been meaning to fire him anyway. He was an unwanted connection to Liam.

Eve climbed off the bed. She combed her hair and applied a hint of makeup before slipping out of her silk pajamas and into a sheer lace teddy. A glance at her bedside clock told her she had a few minutes, so she packed her suitcase, careful to hide the wigs and flashy, cheap clothes, and put her luggage in a pile by the door. She was spraying perfume on the sheets when she heard a knock at the door.

"Come in."

Jack strode into the room, shoulders back and chest puffed, ready for an argument. When he saw Eve, he stopped moving. He looked confused.

Eve said, "Take your clothes off. Everything."

Jack shook his head. "I thought—since Flora wouldn't cooperate, I thought you asked me here to—"

"You thought wrong."

Eve helped him strip out of his shirt and jeans. Greedy eyes searched Eve's while he climbed into bed, then pulled her with him. His mouth found hers, but she turned away. She pushed his head down the length of her body until he reached the right spot. His tongue was warm; she lifted her hips, rewarding him with a moan.

"Eve." He pulled her hand to his cock.

"Not yet," Eve whispered. She pushed his head down farther, harder. She wanted to feel the pressure of his tongue against her. She wanted a moment of oblivion.

*   *   *

"You're leaving." Jack said the words casually, a friend noticing a detail about another friend's life.

"I'm flying back East soon." Eve took a long draw of her cigarette before handing it to Jack. "Will you miss me?"

Jack rubbed the top of Eve's thigh, creamy white and exposed on top of the sheet. He rolled over so he was facing her on the bed. "I think perhaps I will. Will you miss me?"

Eve graced him with an enigmatic smile. She lit a second cigarette and inhaled deeply, sighing with the exhale.

"Anyway," Jack rolled over again, so he was on his back, gazing up toward the ceiling, "are you giving up on finding your daughter?"

"Not giving up, but I can't afford to stay here any longer. I want to talk to Kyle Summers. After that, I'll have to leave it to the police."

Jack contemplated his cigarette. "Why are you so fixated on Kyle?"

"Because the people of this town are protecting him. I did my research. There have been a series of murders in Nihla. Girls have been raped, killed, yet no one is talking about it. I ask questions about my daughter, and I'm treated like a pariah. If your daughter disappeared in a town with a local reputation like Nihla's, wouldn't *you* be concerned?"

"Of course, but why Kyle?"

"Because no one wants to talk about him. Because he seems untouchable, and that's odd." Eve propped herself up on her elbow. "Why are *you* protecting him?" She thought of Jack's connection to Raul. She didn't trust Jack to be honest, but she asked him anyway.

"I'm not protecting anyone. I'm here, with you. Kyle is a big boy. This is just a close-knit community, and people don't know you. Have you considered that?"

"Why wouldn't a close-knit town want to protect a young girl over a grown man?"

"Because the members of that town don't believe he's done anything wrong."

Eve climbed out of bed. She took her time finding her robe and slipping it on, thinking. "Is that really why you're protecting him, Jack? Or is the true reason that Kyle Summers is related to the man who holds the most power in Nihla and you're beholden to both of them?"

"Judge Leroux?"

"Seems to be the guy everyone is afraid of."

Jack's eyes squinted in amusement. "You can't say that after such a short time in town."

"I saw Kyle's girlfriend, the Mexican. Her face . . . Kyle beats her."

Jack's face flushed. "It's unfortunate, but he's not the only guy who loses his temper. Doesn't make him a serial killer."

"For a town so worried about justice, it doesn't look like there's much justice for Flora Fuentes. Seems to me that Kyle is being protected for a reason, and that reason is power."

"Not everything is as it seems in a town like Nihla."

Eve turned around, clutching her robe shut. "What's that supposed to mean?"

"It means exactly what I said. Just because someone has a title or owns property doesn't mean they hold the power."

Eve's smile was coy. "Then who holds the power in Nihla? Tell me, Jack."

"Good question, Eve Foster. Good question."

*   *   *

With Jack gone, Eve dressed in cream linen pants, a matching belted tunic, and a pair of heels. She wore a wide-brimmed hat with a black ribbon, a grand hat that couldn't be missed, and packed her luggage in the trunk of her car.

Out of the corner of her eye, she watched the cop in the unmarked car as he watched her.

With the car packed and ready, she checked out of the motel and returned her room key. She climbed into her sedan and pulled out her directions for Kyle's office, the address her lawyer was able to find. Eight minutes later, she arrived at a nondescript apartment building on the edge of town. Kyle's office was on the ground floor, in what had once been a caretaker's apartment. The sign on the door said open, so Eve strode in, clutching her bag.

The woman who sat behind the receptionist desk looked annoyed but not surprised. Blue-lined eyes rounded. She put a manicured hand on her phone, another against the desk.

Eve said, "I'm looking for Kyle Summers."

"I'm afraid he's not here."

"Isn't that his BMW outside?"

"He stepped out for a bit."

Eve sat on the edge of the woman's desk and looked down at her. She was all of twenty-two and wore a clingy yellow dress that accentuated a full chest. Eve despised her on sight.

Eve said, "I'll wait."

The woman picked up her phone. "I'm calling the police."

"No need, Ellen." The man who emerged from another room was wiry, nondescript in a clean-cut, buttoned-down sort of way. He wore a well-tailored business suit and carried a stack of papers. His blond hair was cut short and had been blow-dried into place. He put the papers on the receptionist's desk. "Take care of those for me, will you?" He smiled broadly at Eve. "You must be Eve Foster. I'm Kyle. I've heard so much about you."

I'm sure, Eve thought. Eve stood up from Brenda's desk. In heels, she was at least an inch taller than he was. "I'd like to talk with you. Is there somewhere private we can go?"

Kyle glanced at Brenda. "We'll be in my office. If you need me, call."

Eve followed Kyle to a large, bright office off the main reception area. A massive cherrywood desk sat next to a matching credenza. On its shelves, stacks of business books competed for space with awards—best business, good citizen, even a church fundraising award. His office screamed "all around great guy." His smile screamed "compulsive liar."

Eve recalled Kyle's ex-wife's description of him—controlling, absent. She said, "Impressive office."

Kyle smiled again. "This is where the magic happens. Please, sit." He gestured toward an upholstered armchair across from his desk. When Eve obliged, he sat on the edge of his desk, much as Eve had done with his receptionist. "How can I help you, Mrs. Foster? As you can imagine, having you slander my good name all over my hometown has been . . . trying. I know you're frantic about your daughter. I can understand that."

"You were the last person to be seen with Kelsey."

Kyle sighed. "A mistake. I gave her a ride into town. She was at a party out in the desert with my nephew, Antonio. I was there checking on Antonio. Your daughter was unhappy, I was leaving anyway, so I offered her a ride. I shared this with the police already."

Eve held his gaze. "What time was that?"

"About midnight."

"And where did you drop her off?"

"Downtown."

"Just the middle of the road? At midnight? It's not much of a town, so surely you can be more specific."

"She was going to stay at the boarding house for the evening. A place called The Cat's Meow. Then she planned to get a bus home the next day."

"That's what she told you?"

"Yes."

"The Pussy Palace? A bus home? You're sure?"

Eve saw the first crack in his façade. His eyes shifted, he looked down at his desk, then out toward the window. He must know that Kelsey would never sleep in a place like The Cat's Meow, would never take a *bus* across the country, Eve thought, and she would never return home under those circumstances. In Kelsey's mind, coming home would be losing.

Eve stood. "Raul at The Cat's Meow says he never saw her." When Kyle didn't respond, Eve said, "Why in the world would you drop a sixteen-year-old in the middle of a deserted town at midnight and think that was okay?"

"She said she was twenty-one. Your daughter is very . . . mature."

Eve heard the front door open, the soft murmur of the receptionist's voice. Soon the cops would barge in. She only had a few minutes alone with Kyle.

"Tell me about the party. Was there anyone there who could have been a threat to my daughter? Anyone at all?"

Kyle glanced out the window again. His eyes narrowed, his pupils were black holes. "You really don't get it, do you?"

"What is it that I don't get?"

"Your daughter is a partier. She came to town with an open wallet and open legs, inviting anyone to join her for a good time. I bet she'd slept with half the men in Nihla by the time I dropped her off that evening."

Eve's smile seemed to knock Kyle off balance. If he meant to offend her, he was sorely mistaken. Eve knew her daughter, and she knew she probably *had* come to Nihla looking to fuck as many locals as possible. What better way to get back at her mother. So what? That had nothing to do with whatever she was certain Kyle had done.

Eve studied the man before her. He didn't seem shaken or worried. He seemed calm, self-assured, even amused. Everything about him was precise, from his neatly trimmed nails to his perfectly shined shoes. But Eve recalled Flora's face. Underneath the veneer of civility was a man of temper and appetites. Appetites he liked to keep hidden.

Eve said, "None of that matters. I had Kelsey followed across this great nation all the way to Nihla, and then the trail stopped dead. One day she was at a desert rave, and the next day she went missing." Eve leaned in so that her face was inches from Kyle's. She inhaled him, hoping for a whiff of Kelsey's perfume. Hoping for the smell of fear. Disappointed, she said, "The last person to have seen my daughter was you."

"I told you what I know."

"You told me lies."

The door to the office opened. In walked two men—Officer Mayor and another man, shorter, squatter, bald, and holding a gun.

"Judge Leroux," Eve said. "I was hoping you would join us. I've been wanting to meet you."

The judge shared a look with Kyle before putting the gun into a holster around his ample waist. "I hear you've caused quite a stir around here."

"The people of Nihla are enabling a kidnapper and a murderer."

Leroux rolled his eyes. "Mrs. Foster, this stops now. You have twenty-four hours to leave town, or this man will arrest you." He nodded toward Mayor. "I'm not joking around. Your money and your attitude won't get you anywhere in Nihla."

"You'll arrest me for what? My daughter—"

"*Is not here.*" Leroux walked around the office until he was by the window that overlooked the street. "Officer Mayor did a thorough investigation. Your daughter came to Nihla, made her way around—hard to hear, I know—and left. Where is she now? Probably in California or Vegas or Mexico. Truckers pass through daily. Kyle dropped her off, she hitchhiked to her next destination. You're wasting your time in Nihla."

Eve slid her hand under her thigh and pinched herself hard enough to make her eyes water. She hung her head. When she looked back up at the judge, she gave a small nod.

"You'll leave then?" Mayor asked.

"I'll think about it. Do you have a lead for me? Anything? The next town I can search?"

"Tell her," Leroux said.

Mayor rubbed his eyes. "We spoke to a trucker who claims to have seen a girl matching your daughter's description at a highway stop north of Taos."

Eve looked back and forth between the three men. "And you're just telling me now?"

"It just came up," Mayor said. "We questioned him this morning."

Eve swallowed. "Was she with another trucker?"

"He thought so," Mayor said. "Looked like she may have been . . . um . . ."

"Hooking," Kyle said with a sardonic smile.

Eve took a deep breath. "Thank you, gentlemen. That gives me something to go on, at least." She sighed. "It's tough being a parent. I know you all understand."

Leroux smiled. His teeth were white, sharp, perfectly capped. A carnivore's mouth. "We do what we can for our kids, Mrs. Foster, but sometimes . . . well, sometimes it's just not enough."

33

Constance Foster
Nihla, New Mexico—Present

I CALLED LISA FROM the relative safety of my house later that night. It was after eight, and outside darkness had begun to descend. I scoured the corners of the house for snakes as I spoke with my sister. She sounded tired, groggy, her speech garbled around the edges. I asked her why.

"I'm fine."

"Lisa, you know I know you better than that." Silence. "*Lisa.*"

"It's just the house." A beat. "Come home."

"We've been through this." *Nonstop, every conversation.* "I can't."

"I want you to come *here.* Be with me." More slurring. "I have a plan. For both of us. You'll see."

I sank down into a living room chair. "Lisa, what are you taking?"

"Just a sedative." She laughed—a loud, shrill laugh. Not my sister's normal laugh. "It's happening again."

I sat up straighter. "What's happening?"

"The noises."

Lisa didn't need to say more. The basement, the locked room. How many nights had I lain there, listening to noises, scared witless? I looked up to see my own face in the window. Chalky skin, wide, tired eyes. I didn't like what I saw, a ghost of myself.

"There's no one in the basement," I said. "Eve planted those thoughts in our head. Ghost stories used to scare us."

"I know what I heard."

"I spoke with Eve's cousin, the one from Philadelphia. Kelsey disappeared. She didn't live in Vermont. Those stories were meant to scare us, control us."

"I know what I heard."

"Stay out of the basement, Lisa. You'll drive yourself mad."

"Scratching. Rustling. Moaning. What if she is down there, starving now that Aunt Eve is gone?"

"She was never there to begin with. Are you hearing me? It was all part of Eve's sick mind games."

Lisa sobbed. "I heard someone. Please, please come home. I'm scared, Connie."

"Lisa," I said sternly. "Stop. If you're that worried about it, have Dave or Cook go down and see what's in that room. Find the key to the padlock and open the door. You'll see. It'll be empty, just like it's always been."

"You really think so?"

"Even Eve wouldn't keep a woman locked up in the basement for over twenty years."

"You're right. Of course you're right," Lisa said. I could hear her fading. "Good night, Connie."

"Stay strong, Lisa. Please." But she had already hung up.

I lay in bed that night listening to the desert noises. Wind against the loose boards of my house. Coyotes echoing across the vast expanse of flat, scrubby land. A rabbit's scream.

Night noises.

In Vermont, when I slept with the windows open in spring, I'd hear the peepers—the tiny frogs whose calls became deafening when the sun went down. And owls. And coyotes. And the occasional loon nesting on the banks of Lake Champlain. And if I had been locked in my basement room, I'd hear other noises.

Rattling. Boards creaking. Moans.

"It's her," the housekeepers would whisper. "The daughter. The one who ran away."

"Big old house like that? Mice," Dave, the driver would tease us, grinning. "Maybe rats, too."

"Your imagination," Aunt Eve would say. She always seemed sincere. It made me doubt myself, my sanity.

But Lisa heard the noises, too.

I suspected Cook was in on the secret. That if Eve's daughter Kelsey had been locked in that godawful basement, Cook was in charge of feeding and caring for her. Ageless Cook, with her steel-colored bun and her no-nonsense loafers, had the look of a woman who knew more than she'd like to. Somehow, she'd survived in Eve's household when so many other staff members had been fired. She and, eventually, Eve's driver, Dave Dagger.

The wind railed against the house. Something slammed against my window, once, twice. I turned over and buried my head in my pillow, blocking out the noises. Loose boards. Maybe I should ask Jet to fix them.

If Lisa was hearing things in the basement, then perhaps the maids were right. Maybe Kelsey *was* down there. But wouldn't Eve have put some provision in her will for Kelsey's care? Eve was a heartless bitch, true, but she was, in her own way, practical. Leaving her own daughter to rot—quite literally—was too messy.

No, it was more likely that Lisa was hearing mice. And rats. Or the machinations of her own mind.

My eyelids felt heavy with sleep. Another bang outside made me gasp and plunged me into the first of a long night of nightmares. My little red house became a room buried far beneath the Vermont mansion, and Lisa and I were trapped in its basement. No matter how much we clawed at the doors, no one came to save us. Dripping red handprints ran the length of the walls. I couldn't breathe, couldn't move. I was buried alive.

* * *

By morning, the winds had subsided, and the sun flooded my room with a yellow-orange glow. I crawled off the blow-up bed feeling groggy and off center, the remnants of my nightmares like dusty shadows in the corners of my mind. I brushed my teeth, changed clothes, and put my hair into a loose ponytail. One look in the mirror, and I splashed cold water on my pallid face. It didn't help.

At 8:14, I walked outside. It was then I saw the blood smeared on the wood. Streaks of what looked like blood, thick and dried now, staining the length of my door. I ran outside to look at the window, remembering the noises I'd heard the night before.

More blood, in a star pattern against the glass.

I stared at the bloody prints, feeling confused and afraid. The sun, with its false comfort, distorted my vision, muting the color of the blood, creating a macabre impressionist painting on my door. I felt dizzy.

Who had been here last night? Whose blood was it?

In a panic, I yelled for Jet. He poked his head around the corner of the house.

"What's up?"

I pointed.

He stared for a very long time. "Do you have any idea where this came from?"

I shook my head. "Do you?"

"Of course not." He glanced back, toward his house. "Micah was barking last night. I figured it was the wind."

"I heard thumping against the house. I thought . . . I thought it was wind, too."

We stared at each other. I was thinking of earlier that week, of being held, naked, in his arms. Could I have been wrong about him? Was it possible that he was behind this prank—I sure as hell hoped it was a prank—and was trying to drive me mad?

Jet whistled for Micah, and she ran around the side of the house, toward us. "Come on, girl." To me he said, "I'm going to search the perimeter and the surrounding desert, in case someone is injured. I'll take Micah. Why don't you call the police?"

I watched him trek to the far corner of the property, his broad shoulders back, loyal dog by his side. I had to believe he was trustworthy. I also had to believe Lisa was safe. For my own sanity. Only part of me was afraid last night's nightmare had been real. That Lisa had been trapped outside my house, left to beg for entry, her hands reduced to bloody stumps, while I slept through her terror.

34

Constance Foster
Nihla, New Mexico—Present

M Y FEARS SEEMED unfounded—but then why the continued uneasiness? When I reached my sister that morning, she sounded more alert than she'd been the night before. She didn't mention the basement, and I didn't mention my nightmares or the ominous blood on the door. I hung up when the police arrived.

The responding officers were curt. They looked at my door and window, asked a few questions, and cast a skeptical eye toward Jet's shack. They wanted to talk to him, too. I have no idea what was said to Jet, but they left thirty minutes later and seemed utterly disinterested in what had happened.

Jet and I watched them pull out.

"What do you think?" I asked.

"I think they don't give a fuck. You won't get any follow-up."

We were standing by the road, its length a dusty path to nowhere, and he was holding a chisel. For a brief moment, I pictured him stabbing someone with that chisel. Someone who would later run to my house and pound on the door, begging for help. I shut my eyes against the image. I had no reason to suspect Jet. So far, other than hanging the cross, he'd done nothing bad other than work for Eve.

I headed for the house, but not before I saw Oliver watching us from the edge of his property.

"Where are you going?" Jet asked.

"To get some bleach. I need to scrub the blood off the house. Unless that's part of *your* job?"

Jet held out his hands. "I have to go into town, but I can help for a little bit."

"That's okay."

He came toward me, and I took a step back. Our night together lingered in my mind, but so did the doubts.

"If you need anything else," he said.

I nodded, opened my front door.

"You believe it wasn't me?" He swallowed, his Adam's apple bobbing against his tan, muscular neck. I focused on his sinewy, thick neck, thought about how much stronger he was than I was.

I said, "Sure."

"I don't know why I care whether you believe me, but I do."

I managed a smile. I believed him as much as I believed anyone in Nihla. I just wanted to wipe away that blood and get on with my day. Jet seemed to be studying me intensely. I saw the set of his jaw, the red flush on his face. His anger was growing. No one understands the signs of burgeoning rage like someone who lived with an abuser.

"*Jet.*"

"I'm not that person," he said tightly. "Not—"

Not what? Not anymore?

Jet looked ready to hurl the chisel through my bloody window. Instead, he tossed it on the ground and walked away.

* * *

I reached Alberto Rodriguez on the first try. "I need to talk to you," I said.

"Leave it be, Connie."

"Today. Say one o'clock? I'll buy you lunch."

"Connie, I don't think this is a great idea. Listen to me. *Please.* You need to stop asking questions. You're raising alarms. Calling attention to yourself." He paused. "I don't need that on my conscience."

"I absolve you." I named a little restaurant off the main drag. "I'll see you at one."

* * *

There was someone else I needed to see before meeting Alberto.

The Olive Branch was a small store in downtown Santa Fe specializing in olive oils, vinegars, and high-end comestibles. I arrived shortly after it opened, and already a small crowd was milling about inside. The only salesperson was about my age. She had red hair and an open smile and seemed at ease with the customers. I waited until she'd helped an older man sample an oil from Greece before approaching.

"I'm looking for my Aunt Anita," I explained, lying. "I haven't seen her in ages, and because I was in town, I figured I'd stop by."

At the mention of Anita, the saleswoman's face lit up. "I had no idea she even had family. She'll be thrilled. Unfortunately, though, she doesn't come in until noon."

I sighed, thinking of my appointment with Alberto. "I'm afraid I can't wait around that long."

"That's too bad." A middle-aged man in a fedora held up a bottle of vinegar and asked for a price. As she answered him, the saleswoman snapped her fingers. "Anita usually has a late breakfast at the café down the road before coming to work. Betty's. A small coffee, two creams, a yogurt with berries, and a blueberry scone. She loves her routines. You could try her there."

I smiled, genuinely grateful for the help.

"If you miss her for some reason, should I tell her you stopped by?"

"Please don't," I said. "I'll save the surprise for another day."

When I arrived, Betty's was nearly empty. An unpretentious coffee shop with a long wooden counter and a dozen tables, Betty's welcomed me with the warm scents of cinnamon and coffee. I asked for a tall coffee and a breakfast sandwich. The waitress asked my name, and my order was up five minutes later. I slipped her a twenty and asked her to cover the order for a woman named Anita. She nodded, clearly knowing who Anita was.

I ate my breakfast and waited.

At 10:36, an older Black woman with soft features and closely cropped hair entered the café. The barista seemed to recognize her.

Trim and well-dressed, she balked when the barista told her the order had been paid for. The barista pointed to me. I waved. Anita shook her head, frowned, and handed the barista her credit card. The barista shrugged, took it.

Anita walked to my table. Those soft features hid a fierceness in her eyes, and she glared at me, hard. "Who are you, and what business do you have following me?"

"I'm not following you. I promise."

"Then how did you know my name and that I would be here?" She leaned toward me. "You a reporter? I'm done with reporters."

"No ma'am, I'm not a reporter. My name is Connie Foster. I live in Nihla."

The barista called Anita's name. Anita waved to her to wait. I took advantage of Anita's momentary distraction and said, "I'm here because of your husband, Mrs. Smallwood." She started to object, and I put up a hand. "Please, hear me out. I know Norton was innocent. I know he and the other man were framed." I motioned toward the empty seat. "There have been more murders. The police seem to be covering them up. Please, hear me out."

"You a civil rights activist?"

"No, just a scared woman."

Anita's face turned ashen. She sank down into the seat.

I said, "I am so very sorry for your loss, but I need to know if you know anything that could help. Something that could clear your husband's name, save lives."

Anita looked around the café, let out a long, slow whistle, and threw back her head.

"Mrs. Smallwood?"

"I'm not doing this again. No way."

"Doing what?"

"Pointing out the obvious. Waiting for someone to get a clue, then watching as our notion of justice is thrown in the garbage can."

"I'm on your side. I believe Mr. Smallwood was innocent."

After a long moment, she said, "Show me your ID."

I pulled my Vermont driver's license out of my wallet and handed it to her. "I live in Nihla now, in a house I inherited. Ever since I arrived, weird things have been happening. No one talks about it. I'm . . . afraid." As I said the words, I realized just how true they were. Years of bravado, of having nothing to lose, and this not knowing is what scared me to my core.

Anita stared at the license. "No one in Nihla sent you?"

"No, ma'am."

She shook her head. "You don't get it, but why would you? Of course my Norton was innocent. They both were. No one doubted their innocence for a second. Not that dim-witted puppet chief of police, not the DA, not even the judge who heard his case. They all knew Norton was innocent, and they railroaded him right to prison anyway."

"Why? Why would they do that? For political reasons?"

"That's what they wanted people to think. They needed a quick resolution, and if there was doubt about the men's guilt later on, they could say they pressed forward to reassure the public."

"But that wasn't true?"

Anita Smallwood looked around, lowered her voice until it was barely a whisper. "They were covering up for someone else. Some- one in that town." She sneered. "Nihla." She spat the word like it was poison.

"Who were they covering for?"

"I have my hunches, but the truth is, I don't know. Whoever 'they' were, they must have had some pull."

The barista brought Anita's food to the table, and I waited until she'd left to say, "Do you know a man named Josiah Smith?"

"Know him? That's the coward who prosecuted the case." She shook her head again, eyes blazing. "He knew they were innocent. I could see it in his face. Would never look me or Norton in the eye. *Never*."

I watched as a couple of teenage boys brought whipped cream–topped mugs to a table beside us, seemingly oblivious to Anita's distress. "The women who were murdered—they were mostly run- aways. Young, many of them not from around here."

"That's right."

"Why would they have pinned this on your husband and Mark LeBron?"

"Two Black men at the wrong place at the wrong time? You really need to ask me that question? Nothing feeds the beast of public outcry like two Black men and a bunch of young girls."

"Did you know more women have died over the last few months?" When Anita didn't reply, I said, "And no one's talking about it."

"And no one will."

"Why?"

"I don't know." Anita sighed. The rage seemed to have left her, and she took a half-hearted bite of the scone. "For some reason, this is a taboo subject around Nihla."

"If there was a cover-up, if your husband and LeBron were framed, do you think the same people could be involved today?"

Anita ate her yogurt, considering my question. Quietly, she wrapped the remainder of her scone in a napkin. She placed the scone in her bag.

"Anita?"

"I need to get to work."

"If the same person is murdering girls today, and it can be proven, that would clear your husband's name."

Anita walked to the trash with her tray. When she returned, she gave me a look heavy with sorrow. "Look, I don't know why girls are turning up dead again. The judge that presided over Norton's case is dead. I don't know about the rest of them." She picked up her coffee. "Whatever's happening there, it's no longer my problem. I've made my sacrifices. I don't need to clear Norton's name. It was never sullied. No one in their right mind believed that story."

"More women could disappear, die. That doesn't worry you?"

"I learned the hard way that there's no fighting injustice around here. More girls could die, more men could lose their lives in prison." Anita threw her bag over her shoulder, met my gaze with a stony one of her own. "Don't give me those accusing eyes. My husband was a good man. Churchgoer, volunteer fireman. He had his whole life ahead of him. *We* had our whole life ahead of us."

"Anita—"

She blinked, and I saw the moisture pooling in her eyes. More softly, she said, "The girls died, Norton died, and most of me died, too."

CHAPTER

35

Eve Foster
Nihla, New Mexico—1997

E VE DROVE STRAIGHT to the airport in Albuquerque. She spotted the plainclothes cop out of her rearview window just past Santa Fe. He stayed with her until she arrived at the airport parking garage. After that, he disappeared. Eve wasn't taking any chances. She grabbed her luggage, returned the rental, and entered the airport. She sat in an uncomfortable vinyl chair for forty minutes before deciding she was no longer being followed. Her next stop was the bathroom.

There, she changed into jeans, cowboy boots, and a flowery blouse. She pulled a black, curly wig from her bag and carefully placed it over her own blonde head. It was an expensive wig, and the change was dramatic. Gold hoop earrings and a pair of over-sized sunglasses finished the look.

Back out in the airport terminal, Eve climbed into the car that was waiting for her in the limo section. It was a plain Chevy, nothing fancy. With a nod to the driver, she gave the address of a different motel near the highway on the outskirts of Nihla. She asked him to take a meandering route and increased his fare by $200. He happily obliged.

"Why all the trouble?" he asked, peering at her through the rearview mirror. "You running from someone?"

"Running *to* someone," Eve replied.

Eve saw the driver's overgrown eyebrows weave together in confusion. "Wouldn't it be best to take a direct route then?"

"Please. Just drive."

Eve gazed out the window at the passing landscape. The air was dry, the sky clear. Her mind was made up, but some of the bravado had faded like the paint on the signs she saw as they careened down the highway. She closed her eyes. Kelsey was in Nihla. She knew that with a mother lion's instincts, and like a mother lion, she planned to kill anyone in her way. Summers and Mayor and the others had raised the stakes. She'd be damned if they were going to win. She touched her bag. Just knowing the gun was there gave her strength.

"What's your name?" the driver asked.

"Georgina."

"Pretty," he said. "You look like a Georgina."

"Is that so?"

"Are you from Georgia?" He laughed heartily at his own joke.

"Nebraska by way of Kansas."

"A corn-fed girl. I hope the man you're running to knows how lucky he is. Midwestern gals are the best in the kitchen *and* the bedroom." Eve saw his wink through the rearview mirror.

Eve forced her eyes not to roll. "I don't think he'll see it that way."

The driver shook his head. "In my day, a man would be grateful."

"What's your name?" Eve asked, not actually caring. The conversation was a distraction, and the more he thought of her as Georgina from Nebraska, the better.

"My name is Ed. Born and raised in New York. Retired here a decade ago. Never looked back."

"Nice place to retire to."

"Most of it." He glanced back at her. "This beau of yours, he live in Nihla? Or is he a trucker?"

"His . . . uh, lady friend . . . lives near Nihla."

"Ah. I'm sorry."

"Yeah, well. Men can be bastards."

Ed's eyes rounded. "And women can't be?"

"Women? Hmm. Sometimes the world forces us to be victim or vixen."

"And you, Georgina?" Amused eyes stared at her through the rearview mirror. "Which are you?"

"Me? Vixen, I guess." Eve returned her attention to the landscape. The words, like the air, were sawdust in her mouth. "I will never again be a victim, so I guess that's what's left."

*   *   *

This motel was worse than the last one. Stained rug, tacky décor, pervasive smell of cigarette smoke throughout the hallways and in the room. But Eve was willing to sacrifice, and so she willingly accepted her quarters under the name Georgina Hawkins. Who needed comfort? She wouldn't be sleeping anyway.

A rental car had been left for her, an unappealing tan Buick, and she used this to first pick up some food and supplies in Taos, and then to stake out Kyle's house.

Without the police on her tail, without the judge breathing down her neck, she would be able to see what was really going on in Nihla. And then she would strike.

36

Constance Foster
Nihla, New Mexico—Present

ALBERTO WAS ALREADY at the restaurant when I arrived. He was holed up in a booth in the back, a sour expression on his face. I slid in across from him and thanked him for coming.

"You have a fucking death wish," he muttered.

"You're the one who writes about this stuff. Why am *I* the one in danger?"

"It's a matter of method. I focus on the victims from the safety of a legitimate paper. Notice I'm not in Nihla. I stay away from the fire." He sipped a mug of what looked like coffee, wiped his mouth with a crumpled napkin. "You are dancing *in* the fire."

The waitress came over, and I ordered a taco plate special and water. Alberto ordered three enchiladas, rice, beans, a sopapilla, and a salad.

"Since you're paying," he said with a half smile. When the waitress left, he sat back in his seat and frowned, chewing his lip as he did so. "What do you want? Be quick—my time is limited."

I told him about my exchange with Anita Smallwood. "She said no one believed that Norton or James could have been guilty. That even the DA and judge didn't seem to believe it. Is that true?"

"If she's right, they put on a good show."

"The judge who oversaw the trials, do you know who he was?"

Alberto's eyebrows knit together. "Guy named Leroux. Died about six years ago."

"Did you know him?"

"Only to watch him during the trials."

"Anita mentioned that Josiah Smith was the prosecutor at the time."

"I told you that. Assistant DA." Rodriguez twisted a napkin into thin shreds. "Connie, what's your angle here? We already know the trial was a sham. We both know LeBron and Smallwood were innocent. Why are you bothering Anita?" He threw the napkin in the table. "Why are you bugging me?"

"I don't know."

"*You don't know?*"

I told him about last night. About the thumping, about the blood. About Jet.

"That's a lot to take in. The prints—do the cops think it's actually blood?"

"That's just it. They showed up, asked some questions, walked around, and left. They were in and out in the time it takes me to shower. Didn't even mark it a crime scene."

Alberto looked pensive. "And this guy, your caretaker—he was accounted for last night?"

"Bernard Jetson Montgomery is his full name. Originally from Texas. And no, not really."

"Name doesn't ring any bells."

I knew I was asking a lot, but I said anyway, "Can you do some digging into his background?"

"I'm not a private investigator."

"Yeah, I know. But I don't have the money for an investigator, and you said yourself that I need to be discreet."

His eyes widened. "One, since when do you listen to me, and two, no."

"Please?"

The food arrived, and as soon as the waitress was gone, Rodriguez tucked into his plate. Midway through his fourth fork-full, he stopped eating and looked up at me, bits of corn tortilla in his beard. "You're serious, aren't you?"

"I'm serious."

"You think this Jet has something to do with the murders?"

"No, I don't—not really. But I can't fire him because of a stupid clause in the will, and I don't trust Eve's judgment. She . . . she had a cruel sense of humor." I poked at a taco. It smelled delicious, but my appetite was gone. "I really want to trust this guy, but it's all a little too convenient."

"You realize you may never actually know for sure. He could be clean as a baby's backside after a bath and still be a pervert. Or he could have a record a kilometer long and be Mother Teresa now." Alberto waved a chip in the air. "Look at serial killers like Ted Bundy. They seemed like model citizens. It's the quiet ones, you know?"

I smiled. "I know. But something is better than nothing."

"No promises," Rodriguez mumbled, mouth full.

"Thank you," I said. "I mean that."

He pointed a fork at me. "Paybacks, Connie. I know you're not going to stop digging around. You find something, you call me." He shook the fork. "Promise."

"You have my word."

"That'll have to do." He picked up his sopapilla from a side plate and tore a piece off. There was a squeeze bottle of honey on the table, and he poured a glob on the bite before popping it into his mouth. "The only thing I can count on in this train wreck of a world is that politicians will disappoint and this place won't."

I glanced down at my plate, realized I should eat, and picked up a taco.

"Your mother," Alberto said between bites. "She sounds like a real gem."

"If by 'gem' you mean sadistic nut job, sure."

"What was her name?"

"Eve. We called her 'Aunt Eve.'"

"And she left you that house on Mad Dog, huh?"

"Yeah. A house I didn't even know she owned."

Alberto put down his fork. "Hmm."

"What's hmm."

"Just wondering how she came to own that place? Sat abandoned for a long time."

I glanced at him. "Did you know the person who used to live there?"

Rodriquez shook his head. "Nah, only know the road because of Esmerelda. I remember driving by, though. Empty. Sad looking."

He glanced toward the door, a distant expression in his eyes. "Truth is, I tried to get in. Thought maybe the house had something to do with my sister's disappearance. It was locked up tight." His gaze returned to the present, to me. "Your mother, how'd she die?"

"She drowned."

"That's an awful way to go."

"She was a strong swimmer. Kept herself in shape. Claimed the cold water in Lake Champlain was what kept her looking young." I shrugged. "Joke's on her."

"In my culture, we have respect for our parents."

"You didn't know her," I said quietly.

"Difficult?"

"You could say that." I watched as a mother and a young toddler settled into a nearby booth. The mother waited patiently while the toddler, a little girl, took every toy animal from her tiny backpack and spread them on the table. "She lost a daughter. I don't think she ever fully recovered from that. She became . . . twisted. Cruel."

"Losing a child is a terrible thing."

I nodded. "The daughter, Kelsey, ran away. Disappeared. Sometimes Eve's staff teased us, insisted she had returned, deranged and unmanageable. They used to tell my sister and me that she was forced to live in the basement."

"That's horrible."

"The staff never saw her, of course—just heard the noises. They got their kicks by scaring us. No one lasted in Eve's employ long, anyway." I sat back, remembering. "Anyway, Kelsey never returned." I shrugged. "She's dead. Or she ran away and managed never to be found. The staff didn't like my mother any more than I did. I think those rumors were their way of getting back at her *and* us. They knew Kelsey was a sore subject."

"The staff?" His smile was condescending. "So you're a poor little rich girl?"

I threw my napkin down on my plate and signaled to the waitress. Eve was rich, sure—but *that* was what he got from this conversation? I shoved two twenties at the waitress and stood.

"Thanks for checking on Jet," I said coldly.

"Whoa, wait a minute, Connie. You joke, I joke. That's how this works." He looked up at me. "Seriously, don't get your thong in a twist. I'm sorry I said anything about your family."

I nodded. "Call me if you learn anything. I'll do the same."

"You're still angry."

I glanced again at the young mother with her young daughter. "I'm tired. Just very, very tired. And I think I'm owed some answers."

* * *

It was after nine when James Riley called my cell phone.

"I heard what happened. Are you okay?"

"I'm fine."

"Would it be all right to see you tomorrow?"

I was surprised to hear from him. Even more surprised that he wanted to see me.

"I'm working," I said. "You can come by Manuela's. I'll be there until six."

There was a pause. Then, "It would be better if it were after my work hours. How about later? I can bring some dinner to your place. Pizza or something."

I would have been happy had it not been for the tension in his voice. He seemed like easy company. He was certainly easy on the eyes. "Sure. That'll work, I guess. Is everything okay?"

"I don't know." Another pause. "See you tomorrow. I'll be there by seven."

CHAPTER

37

Constance Foster
Nihla, New Mexico—Present

JAMES ARRIVED AT seven o'clock on the dot. He was still wearing his uniform, and he looked proper and serious in his dress blues. I was happy to see him at the door, despite the grim expression on his face. He was carrying a pizza and a six-pack of Santa Fe Pale Ale, and he held up the beer and smiled. I led him to the kitchen, and he placed both on the table.

"I didn't know what you drank, so I played it safe. Same goes for the pizza—boring and plain."

"These days, boring and plain work for me. Thanks."

"Thanks for having me."

I smiled. "You didn't give me much choice."

He glanced around, not returning my smile. "We alone?"

I nodded. "Why? You look like you saw your dead Great-Aunt Edna in my driveway."

He pulled two beers out of their box. I tossed him a bottle opener from the drawer. He wedged off the caps and handed me one of the beers. "How about we eat first?"

"I can't. Not with that look on your face."

This seemed to reach him, and his shoulders relaxed. So did his mouth, and I noticed—not for the first time—that his rough-guy exterior was balanced by soft, kind eyes. I trusted him. Whether

I was just dying to trust someone in this hellhole of a town, or whether he was truly trustworthy remained to be seen.

"Suit yourself." He sat down. I joined him. "Is this about the data you were looking for—similar murders?"

He shook his head no. "That report you made yesterday, anyone follow up?"

"Just the initial call."

"Do you remember the officers who came by?"

I described them, and he frowned. "Huh."

"You know them?"

"I know of them. Same precinct. Good reps."

"What does that mean? They determined the prints were just a cruel prank?"

"No, that's the thing. I tried to pull the report and there was none." He put his beer down. "You're absolutely certain you gave them a statement."

"Of course."

"And you're sure it was blood."

"As sure as I can be. But I think it's their job to decide, right?"

"Can you describe what happened one more time? In as much detail as possible." He leaned closer, his face a map of unease. "I'm sorry to make you relive it, but I need to hear it again."

I recounted everything I could recall—from the sounds outside late at night to waking up to those horrible prints on my windows.

"Smears and star shapes, you said?"

I nodded. "Not like purposeful prints, more like random smears and shapes. Like someone—" I paused, swallowed. "Like someone was desperate to get inside."

James stood. He walked to my sink and stood there, staring into the basin. "Who knows you live here? Besides me and your tenant?"

"Not many people. Manuela. The cops who responded. Oliver and his brother. They're my neighbors."

"No one else?"

I tilted my head back, thinking. "I don't know, James. I may have told some random people in passing."

"Right." He turned back around. "Here's the thing. Another woman turned up last night. Caucasian, mid-twenties, no ID."

"When you say 'turned up' you mean—?"

"Dead."

My skin prickled again, my chest tightened. "Near here?" His silence was enough. "Dear God. No idea who she was?" And then it hit me. Amy—the girl from the bar. I'd given her my address. She'd been alone, vocal, restless. If this guy only killed those from away, she'd be a sure target. "Did she have blue-tinged hair and an angel tattoo on her stomach?"

His eyebrows shot up. "Yes."

I forced myself to be calm. *Stay with it, Connie.* There was no use freaking out. "I know her. Well, at least I know who she is. Her name's Amy. She was staying at the boarding house."

"Was she alone in town?"

"She mentioned a boyfriend, but I think they'd broken up." I asked him to sit back down, and he perched on the edge of his chair, legs out straight, hands clasped. "The first time I met her, she was drunk. Really drunk. And all she could talk about were the murders. The second time I ran into her, she seemed like a different person. Colder, controlled, nervous." I shrugged. "I tried to find her a few days ago, but she wasn't home. I thought maybe she'd left town. Are there any leads?"

James shrugged. "I have no answers, Connie. Just questions, like you. The precinct is shut down when it comes to this issue. No information. I've been accessing the database, but haven't found anything conclusive—yet."

"How'd you know about Amy?"

"Derek, a guy on the force. He's lived around here longer, but he seems as perplexed as I am. I told him what happened to you, he told me about the latest victim."

A terrible possibility crossed my mind. "Had she been tortured like the others?"

"I don't know."

"Were there injuries that could have caused the prints I saw?"

"Possibly—yes." James reached out a hand and touched my wrist. "Look, I wanted to tell you this in person, but it's confidential. It's not public yet, and I don't want to interfere with the investigation. I had been hoping that someone from the precinct had contacted you."

"They should have." And then it occurred to me—the real reason he was so agitated. I asked, "When was she found?"

More silence.

Fuck. These bastards had known when they showed up at my house that a woman's body had been found. That's what James was trying to tell me. That's what this visit was about.

"They'd already found her when they came to my house, right?" I jumped up, slammed my hand against the wall. "Fuck, James, they *knew* a woman had been killed near my house. They *knew* that blood could have—who the fuck are we kidding?—probably did—come from her." The implications hit me. "If the victim is Amy, she may have come to my house for help. She may have been running from whoever this asshole is. She could have been trying to get away—*oh, shit.*"

"What is it?"

"I could have saved her. Had I let her in. Had I taken certain things more seriously."

"What things, Connie? What are you talking about?"

I jogged to the bedroom and dug the newspaper crossword from my bag. I put it on the table, in front of James, and tapped my finger on the puzzle.

"*Little red house,*" he read. "Where did this come from?"

"The diner."

"Who wrote it? Did you see who did it?"

"No. I mean, customers do puzzles all the time when they eat alone. I saw a few men working on puzzles that day, but I can't say which one did this."

James looked back down at the paper. "When did this happen?"

I told him. "Maybe there's a connection between the house and my mother, Eve Foster." When he looked at me quizzically, I waved away his unspoken questions. "This house has a history, James. Something happened here, I can feel it in my gut. I can't help but wonder if Amy's death and whoever wrote 'little red house' in the puzzle are connected."

James didn't look convinced. "One thing's clear—you can't stay here."

I opened the cabinet above the sink and took out the bottle of vodka, the good one, the one I saved for crises. I poured a glass for myself. "Join me."

"No, thanks."

"You're not on duty."

"After this conversation, I think I may need to go back to see if I can help identify that woman."

I nodded, took a swig. It stung my mouth and throat going down, so I took another. Finished it and repoured.

"You need to go somewhere else for now. If you're right and there's a connection, you could be next."

"I'm not leaving."

"Someone was taunting you with this puzzle. Or worse, warning you."

I picked up the paper and took it back to my room. I didn't want to look at those even red letters anymore. From there, I went into the bathroom and splashed cold water on my face. He was right, of course, but that didn't mean I would leave.

Back in the kitchen, I opened the box and took a slice of cold pizza. "Want one?"

"Connie, you know you can't stay here. And pretending like nothing is wrong isn't going to solve anything."

I downed a gulp of vodka, chased it with a mouthful of beer, and then took a bite of the pizza. It was greasy and heavy and I immediately regretted it. I took another gulp of beer to get rid of the taste.

"Connie—"

"Fuck, James, *this* is *my* house. It's all I have. I'm not running." My mind shifted to Eve, to all those nights in cities across the globe, to her mind-fuck games and her cruel competitions and her red fucking slash of a mean mouth. To strangers' beds and hunger pangs and raw, gnawing fear and loneliness. "No one's chasing me away."

He shook his head, grabbed my wrists gently, and looked down into my eyes with that do-gooder gaze. The concern and kindness threatened to drown me in a tsunami of emotion. It was too fucking much. It was all too fucking much. I twisted my wrists away. He opened his mouth to say something else, and I shoved my body against his. I kissed him, hard, reaching for his belt buckle. I'd never fucked a cop before.

"*Connie.*"

"Shut up." I pulled off my shirt, started to unbutton his. "Please, James, just shut up."

We did it there, on my kitchen table, my legs wrapped around his tight torso, his body pounding away at the fear and loneliness and anger. When we were finished, he lingered in my kitchen, those soft baby-brown eyes a little unfocused, a little confused. I wanted him to stay for the night, maybe for longer. But I let him go—back out into the darkness of Nihla.

CHAPTER

38

Constance Foster
Nihla, New Mexico—Present

Becky Smith woke me from another shitty dream at seven thirty the next morning. She had to repeat her name three times before I remembered who she was. Squat woman, muddy knees. Her uncle was the former assistant district attorney. "I kept my word. Josiah's lucid," she said. "And he's willing to see you."

I sat up. "Yeah, sure . . . when can I come over?"

"You have a window now, I'm afraid. I have no idea how long it will last or whether he'll change his mind when you get here."

"Got it." I hopped out of bed, pulling jeans on while I cradled my phone with my shoulder and chin. "Leaving now. I'll be there in twenty or so."

I hung up, brushed my teeth, and threw on a shirt. My head was pounding from last night's booze. After James left, I'd drowned my worries in a few more shots before succumbing to a restless night's sleep. Now I regretted the vodka, but not James.

I called him from the car. Right to voice mail. I hung up—I'd try him later.

It took me fifteen minutes to get to the Smith residence. I found the front door open and Becky and her uncle sitting in a claustrophobic living room that smelled faintly of Bengay and cat urine. Becky waved me in. She was curled up on a navy blue couch, a cat on her lap. An elderly man was reclining on a matching easy chair. The man had his eyes open. His mouth was working, but no words were coming out. Stacks of books and papers covered every surface, including most of the beige-carpeted floor. Clean clutter. A silver tabby greeted me with a firm rub and a loud yowl.

"That's Cookie," Becky said. "His sister is hiding under the table. She's scared of people. And this is Princess." She stroked the orange cat on her lap. "They're our babies."

"Your babies," the man growled.

I bent down and petted the cat, feeling all five sets of eyes staring at me.

"Uncle Joe, this is the woman I told you about," Becky said loudly, over-enunciating her words. "Here, you can sit on the couch." She moved a pile of old photo albums, patted the cushion, and I took the seat, uncomfortably close to her. "Uncle Joe is partially deaf, so—"

"I hear just fine."

"Funny," Becky snapped. "Then you must be ignoring me most of the time."

The man on the recliner gave a harrumph and closed his eyes. He was all bones and sinew, with an island of white hair and the rough, ruddy complexion of an alcoholic.

"Iced tea?" Becky asked.

"She doesn't want iced tea."

"Mr. Smith," I said. "I was hoping to talk to you about what happened here in Nihla. Back in the nineties."

One watery red eye opened and gave me a sideways once-over. "Leave," the man said to his niece. Then in a kinder voice, "Go outside, Becky. Have some fun in your garden. I know you like that."

Becky rose dutifully and left. When she was gone, Josiah pulled the recliner into a sitting position and turned to face me. "Don't think she does this out of the kindness of her wilted heart. I pay for this place. She had nowhere to live after her bastard of a husband left, so she stays with me. It's a fair exchange—my care for a roof over her head. Distasteful for both of us. I have to deal with her hovering and her godforsaken cats and this mess, and she . . . well, she has to deal with me." He coughed into a handkerchief. "Sometimes life is about distasteful trade-offs."

I was surprised by the strength of his voice. He didn't seem like the same man Becky had described. "You know about distasteful trade-offs."

He smiled. "Smart girl. These days I'm supposed to say 'woman.'" He shook his head, wiped a rheumy eye. "Can't call a person black or Chinese or gay. Everyone is so sensitive. People are who they are. Since when did descriptions become a bad thing?"

I wasn't about to go down that rabbit hole with this guy. "You were the prosecutor who oversaw the case against Norton Small-wood and Mark LeBron."

"Is that a statement or a question?"

"A statement."

His nod was barely perceptible. He closed his eyes again, shut-ting me out. It seemed he was very good at blocking out the world when it suited him. How much of his illness was real—and how much was façade? For how long would I have his attention—until he got bored?

"They were innocent," I said. "The real killer got away."

"*Killers*. More than one."

I let that sink in. "You seem certain."

"I don't know if his partner was a murderer, but I can say with certainty that he had help."

I was confused. "If you knew they were innocent, why pros-ecute LeBron and Smallwood? Why ruin their lives?"

Silence, another phlegmy cough.

"You knew and you did nothing. You let two innocent men rot away in prison."

He sat up straighter, glared at me. "No, I didn't know anything for certain. I knew the evidence was thin. I knew these were bad men. I knew society would be better off if they were put away—"

"That wasn't your judgment to make."

"Norton was a pervert."

"According to his wife, he was a churchgoing volunteer fire-fighter with a family."

"He had a stash of underage porn in his truck. Nasty stuff."

I cocked my head. "His porn—or porn someone planted?"

Josiah made a guttural noise in the back of this throat.

I said, "While they were jailed, the real killer—or killers—remained at large."

"It's my one regret."

I said, "What is?"

"That the killers walked away unscathed. I have to live with that every day."

"So you do know who they are."

Silence.

I said, "Why didn't you do something back then?"

His face reddened. "That's the problem with your generation. You see things as cut and dried, right and wrong. That's not how the world works."

"I know," I said. "Distasteful trade-offs."

He gave me a twisted, bitter smile. "Sit over there and be holier than thou. I can tell you've never worked a day in your life. Some of us have faced hard choices. You have no idea what it was to walk in my shoes."

"Enlighten me."

Josiah studied me. His eyes suddenly widened. I saw a hint of fear. "You look like her."

"Like who?"

He shook his head, sighed. "Nothing good will come of you being here. You should leave. Go back to wherever you come from and let this go."

"Let *what* go? The murders?"

"They're still out there." Then, in a weaker voice, "You can't stop this."

His eyes were losing their spark. I stood, hoping to catch his attention before he drifted off into whatever other world he mostly lived in. "Mr. Smith," I barked. "Why did you agree to see me?"

His head toggled to the right. I walked around his recliner, forcing him to look at me. "You can get this off your chest. Now, here. Make a difference. Just tell me . . . what do you know? Why did you agree to see me?"

"She was kind," he said. "Pretty, too. She didn't deserve it."

"Who is she?"

"There are more," he said. "It wasn't her fault. There are more."

"More what? Women? Victims? Murderers? You're not making sense."

I knew I was yelling, but I didn't care. I heard Becky open the front door. I said, "I understand you have regrets, but help me understand. Who is she—and what are there more of?"

But he was already gone. Those watery eyes were closed, his mouth wide open. My chest felt weighted, heavy, my own breath coming in painful gasps. Who the fuck was *she*, and what were there more of? I was so close to understanding some clue to this goddamn place. So close—and once again, nothing.

"Bodies," Becky whispered behind me. She said it the way you would mention the name of the monster under the bed. Carefully, timidly. "There are more bodies out there."

I spun around. "How do you know that's what he meant?"

"Because he talks in his sleep. He mumbles about girls disappearing. He's done it for months. Ever since . . . ever since the murders started here again." Her smile was apologetic. "He thinks there are more victims. He blames himself."

"And the 'she'? Did he say who that was while he was sleep talking?"

"No," Becky said. Her knees were clean, but she picked at them anyway. "But I know who he was referring to."

"Tell me."

"She was the only woman I remember him actually caring about when I was young."

"Who is she, Becky? Whom is he talking about?" *Who do I look like?*

"Who *was* she, you mean. Her name was Flora Fuentes. She was murdered in Nihla over twenty years ago."

*   *   *

Underneath the vast expanse of desert, the dusty, forlorn downtown, the despair that seeped from the sidewalks, underneath the unrelenting red sun, there was beauty in Nihla. I saw it in the distant mountains, their rugged peaks reaching out to an unobtainable sky. I saw it in the way Manuela's customers rallied around her. I saw it in Stella-from-the-hardware-store's maternal concern, and I felt it in James's kiss.

I did not find it in Josiah Smith. In Josiah, I found an ugly coward. He was both a cause and a symptom of all that was wrong in Nihla.

My conversation with Josiah stayed with me the remainder of the day. I couldn't get the thought of those two men, Smallwood and LeBron, out of my head. Why would a town knowingly sacrifice people to protect a killer—or killers? Was it the ridiculous notion that their kids would somehow be spared, like James had said? Or were the actual killers just too slick or too powerful to be caught, and rather than admit defeat, the powers that once were chose scapegoats? I may never know.

And who the hell was Flora Fuentes?

That afternoon, during my break at work, I called James again. Still no response—right to voice mail. I was beginning to worry. Every time the door opened to the diner, I looked up, half expecting it to be him. From the little I knew of him, it seemed he was too much of a perfectionist at his job to turn off his phone for so long, and he'd been planning to follow up on the identity of the woman who'd been murdered. I wanted to know if it was Amy's body, but more than that, I wanted to hear his voice. My second call went to Alberto. Voice mail again. I left him a message about Flora Fuentes, and I asked him for an update on Jet.

It was after eight when I pulled into my driveway. The sun had set, and the full moon cast shadows on the property. Jet's lights were on—both in his little house and in the workshop—but my house was buttoned up tight. I unlocked the door and made my way to the kitchen. My hand was around the vodka bottle when my cell phone rang. Lisa. I slid the bottle back in the cupboard and answered the call.

"Hey," Lisa said. "What are you doing?"

"You're taking something again. I hear it in your voice."

"Nothing I shouldn't be." She sighed. "Dave picked up my prescription. Just some tranquilizers for nerves." In a lower volume, she said, "Cook is quitting. She gave notice today."

I sat down at the table. Without Cook, Lisa would be practically alone in that huge house.

"Are you okay with that?"

"Not really. What do I know about hiring a new cook? And the house is . . . well, I don't need to tell you. It's big."

It was big, big enough to house three families comfortably. Big enough to lose your mind. "Why don't you sell the house, Lisa?" I said. "Sell it and move to something smaller and more manageable. Something that doesn't have the . . . memories."

"Am I even allowed to sell it?"

"I don't recall the lawyer saying you can't."

But Lisa had already lost interest in the subject. She said, "My God, Constance, I miss you. I'm like a ghost wandering these damn halls. I guess Aunt Eve got her wish after all."

"What do you mean?"

"To get me all to herself. We're just two ghosts now, rattling around this monstrosity of a house, as pathetic as we were in life."

"Stop talking like that." Then, softer, "I miss you. You're not alone. You have Dave there, and the gardener, and I'm always watching out for you. Remember that. Just like . . . like when we were little."

"Yes, I know."

"But listen to me, okay? You can't continue like this. You're driving yourself crazy. Ask Dave to help you. Call the lawyer if you must, find a realtor. Without Cook, that's too much house." Even with Cook, it was too much house. *And you have no idea how to cook*, I thought. Lisa was a poor eater on good days; without someone prodding her to eat, she'd waste away. "Move."

"I found the key to the basement padlock," she said. "The noises. I want them to stop."

The noises again. She was imagining things. All that house, all that time. It was too much for my sister. "Just go to a hotel, Lisa. Get out of the house and stay somewhere clean and quiet for a while, okay?"

"I have a plan. Check your mail. I sent it to the P.O. box. Promise?"

"Lisa—"

"Her jewelry," she whispered. "It's not traceable. I've been squirreling it into a safe deposit box in Burlington. Soon there will be enough . . . enough for us to go somewhere together."

"Lisa, we don't need to do that—"

"I want you to have a key, too. In case." She took an audible breath. "In case something happens to me." Something clattered to the floor, and she muttered *damn*. In a more resolute voice, she said, "I'm resourceful. I can handle this. You and Eve always thought I was weak. Strong, able Connie and weak, silly Lisa. Well, I'll show you both. I can do this."

She hung up. I called her back and no one answered. I called Cook and Dave and left messages for both to check in on my sister. She needed to be out of that house, but with Eve's stupid rules, there wasn't much I could do to force her hand. I was certain Lisa was right. Split us up. Let the money divide us. I could go without—hadn't I for years?—but Lisa was used to a certain lifestyle. Eve had made sure of that. Walking away from a fortune wasn't something my sister would do, so she'd rot in that fucking house, a madwoman haunted by imaginary sounds in the basement and what could have been.

My phone buzzed again. This time it was Alberto.

I said, "What do you have for me?"

"Whoa there. Who says I have anything?"

"You never call me just to chat."

Alberto laughed. "I wish I was just calling to chat. No fun being the bearer of bad news."

"Isn't that basically your occupation—to be the bearer of bad news?" I joked, but I could feel the tension in my temples. Whatever Alberto had to say, it couldn't make things much worse.

"That name you left on my voice mail, Flora Fuentes. I didn't have to look her up because I remember her. She died back in the nineties."

I stood, walked to the window. "Another victim?"

"Unclear. Her body was found in a house fire over by the original Jack's Place. Incinerated, so authorities couldn't tell whether she'd died in the fire or whether she'd been killed first and her body left behind. The fire took the house she was in and some of the original bar, too."

"Whose house was it?"

"Belonged to the bar owner. A man named John Cozbi. Went by—you guessed it—Jack. He denied knowing anything about it, though. Claimed the house was vacant, had been for years, and that whoever was in there was in there illegally."

"Was it arson?"

"Possibly. The reports were inconclusive."

Convenient. "Then she *may* have been another victim."

"The cops and the DA tried to pin her death on LeBron and Smallwood, but it didn't stick. No evidence whatsoever connecting them." He paused. "The real tragedy was her kids."

"Her kids?"

"She had two daughters, about two at the time. Their bodies weren't with her in the fire, so no one knows what happened to them."

"Twins?" Twins, like Lisa and me.

"Yes."

A wave of foreboding went through me. The items I found in my basement. The crosses, the clothes. "They lived here, didn't they? This Flora Fuentes and her daughters."

Another pause. "Your house was once her house. When she died and the children disappeared, it eventually went up for auction. A corporation purchased it."

"The name of the corporation?"

"Hold on, let me see . . . Apex Burton. A realty subsidiary of—"

"Foster Enterprises."

"How did you know?"

"That's my mother's company. *Was* my mother's company, anyway. So she bought this property at auction. But why?"

Alberto said, "I can't answer that, Connie. I can tell you that Flora's death weighed on the town. She was well liked. She was here illegally, and some believed her family or the kids' father kidnapped the daughters. Others think they were victims, their little bodies still buried somewhere in Nihla."

Josiah's insistence that there were more bodies. I tried to wrap my mind around what Alberto was telling me. Another possible victim, twin girls, the house bought at auction. I closed my eyes and saw and felt colors. A flash of a twisted red smile. A blood-red orb in the distance. The searing red pain of burned flesh. There was something there, something just beyond my reach, but I couldn't figure out what.

Could we be the twins? Could that be the connection?

Eyes still closed, I said, "What could this all have to do with Eve?"

Alberto's response was slow in coming. "One of the people who disappeared in Nihla, whose body was never found, was Kelsey Foster."

"Eve's daughter."

Alberto said, "Maybe Flora was helping Eve find her kidnapper. Maybe that's the reason you're looking for."

I considered Alberto's theory. Eve had given me the house that once belonged to a dead woman—in the town where Kelsey had disappeared—as homage? "That makes no sense."

"I never said any of this made sense."

"How about the father? Who was the girls' father?"

"A man named Kyle Summers. He disappeared, too."

"Fueling the belief that he took the kids."

"Right." Another beat. "Or that he had something to do with the murders."

"Is that what you believe?"

Alberto hesitated. "I remember Summers. Brother-in-law of the judge who presided over the murder trials. Buddy-buddy with the lead detective."

"You're dancing around my question."

"Summers conveniently disappeared after Flora died. Was he bereft at the loss of his family, or was something more sinister going on? I don't know."

"But you have an opinion."

"Yeah, I do." He sighed. "Look, Connie, from what people are telling me, back then, Nihla was infected by nepotism and graft. Everyone owed Judge Leroux—not hard to figure out why. He did favors behind the scenes. A DUI would disappear, a kid would get probation instead of juvie, an abused wife would be denied a restraining order, child porn would be conveniently lost. And Summers owned half the properties in Nihla. He was landlord, employer, church usher. Together they were a formidable force. And then one day Summers was gone."

"And the murders stopped."

"And the murders stopped happening in Nihla for over twenty years."

But they've begun again—the words he didn't have to say. I had a lot to ponder. Alberto's information held the ring of truth. I had known there had to be a link between Eve and this house, and the fact that it had once belonged to this Flora Fuentes was the nexus I was looking for. It didn't really explain why she'd left the house to me, but Kelsey's death and Flora's possible help following her disappearance explained at least some of it. Perhaps she'd bought it out of gratitude, or for the connection to her daughter. Maybe she was trying to make amends after her death. My mind flashed to the two crosses. Maybe there was something more.

One way or another, I had some names to work with. Flora Fuentes. Kyle Summers. Perhaps I could even track down Jack Cozbi if he was still alive. I thanked Alberto.

"Don't thank me yet," he said. "That's not the only reason I called."

I opened the window, in need of air. Despite the hour, I could hear Jet working away in the shop—his machines grinding away at something or other. Lightning flashed in the distance, and I watched it snake to the ground.

I said, "Go on."

"Jetson's records are sealed, which is weird, because he wasn't a juvenile. This tells me there was something serious in there."

"Or that he has friends in high places." *Like Eve.*

"Maybe. Anyway, this bothered me. And because I had nothing else to do—that's a joke, in case you were wondering—I dug a little further. Nothing. No online history, no social media, no college alumni listings. Weird, I thought. I called a buddy from this guy's hometown. Asked him to do some asking around. Anyway, I finally got a hit. Megan's Law."

"The sex offender rule?"

"Yeah. Every state has a version, especially when it comes to the public notification part. He's listed as an offender."

Jet was a sex offender? I sat down, hard. I wish I could have said I was surprised, but I wasn't. I knew there was something odd about him, about his relationship with Eve. The very fact that she chose him meant he was willing to do her bidding, and in my experience, desperate people were most likely to do Eve's dirty work—for a price.

"Do you know what he did?"

"No. I only know he's registered. If I had to guess, I'd say he came to Nihla looking for a quiet place to disappear. Normal life can be hard for sex offenders. There is no absolution."

And there was no peace for the victims—or their families. "Thanks, Alberto. I appreciate the help."

"Now will you let it go? Fire that asshole and maybe even get the hell out of New Mexico?" His phone beeped, and he asked me to hold. When he came back on, he said, "Sorry. No more questions, okay? I've already finished my volunteer hours, and I gotta go. That cop who crashed. Shitty night for him. Anyway, duty calls."

I sat up straighter. "Cop who crashed?"

"Yeah, yeah. Young guy. High as a rocket, or so I heard. Happened late last night down your way, and I just got word that he's still in critical condition."

"What's his name?" I asked slowly, although deep down, I knew the answer.

"James Riley. Why?"

James, who left here sober. James, who refused my offer of a drink. James, who was asking questions around the station. James, who did nothing wrong but try to help me.

"I gotta go," I said.

"Are you alright, Connie?"

"I just have to go."

After I hung up, I looked down to see blood trickling across my forearm. I'd been clutching my skin so hard that my nails had ripped through flesh. *James.* A crash. My fault. I'd gotten him into this.

First Amy, now James.

Someone in Nihla was still worried about these murders, and now an innocent man was taking the hit.

CHAPTER

39

Eve Foster
Nihla, New Mexico—1997

EVE WATCHED AS Flora locked the front door of Kyle's house and made her way down the stone path. It was nearly seven, and the sun was just starting to set, bathing the cacti and yucca in the desert beyond his house in a golden halo. Behind the fence that surrounded Kyle's backyard, that desert stretched to the horizon, giving Eve the feeling of eternity, of timelessness—a feeling, she knew, that was deceptive. Time was quickly running out. If she didn't find Kelsey soon, she may never know what happened to her daughter.

Flora was clutching a paper bag to her chest with one arm while carrying a grocery bag with the other. A bruise had blossomed along her forearm, and it peeked out like an algae bloom from beneath a cheap pink blouse. Her shoulders were hunched, and her head was cast down toward the ground. She seemed broken and submissive, a frightened mole of a woman scurrying from a place she didn't belong. Eve took no satisfaction in her pain, although Flora was proof that her theory was right: Kyle wasn't the man he pretended to be.

Flora placed the bags into the trunk of her car, then climbed behind the wheel. Her blouse had hiked up in the back, and she tugged it down, looking around anxiously as she did so. She put her head against the wheel momentarily before starting the car.

Eve placed her binoculars on the seat beside her and patted the top of her dark wig. A glance in the rearview mirror confirmed the success of her disguise. No police tail. The town thought she had left. Poised, polished Eve Foster *was* gone, replaced with a woman even Eve barely recognized. Nevertheless, she would wait a few moments before heading out behind Flora. She needed to seem natural, and in a neighborhood as quiet as this, a person used to being wary might notice a stranger in her midst.

Abused women needed to be wary. They learned to read others in ways normal people with normal lives would never understand. Eve certainly understood. And she'd use that understanding to her advantage.

*   *   *

Flora's destination was a small, rectangular building on the outskirts of town. It sat alone, a rundown, forsaken box an eighth of a mile from the highway. Scrubby ghost plants dotted the dusty rock garden lining the exterior. Diesel fumes permeated the air. A sign attached to a chain-link fence announced "Gerta's Daycare," the "D" scribbled out and replaced by a spray-painted "G." Behind the fence, a half dozen Big Wheels and a sandbox sat amid a scattering of brightly colored pails and shovels. A single pink sock had been draped over the edge of the fence, its once white lacy trim stained brown.

There was nowhere for Eve to park unobtrusively, so she drove past the daycare and turned around, idling on the side of the road while she waited for Flora to emerge.

Gerta's Daycare. Either Flora had a second job, or she had a kid.

It didn't take long to figure out which. Twenty minutes later, Flora emerged. She held a child by the hand and another in her arms. Two little girls: one tiny and blonde, the other taller and dark-haired like her mom. Unless one belonged to someone else, they were too close in age to be anything but twins. The blonde one had her arms wrapped tightly around Flora's shoulder. The other one was trying to run ahead on stubby toddler legs. Eve adjusted the binoculars, her heart racing.

Finally, she had leverage.

Flora opened the back of her car, seemingly oblivious to the stranger watching her from a distance. She put the blonde in the car and reached for the hand of the wilder brunette, who pulled away and darted into the street. Flora grabbed her arm, but the child stood in the street with her shoulders back and her feet planted firmly on the ground. Eve was about to put the binoculars down when she caught the toddler looking her way. Dark eyes, stormy with intelligence even at her tender age. Full mouth set in a half scream, ready with an id-fueled opinion. She would be a handful one day. She was probably a handful now. Like Kelsey.

Eve knew she was too far away for the child to see her, but the way the little girl was staring made Eve feel like she *could* see her. Could see *through* her. Eve felt suddenly exposed, naked. Judged.

Judged and found wanting.

40

Constance Foster
Nihla, New Mexico—Present

THE RUMBLE OF thunder echoed the pounding in my chest. I couldn't breathe. In all the situations Eve had put me in, somehow this felt the worst. Maybe because I didn't know what the rules were. Maybe because I had started to have real feelings for James. Maybe because I was just plain terrified.

I searched for the names and numbers of local hospitals. I called one after another, but no one would tell me anything. I tried James's station house, but all they would do was confirm that James had been in an accident. They wanted my name and number. I refused to give them, worried the wrong cops would show up asking questions.

Thunder boomed, and flashes of lightning hit ground in the distance. I wanted the cold, wet, cleansing beat of drops against my skin. But this was an impotent storm. All noise and flash, but no rain.

I threw my head back, feeling hopeless and helpless and angry. I tried calling Alberto back but reached his voice mail. I was about to call the station again when I remembered the name of the man James said he trusted. Derek. I should be able to figure out who that was easily enough. James had said he was a cop, too. Fifteen minutes of mad scrambling on my computer gave me the name Derek Pressman. Another fifteen minutes and I'd found his home phone number. A woman answered on the third ring. She sounded tired, as though I'd awakened her.

"I'm looking for Derek Pressman," I said.

"May I ask who is calling?" Clipped, wary tone.

My mind shuffled for an excuse. I landed on, "This is Nora, a grief counselor with the state."

"Oh, yes, yes, because of James. Derek is still reeling. In fact, he's at the hospital now."

I perked up, wanting badly to know which hospital, but before I could ask, she said, "Baby's crying. Quick, give me your number and I promise I'll have him call you back. He could use the help. Something like this, wow . . . it'll stay with him."

I gave her my cell, and we both hung up; I lowered my head, stretched my arms, forced myself to think. I poured a glass of vodka, thought better of it, and downed it anyway. It stung my throat, and I swallowed another, mulling over what Alberto had told me. Flora, an illegal immigrant who died mysteriously in a fire. Two babies. This house.

And Jet. Fucking Jet, with his fake overtures of friendship. That cross he'd hung on my wall. The bloodstains on the floor of his workshop. His body in my bed—warm, comforting, strong. Jet, Eve's puppet. Or worse.

I downed one more glass of booze before storming out the door toward Jet's house. A flash of lightning lit my path as I sprinted between buildings. The machine had stopped whirring, but I could hear him in there, whistling while he worked. Fucking *whistling*. I wondered if he had fucked Eve. Had they been lovers at some point, screwing in my little house and cooking up a plan to drive me crazy? Gaslighting would be right up her alley, with Jet as her sex-offender accomplice.

To think I'd trusted him.

The door was open, so I ran in, breathless, blood full of lye and outrage.

"You motherfucker. How could you?" I ran toward him, arms outstretched. His face was buried in the shadows, but the dim light from an overhead bulb reflected in his eyes. I saw shock and fear.

"Connie!" He darted backward and grabbed my wrist, pulling me tight against him so I couldn't move. "What the hell are you doing?"

I struggled to get my hand loose from his grip. He pushed me back, keeping my wrists in an iron grip.

"Connie, please. Talk to me."

"You lied to me. What'd she do, pay someone a million dollars to expunge your record? Why?" I could feel reality slipping away, a life raft of reason drifting into darkness on choppy waves. I saw my friend from Corfu so many years ago, his terror in the water. I saw Lisa's face, tear-stained and terrorized after being locked in the basement. I was ready to raise the white flag. I couldn't win. Even from beyond the grave, she hated me enough to make me miserable. My vision blurred, I felt faint.

I had no one.

I stopped struggling. Jet bent down and looked into my eyes. "I can explain if you give me the chance." He let go of my wrists and led me to a stool that sat by itself, away from anything that could be a weapon. He pushed me down gently. I let my head rest against the wall, tried to control my breathing.

"I don't know what you think you know about me, but there was no record to expunge. No real record, anyway." He pulled up another stool. "I was twelve when my dad was locked up, fifteen when my mom OD'd. The courts sent me to live with my grandfather, a mean, racist asshole who preferred a bottle of gin to a day's work. No surprise that my teen years were littered with petty crimes and drugs."

I breathed deeply, calming myself, and watched him, looking for signs that he was lying. Shifting eyes, rapid breathing, nervous gestures. But he was speaking to me calmly, firmly, like I was a child or a hyperactive puppy. I didn't trust my instincts. I just listened.

"A local teacher stepped in to help me. Taught me woodworking, helped me get my GED. I was still angry and confused, but I had some direction. The day I turned eighteen, I went out with friends to celebrate. The night ended in a fight outside a bar. Got beat up pretty bad." He ran a hand through his hair, frowned. "I was pissing blood into a bush outside the bar when the cops arrived. Caught me with my pants down, literally. I'd been a pain in the ass to them for years, and now they had me."

"I don't understand."

"My juvenile record was sealed as an adult. But where I'm from, pissing in a public place can be considered indecent exposure."

"I still don't get it."

"Public urination can be charged as a sex crime. And that's exactly what those jackasses did. They charged me with assault and battery and indecent exposure, along with a host of other stupid shit, but the exposure charge stuck. I was eighteen, an adult, and branded a sex criminal."

"What does Eve have to do with any of this?"

Jet was silent. He stood up, walked to the piece of wood he'd been sanding and ran a finger along the smooth edge. He was wearing a dirty sweatshirt, and he used the sleeve to wipe away dust. His touch was light, reverent. Would someone like that defile his workshop with violence? I didn't know. I didn't know anything anymore.

Finally, he said, "She had the charges erased from my record. Is that what you want to hear? I met her in Memphis. She was there on company business, or so she said. We had a drink together, I had a few too many and shared my woes. I was twenty-five, poor, and still angry. She offered me a deal."

"She wanted you to mess with me."

He spun around. "This had nothing to do with you. She had a house she needed a caretaker for. I needed a new life, some privacy. She let me fix up the outbuildings, do what I wanted, paid me a good sum, and in return—"

"You sold your soul."

"I signed her silly contract." He reached up and gave the bulb a twist, wincing when he touched the hot glass. "A year after I started, she told me she'd had my record cleared, got rid of any public mention of me. The Megan's Law stuff is still out there, nothing either of us could do about that, but she did the rest on her own."

"You owed her loyalty. But what about the cash?" I asked. "That's a shit ton of cash for a caretaker to earn."

"Cash?" His face contorted. "You've been snooping."

"When I first came here, I looked around. I do own the property."

His jaw tightened. "Based on the rules Eve set down, this is mine to use. You were trespassing."

"Look at it from my perspective. I was given a rundown house that came with a caretaker I couldn't fire. Wouldn't you want to know who you were living with?" I waited until the color had receded from him face. "Just tell me why you have so much cash. And why there are blood stains in the workshop."

"Blood?" He looked at me questioningly. "Cash, yes. Blood, no."

I stood, feeling wobbly, and walked to the spot where I'd seen the stains. I pointed, but the light toward the back of the workshop was too dark to see. I pulled my phone from my pocket and flicked on the flashlight, pointing it downward. "See?"

He squatted, his gaze on the wooden boards. "I'll be damned. Never noticed that." He glanced up at me, his eyes searching mine. "I'm not lying, Connie. This had nothing to do with me."

"How do you explain the money?"

"Just savings. I don't need much here. All my rent and utilities are covered. Only food and business expenses. The rest I squirrel away. That plus the earnings from my furniture, and I'm set."

Reluctantly, I nodded. He did live frugally, that was evident, and if he'd hoarded the cash over the years, it would have added up. I traced a finger along the stains. "What do you think happened here?"

When I looked up, Jet was staring toward the main house. He seemed unnerved.

"What's wrong?"

Focus still on my house, he said, "When I first came, Eve told me to stay out of the shotgun house. She wanted it preserved just the way it was. I always wondered why, but I was young and grateful and scared she'd fire me, so I complied."

I knew this already. "What are you saying?"

He shrugged. "Just that looking back, it was a strange request. Why would you hire a caretaker whose job it is to let a house fall into disrepair?"

I had wondered that, too. "Unless you wanted to hide something," I said, the pieces clicking together in my mind. "What better way to keep something secure than to hire a guard to watch over it? No looters, no curious kids." I rose, the shaking in my voice matching the quiver in my hand. The basement—an afterthought with a dirt floor. "Do you have a shovel?"

"Yeah, why?"

"Can I borrow it?" I spotted it against the wall at the back of the shop. I climbed my way over his equipment to grab it before heading back out into the night. The rain was coming down in sheets now, a quick desert storm, and I let the pounding drops wash away some of my fear.

"Where are you going?" Jet called.

I didn't answer him. I wasn't going anywhere. Not just yet, anyway.

*　　*　　*

The basement was hot and dusty and full of things that crawled and scuttled. We'd emptied most of the junk, so I stared at an expanse of packed-down dirt. The liquid courage had long since left my system, and I was running on pure adrenaline. But it was enough.

The ground beneath me barely moved under the shovel. Each stab gave forth tablespoons of dirt, but I persisted, venom running through my veins. This house had secrets, and I was going to make her give them up. Sweat trickled down my neck and between my breasts. My breath came in chunky gasps, and my hair had escaped from its holder and hung against my face in wet clumps. I looked, I was sure, like the madwoman Eve had wanted me to become.

My phone rang. I ignored it.

I had cleared about two square feet of soil, six inches deep, when I heard footsteps behind me. Jet joined me in the basement, another shovel in his hands, Micah beside him. Silently, he began digging. We worked like that for what felt like hours—the rain pounding outside, the cracks of thunder, and our heavy breathing. My arms were sore, my back burning, but we kept digging.

Around eleven, Micah became excited. She scratched at the ground, her tail waving furiously. We increased our speed, encouraged by the dog's agitation. After midnight my shovel hit something hard. I stopped, looked at Jet. He shoveled beside me, carefully digging around whatever it was.

"Oh, man," he said under his breath. We could both see something poking through the dirt. Micah whined and pawed at the object. "Micah, no." To me, "Smell that? It's subtle, but there."

All I could smell was musty air and my own sour sweat.

I took another shovel full of dirt and the bony shape of human fingers began to emerge. On my hands and knees, I started to dig dirt away from the bones, exposing more skeletal remains. Jet knelt down next to me, his face a stony fortress.

"Connie, stop."

I kept digging, my fingernails ripped to bloody shreds. My phone rang again; again I ignored it. I scraped dirt away from the remains, ran my sore hands through the disgusting dirt, but just as quickly, the sandy soil slid back into place. I worked harder, faster, uncovering more bones. Micah whined, gave out a sharp bark. The remains of a foot came into view. Then the curved top of a skull. I could see another hand emerging, this one larger, longer, its macabre wrist still encircled by a gold bracelet. The smell had reached me. Sweet and rotten: the calling card of death.

"They're layered under here," Jet whispered. "Just bones. God knows how many there are."

I kept digging.

"Connie, you need to stop. This is a crime scene." He glanced around nervously, his hand in his pocket. "Shit, shit, shit."

"We'll call the police, but not now. Just help me dig."

Jet shook his head.

"The walls," I said. The funky basement walls. "It's bothered me . . . the way this basement was built. What basement is smaller than the house foundation? And you said so yourself: most houses around here don't even have basements. Especially not a little shotgun thing like this."

Jet wiped his hands on his pants, rubbed the sweat from his forehead with the back of a hand. "What are you getting at?"

I took the shovel and swung it at the wall, knocking myself down with the effort.

"Here, let me."

Jet dug into the wall with the point of the shovel. It broke surprisingly easily. He swung again and again. I joined him, tearing away at the façade with the tip of my shovel as quickly as my tired body allowed. We finally reached the foundation. And a door.

"What the hell? Connie, please stop. Please. Look, we need to talk—"

I wasn't listening. My mind jumped to the kitchen layout. The patched-up spot behind the refrigerator. The old refrigerator I hadn't had the courage or will to clean. I climbed the steps to the outside two at a time, shovel in hand. The rain had stopped but the wind had picked up, and bits of scrub whipped my face as I pushed my way into the house. I shoved aside the refrigerator and stared at that patch on the wall. I aimed the shovel at it. When that didn't work, I pulled a butcher knife from the drawer and started hacking away at the wall, twisting and prying until I had pulled away some of the drywall. Blood streaked the wall from my broken nails and injured fingertips. I didn't care. I just wanted to find whatever was underneath.

I wedged my fingers behind the small opening and pulled. I did it again, and again, and again, until finally it came away enough to see behind. Another boarded up door. Someone had gone to a lot of trouble to hide this stairwell.

Someone had gone to a lot of trouble to add a basement. The bodies explained why.

I felt a presence behind me. I spun around in time to see Jet, standing close, pointing a pistol at my face. Micah was beside him, but she glanced back and forth between us, whining.

"You fucking bastard. I knew it. You *are* with her."

"Stop, it, Connie." He waved the gun. "I'm not with her, and I'm not going to shoot you. I just wanted to get your goddamn attention."

Eyeing the gun, I said, "Well, you have it."

"Those are bones, human bones, in case you didn't notice. Lots of them."

"No kidding."

"You just got here, but I've been living here for years. *Years.* And like I told you, I have a record. Expunged or not, you know the government can find out all sorts of shit on a person." He threw his head back, moaned. "I want to help you, I really do, but this is sick. I can't afford to have cops nosing around. I can't get caught up in all that again."

I wiped my forehead with the back of my hand, eyed the gun. "You're afraid they'll suspect you."

Jet's nod was barely perceptible. "I didn't do it, but they'll look at me first. You know they will."

He was right, of course. Ex-con living in a remote area alone. Lots of hidden cash. Blood-stained floorboards. Missing women and girls.

I said, "Put the gun away."

Jet looked from the dog to me to the gun. His resolve was wavering, I could see it in his eyes. My earlier anger and panic had subsided, and I was left feeling exhausted and annoyed. Even if it hadn't been for Jet's pleas, how could we call the local cops? Not after what James had told me. Not after what had happened to James. I needed a better plan.

Jet tucked the gun into his pocket.

I said, "All right, I get it. But we can't sit on this for long. Covering up a crime scene is a crime, and I'm not going to prison for Eve."

"Then what?"

"Derek," I said.

"Derek?"

"James's friend. He's a cop. James said he's trustworthy." He eyed me questioningly and I gave him a quick recount of my time with James. "It's all we have."

Jet didn't look convinced.

I eyed my newly destroyed wall, thought about the bodies in the basement. How could I sleep here tonight, knowing what was underneath my floor? They had to be tied to the serial killings, to Flora Fuentes and Kyle Summers and Kelsey Foster. If the murderer—or murderers—had buried bodies here then, would they be back now? Amy's murder, so close to my house, said the connection remained. What other bodies had been left behind in this house of horrors? Had they been killed here, tortured? The bloodstains in the workshop . . . the fact that there were only bones in the basement. Had someone used the shop to kill the victims, dissolve the flesh from their bones so they wouldn't smell? Maybe this house wasn't just a burial pit. Whoever was to blame had used it as their lair at some point.

"The little girls," I said, horrified.

Jet cocked his head, frowned.

"The woman who owned this house years ago. Flora. She had two daughters. They disappeared." My body gave an involuntary shiver. "What if . . . what if they're down there, too?"

"Nothing would surprise me." He tapped his hand against the hidden doorway, its opening raw and exposed. "Nothing at all."

* * *

"You can have the bed, I'll sleep out here." Jet threw a blanket and a pillow down on his couch. He'd changed into sweatpants and a T-shirt, and now his pistol sat on the small kitchen counter.

"I'm fine on the couch. Really, I'd prefer it."

"Suit yourself. Want some tea? I don't do alcohol, or I'd offer you a drink."

I really wanted a shot of something harder than chamomile. "I'm fine."

While he made himself a cup of tea, I arranged the blanket and pillow on his couch. I didn't know how I was going to sleep. It was after two, and my mind was still swirling. Jet seemed calmer, but I was watching him—and the gun.

He brought the tea to the couch and sat down on the blanket. "This is some fucked-up shit." He shook his head. "All this time . . . I had no idea."

"After a day like this, how do you not add a little something to that tea?"

"A little something is what got me in this mess." He looked at me over the rim of his mug. "After a day like this, how do you not run from that house and this town?"

Why, indeed? Tonight I was too tired to evade the question. It was a good question, and it deserved a thoughtful answer. "I don't know," I said finally. "I've been a pawn in Eve's evil chess game for so long, I think I've lost sight of what's real." I nuzzled in against the couch, letting my head rest against the back.

"That's not a real answer. You told me yourself, you've been playing her games for years. Why? Why didn't you run away long ago?"

That was an easy one. "Lisa."

"Your sister?"

"Yeah."

"You could have run away together."

"Where would we have gone?"

Jet said, "Where would you like to have lived?"

I shrugged. "Somewhere mountainous and remote. Maybe Alaska. Or Montana. I used to kid myself that I could survive in the wilderness." I imagined Lisa's fine-boned face, her spindly arms, her clumsy gait, the now-muted red scars down her back, like a twisted tree of life. "Lisa's not built like me. She's . . . vulnerable. Eve knew that. She used it to her advantage."

"How so?"

How do you explain years of psychological warfare to someone who hadn't lived through it? I knew I sounded like one of those kidnapping victims who did their kidnappers' bidding. For some reason, I wanted Jet to understand. It seemed at that moment the most important thing that he comprehend what we were up against. Even dead, Eve was a formidable enemy.

"I threatened to run when I was sixteen. I'd met a friend whose parents would have helped me. I was being homeschooled, and I'd just gotten back from four days stranded in some small town outside Detroit. I'd had enough."

"You didn't go through with it, obviously," Jet said.

"I made the mistake of arguing with Eve, letting her know I had someone on the outside."

Jet put his cup down on his knee. "Let me guess. She paid off the family to go away and leave you alone?"

"That would have been better." I recalled that day in September. The brilliant fall foliage. The marshmallow clouds gathering over Lake Champlain. The bonfire in the clearing beyond the house. "The gardener was burning some brush, probably illegally. He left the area and my sister conveniently tripped over something and fell into the fire." I wrapped my arms around my chest. "It was a clumsy accident, Eve said. Lisa, always so ungainly and unobservant, she said."

"It wasn't an accident?"

I stood up, feeling claustrophobic in the tight space. I peeked out the windows, toward the little red house, but all was dark, it's secrets held close—for now. "Nothing with Eve was an accident. I don't know how she managed it, but she did. Lisa was hospitalized with severe burns on her back and thighs. The gardener never returned. I stopped seeing my friend."

"A veiled threat."

I turned toward him. "A not-so-veiled threat." I shrugged. "Anyway, you wonder why I did the things I did at Eve's direction? Because she held someone over me. She never really cared about Lisa. I knew that, and I think deep down, Lisa knows that, too. But I also knew that if I didn't do what Eve wanted, she would take it out on my sister. And my sister is all I have."

Jet got up and placed his mug in the sink. He leaned back, against the counter, looking thoughtful. The rain had stopped, and a pack of coyotes howled in the distance. I was getting used to their noise.

Jet said, "Ever wonder why she wanted you to do these things? The travel games in particular?"

It had been such an integral part of my relationship with Eve that I always just assumed it was her strange, sadistic form of control. I said, "She hated us."

"Then why adopt you?"

"I have no idea. Someone to torture, maybe?"

Jet shook his head. "I knew Eve as a controlling, highly organized woman. She did nothing without a reason."

"What are you getting at?"

Jet sat back down on the couch, and Micah immediately hopped up and curled next to him. He looked tired, but his dark eyes had taken on a spark. "Think about it, Connie. Think about the big picture. Eve adopts twin girls. Why? Why would such a sadistic woman adopt two little girls? Seems awfully altruistic."

"Horrible people adopt pets all the time, and then they treat them cruelly. One could say the same thing about them."

"Fair enough. But think about it—Eve takes one of the girls and sends her out into the world with nothing. A destitute throwaway in a strange region. Sound familiar?"

"Not really—"

"You never noticed any pattern to your travels."

"No."

"Were they all big cities?"

I thought about the places she'd sent me. "Chicago and New York. Other than that, mostly small towns or rundown burbs."

"And you never questioned *why* she chose these places?"

I was getting annoyed now. "Jet, I was a kid. My whole fucking world was Eve, my sister, and that house. Other than living in Greece when I was pretty young, we lived in one house. I was homeschooled. I had nothing other than what she gave me, and if I'd left, that was the end for my sister. No, I didn't ask why those locations. I assumed they were the worst spots on Earth or she wouldn't have made me go."

Jet disappeared into his bedroom for a moment. When he came back, he was carrying his laptop and a pad of paper. "Tell me the places she sent you. In order. Do your best to give me the dates, too."

"Why?"

"Just do it. I have a hunch, and I want to see if I'm right."

I listed the places she'd sent me, trying hard to remember the order, exhaustion winning out over curiosity about this hunch. Jet jotted down the dates and locations. "Nowhere else?"

"Isn't that enough?"

While he worked, I flirted with sleep. My dreams were a murky red haze, though, and I'd awaken in a twilight state unsure of where I was until Jet reminded me. Finally, after what seemed like hours, Jet pulled me off the couch and to his computer.

"Look at this." He pointed to an article from *New York Daily News*. It was about a rash of disappearances in and around SoHo and other spots in New York. Prostitutes, runaways, drug addicts.

"Okay, so?"

He tapped the date. Four weeks before Eve died. "And this."

Another new article. This one about a Detroit suburb where she'd sent me at sixteen—two girls had disappeared from their parents' trailer. Their bodies were found in two garbage bags a month later. They'd been raped and tortured.

"And this."

The piece was about a small city she'd sent me to in Florida several years ago. The article detailed the hunt for several missing women and girls over a period of a year. I'd been nineteen when she'd sent me there. *Oh my God.* Suddenly so many things clicked into place.

"*Kelsey.* Her disappearance. She must have been looking for the man who kidnapped her daughter."

"Now you get it," Jet said. He tapped the computer with a callused finger. "This can't be a coincidence. Every place you were sent has a story like this. Runaways, illegal immigrants, prostitutes. All women between the ages of fourteen and thirty. The only thing that connected them was that no one was looking for them. They were castaways in strange towns, their disappearances warranting only small blurbs in the backs of newspapers."

The quiet was, for a moment, deafening. I could hear my own pulse, Micah's breathing, sense the sudden tension in the air. What I felt was a *knowing* that went deeper than this discovery. It invaded my blood and wrapped its bony, skeletal fingers around my heart.

"Eve was using me for bait," I said. We looked at each other, and I could see my own alarm reflected in Jet's eyes. "And she still is."

CHAPTER

41

Eve Foster
Nihla, New Mexico—1997

FLORA DROVE ALONG a meandering path of dusty back roads, causing Eve to wonder whether she knew she was being followed. Eve maintained her distance, which was easy given the scarcity of headlights. Night fell fast and hard in the desert, and the reddish glow of the moon along with the absence of streetlights made it feel as though she and Flora were the only people on Earth. Eve rolled down the window, letting the cool air blow against her face. She was getting closer to her daughter. She felt it deep down in her gut, that buzzing sense of anticipation that heralded things to come. Good or bad, she couldn't tell. But that was always the way with Kelsey. No one was as predictable in her unpredictability as Kelsey.

One way or another, though, Eve would find Kelsey. And then she'd make every last one of these people pay.

Flora braked suddenly and turned down another dirt road. Eve slowed, watching her progress. The road was narrow, dark, and lined with only three houses, each modest and one-story. Flora parked in front of the last one.

Not willing to risk being seen, Eve drove past the turnout, pulled over, and killed the engine. In this part of Nihla, the land was flat and open, and even without her binoculars, Eve could see the house, which sat forlornly in a dead end, against a backdrop of shadowy cacti and brush. A ramshackle set of buildings loomed behind the house like an ominous set in a horror movie. She watched as Flora opened the front door and turned on the indoor and outdoor lights, the children still in the car. She juggled a bag of groceries against one hip and left the front door open. A moment later, she was back outside for the children, whom she wrangled inside the house with a few impatient nudges.

The front door closed. The outside light went dark.

Eve climbed out of the car and leaned against the side, her binoculars trained on Flora's home. Through backlit open windows, she watched Flora's pretty head bob about as she went about her evening. Coyotes howled, their eerie collective voices too close for comfort. Eve took a deep breath, listening. She heard other noises, night noises—predator noises. A smile flitted across her lips. She was one with them now—a night predator out for prey. The thought cheered her, and she settled against the car, in for the long haul.

The sound of a distant car engine startled her, the glow of headlights shone in the distance. She climbed quickly into her car and ducked down, unwilling to be seen stalking Flora's street. The car slowed before Mad Dog Road and turned onto it. Peeking over the doorframe, she saw Kyle's BMW pull in front of the house. Kyle got out, leaving the car running, and strode toward the door like a man who owned the place. But then, Eve thought, Kyle was confident of his place in Nihla, of his place in the world.

Lord, how she hated him. Hated his pompous head of neatly coiffed hair. Hated his manicured fingernails and his unnaturally white teeth. Hated the way he'd looked at her—dismissing her as though she were nothing.

Eve sat up, hidden by the cloak of darkness. She gripped the car door handle and immediately thought better of it. In the silence of the surrounding desert, sounds carried. She settled for rolling down the window slightly and watching from the car as Kyle knocked, then banged on the door. He jammed a key in the lock and turned, but was met with a chain that blocked his entry. The interior of the house had gone dark, and Eve gazed, mesmerized, as the cool and collected businessman became more and more enraged. He slammed on the door with an open fist, yelling for Flora to let him in. He kicked at the door, stuck his hand in and reached for the chain's latch. Unable to gain entry, he settled for yelling expletives, promises to get her back.

Promises to make her pay.

As he turned back toward the car, Eve slid down into her seat, hoping he wouldn't notice the beat-up car parked along the road as he drove away. She listened for the sounds of him leaving—the slamming of his car door, the revving of his engine—but heard only the coyotes in the distance. Curious, she again popped up to look outside. Kyle was back in the car, his head against the seat, staring off into the distance. He'd turned off the engine, waiting for Flora to change her mind.

Eve debated what to do. Wait and watch, risking eventual discovery? Or leave—and risk bringing attention to herself and her car. She was hungry, and she had to pee, but she knew she was trapped. If he heard a car pull away now, he'd know someone had been inside, sitting in a car parked in the middle of nowhere. As camouflaged as she felt she was, she couldn't risk it.

Food would wait. She'd have to hold her pee. She reached for her purse and pulled out her small handgun.

Eve settled in on the floor of the car, the gun in her hand. She reminded herself that she was the predator, not the prey.

Then why did she feel so vulnerable?

*　*　*

At 10:46, Flora turned on the outside light and finally let Kyle inside her home. Eve snuck out of the car and relieved herself in the desert before climbing back into the car. *How low I've sunk*, she thought, and aimed her binoculars back at the house.

At 10:51, she heard screaming.

At 11:07, the front door slammed again, and Flora stormed outside. She stood against her car and smoked a cigarette, sucking on the stick in short, angry puffs, her face half illuminated by the watery yellow glow of the porch light. Flora threw the half-used cigarette on the ground and stomped on it, kicking it under her car. A moment later, Kyle opened the door, a towel draped over his midsection. He said something Eve couldn't hear. Flora looked toward the desert before heading back inside the house. She walked slowly through the door, head down.

Kyle closed the front door and turned off the porch light. Eve waited, but the only light came from the moon, the only sounds were the rhythmic whoosh of her own breathing and the eerie cries of desert night animals.

Whatever had transpired between Flora and Kyle, it was over now. The house was dark, quiet. Eve started the engine and pulled away.

* * *

As the nights grew longer, Eve's patience grew shorter. She needed to know whether Kelsey was being held in Flora's little red house. It was the perfect spot—isolated, derelict, a sturdy little box where no one would think to look. Two days passed before Eve had an opportunity to check it out for herself. Kyle had left the morning after the incident, but for those two days, Flora remained inside, windows shuttered.

Eve traded her car for a Jeep and parked far down the road that intersected with Mad Dog. It was a desolate stretch of nothing, and although she worried that someone would question her, no one bothered.

At nine thirty in the morning on the third day, Flora finally emerged. Her girls each straddled a hip, the blonde one half asleep against her chest and the brunette picking at Flora's hoop earring. An overstuffed diaper bag and beat-up black purse hung from her elbow. Eve watched as Flora strapped the children into their car seats and climbed behind the wheel. Her movements were stiff and robotic. The movements of someone in pain.

Flora hadn't walked that way when she had gone into the house two days ago. A parting gift, perhaps. Eve felt a frisson of pity. Weak or not, Flora was dealing with a sick bastard.

Flora pulled away from the house and made her way slowly down Mad Dog Road. At the intersection, she turned left, heading toward town and presumably the daycare. Eve didn't follow. Instead, she waited until Flora was out of sight before pulling a Mary Kay Cosmetics sign from the back of the car and placing it inside the Jeep's rear window. She'd dump the car later, but if anyone saw it, they'd remember that pink sign, and, hopefully, little else. She drove the car to the house and parked in front. She glanced at the other two houses on the street. No one seemed to be home.

Eve turned the knob, but the door was locked. She walked around the side of the house, taking in the simplicity of the design, searching for entry. One story, longer than wide, its paint peeling in places. Behind the house sat two outbuildings: a small garage and a one-room shack. Both were boarded up. Eve would start with them.

The small shack was empty. The boards on the back side had been pulled away, and the rising sun provided enough illumination to make out a vacant, dusty space. Eve moved on.

The garage presented more of a problem. It was tightly boarded up, its main entrance padlocked. Eve cursed herself for not bringing a tire iron or something she could have used to wedge apart the boards. She paced around the far side of the building, careful not to step on the cacti that dotted the landscape like stray hairs on an old chin.

She was about to give up when she noticed a board that was incompletely nailed across a window on the rear side of the garage. She pulled at it with her fingers. It started to come away further—at the cost of three fingernails and a splinter. She pulled her keys from her pocket and used them instead, digging down under the wood and pulling up as hard as she could. Finally, with a squeaky groan, the board tore away. She used that board as a wedge under the next board, slipping it under and moving it roughly back and forth until the dry wood split. She heard a creak, and with one more pull it broke off, leaving only a jagged edge hanging from the window.

The window wasn't big enough to climb through, but with the sun shining from that side of the garage, she could see through the murky glass. She pressed herself against the building, and cupping her hands around her face, peered inside.

She gasped, stepped back.

The outline of a woman had stared back at her from behind the streaked and dust-coated glass.

From somewhere behind her, there was a rustle in the sage bushes. A snake slithered out of the sun and darted under a rock. She stepped closer to the garage, away from the rock. Again she peered inside, blinking repeatedly.

There it was—the female figure shrouded in shredded linen. It was an old dress form, now colored by dust and neglect and partially shrouded by a piece of gray cloth. Eve put her hands against the glass and scanned the rest of the interior. She saw cardboard boxes, large buckets, a garden shovel, a broken desk, and a box of tools. A pair of pliers stuck out from beneath a wooden hammer, next to a wash bin.

Normal garage junk.

She'd started to turn away from the garage when her eye caught motion—the sun reflecting off an object inside the building. She squinted, but unable to clearly make it out, she spit, then rubbed at the dirty glass with her blouse and looked inside again. Clearer now, she saw a silver stone-studded earring bright and new amid the old clutter in the garage. It could be Flora's, Eve thought, although it looked expensive and not Flora's style. But what caught her eye more than the earring was a stain on the flooring underneath. A dark red snake that, like that reptile, slithered from the bright middle of the garage to a spot somewhere under the shell of the old desk. She was familiar with that hue. Too familiar.

Blood.

She backed away from the building. Suddenly the rest of the objects in the garage took on a more ominous tone. A shovel. Pliers. A hammer. The buckets and bin. Even the earring. She didn't recognize it, but it could have been something Kelsey had purchased during her trek across the United States. It looked to be her style and her size.

Eve glanced toward the small red house. It, too, seemed more ominous now, its simple façade a mask for something sinister.

She knew what she needed to do.

42

Constance Foster
Nihla, New Mexico—Present

B Y THE NEXT morning, the weather had cleared, but the fog in my head had grown worse. I stopped by the post office. True to her word, my sister had sent me a small package. Inside was a short, hand-written letter and a single bronze key. The letter held directions to a safe deposit box. The letter said simply, "*Soon there will be enough for us both. —L.*"

I tucked the key into my wallet and crumpled the letter. Lisa was living in a fantasy if she thought it would be that simple.

* * *

At the diner, Manuela watched me with that sideways appraisal she saved for regular customers who looked like they'd slept in a port-a-potty the night before. I'd awakened that morning with a splitting headache, spit like putty, and a bloody nose. A quick phone check showed I'd missed three calls from Lisa, but she didn't pick up when I called back.

"You can either explain to me why you're pouring half and half in the syrup pitchers or go home and get some sleep." Manuela picked up a small glass pitcher, tapped the surface with a tip of magenta nail. "I'm not kidding."

I gave Manuela a tired smile. "Didn't sleep well."

"What's going on, Connie? I might be able to help you, you know."

"Nothing's going on." I forced a smile. "Promise."

I hated lying to Manuela. After Amy and James, there was no way I was putting someone else I cared about in danger. The small bell hanging from the diner door chimed. I looked up to see a man in his sixties take the far booth.

I said to Manuela, "I'll take this one."

Manuela looked from him to me and back again. "Last one. Then *sal de aquí*."

"Yeah, yeah, I'm out of here. Just let me get him."

Before I could walk away, Manuela put a hand on my shoulder. "I've had my own issues, so I get it." Her finely penciled brows knit into a frown. "If you need money, a place to stay—"

"I'm fine." I shrugged her off. "Really. Just exhausted."

The customer was an older guy with a full head of blond-gray hair and stingy lips, the kind of lips that disappeared into his face. I'd seen him in here before. His fussy sweater vest seemed out of place at Manuela's, and I reminded myself not to screw up his order. I didn't need a pissed-off customer today. After ordering a cheese omelet and hash browns, hold the toast, he watched me intently as I jotted down his requests.

"You wrote down extra cheese?"

"Yep," I said.

"I want the eggs buried in it."

"Okay. Got it."

As I turned to go, I felt his hand on my elbow. I spun back around.

"What's the nicest hotel in the area?"

"Best you're going to do is a roadside motel unless you head to Taos or Santa Fe."

"How about that rooming house on the Main Street?"

"Wouldn't know."

The guy looked annoyed and more than a little disappointed. It was my day, it seemed, to let people down. I passed the message about cheese to Manuela in the kitchen and helped her pull together the hash browns. When I returned to the dining area with the food, the customer was gone. At his seat were two twenty dollar bills, nothing else.

"Asshole," I muttered. "Wonder what I did to piss him off. Do you know him?"

Manuela shrugged. "Not that I recall, but some days, they're all just hungry mouths, chewing and talking. I learn to ignore the chatter, concentrate on cooking." When I frowned, she smiled and poked me gently with two fingers. "Doesn't matter, Connie. Lighten up! Eat the omelet. Now you get a good meal *and* a hefty tip."

I nodded, my thoughts on those miserly lips. There was something familiar about the man, but my harried mind was too worn to figure out just what.

*   *   *

I stared down at the bones. Dirty white splinters poked from beneath their graves and reflected the light from my flashlight, calling me to make this right. My eye caught a sparkle just under the surface of the dirt. I wiped at the spot with the toe of my shoe, pulling the dirt away from the skeletal remains. My breath caught in my throat, and I felt like someone was sitting on my chest. Like I was suffocating. *Buck the hell up, Connie.* It was the gold bracelet. It had fallen off when we'd been digging the night before. I bent down to get a closer look, then pulled it from the ground and wiped it with my shirt. Small rubies were centered on a delicate gold chain. I stared at it a moment, debating whether to put it back, when my phone rang. On impulse, I stuck the bracelet in my pocket. It wasn't doing anyone any good here.

A call from an unknown number.

I raced upstairs and into the daylight. I'd just stolen a bracelet from a dead person. Bones littered my basement. I was in a strange state and a strange town and a strange house, living next to a practical stranger who was somehow my only confidant. But all I could think about was James.

I answered the call.

A baritone voice said, "I'm looking for Nora."

"This is she," I said, breathless.

"Nora, this is Officer Derek Pressman. My wife said you called." He paused, then in a hushed tone, "About mandatory counseling."

"Yes, see . . . this is actually about James. I'm not a grief counselor. My name is Constance. I'm . . . I'm a friend of James. He said I could trust you."

Silence on the other end. I was beginning to think he'd hung up when he said, "Go on."

"How is he?"

"Not well."

I blurted, "He wasn't drunk, and he wasn't using."

"How can you be so sure?"

"I was with him that night." I took a deep breath, forced myself to slow down, to think. "I have some information for you, information that may support that this was no accident."

Another long pause. "Where are you?"

I didn't want to give him my address. Not until I knew I could trust him. "Meet me in town. At the taco shop next to the rooming house."

"I need an hour," he said. "I'll be wearing a bright red sweatshirt. And Constance—"

"Yes?"

"Don't tell a soul."

*   *   *

Any trace of the storms from the day before had disappeared, and downtown Nihla was the same dusty bowl I'd witnessed on my first day. The street felt deserted. I watched a raven pick at a whole soft pretzel on the street in front of the boarding house and thought about Amy and the vagaries of fate. It could have been my body in a trash bag beside the highway. Had I only answered the door that night, she might have still been alive.

A glance at the Integra clock told me I was thirty minutes early. I climbed out of the car. I needed to walk. I followed the main road, lost in a murky labyrinth of thought, until I arrived at the hardware store. Outside, a child's pool stood upright against the exterior façade, the smiling puppy pattern on molded blue plastic mocking my anxiety. Next to it sat two camping chairs, and Stella, the cashier, was reclining in one of them, a cigarette dangling from her fingers.

"I figured you'd be back." She took a long draw on the cigarette before tossing it on the ground and snubbing it out with a sneakered toe. She picked up the butt.

I took the seat next to her, uninvited. "I saw Josiah."

She nodded, her weathered face impassive. Her breath was mostly wheeze, her hand shaky, and I noticed the cotton ball and band-aid in the crook of her elbow, the skin around it a bruised yellow. It took her a full minute to stand, and she walked into the store without another word. I followed her inside.

The place was empty aside from the two of us. Stella disappeared in the back, and I thought she'd gone for good, but she returned with a thermos in her hand. She drank its contents in short gulps, mouth twisting in pain.

"Throat cancer." She tossed her head back, grimaced. "Even plain old water's a bitch. I should've quit smoking years ago. Folks in my family never listen. But you don't want to hear about an old lady's troubles. You have problems of your own."

"I'm sorry," I said, unsure what to say. Then, "Another woman died."

"I heard."

I shook my head, angry and baffled. "That's how many this year?"

Stella stared into her thermos as though it held the answer to my question. After a pregnant silence, she shrugged bony shoulders. "I stopped keeping track."

"I haven't," I said. "That's four. Four women in five months." When Stella didn't respond, didn't so much as acknowledge what I'd said, I grabbed the thermos from her hand and pushed it aside. I crouched down so I was looking directly into her face. "You gave me Josiah's name for a reason. What was it?"

She turned away.

"Dammit." I slapped my hand against the counter. "My house is the key to all of it. I understand that now. I know it used to belong to a woman named Flora Fuentes. I know she died in a fire." I walked around the counter so I was staring into Stella's sad, hollow eyes once again. "I know two men died in prison for crimes they didn't commit. I know my mother's daughter disappeared in Nihla years ago and was never found." I could feel my temples throb, my chest constrict. Stella's face had paled. I didn't care. "I know that the people of Nihla have some ass-backward belief that if they turn the other cheek, *their* kids will be spared."

"It's not ass-backward." Her words came out in a guttural heap, eyes flashed fire. "You have *no right* to waltz into town thinking *you* understand *us*. You don't—and you can't."

"Then tell me. Explain it to me. For starters, why did you give me Josiah's name?"

The bell on the door chimed, and a man entered the store. He glanced at us and quickly averted his gaze. I took a few steps backward, away from Stella, deflated. There was nothing for me here.

As I was leaving, she whispered something.

"What?" I asked, spinning back around.

"Josiah Smith owes a debt. For the girls who are lost. For . . . well, others who have suffered."

"Like the men who were wrongly accused?"

She shook her head. "Those men in prison are gone. But you're not."

"Me? What do I have to do with Josiah's penance?"

"Everything." She blinked, wiped her eyes with a weathered hand. "You, Constance, are a murderer's daughter."

43

Eve Foster
Nihla, New Mexico—1997

E VE DROVE THE Jeep down Mad Dog Road, past the other homes, made a right, and parked the beast along the side of the road, far from the sight line of Flora's house. She removed the license plate and stuffed it in her purse—better to delay any chance that the local cops would connect the car to her. Then she pulled a charcoal gray knit poncho from the trunk, slipped it on, and pulled the hood over her head, ensuring that the dark curly wig would stick out beyond the hood. To this she added large sunglasses and a scarf. Hopefully if she was seen by any neighbors, their description would throw the locals off her tail.

She sauntered along the street, trying to look as though she belonged there, her heart pounding and a knot forming in her stomach. There was nowhere to hide. She felt exposed and increasingly angry as she walked down Mad Dog Road. If the police had taken her seriously, she wouldn't need to be sneaking around. She'd call them now and report the blood in the garage, but she knew damn well they'd do nothing about it other than chase her out of town. They were complicit, in her mind—as guilty as Kyle.

She reached the house and walked around back. There was only one window at the rear of the building, and it was too high off the ground for her to reach. The other long side of the rectangle, however, was protected from the neighbors' line of sight but visible from the road. Two larger windows sat close to the ground. No cars were coming, and only the desert, stretching on for what felt like eternity, was there to witness. She'd take her chances.

She removed the poncho, wrapped it around her wrist and hand, and punched the window closest to the rear of the house. She did this two more times, careful to avoid slivers of glass, until she could reach in, through the curtain, and unlock and raise the window. She skirted over the threshold, landing in a cramped bathroom. She did her best to clean the glass from her clothes and the sill before drawing the curtain closed.

The bathroom smelled of lemon disinfectant and baby shampoo. A plastic basket had been tucked in the corner and held a handful of rubber toys and waterproof books. A single yellow towel was draped over a stainless steel sink, and a baby's plastic comb lay under the sink's exposed pipe. A water stain meandered from the ceiling to above the window, making the cheerful yellow wall paint feel like it was trying too hard.

Seeing the kids' things only fueled her resolve.

Eve opened the door into a kitchen. Like the bathroom, it was clean and neat and utterly depressing. White paint had turned gray and dingy. An old stove and a beat-up refrigerator were the only appliances. A linoleum-topped table for two had been propped against a wall. The only thing on its surface was a glass bowl that doubled as an ashtray, the remnants of someone's cigarette floating on top of a small pool of ashes.

Eve followed the simple path of the house, moving from the dark kitchen to a bedroom. On one side of the bedroom stood two small cribs, their metal bars painted the same yellow as the bathroom. A plastic basket, the twin to the bathroom basket, sat under a window and was filled with worn toys. Two majolica crosses hung on the wall, one over each crib.

On the other side of the room was a double bed. It was placed up against the wall, its covers mismatched but neatly made. A single dresser was wedged between the bed and the wall. A single dresser for everyone, Eve thought. Again, she almost felt sorry for Flora. *Almost.* But then she thought of the blood in the garage and her missing daughter and Flora's refusal to even speak to her, and her pity morphed back into rage.

She moved on.

The final room was the living area. Like the other rooms, it was sparsely furnished, dingy, and utterly without charm. It was also the only room that hinted at Kyle's existence in Flora's life.

Two armchairs sat on either side of a small table. A desk had been wedged against a wall, between a low bookshelf filled with children's books and another dresser. On the dresser was a man's leather belt, a button-down blue shirt, a pack of Marlboros, and a set of keys. Eve picked up the shirt and sniffed it. She could smell him—his musky aftershave, tobacco, and sweat. She threw the shirt back down and grabbed the keys. There were two—a small padlock key and a larger door key. She unlocked the front door and tried the latter in its lock. Not a fit.

She hadn't seen any other locks in the house. Maybe these were to the garage?

She walked back through the shotgun-style building, lingering in front of the single photograph of Flora. The face staring up from the photo looked young, hopeful, beautiful—a face telegraphing naïveté and joy and faith. The photo lay face up on the dresser, its glass shattered into a thousand shards, held together by the flimsy plastic frame.

Was there a time when I was like Flora? Eve wondered. She'd been married at fifteen at the insistence of her parents, and she'd become a mother later that same year. If she looked back at a photo of herself at eleven or twelve, would her smile have been genuine? Had she ever been guileless and hopeful?

Perhaps if she went back far enough, before her father's threats and daily shame sessions. *I have no illusions about who I am*, Eve thought. In her mind, she had made the choices she needed to make in order to keep Kelsey out of poverty. *That's what separates me from Flora. I never enabled Liam. I fought back.*

But what do I really know about Flora's life, her choices?

Eve forced herself away from the photograph and back into the kitchen, the keys in her hand. She was reluctant to go back outside for fear Flora would return and her plan would be ruined, but she needed to see where this key led. As she made her way to the back door, something in the kitchen caught her eye. Behind the refrigerator, she could see a line of cracks in the wall. Faint but unmistakable. A glance down at the floor confirmed her suspicion. Lines had been etched into the wood flooring—scrapes from repeatedly dragging the refrigerator away from its spot.

Eve glanced outside. Satisfied that no one was here or coming down the road, she pushed the refrigerator aside to expose a small entryway. It looked as though that wall had been reframed and moved forward, and a small door—half the size of a regular one—had been fashioned from matching drywall. A piece of rope hung where a doorknob would typically be.

Eve tugged on the rope and after a few pulls, the door opened a crack. Pulse racing, she pulled the door open farther, her hand shaking. She felt around for a light switch. Finding none, she searched the kitchen for a flashlight, which she located under the sink. The light revealed a rustic, cobwebbed staircase. Eve held her breath, listening—for what, she wasn't sure. Her daughter's breathing. The rustle of cloth. A moan. Any sign of life.

Instead, only silence.

Steeling herself, Eve pulled the door open all the way and placed a foot on the top step. The wooden stair, though narrow and low-ceilinged, felt solid. She held the flashlight with one hand and the wall with the other as she descended. The air felt dry and hot, the tomb-like space, claustrophobic. Light-headedness threatened, but with sheer will, Eve kept her focus on the task ahead. She'd been in other basements, other tomb-like spaces, after all, and had lived to tell about it. She'd live through this ordeal, too.

Beneath her, the steps creaked. At the bottom of the staircase was another door. This one had no handle. She moved the flashlight beam along another makeshift wall until she could see the edge of the door. She pushed with one hand—nothing. She kicked at it—still nothing. Reluctantly, she pressed her body against the door until she felt it give way.

The smell hit her first, acrid and musty with an underlying stench of something sweet, like a trough of decaying apples. It took a moment for Eve's eyes to adjust, but once they did, she scanned for some sign of her daughter. A few cardboard boxes, a large, empty plastic container, some assorted tools. The floor was dirt, its surface fresh and hard-packed. The low ceilings had continued down here, and the room was a narrow rectangle, a smaller footprint of the structure above.

Eve's temples throbbed, her breath caught in her throat. Every cell in her being screamed "danger." Someone had dug this basement and had gone to the trouble of creating the hidden staircase and doors. Why? So they could store some junk? Doubtful. This was no normal cellar. She breathed in, past the sickly sweet smell, past the dirt and mustiness. She wanted to smell some hint that Kelsey had been here—her perfume, her shampoo—but this hole was devoid of life scents. It felt like a tomb.

Eve grabbed the closest thing to her—a broom—and wedged it into the doorframe. Getting stuck down here would be a nightmare. She hurried toward the boxes. They were sealed, but she was able to use the key as a knife, cutting her way through the tape. The first box contained an assortment of cleaning supplies and yard goods. The second box contained clothes. She was in the midst of opening the third box when she heard a noise coming from above. She swallowed hard, stuck the key in her pocket, and pulled out her handgun. Her mind flitted to the kitchen door and the possibility of getting stuck down here, entombed in this horrid house.

Never.

She sprinted across the basement and was almost at the steps when a woman's voice called out, "Kyle?"

Flora.

Eve flattened herself against the wall. She held her breath, waiting, following the sound of Flora's footsteps against the wooden treads until she was almost in the basement.

"Kyle? Are you down here?" Flora's voice was uneven, shrill. She poked her head into the room, her face red and tear-stained.

Eve spun around, arm outstretched, gun pointed at Flora. "Don't move."

Using her other hand, Eve shone the flashlight in Flora's face. Flora's eyes widened. She turned around.

"I *will* use this," Eve pushed the tip of the gun into Flora's back, between her shoulder blades.

Flora's body tensed, but she continued her slow progress up the steps. "No you won't."

"What makes you so sure?"

Flora's face half turned into the unforgiving light. "Because with one phone call, I can get you what you want."

CHAPTER

44

Constance Foster
Nihla, New Mexico—Present

D EREK STILL HADN'T arrived. I'd waited at the designated spot for over an hour, Stella's words ringing in my ears like a bad case of tinnitus. Deep down in my gut, I knew she was telling the truth. I *was* the daughter of a murderer. It was the reason Eve had treated me so badly, it was the reason for her cruelty and obsession. She believed my father killed her daughter, and she was going to get me back, slowly and painfully. Jet was right. She'd been using me as bait before, and she was using me again now.

But if I was the daughter of a murderer, so was Lisa.

And Eve would have wanted revenge against her, too.

Thoughts of Lisa flooded bile into my throat, and I coughed and sputtered into an old paper towel, esophagus burning. It'd been more than a day since Lisa's panicked call, since I'd heard from her at all. I glanced around the restaurant; still no one meeting Derek's description, and anyway I couldn't focus without knowing my sister was safe. I picked up my phone and dialed home. Right to voice mail. I left her another message, then I tried the cook and Dave. No answer.

After nearly two hours, I left the taco shop, unsure what to do next. I sat in my car, wavering. The cops couldn't be trusted. I wanted to head back to Vermont to find Lisa, but I knew going there now might only put her in danger. I was tempted to leave

Nihla, but I wouldn't allow myself to, not until this was resolved, one way or another. I would never find peace with Eve lurking. I would never find peace until I understood what this all meant.

Bodies in my basement. Daughter of a murderer.

You look like her.

What if Flora Fuentes was my mother? She'd had twins, twins who disappeared. Was it possible that Eve had taken them? Maybe she'd grabbed them after Flora died. It would explain why we were whisked off to Greece, why she spent her life being so secretive. If she had taken us, was it out of friendship toward Flora or out of revenge? Or—could she have murdered Flora herself?

Josiah Smith. He knew more than he was saying. If Derek was going to stand me up, maybe I'd try Josiah one more time.

* * *

On the way to Rebecca Smith's house, I thought about Flora and Eve. Eve had been here in Nihla, looking for Kelsey. The Eve I knew was vindictive, smart, resourceful—and completely unfettered by a conscience. My mind spun a mad web of possibilities. I pictured Eve nabbing the two little girls, taking them abroad to Greece while she used her money to buy falsified documentation. Coming home to the States later with two adoptees. Moving from Philadelphia to Vermont, a new place where no one would think to ask questions. She would have been simply a rich widow who'd lost her daughter and was filling a gap in her life. No rational person would think like Eve. No rational person would link those "adoptions" with revenge.

Years and years of revenge. The more I thought about it, the more this made sense. It explained so much, including my journey to Nihla.

My phone rang, interrupting my thoughts.

"Connie, we need to talk."

"My God, Lisa, I've been worried. Are you okay?"

"It was all fake. Kelsey never existed, at least not in our basement." Lisa took a breath, gasped. "There was never a girl in that room."

It took me a moment to understand what she was saying. "Did you go into the basement, Lisa?"

"Aunt Eve . . . she was . . . searching. I don't know. I don't understand what I saw."

"Slow down. You're not making sense."

"The room downstairs. It's some sort of . . . some sort of head-quarters." Hysteria tinged Lisa's voice.

I said calmly, "Describe what you saw."

"I can't. It seemed crazy, bizarre."

"Try."

"I need you to come home now, Connie. *Now*."

"*Tell me, Lisa*."

"Okay . . . okay." She was quiet for a moment. "Chalkboards and bulletin boards, all covered in maps and pins and newspaper articles. Some of the articles were yellowed and old, others new. Like . . . almost like she was searching for missing persons or posting celebrity sightings."

"Could she have been searching for Kelsey?"

"I thought that at first, but Kelsey would be forty by now. The girls in these recent articles were younger. Teens. Twenties." She groaned. "And dead. *Murdered*."

"Stay with me, Lisa, okay? I'm going to ask you some simple questions. You said chalkboards and bulletin boards. Was that all you saw?"

She hesitated. "A tape recorder. At first I was so relieved that there wasn't a dead girl in there that I looked around. I saw the tape recorder, pushed it—"

"And?"

"Moans . . . and screams."

The moans and screams we'd grown up hearing, believing it was our mentally ill sister, believing Eve would lock us up there, too. So many punishments I'd endured, lying on that horrid cot and listening to those awful sounds. I pulled over, the sudden tightening in my temples causing my vision to blur. Eve's mind-fuckery knew no bounds.

I envisioned my poor sister down in that basement, alone, pushing the button that would bring back all of the memories. Fragile Lisa. Impressionable Lisa. And I knew in that moment that Eve's will—her decision to give Lisa alone the keys to her kingdom—was as much about punishing Lisa as it was about persecuting me.

The daughters of a murderer.

"What was she looking for?" Lisa asked.

She was tracking a killer. I was sure the map matched the places Eve had sent me. Only Lisa didn't need to worry about that, too. "I don't know."

The more I thought about it, the surer I was I was right. For all these years, Eve had been keeping tabs on a killer—tracking our father. Trying to draw him out. Keeping us away from the basement room to scare us and to hide what was going on. If Flora was our mother, then this man—Kyle Summers, whoever he was—was our father. I wanted Lisa to send me photos, I wanted so badly to know if I was right, but I couldn't ask her to go down there again. I feared for her sanity.

"Lisa, listen to me. You need to find Dave. Get out of the house. Go to a hotel or somewhere far away. Do you understand?"

"Can't you just come home?"

"You know I can't. It's not that simple. You could lose everything." *And I could lure a killer to your doorstep.* I took a deep breath, exhaled. "Find Dave."

"I haven't seen him."

"Then leave by yourself. Go to a hotel and stay there. You can do that. Okay?" No answer. "Okay?"

"Yes, yes. I'll do that." Her voice sounded stronger, more confident. "Did you get the key?"

"Yes, but—"

"I've hidden a lot of jewelry. They won't miss that. I could have lost it, sold it. Don't worry, Connie. I can do this."

She hung up. Her resolve should have given me hope. Then why did I feel so despondent?

*   *   *

Josiah Smith wasn't expecting me. I hoped surprise worked in my favor.

This time, I found Rebecca's car gone and the house dark and closed up, except for two open windows. Knocking brought no response. I was about to leave when I heard Josiah cough from inside. I slammed a palm against the window frame of one of the open windows and yelled his name through the screen. I continued until he screamed back, "Knock it off! Becky's not here."

"It's Constance Foster, Mr. Smith. Can I talk to you?"

"Who the fuck is Constance Foster?"

"You know who I am." I waited a beat. "Flora's daughter."

Another phlegmy cough. "Go away." There was less venom in his voice.

"I need to talk to you."

"No."

"The little red house on Mad Dog. The basement. Please." I took a deep breath. "You were right."

"Go around to the garden," he said finally. "The back entrance. She always leaves it open."

*   *   *

The back door was, indeed, open—although I had to climb over a locked garden gate to get to it. The house was unlit, the smell of cat urine battling it out with disinfectant and the lingering scent of sausage. I found Josiah in his recliner, head tilted back against the worn velour.

"Josiah." I flipped on a lamp and squatted on the couch next to his chair.

"Tell me what you found." He opened his watery eyes. His skin and the whites of those eyes were yellow. He gave a hoarse cough, wiped his mouth with the back of his hand, and said again, "Tell me."

"Bones. In the basement."

"I knew it." There was triumph in his tone. "How many?"

"I don't know. I only dug down enough to see . . . some. Just bones, as though the flesh had been dissolved right off them."

"What will you do?"

"I . . . I don't know. I can't trust the cops."

"No, you can't."

"Who did this?"

"You haven't figured that out?"

"Flora?"

"She was as much a victim as the others."

"Then I don't know." I leaned forward. "But you do. Tell me, Josiah. Clear your conscience."

The old man snorted, barely lifting his head from the chair. "You think telling you will clear my conscience? I told you before, and I meant it. Life is complicated. My only regret is that while those two creeps rotted in jail, bodies stayed hidden. Parents never received closure about what happened to their daughters."

"It didn't have to be that way."

"Oh, but it did. What do you think would have happened if I'd prosecuted one of the most influential men in town? Think others would have stood by me? Things may work that way where you're from, but here, family matters. Connections matter. Loyalty matters." He coughed, and drops of saliva flew from his mouth. "I was never absolutely sure who did it. And frankly, sometimes you have to make a trade with the devil."

I thought about Eve's bulletin boards and news articles, the fact that Kyle Summers disappeared after Flora died. "You did know exactly who did these things. In fact, in return for closing the cases in Nihla, the murderer agreed to leave." When Josiah didn't respond, I said, "You know what else would have kept him out of Nihla? Putting his ass in jail."

"My case would have been challenged. He would have stayed in town. Others were willing to flirt with the rules."

"By 'flirt' you mean lie, tamper with evidence."

Josiah flinched. "Like I said, he had influence."

"Who is 'he'?" When he didn't answer, I said, "You have a chance to right things now. Who is the man you're talking about? Kyle Summers?"

Josiah gave me that exasperating half smile again. Even now, his body twisted by disease, his mind rattled by guilt, he was beholden to a murderer.

"You're a fucking prick, you know that? You have the chance to save lives. Forget regret. Now, here, you can make a real difference. But apparently the whole town—you included—has stood by as this asshole holds it hostage."

"Not everyone."

"Who then? Who had the ovaries to stand up to him?"

Josiah Smith closed his eyes. "Ask yourself who suffered."

"The women who were murdered sure suffered."

"Don't be obtuse. Ask yourself who from Nihla suffered. You'll have your weak link." Josiah met my gaze with those rheumy, yellowed eyes. I saw impatience, anger, amusement. *Monster*. Not the monster the killer was, perhaps, but a monster nonetheless.

He said, "Ask yourself who suffered in the worst way possible, Constance, and you'll understand who traded a loved one's life for the chance to ease their conscience. You'll understand why the town has kept its silence." He closed his eyes. "Why I have kept my silence."

CHAPTER

45

Constance Foster
Nihla, New Mexico—Present

THE NEAREST HOSPITAL was almost thirty miles away, and I drove there at max speed. I needed to see James. The nurse at the front desk refused to give me his room number, even after I lied and told her I was his fiancée. "Call the police station," she said. "I'm not at liberty."

At least I knew he was there and still alive.

A uniformed officer walked through the lobby as I was getting ready to leave. He was older and overweight, and I recognized him as the cop who'd investigated Manuela's ex-boyfriend at the diner. While the receptionist helped someone else, I hid in the tiny gift shop, then followed the cop at a distance. He pressed the button for the fourth floor. I sprinted for the stairway and climbed to the fourth floor, making certain he was gone before emerging into the hallway.

The passage was dimly lit, a patchwork of gray vinyl tiles lining the floor, their edges worn. I hated hospitals—ever since Lisa's experience with the fire, I've been terrified of doctors, terrified of the hopeless loss of control hospitals represented. Nevertheless, I followed the hall toward the sound of men talking outside a room around the corner. I stood with my back against the wall, pretending to look at my phone, while I eavesdropped on their numbing, mundane conversation—the weather, the latest sports scores, what they'd last had for dinner. Finally I heard his name mentioned. "Jamie's still in a coma," someone said, someone who sounded like the partner Jamie had come to the diner with all those days ago.

"Better for him. The press loves to crucify a crooked cop," someone else said.

"It's a shame it has to be this way," said a deep voice. A voice I recognized. "He just wouldn't let up."

Derek, the cop James had trusted. My chest tightened. James must have called him, told him what he suspected. If that was the case, it meant Derek was dirty. It also meant James was a threat, that whoever was responsible for the murders two decades ago was back at it, and James had gotten too close for their comfort. Otherwise, why silence him?

Footsteps echoed down the hall. I turned and sprinted back toward the stairwell and disappeared inside, letting my breath out as I ran down the steps, taking them two at a time. Outside, I bolted for my car. James was alive—for now. But he was under guard and being branded a crooked cop. All for asking questions.

Aside from helping me, trusting Derek had been James's biggest mistake.

I unlocked my car and started to slide into my seat when I noticed a piece of folded paper under the window wiper. I reached around, snatched the paper, and sat behind the wheel, locking my doors as I turned on the ignition. I opened the paper. Neat, rounded letters spelled out:

Little. Red. House.

* * *

The house was silent. I half expected to find police staking out the place, or the front door smashed open. Instead, the shotgun house stood like a bastion against a brewing dust storm, as I imagined it had for decades. I could feel the wind picking up. Down Mad Dog Road, Oliver's chickens were squawking away, but aside from that, the brothers' houses were silent as well. Even Jet's little shack seemed barren, although his truck was parked in its usual spot. No sound came from the workshop. Maybe he was asleep.

Little. Red. House.

The words had become a mantra in my mind. I dreaded going inside.

I sat in the car for a long minute. So many emotions to process, so many threads to connect. Flora was my mother. I looked like her, and although Lisa did not, we were fraternal twins and she might have looked like our father. Alberto had mentioned Kyle Summers, and I guessed that was my father's name. Eve had sent me to Nihla, to this house, for one reason: revenge. She knew my presence would draw the killer out, so whoever it was, I merely had to wait for him.

If I had the courage.

My father, the killer, was playing with me, trying to turn any safe havens—my home, my car, Manuela's—into places of fear. But I wouldn't let him do that to me. After all, I'd been through worse.

I called Manuela and left her a message that I wouldn't be at work for the next few days. She'd be worried and maybe even a little angry, but she'd manage without me. I had enough food and water to last a week. I still wasn't certain I could trust Jet, but having him around gave me some comfort. I wished I'd found a way to purchase a gun, but it was too late now. If Kyle was my father, perhaps he'd spare me. Perhaps I wouldn't need one.

I put my head back against the seat, groaned. Maybe this was all my imagination. Maybe the whole town was conspiring to make me go mad.

Only I didn't think so.

I had to hand it to Eve: pitting me against him was ingenious. One of us would die—and it was likely to be me. But she would have forced him to be killed or murder his own daughter. One way or another, she'd get retribution.

Since I could remember, Eve always won in the end.

*   *   *

My earliest memories were from our time in Greece. I don't recall people, exactly, but rather images and sensations and feelings that left ghost imprints on my mind. Not all memories were bad. The warmth of sunshine and the coolness of saltwater spray. The joy of seeing my sister's face first thing in the morning, the day spread before us in the same way the ocean reached out to the horizon. The burst of sweet brightness the first time I remember eating freshly picked watermelon. The alien but comforting chatter of Greeks in the Corfu Town marketplace. My mind will recall colors and shapes and smells and sounds, and always, always, the way they defined my emotions.

Within the patchwork of these early recollections lurked the shadows. I saw a red orb, hanging suspended in the air over an angry ocean. I saw long blonde hair, gold and wavy like one of Lisa's Disney princesses. I heard a sharp voice, full of venomous anger and, at the worst times, cruel amusement. I remembered mesmerizing, hateful eyes—cat eyes that watched me constantly, always ready to pounce.

Always, always waiting.

*　*　*

I stared at the red paint on my house, remembering all of the ways Eve had tried to tear Lisa and me apart. I was tired of being the rodent in her game of cat and mouse, the target in her vicious rounds of darts. I turned off the ignition and climbed out of the car. If the murderer was coming to me, if Eve had laid a trail to my doorstep, I'd be ready.

CHAPTER

46

Constance Foster
Nihla, New Mexico—Present

THE WIND WAS picking up, and along with it, needle-like dust and sand. I pulled open the door to the house and slipped inside, pausing to listen, but the wind blocked out all other sounds. I grabbed a scarf from my dresser and wrapped it around my face, leaving only a slit for eyes, and left through the back door. I pounded on Jet's door, but he didn't answer. The door was locked; Micah was going nuts inside. After checking the cab of his truck, I swung by the workshop, shielding my face with my hand to keep the stinging sand out of my eyes. He wasn't in his workshop, either, but the door was open. I let myself inside and closed it behind me.

The place felt different. I looked around, trying to decide why. His tools were still neatly stored in their cabinets, half-finished projects still sat stacked by the wall, and cans of finishes still lined the shelves next to his workbenches. I couldn't put my finger on what had changed, exactly, but *something* had. I didn't have time to dwell. I scoured the cabinets and shelves for things I could use. I pulled a plane, a nail gun, and two chisels down from an overhead cabinet along with a can of paint thinner, a box of nails, and a hammer. Old boards stood against one wall, and I grabbed as many as I could carry. On the way out, I took some tacks, a flashlight, and a roll of electrical tape.

I was about to leave when I thought of one more thing. I glanced back at the cabinet where Jet kept his cash. The drawer sat partially open, unlocked. I pulled it the rest of the way and stared inside. Empty.

Had he run with his cash, leaving me here to face Eve's vengeance on my own? No. Whatever my misgivings, Jet would not do that. And he certainly would never leave without Micah.

For now, though, I was in this alone.

* * *

I started with the windows. Using Jet's hammer and nails and some of the plywood, I nailed every window shut and secured plywood across the glass, leaving myself a peephole in each window. I took a larger piece of wood and nailed it across the back door before taping my bear bells to the doorknob, just in case.

I left the front door untouched but secured bear bells to the knob and aimed a nail gun toward the entrance, its trigger attached to a string around the knob.

Tired, I stood back to judge my handiwork. It was sloppy and amateurish, but it would do. When this asshole arrived, he would have one way in, and I'd be ready.

Outside, the wind continued to howl, and a frenzy of dust whipped at the house, rattling the windows. I pressed my face against the peephole, but the storm blocked what remained of the sun, and I couldn't make out anything other than a faint light coming from Oliver's house.

My exhausted mind wandered from Oliver to Jet to Lisa. Lisa made me think of the bodies in the basement, and in a panic I remembered the basement door. If someone got into the basement, they could climb up the hidden staircase to the kitchen.

Quickly, I hammered a board across the interior door that led to the basement. The Bilco doors already had a lock, but it was a flimsy one. I needed to check the exterior doors just to make sure they were secure, too. I wrapped the scarf around my head and face again and pulled on a hoodie. My hand was on the knob to the front door when I heard a sharp sound coming from somewhere toward the back of the house. *Scratch, scratch, scratch.*

I stopped, pausing to listen, straining to hear over the wind raging outside.

Scratch, scratch, scratch. I *felt* it more than heard it. It was coming from behind me. I tore off the scarf, tucked a razor in my pocket, and picked up a chisel. Holding the chisel over my head, I walked quietly through the house. Silence mocked me.

A mouse, perhaps. Or a loose board grating against the house because of the wind. Or my pumped-up imagination.

I returned to the living room, pulled a chair in front of the door, ready for a long wait. Five minutes later, I heard it again, this time louder, more distinct. *Scratch, scratch, scratch.* Rhythmic, demanding, like a chant. *Scratch, scratch, scratch.*

Little. Red. House.

God, I wanted a drink. I wanted to down the whole fucking bottle and crawl under my blankets and fall into the deepest, meanest, nothing-est sleep.

Scratch, scratch, scratch.

Back in the kitchen, I placed my ear against the door to the basement. I couldn't hear anything other than the howl of the wind and the sand assaulting the windows. I rubbed my eyes, shook my head, praying for some sanity to return. I was hopped up on adrenaline, scared. I needed my wits about me.

Scratch, scratch, scratch.

Now the fucking sound seemed to be coming from underneath the house. A visceral, repulsive sound, like nails across wood. Human nails. In that moment, I was a kid again, locked in Eve's godforsaken basement with those moans and screams and horrid scratches echoing from the other room. Fucking Eve with her fucking games. And all that time, it was a recording.

Fuck Eve.

I used the chisel to pull away the board I'd just nailed to the door, and then with all the strength I could muster, I pulled open the door to the basement. A dark abyss.

It had been a mouse. Or a branch. Or my overactive imagination.

I was about to close the door when I heard the unmistakable sound of a human moan. The light switch wasn't working, so I grabbed a flashlight from my kitchen table and aimed the beam onto the stairwell. Just dust—and the imprint of a man's shoe in that dust. Jet's from last time we were here? Another moan, masculine and deep and pained. It sounded like Jet.

I needed help, but who could I ask? Not the cops. Manuela? She'd come, I was sure—but I didn't want to drag her into this mess. Oliver and Raymond? They would sooner kill me than help me. It was just me, and if Jet was down there and needed saving, I was all he had. I'd need something better than a chisel.

I sprinted toward the living room to grab the nail gun. I was two-thirds of the way through the bedroom when I felt a hand grip my ankle. I tripped, fell, and slammed onto the floor, hitting my head on the old cast iron tub.

"Didn't your mother teach you that the boogie man always hides in the shadows?"

Terror and confusion gripped me. I knew that voice. I struggled to stand, to catch a glimpse of my attacker. Blood trickled down my scalp and into my eyes. I groped for the chisel, came up empty. I scrambled on all fours toward the living room and the front door, but I felt myself being pulled backward. A hand tugged viciously at my hair, yanking me up.

The scents of cherry pipe tobacco and menthol. Familiar smells. "Dave?"

My attacker placed cold metal against my temple. "It would be best if you didn't give me a hard time."

My eyes had cleared enough to see him. Dave, Eve's driver. My mind reeled with the implications. Was Dave the man responsible for all these deaths? Had he been the powerful Nihla presence everyone seemed so scared of? Dave the driver, who lived in the guesthouse, and spent his time taking orders from Eve.

I said, "I don't get it—why?"

Dave pushed me toward the kitchen. He opened the door to the basement and shoved me through, the gun now aimed at the back of my skull.

"Down," he said and waved the gun toward the dark, narrow basement steps.

"No."

He pushed me. I tripped and fell, slamming my hip against the wall and my knee on the step. He pulled me up and pushed me forward, his hand an iron claw around my arm. My knee throbbed. I was starting to feel wobbly and nauseous from the hit to my head.

He said, "Get down there."

I walked obediently in front of him, biding my time, looking for a way out. At the bottom of the steps, he flipped on the light. It took a moment for my eyes to adjust. Jet sat on one of three chairs placed toward the exterior wall of the basement. Sat was a kind word—he was restrained on the chair with rope and duct tape. His head lolled to one side; dried blood had pooled under his lips and around his eyes. I wondered how long he'd been down here. I wondered how long I would be, too.

"Sit." Dave pushed me down onto the second chair and secured my wrists behind me with rope. With one finger, he traced a line on my forehead, then glanced at the blood now staining his skin.

"Dave," I said, trying to sound reasonable. "We've known each other for years. If it's money you're after, we can work something out—"

Dave walked over to the spot where Jet and I had dug up the bones. He looked dispassionately down at the morbid gravesite, his face an unreadable mask.

"You did that," I said. "You killed those women."

He glanced my way, and in that split second, I saw genuine surprise before he had the chance to rearrange his features once again.

"Dave—"

He strolled back to the steps with that rambling gait I knew so well. He flicked off the light, then made his way back upstairs, leaving me with an unconscious Jet in the blackened basement of this hell house.

"Dave!" I screamed. "Let me go!"

A low moan escaped Jet's lips. That moan, and the howling of the wind outside, were the only answers to my desperate plea for freedom.

*   *   *

The darkness swallowed me. Jet's moans were more sporadic now, his voice weaker than before. Something scurried along the dirt floor, the asshole's heavy tread echoed from upstairs. My throat was dry, my head pounding. I had to pee.

"Jet," I hissed. Then louder, "*Jet.*"

He groaned. What had Dave done to him down here? I thought of the years Dave had been with us. Plain, vanilla Dave.

Dependable, quiet Dave. The antidote to Eve's erratic moods. Dave was a serial killer? Nothing he had done ever indicated his part in all of this. And if he had come after me now, then that meant he'd been hiding in plain sight of Eve for the past five years. While she played secret agent in the basement, he'd been driving her around, laughing behind her back. Which meant Eve didn't recognize him. Either he was very good at disguise, or she'd never met the man who'd killed her daughter.

But if Dave was Nihla's serial killer, why hadn't he done something before now? He'd had five years to go after Eve. Five years to kill me and Lisa. Five years to finish what he'd started with the Foster family. Either he was like a cat, playing with his prey, or I was missing some crucial element of the story.

My head throbbed. Thoughts rushed at me—nonsensical, half-formed, fluid. Thinking in any organized fashion was like swimming upstream against the current. I closed my eyes, forced myself to concentrate.

Currents. Waves. Lisa's head bobbing just above the water. A flash of blonde hair. Red all around us, consuming us. Smoke, so much smoke. Bits of memories swirled with pervasive, pummeling thoughts. I tried to anchor myself in the here and now, feel the wood under my thighs, the rope against my wrists, but I couldn't focus, couldn't hold on.

Currents. Waves. A red door and a red roof and a red sun over an impossibly aqua Ionian Sea.

Red blood in a bland hallway.

A red slash of a mouth, open, yelling.

Smoke. Suffocation. Terror.

I tried to open my eyes against the assault, but they were heavy, so heavy, and I was tired. *Hold on, Connie.* For the absolute briefest of moments, like an illuminating flash of lightning overhead, I knew everything there was to know about what had happened. Some kind of truth was buried, like these bodies, right beneath the surface of my psyche.

Buried under veils and veils of red.

CHAPTER

47

Eve Foster
Nihla, New Mexico—1997

THE GUN FELT heavy in Eve's hand. *This is too easy*, she thought, as she sat beside Flora in a car that smelled like spoiled milk and baby powder. Her head hurt from the tension and excitement and knowledge that she'd finally find her ungrateful daughter. What the hell would she do with Kelsey once she was found? Lock her in the basement until she was twenty-one? She'd already disowned her, and that hadn't done a damn thing to change her behavior.

That decision could be made later. Once she saw what shape Kelsey was in. Once she understood whether this little adventure—this fucking fiasco—had made Kelsey repent her ways at all. Doubtful. Kelsey, like her father, was what a psychiatrist had once called a sociopath in the making. Sociopaths don't repent. They just go on hurting people until someone makes them stop.

Eve took a long look at Flora. A few kinky gray hairs corkscrewed from her otherwise flawless black hair. Frown lines etched into her young skin. Eve noticed the clenched jaw, the white knuckles, red eyes, those horrid neck bruises. In another life, perhaps she and Flora could have been friends. Friendship born of suffering. Maybe even a friendship forged with understanding.

But right now, Flora was her enemy. And Eve would do what she had to do to protect her own.

Flora drove silently along Nihla's main road. She pulled down an alley and behind a row of houses, wedging the car between two dumpsters. Eve recognized the back of Jack's bar. The neighborhood was cramped and ugly, each narrow house more rundown and derelict than the next. She glanced at Flora in confusion.

"We'll park and wait," Flora said. Her leg was shaking, her skin had paled to the color of sour milk. But her tone was all iron.

"Is this where my daughter is being held?"

"We park and wait."

Eve waved the gun. "You remember who's in charge."

"Use it. It will be a blessing." Flora's smile twisted like a snake across her face. It was a bitter smile, full of anger and disgust, and Eve felt herself recoil. "Neither of us is in charge."

Seconds morphed into minutes until almost half an hour had passed. The car was warm, the baby stench strengthening as the air grew stale. Eve reached for the window handle, and Flora's arm shot out to stop her.

"Leave it," she said. Like her neck, her wrist, visible beneath the cheap material, was mottled by a circular bruise. Eve looked up from her wrist to her face.

"He likes to tie me up," Flora said, voice flat. "He wasn't always like this. Once he was kind, generous. But now . . . I never know what I'm getting."

Eve took a deep breath and stared into the deserted alleyway. "My late husband was fond of games, too. His favorite game involved tying me up for hours on end and leaving me like that, with no idea when he would return." She turned her attention to her own hands. Their neon fingernail polish, done as part of her disguise, created a stranger's hands. "Once he left me like that for over a day."

"What did you do?"

"I managed."

Eve flexed her hands. She could still feel the sting of metal cutting into her wrists, the wire binding her ankles to the bed. He'd left her a hamster bottle of water suspended over her head, but no food. Sheer hatred had turned to panic and, eventually, despair. She'd managed all right.

Kelsey had been seven. She'd escaped the nanny and come into their room, looking for her father. Instead, she'd found her mother tied to the bed in a pool of her own waste.

"Help me," Eve had said, swallowing her shame. "The key is over there, on the bureau. Give it to me, Kelsey."

Kelsey's look was one of surprise, then disgust, then cool appraisal. Her little chin had jutted forward. "Why'd Daddy do this?"

"He forgot about me, that's all."

"Were you bad?"

"Of course not."

"Huh." Kelsey had walked over to the dresser, picked up the key. She'd turned it over, studied it.

"Kelsey, give me the key."

"Daddy tells me that half the fun is doing it yourself. He must have wanted you to figure it out."

Daddy is a monster. "Daddy lost track of time, that's all. This is no game, Kelsey. Give me the key."

Kelsey placed the key on the edge of the bed, outside Eve's reach, and turned to leave.

"Kelsey, dammit, *give me the key.*"

"You have to earn it, Mommy. By figuring it out yourself." She left the room, closing the door behind her.

Liam had returned four hours later. He'd laughed when he heard about Kelsey.

"Did you hate him?" Flora asked, interrupting Eve's thoughts.

"Yes."

"How did he die?"

Eve stared at the rundown houses. When she found Kelsey, would she bring her home? Would she make her pay?

"Eve, how did your late husband die?"

Eve turned toward the younger woman. "He had an unfortunate car accident."

Flora nodded slowly. "I'm sorry for your loss."

This time it was Eve's smile that was reptilian and ugly. "Don't be," she said. "I'm not."

CHAPTER

48

Constance Foster
Nihla, New Mexico—Present

CALL ME MOTHER. Terrifying sensations of panic, pain, terror. *Mother.* I couldn't wake up, couldn't escape. I slept for hours, maybe a day, trapped in a nightmare.

Cold water splashed me lucid.

"Get up, Connie. Come on. Don't make it worse than it has to be."

Mother. Cold water. Searing heat. Suffocation. Panic. *Mother.* Not a dream—a memory. A series of memories. A series of memories that swam in and out of focus like an impressionist painting or a fuzzy photograph. *Call me Mother.* A red slash of mouth. A red door. Two little red wires.

Call me Mother.

I blinked against the harsh light. Dave's voice came through as though he were speaking through a tunnel. My head hummed, my heart was pounding. Dave's fingers clenched my jaw, pulling my head up and forward.

"Come on, Connie. Look at me."

I forced my eyes to open. Dave's gaze met mine before darting away guiltily.

"Do you know why you're here?" he asked.

"No."

With his gold watch gone, his tattoo was visible. A mermaid, her blue and silver tail wrapped around his wrist and meeting at a pair of perky tits, smiled from tan flesh. A mermaid I'd seen before. I saw Amy's face, remembered our conversation at the bar. Jack's Place. The mermaid painted on the wall over the pool table in the back.

Mermaid. Surf. Waves. Lisa's head being forced under the water. Wild, terrorized eyes. My own screams, high-pitched and frenzied.

Call me Mother.

"You're Jack Cozbi. You owned the bar."

"Why are you here, Constance?"

I didn't respond. He tossed more water on me. I shut my eyes and was transported again. Thick, choking smoke. A red pump, sitting in a pool of red liquid. Two eyes, staring. *Mami.* My Mami.

Stingy red lips: *Call me Mother.*

"You're the serial killer," I managed, trying to ignore the chaos in my head. "You're the fucker who's been murdering these women. These *girls*." But even as I said the words, I knew they weren't right. Deep down . . . deep down where the memories were buried, I *knew*.

He shook his head slowly back and forth. "I thought for sure you'd have it all figured out by now. You were always the smart one. Too smart. Your *mother* couldn't keep up with you." He said "mother" with a sneer. "She didn't deserve you." He reached his mermaid hand out and caressed the side of my face. My skull was still tender, and I flinched.

He said, "I'm not going to hurt you. Not if you cooperate."

"What do you want from me?"

"You'll see in time."

A sound escaped Jet's mouth.

"You're killing him."

"He'll be fine."

"Let him go."

Dave rose, disappearing into a dark corner of the basement. He returned with a thermos of water. He held the water to my mouth, and I clenched my lips together. I didn't trust whatever was in the container.

"Suit yourself."

He pulled Jet's head back and poured liquid into his mouth. Jet sputtered, spit, and coughed. Dave did it again, this time pouring some of the water on Jet's head, splashing his face. Jet's eyes opened. He blinked, turned toward me, blinked again. His eyes looked bloodshot and unfocused.

Dave gave Jet another sip before offering it to me. I accepted this time. I needed my strength if I was going to get out of this alive. The water was lukewarm, but I gulped at it hungrily.

"How long have I been down here?" I asked between gulps.

"Maybe not long enough," Dave said. "Tell me, why are you here, Constance? Things will be much easier if you just remember."

I took a deep breath. My ribs hurt, pain like knife stabs seared behind my temple. "I think I have a concussion. And I pissed myself."

"You're fine." He squatted down, gazed into my face. "Why are you here?"

I looked away. Said softly, "Because I'm his daughter."

Dave stood and stepped back. "Good girl. You *are* his daughter. In more ways than you know."

"I don't care. I don't even know who *he* is." I spat on the ground. "Get me the fuck out of here."

"Calm down."

"Don't tell me to calm down. What is this all about? And why is Jet here? You're killing him. Can't you see? Let him go!"

But Dave was finished talking to me. He reached again into the shadows, and this time he brought over a black bag. His hand disappeared inside and came out holding a syringe.

"Just a small pinch and you'll feel better. Do you know why I'm here yet?"

I refused to answer him, refused to look at him. He held my arm in one hand and squeezed the flesh before jabbing the needle beneath my skin.

"Good night, Ana."

Ana? I tried to tell him to fuck off, but I was already flailing beneath the current again.

Ana?

A red orb over a raging sea. Searing heat, this time in my chest. The hand that holds is holding me down. Holding me under. Pulling me up. Again and again and again.

Call me Eve.

*   *   *

I woke up in a cold sweat. My body ached and my head throbbed, but otherwise, I was still alive. It was pitch black in the basement, but I could hear Jet's ragged breath. He was alive, too.

"Jet," I whispered. "Are you okay?"

"Been better. I think the motherfucker broke my wrist." Jet's voice was weak and uneven. "Bashed my head pretty good, too. Ribs as well."

"How'd you end up down here?"

It was a moment before he responded. "I heard something at your house. Came to check." He groaned. "He caught me by surprise, from behind. Hit me over the head, whacked me with a bat. Who the hell is he?"

"Eve's driver. I don't know why he's here."

"Eve's driver?" Jet's voice trailed off. "Really? That can't be right."

I strained against the rope around my wrists. "Why?"

"His tattoo. The mermaid one on his wrist. Did you see that? He's from Nihla."

"Yeah, I noticed that. The same design as the mermaid in the bar. I never noticed it when he was at the estate. His watch covered it. I think he's the bar's former owner, Jack Cozbi."

"Does that mean he's the guy . . ." Jet gasped in pain, let out his breath slowly. "Is he the one . . . doing all of this?"

"I don't know. It doesn't really add up. Eve would have known who he was." I told Jet about the setup Lisa had found in the Vermont basement. "Even if she didn't know who he was, if he was in Vermont with us, who was she hunting?"

"Good point." Jet was silent for a few moments, and when he spoke again, his voice was weak and raspy. "Do you think he killed Eve?"

I chided myself for not considering that. Her death in Lake Champlain was suspicious. Eve *had* been a strong swimmer. Strong and sure and confident—and careful. She wore an open water swim buoy tethered to her waist, which is how they located her body. The buoy was still bobbing. Lisa said that day the wind had been gusty, and the lake's chop had been higher than normal. I—we all, I guess—assumed she'd gotten a mouthful of water and lost control. But Eve never lost control.

"Biding his time, like a predator," I said. "Eve finally met her match?"

"Perhaps."

We sat in silence for a while. Jet's labored breathing worried me, although silence from him would have worried me more.

Jet said, "I was afraid he'd killed you."

I smiled, despite the situation, and even though he couldn't see me. "I was afraid you'd run with your money. But I heard Micah. I knew you'd never leave her."

"Considered it. Went so far as to move the money, just in case the cops came snooping around. Should have, it seems." He coughed. More quietly, he said, "I may not make it out of here, Connie. And if I don't . . . take my truck. It's all there."

"We'll both make it out just fine."

He coughed again, tight and painful sounding. I felt myself flinch. I squinted, trying to see Jet—see anything—in the basement. It was a pure black abyss.

I asked, "Do you have one usable hand?"

"Why?"

"There's a razor in my pocket. Maybe you can reach it if I can get myself behind you."

"In the dark? Next to the pit?" He made a half-hearted attempt at a laugh. "I don't see that working."

"So we sit down here waiting for him to kill us?"

"I didn't say that."

"Let me try, then. My ankles aren't secured. I think I can move the chair."

I took a deep breath, pushed my feet against the hard-packed dirt floor, and scooted the chair backward about five inches. I could picture the layout of the basement: the pit, Jet's chair next to mine, and the ominous third chair. I just needed to move back about a foot—that would be the easy part—and then over about three feet. It was the latter move that would be tricky. Somewhere near the pit, we'd left our shovels. If I dumped the chair over, or worse, fell into the pit, I wouldn't be able to right myself.

I shifted backward again, sensitive to the sound of the chair's feet scraping against the ground.

"Say something," I hissed. "I need to check your location."

Jet muttered a few nonsensical words, and I angled myself in the direction of his voice before scooting the chair to the side a few inches.

"Again," I whispered.

He coughed, then said, "Fuck, fuck, fuck," over and over.

"Nice."

I reached out with my foot, hoping to feel for anything on the floor. I could only extend my leg so far to the left, but from what I could tell, the floor near me was clear. I moved to the side a few more inches. We did this a few times until I felt like I was behind him. I just needed to turn the chair ninety degrees and back it up, so he could reach into my pocket.

I swept my foot out, then moved the chair at an angle, picturing an axis in my mind. I did this again. And again.

I said, "Say something."

"Shit."

"Very original." I didn't like the sound of his voice. He was weakening. Whether from dehydration, blood loss, pain, a concussion, or some combination, I wasn't sure. But I was sure he needed to get out of this basement, or he would be joining the bodies in the pit. "Hold on, okay?"

I thought I had the right angle, but now I needed to edge closer to Jet so he could reach my pocket. Only I couldn't remember which pocket I'd slipped the razor in. I closed my eyes, tried to picture picking it up, slipping it inside, but my brain was forging ahead too quickly and no image came to mind. I moved an inch, swept with my foot, and felt the back of Jet's chair. Good. Just a few more inches. I repeated the process twice, and I could feel heat from his body nearby. I reached a foot out and was met with the sturdy wood from his chair.

"Ready?"

"Why not."

"Which is your good hand?"

"My left."

I pressed the side of my chair and my hip against his chair, trying to avoid his injured wrist in the dark. I heard him gasp, then let out a slow, deliberate breath.

I said, "Sorry."

Jet didn't answer, but I could feel his hand against my pocket. I shifted, trying to move closer. His fingers swept the top of my jeans.

"It's no use. I can't get in there."

"Keep trying."

"Connie, your pockets are too tight and I don't have enough give. I can't reach."

Damn. "What the hell are we going to do now—" I stopped. Sounds overhead caught my attention. It was the sound of the front door opening and footsteps overhead. "Shhh," I said. "Listen."

I heard two, no three, sets of footsteps. Two sets of steps were heavy and one light. A child or a woman. A man spoke. I could hear the tone and pitch—conversational and deep—but not what he was saying. The reply came from another man, a man Dave called "Kyle." The tone was authoritative, the voice surprisingly high-pitched. Voices escalated, and I heard the unmistakable plea from a woman. She was sobbing.

"Hear that?" I whispered to Jet.

"Yes. Two more people. One is a woman."

Kyle Summers is upstairs. With another victim? I didn't even want to consider that possibility. There was a thud overhead, followed by a scream. The sound was a knife stab to my temples. Again I saw a red orb above a roiling ocean, a mean, slash of a mouth. *Call me Eve.* I closed my eyes, clenched my fists. A face, barely bobbing above the sea, melding with a hot red sun, eyes wide with terror.

Jet said, "Connie—"

A tiny mouth trying to let out a scream. A hand holding her under the water, pulling her up. Over and over again. I knew the hand, I knew the cruel slash of a mouth. I knew the tiny head being held under the water. *Call me mother. Call me Eve.*

The woman above screamed again, bringing me back to the here and now.

I'd recognize that scream anywhere.

CHAPTER

49

Eve Foster
Nihla, New Mexico—1997

A PAIR OF HEADLIGHTS flashed in the alley entrance.
Flora sat up straighter. She crossed herself. "*Gracias a Dios*," she said. "He did it."

Eve glanced at her. "Did what?"

But Flora was already opening the car door. She stopped, her hand on the handle, and glanced over at Eve. "Do you want to see your daughter again?"

Eve nodded.

"Leave the gun. Leave everything. You do what he says. I mean it. You understand?"

Eve nodded again, but Flora's sudden shift in tone and demeanor was not lost on her. The other car had pulled into a spot next to one of the houses and killed the lights. Flora was straining to see inside the vehicle, her eyes searching in panic.

Of course—Kyle had taken Flora's children, and Eve had been Flora's pawn to get them back.

Through gritted teeth she said, "You used me."

"I did what I had to do. Just as you have done."

Eve considered running. She could easily open the car door and sprint into the night, find a way back to the rental car and leave this godforsaken hellhole for good. She said, "Is Kelsey even here?"

"She's here. With my girls."

Eve took a deep breath, nodded. She'd come this far. She needed to let go of the fear and harness the anger. Isn't that what she had done with Liam? Her mother's only practical advice ever had been that some people feed on fear. *Don't give it to them. Don't feed the monster.*

She wouldn't give it to Kyle now.

"Let's go," she said as she opened her door. "I want to see my daughter."

50

Constance Foster
Nihla, New Mexico—Present

L ISA. "My God, it's my sister."
I felt Jet's hand stroking my side, his touch gentle. It was a small gesture of comfort, and I appreciated it, but it did nothing to quell the wave of nausea and fear rising inside of me. My body started to shake, and the pain in my head that I'd been trying to ignore hit me again in waves.

He had Lisa.

"Connie, keep it together. Now isn't the time to lose your shit."

"Seriously, Jet? My sister is at the hands of these cretins, and I'm tied in a basement with no fucking way out—"

"There may be a way out."

"What do you mean?" I waited, willing deep, calm breaths.

"Can you reach my right pocket?"

"Maybe."

"I have a lighter in there. We may be able to use it to burn through a rope."

I considered what he was saying. Even if I could reach it, that meant one of us had to hold a lighter long enough to burn through rope. Rope that was next to skin. Pain was better than the alternative.

"Let's try."

I shuffled the chair backward a few inches. I couldn't sweep the floor behind me with my foot, so I was banking on a clear path. I repeated the process, little movements at a time, until I was next to Jet's right pocket.

"Can you reach?" he asked.

"Not quite."

Carefully, quietly, I angled myself around Jet, holding my breath out of fear that I'd catch a chair leg on the pit or against a shovel. When I was close enough to reach his pocket, I exhaled, tears blurring my eyes. Upstairs, I could only hear the despicable murmurs of the men. I knew now that the third chair was meant for Lisa, and it wouldn't be long before they came down with their latest prey.

By extending my wrist as far as it would go, I could just reach into his pocket. I focused on the painful stretch, ignoring the ropes tearing my skin. My fingers touched something hard and plastic, but I couldn't quite grasp it.

I said, "Can you shift your hips?"

Jet wiggled closer to the edge of his seat. I reached farther, managed to get a finger underneath the lighter. The ropes were digging more deeply into my wrists, and blood trickled down my hand, making it slippery. I clenched my eyes shut, pictured Eve's face, and fought past the pain. I could feel the lighter moving, and I applied steady pressure until it was at the top of the pocket. This was the crucial moment. If I pushed it too hard, it would fall on the floor and there was no way we'd find it in the dark.

"Stay still," I said. As I pushed the lighter the rest of the way, I wrapped my fingers around the base. "Got it."

I waited until my pulse had calmed to start the journey back around Jet, inch by inch. We needed to be back-to-back, with our hands touching. He'd become my rock, my axis, the only thing real in this basement. I wasn't sure I'd ever been so grateful for another human being in my life.

Except for Lisa.

I heard something dragging across the floor upstairs, then footsteps.

"Take this," I said. "Hurry, but be careful. Don't drop it. I'll hold my wrists as far apart as I can. And whatever I do or say, don't stop until the rope has burned through."

"I can't."

"What do you mean you can't? You have to."

"I mean I can't hold the lighter still enough or securely enough. My wrist is . . . you need to do it."

"No way. You've been through enough."

"Want to die down here, Connie? Do it."

The thought of burning Jet's already mutilated flesh was repugnant. Still, he was right. We couldn't risk him dropping the lighter. I felt for the rope binding Jet's arms with one hand, then positioned the lighter underneath and flicked it until I could sense the heat of the flame. I ran a finger underneath to make sure the fire was aimed at the rope, the pain urging me forward, latching on to the building rage.

It was working. Behind me, Jet groaned. Although I couldn't see it, I knew the flame would be flicking at his skin, burning blisters into tender flesh. The lighter was getting hot. I could smell and feel the skin on my thumb burning, and I fought to keep holding the lighter upright against the pain.

"Try to pull the ropes apart," I said.

"Keep going. We're not there yet." Jet spoke through clenched teeth.

We stayed like that, locked in a circle of agony, while the lighter weakened the rope. Eventually my thumb found a will of its own and let go of the trigger.

"Damn it."

"It's okay," Jet said. "I think that was enough."

We were close enough together that I could feel him tugging against the rope with his tortured wrists.

"Let me help." I grabbed two parts of the rope on either side of the scorched area and pulled. The rope gave way. "Yes."

I helped Jet unbind his hands, then moved the chair so that he could reach into my pocket for the razor blade.

"There," he said. "Unbind my legs."

I used what was left of the lighter to illuminate the ground around us. Above us, footsteps moved across the old wood floors. I crawled around Jet's chair until I found his feet. Using the razor, I sliced through the rope.

"What now?" he asked. I didn't like the rattle in his voice.

"You stay here. Find a dark corner and regain some of your strength. I'll call an ambulance as soon as I can." I stuck my burned thumb into my mouth, relishing the pain, letting it fuel my hatred. Then I kissed him, softly and tenderly on parched lips. "Okay?"

"Sure. Connie—"

"What?"

"Be careful." Voice barely a whisper. "What will you do?"

I glanced up, toward the floorboards overhead. "I think they call it patricide."

* * *

Making it to the stairs was the easy part. I half walked, half crawled across the dirt, using the lighter and my hands for guidance. Jet remained behind me, slumped on the floor by his chair. He needed help, badly. I felt around the base of the steps until I found the pick we'd used to loosen the dirt around the graves and held this to my side as I climbed the darkened steps.

The door at the top was partially ajar, and I could hear them talking, laughing, as though this were an ordinary day.

I started to push on the door when the third voice chilled me to my core. *Eve?* What was she doing here? Eve was dead. It took me a moment to realize it wasn't Eve's voice, but Lisa's. And it wasn't the sound of her voice, exactly, that was the same, but the way Lisa punctuated her words, the lilt with which she curled her vowels.

How had I not noticed that before?

I slipped out of the basement and into the kitchen. Because of the house's layout, I knew as soon as I stepped into the central portion of the kitchen that they would see me. I was deciding how to approach them when I realized they'd stopped talking all together.

"Ana," a voice called. "Please come here."

I froze.

Dave's head popped around the corner. He reached for the pick and took it from me. "Come this way."

Numb and confused, I followed him into the front room. Lisa was sitting on the floor, hugging her knees. She looked up at me. I watched a collage of emotions color her features—surprise, then relief, and finally, shame.

Dave said, "Sit, Ana."

I turned to the second man, recognizing him as the gas station attendant near Manuela's diner. Blond-gray hair, medium build, pale skin. Nondescript, tidy, maybe a little on the paunchy side.

Kyle. My father. He was everyman and no one, a human chameleon. He certainly didn't look like a serial killer.

But then, I guess they never did.

He said, "I'm glad you decided to join us. This makes things easier. How is your friend?"

I refused to answer.

"A travesty of circumstances. Your fault, you know. The basement . . . let's just say there are a lot of memories down there."

I met his gaze with a cool one of my own. Try as I might, I saw little resemblance between us. Lisa, perhaps—with her blonde hair and fair complexion. He smiled, and his eye teeth shone sharp and cruel. I had eye teeth like that. Perhaps we shared something after all.

Dave pulled a chair from the kitchen and placed it next to the wall. He pushed me down. I skirted to the edge.

Kyle said, "I was just offering your sister a deal."

I turned my attention to Lisa. She seemed a smaller version of herself—collar bones jutting, her hair in a thin, wispy ponytail, her linen blouse hanging on her narrow frame. My first inclination was to comfort her, but I couldn't get her to acknowledge me, much less meet my gaze. I wondered about this deal. I wondered what was happening.

Kyle said, "You've hurt yourself."

"Look, I don't know what the fuck is happening here, but I don't know you and you don't know me, so stop feigning concern."

"You do know me, Ana Maria. Granted, it's been a while."

I stood up and reached for the pick in Dave's hands. He moved at the last second, throwing me off balance. I stumbled.

"We're not going to tie you up again," Kyle said. "There's no need for the drama. Just sit, please."

"No."

"Sit." When I remained standing, Kyle said, "Fine, have it your way. As you've probably figured out by now, you and I have a blood bond." He nodded toward Lisa. "Same with Teresa here."

"Kyle Summers. I know your name." I turned to Dave. "How are you two connected?" I glanced at his wrist, which was once again covered by the gold watch. "You owned the bar in Nihla. That much I've figured out, but what's your relationship with him?"

Dave smiled, but it was Kyle who answered. "Jack and I have been friends since grade school, right, Jack?"

Jack nodded.

"I financed his first business, the bar downtown, and he gave me access to certain . . . real estate." Kyle gave Jack a solemn nod. "Now he's just a friend who wants in on the deal."

"You killed those girls," I said to Dave. "Their blood is on your hands."

Dave shook his head. "I never touched any of them."

"You made it possible. You looked away while he did vile things." Josiah believed there had been more than one murderer. He had been half right.

"We're not here to talk about Jack," Kyle said. I saw the slightest shift in that sanguine demeanor. He had a sharp edge, a narcissist's need to be the center of everything. It would be a matter of getting him to go over that edge.

"Why didn't Eve recognize you?" I asked Dave.

"Because I looked different back then. And because your adoptive mother had never really spent much time with me."

"She wasn't my adoptive mother, was she? The orphanage in Greece, a lie."

Kyle said, "Sit. Let's be civilized. We are, after all, family. Or at the very least, we're soon to be business partners."

I turned my attention to Lisa, who'd retreated into her shell. "What deal did you make with him? You can't believe a word that comes out of his mouth. Tell me what you agreed to." I shook her shoulders. "Tell me."

Kyle said, "I merely told her she could stay with you from now on. That you and she could live together at the Vermont estate. That she didn't have to be alone."

"How could you promise her that? That won't ever happen." I glanced at Dave. "You know that. Tell him. It's in the will, in the terms of Eve's trust."

Kyle shook his head. "The will is void. Or at least it can be."

I glanced from him to Dave to my sister, who had retreated further from reality. I needed to get her out of here, but if we were going to escape this, we needed to act together. She had to help me.

"I don't care about the will," I said to Kyle. "I know you're a killer, a cowardly asshole who let two men go to prison for what you did. You murdered my real mother along with countless other women." I stared at him, the full horror of his actions becoming clear. "You murdered Amy. Kidnapped her, tortured her. You've been stalking me. I know *you* wrote 'little red house' on the paper at the diner, *you* put that snake in my house."

"You know more than that." Kyle's voice was chillingly soft. He stood and walked to where I was sitting. "Think, Ana. Think."

I shook my head. Lisa started to sob.

"*Ana.*" He said the name sharply, and I looked up. Gently, almost lovingly, he said, "Do you remember that night? It was so long ago."

As before, I could feel the memories pressing inside me, straining toward the light. A jumbled, infuriating collection of disparate thoughts and phrases. Underneath the chaos, underneath the flashes of memory, lurked the truth. Whether a two-headed monster or an angel of rebirth, the truth, I believed, would set me free.

"Help me remember," I said.

"Are you sure?"

I glanced again at my twin sister, who was rocking back and forth, her arms locked around her knees. "Yes."

*   *   *

Why do men feel the need to possess beauty? Why isn't it enough simply to admire it, appreciate it, acknowledge it? Why must there always be a game, a competition? A conquest. Big game hunter and prey. Fisherman and catch. Art collector and object d'art. Pimp and prostitute.

And why do the worst of men feel the need to not only possess beauty, but destroy it?

*   *   *

Kyle posed these questions as we sat in my living room, as though there weren't dead bodies in the basement and a nearly comatose man in the house. As though my sister and I were his loving daughters rather than hostages. I watched his lips move, fascinated by his self-absorption, his complete lack of understanding of how fucking abnormal this all was.

Kyle said, "Stop and ask yourself, Ana, why men do these things. What drives them? Is it a diseased mind, as many psychoanalysts would have you think? Or is it, perhaps, simply because they can?"

"Simply because *you* can."

He sat back against his chair, crossed his legs. "Ah, but why? And not just men . . . some women as well."

"I'm not sure I care why."

Kyle smiled. "That was an answer your mother would have given. She had no curiosity about the why of things, which is something, sadly, that triggered me on occasion. I regret that."

"I didn't think sociopaths could feel regret."

Kyle laughed. "I hardly consider myself a sociopath. I feel regret, even shame on occasion. While I appreciate Jack here," he glanced at Dave, "I only ever met one person who was a match for my . . . hunger."

"Eve?"

"Kelsey, Eve's daughter. She was a glorious girl. Intelligent, gorgeous, spiteful, and very bright. She was the only girl who ever challenged me, and I'm afraid I let her get the better of me."

"Meaning?"

"Meaning I let her have certain liberties, certain freedoms. I've asked myself why over and over all these years. You see, things would be much different had I made another choice. The simple answer, I suppose, is that she amused me. She was far more fun alive than dead, so I gave in. Eventually, I saw that she enjoyed aspects of the game as much as I did." Kyle's eyes took on a gleam. "A perfectly sculpted neck. A particularly expressive set of eyes. A deliciously tight cunt." He turned those gleaming eyes on me. "She liked the mental part of it. Like a cat torturing a mouse before the kill, Kelsey liked to taunt and tease, nice one minute, cruel the next." He smiled. "We were a pair, she and I, and I relished the partnership almost as much as I enjoyed tormenting her."

Nice one minute, cruel the next. Blonde hair, red lips. A red orb over a choppy sea.

"You're a sick bastard." I spat out the words.

Lisa let out another sob. Her eyes had gone blank, her mouth slack. Was she remembering what I could not?

"I thought maybe this house would have been enough to trigger your memories," Kyle said. "When Jack told me Eve had left it to you, I was admittedly excited by her choice. She knew, of course, that this house held meaning for me. She knew I would find you here."

She had, but I already knew that. While Eve was busy searching for Kyle, he'd already found her, had placed a spy in her house. If I wasn't so twisted up inside, I might have appreciated his cunning. The fact that I was here, though, that even after her death Eve had raised the stakes, was a nod to her planning. And her utter lack of feeling for me or Lisa. She wanted to get back at Kyle, but she also wanted to hurt us.

I watched Lisa rock back and forth, my poor, sensitive, vulnerable sister. I closed my eyes, thought of the red orb, the waves, the hand that held her under. The hand that held me under. What did it all mean?

Call me Mother. Call me Eve.

A red slash of a mouth. A red door. Two red wires.

I knew these memories were from Corfu. I knew the Ionian Sea, the brilliant sunsets and sunrises of my childhood. But the hand, the wire, the mouth. Not wires—matches. Matches. Fire. Smoke.

Kyle said, "Think, Ana."

A *young* mouth, red and twisted and mean. A *young* woman, laughing cruelly. A *young* woman, kicking at a body. My *Mami*, dead on the floor. Matches, fire. A *young* woman forcing Lisa's head under the water. *Call me Eve. Call me Eve.* A young woman taking my kitten. A young woman sending me away.

A young woman. A young woman I *knew*.

I stood, ran to the bedroom. There, I tore through my drawers, looking for the bracelet I had pulled from the bones in the basement. I found it beneath my T-shirts. I turned it over, held the back to the light. There they were: the initials *E. F.*

E. F.

Eve Foster.

It wasn't Kelsey whose bones were buried in the basement of the little red house. It was Eve. The real Eve Foster.

51

Eve Foster
Nihla, New Mexico—1997

S HE FELT THE cold metal against her temple at the same time his chest pressed against her back. Kyle was a small man, but she hadn't noticed just how small he was before now. His chest fit perfectly against the curve of her spine, his slight frame a complement to her own. Such a little man had taken down Kelsey. Who would have thought that was possible? The funny things you think about when you're in danger, Eve thought. She reached up and touched the gun aimed at her brain.

"Really?" she asked. "Is that necessary?"

Kyle shoved her toward the rear entrance of the house. Flora was pulling on the door ahead of her, crying.

"Where are they?" Flora hissed. "You fucking *gilipollas*. You said they'd be here. You said you'd give them back if I brought *her*."

Kyle reached around Flora, opened the screen door, and unlocked a padlock on the bottom of the back door. A padlock—securing the house from the *outside*. Eve's skin prickled. She noticed the barred windows, the drawn shades. Normal people didn't do these things. Hadn't the neighbors noticed? But then, who were the neighbors? A bar? The rest of the houses along this strip looked run-down, condemned, or abandoned. These people had other things on their minds.

"Kyle, where are they? Please tell me." Flora was crying softly now, her shoulders heaving with each word.

"They're here, just like I promised."

"I don't hear them."

"Enough, Flora."

Flora's face paled. "You killed them."

"*Enough.*"

"Oh God, what did you do?" She punched him in the back, pounded her fists against his spine over and over. "What did you do to them? My babies!"

Eve's head was pounding from the tension of the gun against her skin. She fought to focus. Whatever she'd find inside, she needed to stay calm. She had one goal, she reminded herself—get Kelsey out of there. She couldn't be distracted by Flora or Flora's daughters or even fear.

Kyle opened the door and pushed Eve through. The house smelled of mothballs and Lysol and madness. It was dimly lit inside, and her footfalls against the wooden floors echoed. She blinked, her eyes adjusting to the darkness.

Kyle flipped a switch, and the sudden brightness burned. They were standing in a narrow hallway. Flora was alternating between sobs and curses, her back against the wall. Kyle grabbed her hand roughly and pulled her forward. The house was a labyrinth, with a series of small, wood-paneled rooms jutting off a central corridor. It was bigger than Flora's house, but not by much. It felt cramped and hot and claustrophobic. Eve's eyes watered from the musty air, and her head was pulsing now. She wished Flora would shut the fuck up.

"You are mad," Flora muttered. "I should have had you killed when I had the chance. You are both mad. You are both fucking *monsters.*"

Kyle reached back and smacked her. Flora's face reddened. She put a palm to her face, and, wide-eyed, she slapped him back. He pulled back and punched her, knocking her to the floor. Her head snapped backward and hit the bottom wooden step with a loud *crack.*

"See what you made me do?" Kyle poked at Flora with an oxford-clad toe. "Dammit, Flora, get up."

Eve wasn't so sure Flora would ever get up. Her eyes were glassy, her mouth open, and blood was trickling down her forehead. Kyle nudged Flora in the ribs. Her head lolled to the side.

"Damn it," Kyle hissed. He shoved the gun harder against Eve's head. "This is your fault. Move. Now."

Still staring at Flora, Eve said, "You need to call an ambulance."

Kyle grabbed both of her wrists with one hand. He pulled them behind her back. "No funny stuff."

"You killed your girlfriend."

Kyle shoved her, hard, farther down the hallway. The rooms she passed were barely furnished—a singular dingy chair, a floor cushion. But Kelsey was here. She could feel her daughter's energy, like stormy ocean waves lapping at her. A wave of nausea rose in her gut. She pushed it down with a will she'd forged from years of living with Liam.

Survivors survive, she reminded herself.

Kyle stopped at a paneled wall adorned with an oversized, dusty fake fern. He reached behind the plant. With a glance at her, he pulled something, and a seam appeared in the paneling. He pushed against the seam, and the wall popped open, revealing a door. With one hand holding the gun against her head, he unlocked the door, then pushed her through. She stumbled on a small landing, nearly falling down a flight of steps. He flicked on the lights.

"Down there," he mumbled.

"Kelsey!" Eve yelled.

"She can't hear you."

"How do I know she's even down there?"

Kyle tapped her head with the gun. "Do you really have a choice?"

Eve looked around for a weapon—anything she could use in a surprise attack. If only she could push *him* down the steps, use his own weight against him. Before she could angle herself to the side of the narrow staircase, he grabbed her by the hair, pulling off her wig. Then he wrapped his fingers around her skull and twisted her head back, forcing her to look up, into his cold, mocking eyes.

"Don't try anything, Eve. I mean it. Or you and the girl will die."

"I just want to see my daughter."

He smiled, a wicked smile full of contempt and hatred and something akin to amusement but far more cruel. "Just remember . . . you asked for this."

"What about Flora?"

"Her usefulness has passed."

Usefulness? Eve thought about the first time she had seen Flora, in Jack's bar. Pretty, sweet, seductive Flora. What better trap for unwary girls or women . . . someone kind, someone they could trust. Until they met her boyfriend. The little house. The blood in the outbuilding. The tools. The basement with a dirt floor.

My God, Eve thought. Flora wasn't just a naïve victim. He must have been using those little girls as collateral, ensuring Flora's cooperation, ensuring use of her house. With a town unwilling to confront Kyle and her questionable immigration status, Flora was given a Sophie's choice. He'd made her his accomplice. Until she became a liability. Then he'd needed another woman to use as bait. Willing or not.

A sound echoed from the bottom of the steps, and a door swung open. Two little faces peeked up from the doorway—one blonde, one brunette, one crying, the other wide-eyed and curious.

"*Mami?*" the blonde asked.

"Your mommy's coming," a voice said. A voice Eve would recognize any time, anywhere. Low-pitched for a girl. Smooth, mellow, but commanding.

"Kelsey," Eve said.

"Hello, Mother." Kelsey appeared from behind the door. She was thinner, her hair longer, the hungry edges of her face more pronounced. She still had the same Nordic beauty—only she'd lost the soft plushness of youth until all that remained were angles and planes. It was like looking in a mirror.

Kelsey pushed the toddlers forward. "Where's Flora?"

Kyle shook his head.

"Mami," the blonde sobbed. She stuck her thumb in her mouth, and her sister placed a tiny hand on her shoulder.

Kelsey straightened. She was wearing denim shorts, a red T-shirt, and her blonde hair cascaded around her shoulders in waves. Her bare legs were pale and scab-covered, but otherwise she looked healthy.

Kyle pushed Eve toward the open door. "Kelsey, take the girls inside."

Kelsey grabbed their hands and led them back into the base-ment room. The blonde pulled back, refusing to enter, and Kelsey bent down and whispered something that convinced her to cooper-ate. Eve followed the trio deeper into the dank space. Basements here were uncommon, and this basement was rudimentary, at best. A wooden table stood by the entrance, its top covered with a variety of tools and knives, implements that made Eve shudder. A twin bed sat under a boarded-up window. A small dresser, an old-fashioned chamber pot, a large dog bed, and a plastic chair had been scattered about. A single dirty animal pelt had been hung on the wall. Eve could smell it from here.

This wasn't a basement. It was a torture chamber.

Kelsey sat on the bed. A set of leather cuffs was attached to its four corners. Eve's breath caught, the nausea returning.

Kyle settled onto the plastic chair after making the toddlers sit on the dog bed. "On the bed," he said to Eve.

Eve didn't like the emptiness in his eyes. She considered bolting for the door, but he was still holding the gun. Reluctantly, she sat next to Kelsey on the cot.

"Are you okay?" she asked her daughter.

Kyle nodded at Kelsey, who glanced at Eve before rising. Slowly, deliberately, she placed the cuffs on her mother's wrists. Eve started to struggle, and Kyle released the safety on the gun. Eve thought of Flora, dead upstairs. What was one more body to this monster? Eve would cooperate—for now. Between Kelsey and her, they would find a way to get them both out of this hole.

The little brunette started to cry. Kyle reached a hand and placed it on her shoulder. "Ana, that's enough." The girl stiffened and drew herself closer to her sister.

"The feet, too," he said to Kelsey.

Kelsey started to protest. Kyle pointed to the pelt on the wall, and her daughter's eyes clouded. She grabbed her mother's ankles and pulled them straight before securing the leather restraints.

"Your turn first," Kyle said to Kelsey. "Whatever you'd like. Sky's the limit."

"I'll pass."

"Wasn't that the prize for this last round? You get to go first. Have your fun. You don't want your prize?"

"I want more time upstairs."

"That wasn't what we agreed on."

"I didn't think *she* would be the next one."

"Now, Kelsey, prisoners can't be choosey."

Kelsey jutted out her chin defiantly in a way that was all too familiar to Eve. "You need me."

"Don't forget your place." Kyle stood, walked toward the pelt. He touched it gently, ran a pale hand down its filthy surface. The act was gentle, almost sensual. Except for the excited gleam in his eyes. "You can join your mother on the bed. I might like that." He smiled. "You might like that, too."

Kelsey spat on the floor. "Fuck you."

Eve's head was pounding, her mouth was painfully dry—too dry to form words. She could only watch this odd standoff between a madman and her daughter the way she'd watch a confrontation unfold on a plane—simultaneously fascinated and mortified.

She thought of her gun, which sat useless in her bag in Flora's car. If she could get him to release her, maybe she could get out there. The keys were still in the car. She could flee—with or without Kelsey.

Kelsey stood up from the bed, walked across the room, and leaned against the wooden table. "I'll take the girls upstairs. You can do your thing."

"I want to watch you work," Kyle said. "It's always better after you have them amped up."

"Fine. I'll exercise my prize by doing nothing."

Kyle's face was reddening. He waved the gun. "Take off her clothes."

"No."

"You disappoint me, Kelsey. I thought you'd want this. After everything she's done to you—taking away your birthright, having you followed—I thought you'd enjoy some time with her."

Eve's eyes widened. Kelsey had confided in this monster? She watched Kelsey's face for signs of remorse, shame . . . she saw only a chin thrust defiantly forward, eyes that were clear and intelligent and matched his in coldness. *You have to earn it, Mother.*

Kyle moved toward Kelsey, gun outstretched. His voice lower, pleading, he said, "Come on. Take off her clothes. Just that."

"Then can I take the girls upstairs?"

"You know I can't allow that."

Was this one of Kelsey's tricks? Convince him to let her roam upstairs so she could escape. Would she return for Eve? Clearly, Kyle didn't trust her. Eve tried to think past the discomfort, the fear, the foggy head and dry mouth. She pulled at the restraints. She had allowed herself to be trapped, and she knew in that instant that, given the chance, Kelsey *would* escape, leaving her behind.

Eve said, "Kelsey, untie me. I'll put you back in the will. You can come home, no questions asked."

Kyle said, "No one is going home."

Kelsey looked from him to the twins to her mother. She let out a big sigh. "I'm going to let her go, Kyle."

"Don't you fucking move. I'll shoot her, Kelsey. And you'll be back in those restraints."

Quietly, calmly, Kelsey said, "You know I don't really care if you shoot her. And you can't do both. By the time you shoot my mother, I'll have run up the steps and escaped. Better yet, I'll have locked you in here." She nodded toward the entrance. She was a step away, he was across the room.

Kyle smiled, and in that second, Eve knew they both got off on whatever little game was playing out between them. Her daughter had met someone as sick as she was—a sick, twisted match, indeed.

And Eve's life hung in the balance.

"What do you want?" Kyle asked finally. He was looking at his daughters while talking to Kelsey and pointing the gun at Eve. In a huskier tone, "Tell me."

"I'll undress her, if that's what you'd like, and then I let you do what you want to her. But no permanent damage, and afterward, you let her go. In return for her life, she puts me back in the will and otherwise leaves me the fuck alone—and says nothing to no one or we hunt her down."

"And you?"

"I'll stay, but no more basement. I want equal privileges."

"I've been denying your existence in Nihla for weeks. I can't acknowledge you publicly now."

"I'll stay here, at this house, behind closed doors. We can work together." She tilted her head. In a sweet voice, she said again, "You need me."

His attention turned to his daughters. "I do need someone to take care of the girls."

Kelsey said, "I can do that, you know I can."

Eve watched him as he considered his options. She saw a bottomless hole of depravity and hunger and darkness, but it was the hunger that drove him. It would make him stupid with lust, and Kelsey would take advantage of that stupidity. Kelsey knew how to control her urges, to have patience, to lay a trap and wait for the right moment. She'd been doing it her entire life.

Kyle nodded. "Fine."

Kelsey made her way back to the cot. She began unbuttoning Eve's blouse. Eve closed her eyes, swallowing the humiliation, fanning the anger. There was a way out, and this was it. The only way out. When she opened her eyes again, Kyle was staring at them, his hand on his leg. He seemed mesmerized by what was happening, his eyes heavy-lidded. The toddlers were curled around one another, half asleep. Eve was grateful they would not witness what was about to happen.

"I'll do what he wants," Eve said. "If you let me go, I'll never breathe a word of this. Kelsey will be back in the will. In fact, I'll wire money—however much you both want."

Eve felt her daughter's fingers trace a line across her neck. Her touch was gentle, soft.

Kelsey leaned over and whispered, "The problem, Mother, is that I want it all."

With a hard and sudden shove, Kelsey leveraged the bed to push herself outward. She slammed into Kyle, knocking him off balance, and grabbed the gun. Without hesitation, she aimed at his head and pulled the trigger. Kyle dove for the floor. The sound was deafening in the small space, and the girls awakened, screaming, their hands over their ears.

Kelsey aimed again, but Kyle was fast. He ran upstairs just as Kelsey was pulling the trigger again.

"Damn," Kelsey yelled. "Damn you!"

The girls were crying. "Shut up," Kelsey hissed. "Just be quiet." She cocked her head, listening before running up the stairs after him, gun cocked.

Eve heard footsteps overhead, a door slam. She pulled against the cuffs. "Kelsey!"

The little girls were sobbing now. The brunette dragged the blonde toward the steps, but the blonde was crying too hard to move.

Moments later, Kelsey walked back down the steps. Her face was flushed, her mouth set in a frown, but she seemed calm and unhurried, like a woman who'd been planning this for some time and had confidence her plan would work. No doubt she *had* been planning an escape, Eve thought. Weaving her web, patiently waiting.

As Kelsey picked up the blonde toddler and took the hand of the brunette, she said over her shoulder, "I'll be back, Mother."

Kelsey's footsteps echoed all the way up the stairs and into the rooms above.

* * *

Eve smelled smoke, just a hint at first, then heavy enough to make her cough and gag. Kelsey wasn't coming back. She'd die in this hellhole. It was her penance, she supposed, for raising a beast. She was feeling light-headed, her throat burned.

More footsteps. A door closing, an engine starting.

A shuttered window over the cot blocked out even the moonlight. Here, in the dark depths of Kyle's hell house, Eve wanted more than anything to feel the warmth of the sun, taste fresh air, experience a gentle breeze against her skin. All the things she had taken for granted just hours ago. Instead, she felt herself sinking deeper into the muck of despair.

This is what Kelsey dealt with, Eve thought, searching for understanding. Most beings crave the sun. In the depths of a pond, even the slimiest plants reached hopefully upward, toward the surface, toward the light. How Kelsey must have suffered. Day after day, tied to this bed, longing for sunlight. Could she blame her daughter for her depravity? Yes, the potential had been there, but it was Kyle who'd watered it and nurtured it until it bloomed into a full case of sociopathy.

Smoke filled her lungs. She could hear things falling above, then footsteps on the stairs. Her head felt hot and swollen, her tongue thick and parched. Her eyes stung. Her breath came in short gasps.

As her mind clawed against the depths, she felt hands on her, unbinding her, lifting her. She would be saved after all.

"Come on, Mother," Kelsey said through a scarf covering her mouth and nose. "You need to walk. Let's go."

Eve half smiled in her delirium. She used the rest of her strength to help Kelsey drag her up the stairs, past Flora's body, past the flames that were already climbing paneled walls. Her chest hurt, her vision was blurred. Hot air seared her throat, her lungs.

Outside, Eve choked down cool air. She whispered, "Home."

Kelsey pushed her into the front seat of the car. The girls were hysterical in the back. "Mami, Mami," the blonde called, over and over. Kelsey told them to be quiet.

"Home," Eve said again.

Kelsey climbed into Flora's car and threw it into reverse. She pressed thin, stingy lips into a tight, mean line. "In your condition? You're not going home, Mother. Not ever again."

As the last of the blackness enveloped her, Eve saw Flora's little red house in its stolen spot in the desert. And she knew that was where she'd rest for eternity—away from Liam, away from Kelsey. Alone.

52

Constance Foster
Nihla, New Mexico—Present

I WAVED THE BRACELET at Dave. "You knew all along. You *knew* that Eve wasn't really Eve. That Eve *was* Kelsey." I knelt down by my sister. "Eve never talked about Kelsey because she *was* Kelsey. The basement? A stupid lie Eve encouraged to keep us quiet and afraid."

Lisa's eyes were wide with fear. "I didn't know."

The dunking. The beatings. All the times our new mother had withheld kindness, tenderness, as punishment. She had been the ultimate brainwasher, whisking us off to a foreign land, cruelly and methodically replacing our memories with ones she'd planted. *Call me Mother. Call me Eve.* She needed us to call her Eve. She needed us to see her as a mother figure, to forget the past. For her charade to work, she had to convince the world she was Eve Foster; but to do that, she had to convince us first.

I said, "She would hold us under the ocean, terrorize us, until we did what she wanted. It's why you never swam, Lisa. It's why you're so afraid of the lake. For years she manipulated us, lied to us, until we believed it all." I turned to Kyle. "Why would she do that? Why go to all that trouble?"

Only it was Dave who answered. "It all comes back to the will. When Kelsey ran away, Eve took her out of the will, thinking it would influence her behavior. It didn't, of course, but when Eve found Kelsey, Kelsey knew she was beholden to her mother. With her mother alive, she knew under the will she would get nothing. Kelsey took a risk—running off, starting a new life."

"It's too much," Lisa said. "Too hard to take in."

"Kelsey stole Eve's identity," Kyle said. "She waited until Eve's parents were dead, until she'd aged enough to return to the States. She used her mother's youth to her advantage." He gave a wry smile. "She let her own mother die, buried her in this house, and then stole her *life*."

Kyle looked almost proud of Kelsey. I felt sick. "Along with something of yours," I said. "Your daughters."

Kyle nodded. "You and Teresa were collateral. She knew that if I exposed her, she could spill my . . . secrets. But she had a second weapon to use against me—you."

I paced around the small room. So many things made sense now. "The games . . . she knew she was never really safe while you were alive. She knew your style, your preferences. She scoured the news for murders that stank of your presence. She used me to bring you out of hiding. Only with you dead, could she rest."

Kyle let out a twisted laugh. "She didn't give a rat's ass about resting. She could have killed me when she had the chance. She wanted to win, and using you to get to me would make it that much sweeter."

"So you found her and placed Dave in her house," I said. "You got to her before she could get to you." And I was sure it thrilled him to know he had a spy in her house. I wondered what Dave had seen, what he had communicated back to Kyle.

Kyle walked around the room, pacing, a noticeable limp in his gait. "Kelsey's strength was also her weakness. She was overly confident. She'd met Jack a few times, but she'd been young and arrogant and full of herself, and he'd aged since then. I took a risk and it paid off."

"You killed her," I said to Dave.

Kyle's smile was noncommittal. He glanced at Lisa. "Did he?"

"Why are you asking Lisa . . ." I didn't finish the question. I didn't need to. The scarlet flush of my sister's face gave me the answer. I thought of her phone call that day in New York. Stern, commanding, so unlike Lisa. Then her hysteria when the will was read. All along it'd been her. "My God, is it true?"

Lisa was looking down at her hands. Like her face, they were blotchy and red.

I said, "You're afraid of water."

"Swimming, not kayaking," Dave said.

The buoy leash—it wouldn't have been hard to find Eve, to throw her off her game, to wrap the leash around her neck as she struggled. Was Lisa capable of that? I stared at my sister anew. Maybe the travel games had been a blessing, a chance to escape Eve's sick grasp. Lisa had only known Eve, and if she'd wanted me back home, wanted us to be together . . . perhaps she'd snapped.

"So now what do you want with us?" Only as soon as the words were uttered, I knew. He wanted silence and money. "No way. No fucking way."

"It's a win-win, Ana."

"Call me Connie."

"Fine, have it your way, Connie." Kyle stopped pacing and pulled his shoulders back. "It's a win-win. You and your sister, as the never legally adopted daughters of Kelsey Foster, who herself had been disinherited, are technically entitled to nothing. The entire Foster estate will go to some distant cousin. You and Lisa will be pulled apart."

I said, "And you'll be exposed as the murderer you are. That's your real fear. That these bodies, all the evidence that Kelsey had against you for all these years, will get into hands outside of this town and be used to put you away forever. Am I right?" I walked closer to him. "You want the money, sure, but more than that, you want to blackmail us into staying quiet."

His eyes narrowed, a shadow fell across his features. His gaze was cold and black and full of disgust. I saw a glimpse of the beast within, and I was, in that moment, more scared of him than I'd ever been of my mother. For all Eve's faults, she'd been a victim— his victim. Perhaps someday I would find some sympathy for her, or at least some understanding. For now, it was enough to know.

Kyle looked at Lisa, and before I could move, he'd pulled her upright, hugged her against him. She looked frail and pale and surprisingly calm.

"Teresa wants this—right?" He spoke softly into her ear, and my sister nodded. "She wants this all to be over. She wants to go home to Vermont and the estate and her comfortable life, right?"

Lisa nodded again. "Please, Connie. If we don't tell, we can follow my plan. The jewels, the money. Little by little, I can transfer her wealth. Eventually we can leave and be together." She sobbed. "It's all I've ever wanted."

"He's lying, Lisa. We can't trust him. He will never let us be free, not with what we know. If we do what he wants, he gets away with raping and torturing and killing innocent people. And for what? He can't change Eve's will, all the fucking trust stipulations. All he can do is blackmail us and use our compliance against us."

But Lisa's eyes were pleading.

I knew if it was money he was after, he only really needed Lisa. But his real fear was this house, those bodies. I was the time bomb. He'd leave Lisa alive to get to the Foster fortune. I, however, presented unnecessary risk. He wouldn't kill me with Lisa here. If he did that, he'd risk losing her cooperation, which he needed.

"Fine," I said, biding my time. "What about this house? Do I keep it?"

He seemed surprised. "Do you want it?"

I looked around. "The bodies, the workshop. It was the place you dismembered them, stripped the flesh from their bones, and buried them. It was Flora's house, and I imagine it gave you some perverted pleasure to know she and her kids—Lisa and me—were trapped in a house of horrors." My voice was rising, my insides twisting with the realization of the depth of his depravity. "That's why you didn't leave *all* of the bodies for the public to find. Leaving some in the open, exposed, to be violated one last time, gave you a sick thrill, sure, but the women you buried in this house were your special treasures, your reminders to my real mother that she could be next—and so could we."

Kyle stayed silent, but I saw the lift of his head, the subtle stretch of his neck.

"You raped them and murdered them and brought them here for Flora to witness your cruelty, like a hunter bringing home his kill." I shook my head. "You stayed away from Nihla for years, but ultimately it called you back—and the killings started here again." I shook my head. "And now you want us to go along with your evil little plan. But to get away with it, someone needs to stay here. Otherwise a real cop, if there is one around here, will find your cache. And then what?"

"What do you want, Connie?"

"A guarantee that you won't hurt either of us."

"Then you'll agree?"

I glanced at my sister, who seemed to have withdrawn again. "Yes."

Kyle nodded at Jack. As Jack turned toward that horrid black bag, I reached for the pick. Swiftly, I lifted it over my head and brought it down into Jack's back. He screamed, and I pulled it out, slamming it down again.

I felt Kyle's hands around my neck, but the adrenaline coursing through my system gave me strength and speed, and I swung the handle of the pick at his head. It connected with a thud. He fell to the ground.

"Come on," I said to Lisa. "Let's go. Now."

She shook her head, shifted her gaze to Kyle. Tears streamed down her cheeks.

"Lisa!"

"I'm not going, Connie. This is your fight. I just wanted to go home with *you*."

I grabbed her arm and pulled. "*Come on.*"

She sank down, like a toddler becoming dead weight.

"Lisa!"

"I was so wrong. I thought this would be over. I thought we were at the end."

"Lisa, *come on*. Screw the money. We can be together. That's what you wanted."

"Go," she said. She reached under Jack and pulled out his gun. She aimed it at me, tears welling in her eyes. "I'm not running." She shook her head. "There is no happy ending for us, Connie. You're right. If we leave and he lives, we will always wonder . . . when, how?"

"You have the gun. You can take care of that. Then we can run away. They won't come looking, not after everything Kyle did. We don't need the money."

"Then how will we live? The jewelry may be enough for a while, but not forever. What skills do I have? I've never been much of a fighter."

"We can figure all that out. The house, the money—none of that matters. I'll take care of you. Just come on."

She shook her head again, her eyes set and stubborn, and raised the gun higher, aiming it at my heart. "Go."

I said, "You wouldn't. You love me."

I heard something move behind me and saw a shadow slinking along the wall. Before I could turn and confront him, the gun went off. Kyle's body slid down, his head hitting the chair. She'd shot him in the side. He was alive but bleeding heavily. When I glanced back at my sister, she was holding the point of the gun on her own forehead.

"No!" I lunged, and in that instant, she fired again. I stared at my twin's body, now a heap on the floor. Blood and brain matter were splattered on the wall behind her. Bright red, like the matches Kelsey had used to set the fire. Like the lipstick on her sorry slash of a mouth.

With one last glance at Lisa, I ran into the kitchen and down the steps to the cellar. Jet was crumpled on the last step, his body slumped to the side. I pulled him up, pleaded with him, but he was lifeless, his eyes open and glassy. I bit back tears. We could have saved him. I could have saved him. I took the steps two at a time and glanced around the kitchen.

Jack and Kyle had removed the wooden planks from the rear door, and I pulled it open. The storm had abated. Jet's truck was still sitting in its parking spot, covered in sand, and the key was under his seat, where he always kept it. *It's all there*, I remembered him saying. I opened the glove box—nothing. Same with under the seats. On impulse, I pulled the lever that opened the hood. The bag sat on top of the engine, flat and full.

I opened the door to the driver's side. Micah barked and whined from Jet's shack, and I paused to listen. What would I do with a dog? I had no idea, but I owed Jet. It took me a few moments to convince her to come with me. Finally, she climbed in Jet's truck and huddled against the door.

As I pulled the truck back out onto Mad Dog Road, I felt nothing. No relief, no rage, no sorrow. Micah whined, and I reached across the seat to reassure her. The feelings would come later, I knew. For now, I welcomed the peace of indifference.

*   *   *

Alberto took down my statement with a nonchalance that belied his excitement. He would call an ambulance. My house was like the Schrödinger's cat of a crime scene. To me, Kyle was both alive and dead. Not my sister, I was afraid. I'd seen the damage. She was gone. Alberto understood my pain. He also understood that to have called the Nihla police would have been suicide. Everything would have been swept under the rug, and I somehow would have been blamed. There was still hope for James, and still a chance to save the reputations of the two men accused of these heinous crimes. Alberto had his connections outside of Nihla. I could only hope he'd get to them first.

Alberto had something at stake, too. The bodies in the basement—perhaps he'd finally get closure for his sister, Gloria. Perhaps he could rest a little, too.

I made one more call. Afterward, I dropped my phone on the pavement of the Albuquerque long-term airport lot and drove over it. When it was good and smashed, I parked the truck, removed the plates, and waited in the shuttle line with Micah. It would be a while before they'd find Jet's truck, before they came looking for me. In the meantime, I'd buy a car with the cash, drive somewhere far from New Mexico. Start fresh. Micah was surprisingly calm. Perhaps she sensed she needed to be strong for both of us.

I wish I could have stayed to see it through, but I knew my presence would only have complicated matters. Besides, like Lisa, I was done fighting. The only way to stop being a pawn in the battle between Kelsey and her captor was to do, ironically, what they'd prepared me to do all along.

Disappear. Blend. Survive.

CHAPTER

53

Constance Foster
Billings, Montana—Present

HIS NAME WAS Earl. He had a kind heart and shallow pockets and a stomach bigger than either, but none of that bothered me. He knew me as Liz Brown, and he rented his bright red garage apartment for a pittance in exchange for light housework and someone to talk to. He never questioned my refusal to discuss my past, never came on to me. Micah liked him. I appreciated his respect for my privacy, even if the view from my garage apartment was the nearby refinery. I'd take the refinery and the apartment and Earl any day if it meant peace. I cherished my peace.

I knew someone else who cherished her peace. Perhaps now, as she neared the end of her life, she'd finally have it.

Someone lost everything, Josiah had said all those months ago. As I'd hung up the phone with Alberto in the Albuquerque parking lot that horrible spring day, it had dawned on me who that someone was. Stella from the hardware store, with her pained eyes and her dry cough and her kind demeanor. She'd mentioned a daughter in passing but never again. I'd called her that afternoon, right after talking to Alberto and before smashing my phone. She confirmed that her daughter had been murdered shortly after she'd come forward to say LeBron and Smallwood were innocent. It had been punishment for her and a warning to Nihla. I told her everything I knew about Kyle. She could do with the information as she pleased. It was a cowardly act from a woman who'd run, but at the end of the day, I figured Stella needed the closure more than I did.

So on the first Monday in November, a day that was cool and dusty and threatening snow, I opened the national paper to see Kyle's name in the headlines. He'd survived that day in the little shotgun house, his spinal cord severed, paralyzed from the waist down. If there was justice in the world, he would live his final hours in the penitentiary, the bodies underneath the house and Stella's testimony sealing his fate. I supposed there was some cosmic irony in the fact he was imprisoned in his own body. I wasn't sure I believed in karma, but I also wasn't sure what I believed mattered.

Kyle never told the truth about Kelsey, and I believed he would keep that secret to his grave—although the autopsy of the bodies in the pit might declare the truth. Jack was dead—as forgotten as his old bar. Jet was gone, too. James had recovered and moved quietly to Illinois. My sister lay in her final resting place in Vermont, still believed to be the daughter of wealthy widow Eve Foster.

I glanced down at the newspaper. The cloud cover overhead lent a cozy feel to the tiny kitchen, and Micah, curled on her bed by the stove, agreed. The paper said the heir to Lisa's part of the family fortune, Constance Foster, had disappeared from Nihla back in June. Any information leading to Constance's whereabouts would be met with a sizable reward.

I refolded the paper and glanced at the bronze safe deposit box key sitting on the table. As I mixed my morning oatmeal, I thought about Constance Foster and that fortune waiting for her. I thought about my sister, my life until now. Ana Maria, Constance Foster, Liz Brown. What was in a name, after all? As Ana and Connie, I'd had no control. As Liz Brown, I would have freedom.

I rose, lit a gas burner, and held the end of the paper in the fire. I watched it burn for a moment, mesmerized by the flames, before tossing it into the sink. The edges of the newspaper curled, turned black, then scattered into ashes. I turned on the faucet and washed the bits down the drain. *Constance Foster*, I thought. A half smile played on my lips. *Little does the world know the Constance Foster I once was is now dead and buried, like all the other unfortunate souls under the little red house.*

ACKNOWLEDGMENTS

A SPECIAL THANK YOU to my amazing agent, Frances Black of Literary Counsel, who believed in this project from day one. Fran's keen eye and sharp pencil have made this a better book.

Thank you to Faith Black Ross, my editor at Crooked Lane Books, and to the entire Crooked Lane team, including Rebecca Nelson, Melissa Rechter, Madeline Rathle, Dulce Botello, and Kate McManus. I'm so happy *Little Red House* has found such a wonderful home.

Thank you to Sue Norbury and Rowe Carenen for being the first ones to visit the fictional little red house in Nihla, New Mexico.

Thank you to Stephanie Wollman for always entertaining my "could this combination be deadly?" medical questions.

Much gratitude to Ed Aymar, who in addition to being a great friend, writer, and sounding board, always shows up for other authors.

Loving thanks to my family, especially my mother, Angela Tyson, my sons, Ian, Matthew, and Jonathan, my daughter-in-law, Mandy, my godmother, Carol Lizell, and my uncle, Greg Marincola, for being my personal cheering section.

I'm especially grateful to Ben Pickarski, my partner in life and travel, for supporting my dream through the highs and lows of this writing life.